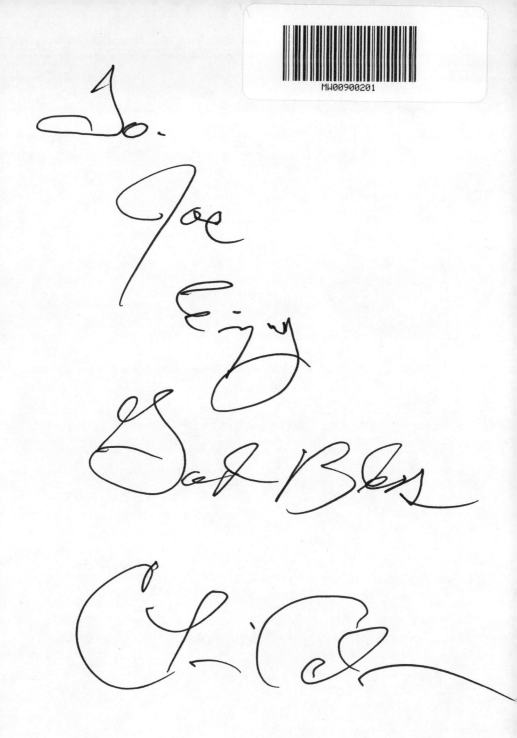

To.

Joe

Enjoy

Get Bless

REQUIEM OF A SPY

CHRIS ADAMS

authorHOUSE®

AuthorHouse™
1663 Liberty Drive
Bloomington, IN 47403
www.authorhouse.com
Phone: 1-800-839-8640

First published by AuthorHouse 7/14/2010

ISBN: 978-1-4520-4434-7 (e)
ISBN: 978-1-4520-4432-3 (sc)
ISBN: 978-1-4520-4433-0 (hc)

Library of Congress Control Number: 2010909437

Printed in the United States of America
Bloomington, Indiana

This book is printed on acid-free paper.

ALSO BY CHRIS ADAMS

Non-fiction

Inside the Cold War: *A Cold Warrior's Reflections* 1999

Ideologies in Conflict: *A Cold War Docu-Story* 2001

Deterrence: *An Enduring Strategy* 2010

Fiction

Red Eagle: *A Story of Cold War Espionage* 2000

Profiles in Betrayal: *The Enemy Within* 2002

The Betrayal Mosaic: *A Cold War Spy Story* 2004

Out of Darkness: *The Last Russian Revolution* 2006

"Any complex activity, if it is to be carried on with any degree of virtuosity, calls for appropriate gifts of intellect and temperament. If they are outstanding and reveal themselves in exceptional achievements, their possessor is called a genius."

Carl Von Clausewitz
ON WAR

Acknowledgements

The Cold War resides in the near past; infrequently referenced, it continues to fade with time. The relevant history of the 45-year political and military impasse however was fraught with intrigue and mystery attributed considerably to the secret operating society within the arch enemy of the period, the Soviet Union. Accordingly, there may be some sensitivity associated with certain aspects of the subject matter in this story which made the project challenging. While the satire is pure fiction, it is drawn from this author's years of experience in strategic air operations during the Cold War and later the opportunity to work in the former Soviet Union. Accordingly, I have gone to considerable lengths to protect any and all information, processes and procedures that might not otherwise even today, to be open to the public.

I am grateful to each of those who made this project possible, especially my many Cold Warrior colleagues who so honorably served during those frantic years. Each deserves some credit for providing the backdrop for the story. In the former Soviet Union, I was privileged to meet and dialogue with many former *enemies* who are enemies no longer, as well as, many ordinary citizens who survived under the tyrannical rule of the Soviet Empire. To each, I wish the very best for their future lives within an ever-recovering society. I also want to acknowledge the professional intelligence agencies of the United States and their diligent surveillance of potential perpetrators who, both then and now, are intent upon doing our country great harm. It is through their professional endeavors that such a caper as this fictional story describes did not actually happen. Finally, and critically important to this writing endeavor, was the extraordinary and meticulous editing of my friend and colleague, Paulette Chapman, and numerous others who assisted in the project. My sincere appreciation to each of You!

Chris Adams

Perspective

*THE FBI ARREST 12 RUSSIAN SPIES...*Newspaper headlines, radio and television networks announced the startling news. A dozen or more undocumented Russian agents were caught operating undercover within the United States. This event might well have occurred back during the last Millennia, and did, but this is 2010; the Cold War has been over for almost twenty years, or has it? Were we surprised? After all, the President of the United States had within the previous week of the arrests, hosted the President of Russia to an Official State Visit. As this book enters the final publication phase, I could not have created a more perfect, although factually unsettling, introduction to the exciting and *factual* story which you are about to begin.

The most powerful and aggressive intelligence and secret police organizations in the world have for centuries belonged to Russia, and during the Cold War, the Soviet Union. The long and sordid history of Russian secret police operations and tactics dates back to the 17th Century and Ivan the Terrible. Peter the Great continued the process by creating an elite guard and personal army which adopted political secret police functions in the name of protecting the czar. The secret police construct survived with flexible persistence through the checkered history of Russian totalitarian regimes.

When communism took the country by storm, Lenin made use of the deep-rooted clandestine organization, the *Tcheka*, to route-out opposing factions. Brutal murder and executions were always the accepted procedures for eliminating internal enemies of the State. After several evolutions, the Committee for State Security, or Komitet Gosudarstvennoy Bezopasnosti (KGB), became the central intelligence and secret police agency of Josef Stalin and the Soviet Union. The advent of the Cold War served to foster the KGB's growth and even more sinister work, and Stalin's successors continued to utilize the foul system handed down to them.

Not as well known outside the Soviet Union, but of equal importance to the security of the State, was the Chief Intelligence Directorate of the General Staff, simply known as the GRU. The GRU had its beginning as a result of a concession by Lenin to his chief lieutenant, Leon Trotsky. The GRU was created principally for the purpose of counteracting the singular work and ravages of the Tcheka. The GRU had a similar mission as that of the KGB—to spy—but focused more directly on collecting technology and weapon systems intelligence from foreign sources. The GRU trained and operated their own spy collection network and maintained a scientific and technical base for the exploitation of foreign weapon systems and technologies.

The Soviets, known for their paranoia and mackorova (masquerade), frequently renamed these agencies in attempts to foil foreign interests. The name changes were largely cosmetic and their foul work never changed. Soviet leaders throughout the Cold War found it expedient to pit the KGB and the GRU against one another for maximum benefit of desired objectives.

Although the story herein is one of fiction, perhaps it is more appropriately one of "faction"—a fictional story derived from factual history, and as we now know persists today. Herein, I have delved into many of the factual truths about these two Cold War secret spy organizations, their sordid and brutal deeds, their recruiting, training and surveillance tactics, agent operations and exploitation of Western technologies. Similarly, the story also weaves into details about U.S. strategic air operations during the period. The manufactured tale is about a Cold War event that could have potentially happened, but fortunately it did not. It is the author's intent to spin a yarn drawn from his personal experiences blended with historical events, facts and truths. These are melded into fictitious people with faces, lives and personalities who may have, in a similar fashion, actually existed during the forty-five year stalemate between the great Super Powers.

Finally, the original manuscript of this story was published some ten years ago under the title of *Red Eagle*; *Requiem of a Spy* takes the story and the reader to the next level. Additionally, in order to provide a flavor for the Russian language and Cyrillic alphabet, I have sprinkled a few words and terms throughout the text and also in the Glossary. I hope these make for both interesting reading and understanding. Enjoy!

Prelude

The two heavily loaded Strategic Air Command B-52G bombers lifted off the 13,000 foot runway, the second trailing the first aircraft after a one-minute interval. These were airborne alert sorties taking off from Ramey Air Force Base, Puerto Rico, on a late October morning in 1962. The co-pilot of the first aircraft called the Wing Command Post at Ramey and reported: "Apache Control, this is Apache Two-Zero airborne; all systems normal."

The Combat Post Controller acknowledged: "Apache Two-Zero, Apache Control, Roger that, have a safe flight."

"Roger, Apache Control, we'll see you tomorrow," the co-pilot aboard Apache Two-Zero responded. The second B-52, Apache Two-One, reported in kind.

On October 22, 1962, President Kennedy had ordered the Commander-in-Chief, Strategic Air Command (SAC), to fully implement the B-52 airborne alert operation plan—"Chromedome"—in response to the growing conflict with the Soviet Union over their intent to place medium range Soviet bombers and medium range ballistic missiles in Cuba. During August and September of 1962, the United States Navy had monitored a steady influx of Soviet cargo ships crossing the Atlantic and docking in Cuban ports. The U.S. had, over a period of several months, steadily tightened an economic embargo on Cuba in an attempt to coerce Fidel Castro into curtailing his bellicose activities in the Caribbean and to cease the inhumane treatment of his people. Stories from Cuban refugees who escaped to the U.S. revealed horrific stories of persecution and torture at the hands of the Cuban police and army. Ever since the ill-fated *Bahia de Cochinos* (Bay of Pigs) incident a little over a year earlier, the United States, in an attempt to support a Cuban refugee over-throw of the Castro government, had grown even more weary of the Soviet influence in Cuba. It seemed that a tough economic squeeze on the island government might bring Castro around. No doubt, the United States' failure in the Bay of Pigs invasion gave Nikita Khrushchev the courage to escalate Soviet influence in the region, only ninety miles from the U.S. coast. Khrushchev was also persuaded to attempt the military venture in Cuba to bolster his weakening position with the Central Committee of the Supreme Soviet, as well as with the Chinese who had begun to doubt the world influence of the Soviet Union after Stalin's death.

Initially, the United States Defense and State Departments interpreted the Soviet cargo shipments as food and supplies to help their ally during the U.S. embargo. But, on October 16th, a SAC U-2 reconnaissance plane brought back startling photos that revealed missile sites were being constructed at several locations on the island. Later, photography showed conclusive evidence of the development of fighter and bomber airfields; neither type of aircraft were possessed by Cuba at the time. Additional U-2 reconnaissance missions clearly showed missile canisters and disassembled aircraft on the decks of several cargo ships. The evidence was sufficient to cause the President to first send a firm verbal warning to the Soviets, and second, to back up the warning by the posturing of U.S. strategic forces.

In addition to the airborne alert B-52's, SAC dispersed 200 B-47 medium bombers loaded with nuclear weapons to various pre-planned civilian airports in the U.S. All remaining B-52's and combat crews were placed on ground alert and their bombers loaded with nuclear weapons. The Navy augmented its POLARIS submarine alert force with additional boats and nuclear missiles. For the first time since the Cold War unofficially began in 1946, the United States and the Soviet Union were rapidly moving toward the possibility of a nuclear war. There had been other tests of will by the Soviets with the Berlin Blockade—their all-out support of the communists during the Korean War and the invasion of Hungary and Czechoslovakia— neither of those blatant incursions escalated to their unequivocal intent in Cuba.

As the two B-52 crews prepared for take-off on this long and potentially world shattering mission, they had reported early that morning to the 70th Bomb Wing Operations-Plans office. After reviewing their mission package including the targets which could be directed to strike with nuclear bombs, they collected their emergency and survival equipment, including side arms. They had divested themselves of all personal identification: military ID cards, credit cards, family photos, personalized jewelry, etc.

They kept only their "dog tags," Geneva Convention Identification Cards and a few dollars, just in case. One last briefing was given on normal and emergency procedures by the Squadron Operations Officer as well as a briefing by the Wing Intelligence Officer on potential threats which could be encountered along the route of flight. The wing and squadron commanders concluded the pre-departure briefing with a few remarks, including words of encouragement, good luck and a safe return. This same event was taking place at about the same time at more than a dozen other SAC B-52 bases around the United States. SAC had been directed to maintain a maximum number of B-52's loaded with nuclear weapons to be on alert, in the air, and to await a possible Presidential Order to execute the war plan.

The combat crews assigned to Apache Two-Zero and Apache Two-One had climbed aboard their respective bombers about forty minutes before their scheduled take-off time, took their crew positions and completed their "START ENGINE AND PRE-TAKE-OFF" checklists. The pilots started the eight turbo-fan engines of their respective B-52's. At the precise time called for in their mission folder, the co-pilot in Apache Two-Zero advised Ground Control, they were ready to taxi.

"Roger, Apache Two-Zero, you are cleared to taxi to Runway One Eight Zero". The pilot in Two-Zero promptly released the brakes of his B-52G and pushed the throttles forward to give the huge bomber the power surge necessary to roll forward and move out of its parking stub. He could feel the unusual sluggishness of his exceptionally heavy loaded bomber and proceeded to taxi the bomber very slowly and deliberately down the taxiway toward the take-off end of the runway. The pilot aboard Apache Two One received his clearance to taxi, eased his bomber out the parking stub and pulled in behind Two-Zero at about a fifty yard interval. The Supervisor of

Flying cruised along the taxiway in his staff car monitoring the two aircraft for any signs of problems—fuel leaks, improper tire inflation and rotation, engine operations—anything that looked suspicious on the heavily loaded bombers.

As the two B-52's approached the apron leading to the active runway, the control tower operator advised: "Apache Two-Zero; Apache Two One, you are cleared for take-off on your timing. After take-off contact Departure Control on UHF Frequency 322.5, and have a safe flight, Sir."

The co-pilots in each aircraft acknowledged: "Roger, copy, thank you, we'll be rolling in a few seconds."

The Navigator in Apache Two-Zero then advised the pilot: "Sir, we can roll on the count of five. Counting now: Five, Four, Three, Two, One!"

The pilot released the brakes, pushed the engine throttles forward slowly and maneuvered the bomber around the 45 degree turn from the apron toward the runway. The co-pilot monitored the engine instruments, while holding his left hand steadily behind the pilot's right hand on the throttles, to insure that neither of the throttles slipped back. As the bomber was aligned down the runway centerline, the pilot continued to push the throttles to the eight Pratt & Whitney J-57 turbo-fan engines full open, and the aircraft began to accelerate rapidly. In spite of its tremendous weight, the B-52 handled and maneuvered easily on the take-off roll.

The Navigator called out the time as they began the take-off roll. The crew coordination was flawless. The co-pilot watched the airspeed indicator, calling: "S-1!", the airspeed which the aircraft should be indicating at a pre-designated point along the take-off roll; and then he barked: "S-2!", the speed at which the aircraft was committed to take-off.

A decision to abort the take-off at the S-2 point would likely end in a crash off the end of the runway. And finally, he called: "Take-off speed!"

The pilot eased back the yoke firmly, and the heavily laden bomber lifted into the air. Once safely airborne, he called, "Gear Up!"

The co-pilot raised the landing gear handle to the Up position. After the landing gear retracted, airspeed again became critical as the pilot maintained both the desired climb speed and aircraft position. He called for the co-pilot to begin to raise the flaps; which he did, incrementally, according to a prescribed schedule. There was an admonition regarding raising the flaps of the B-52 which dated back to the first Boeing test pilots of the bomber: "No distractions during flap retraction!" Flap retraction time on the B-52G was one minute, during which the pilot's complete attention had to be devoted to the airspeed and position of the aircraft lest he find himself in a serious and potentially uncontrollable situation. Raising the flaps became "old hat" to all B-52 pilots as did all of the flying procedures, but they remained wary of the beast's unique flying characteristics associated with this function.

Once all of the "AFTER TAKE-OFF AND CLIMB" checklists were completed the co-pilot contacted Departure Control: "Ramey Departure Control, this is Apache Two-Zero, airborne and climbing to flight plan altitude."

"Roger, Two-Zero," Departure Control responded. "You are cleared as filed; you may switch to your en route flight-following frequency. And, Sir, have a good flight, Two-Zero."

The tension was apparent in the voice of ground controller. Everyone involved knew the potential grave seriousness of these B-52 missions.

Apache Two-Zero climbed to an initial altitude of 24,000 feet with Apache Two One in trail. After leveling off, the combat crews on board the two B-52's began to settle into the long mission ahead. 'Settle', was hardly in the minds of the men on board the bombers. The next 25 hours would require their undivided attention and tax every training discipline in their minds and bodies. The days leading up to this, and previous CHROMEDOME missions, had been trying for all Air Force personnel in the wing, particularly those who had families on the base.

All combat crew members had been required to update their emergency information data files, insurance beneficiaries, next of kin and so on. Family members had been briefed by wing staff personnel concerning the possibility of being evacuated back to the States should their Puerto Rican base come under attack. The period was tense for all, family members and flight crews alike, each deeply concerned for the other. The uncertainty of leaving families behind when departing on missions such as this added to the anxiety of the mission ahead.

Captain Mike Scott was the Pilot and Aircraft Commander (AC) of Apache Two-Zero. Although he was the youngest AC in the squadron, he was also considered one of the top pilots in the wing. He had upgraded to pilot and aircraft commander, with the minimum time required, which reflected both his flying and leadership skills. Following pilot training and B-52 combat crew training school (CCTS), he was assigned as a copilot to one of the first B-52 crews to upgrade in the bomb wing at Castle AFB. He continued his pattern of diligent study and endeavor to comprehend every aspect of the complex bomber. Early on, he demonstrated exceptional flying skills to the unit B-52 instructors and his aircraft commander; he was earmarked by the senior officers in the bomb wing as a "faster burner", a young officer who should rapidly excel and be advanced accordingly.

In the early spring of 1960, Mike had applied for a transfer to Ramey AFB where there were openings for crew members to fly the new B-52G, the latest state-of-the-art strategic bomber just coming into SAC's inventory. SAC looked after its "young tigers," and Mike's request for reassignment was approved. He arrived at his new unit in the summer of 1960 and continued his quest to become a skilled pilot. The best in the wing, he studied and developed a knowledge of the B-52G aircraft systems equal to that of most maintenance technicians. He demonstrated that he was an exceptional pilot who could fly and handle the huge bomber in every situation, including aerial refueling in all kinds of weather and turbulence. At Ramey, he was immediately placed in the aircraft commander upgrade program.

Arriving on this October day, he had flown with his new crew for more than a year and was exceptionally confident of their proficiency. He would accept nothing less than superior attitudes and performance from the other five crew members. During the take-off roll on this momentous flight, Mike allowed several fleeting thoughts to race through his mind:

"I wonder what my father and mother would think of me now. I wonder what a lot of people are going to think of me now. This will be the most incredible day of my life!" But, after only a brief moment, his self-discipline immediately took command of his drifting thoughts and he was quickly in charge of his surroundings.

First Lieutenant Bill Self was Mike's co-pilot. He had been flying in the right seat of the B-52 since graduating from the training school at Castle AFB two years before. He was an Air Force Academy graduate and a sharp young officer and pilot. The Bomb-Nav Team consisted of Major Tom Dalton, the Radar Bombardier and long-time bomber crew member. Having flown in B-36's and B-47's before going to B-52G transition, he was considered one of the squadron's "ace" bombardiers. It was not unusual for a major to be assigned to a combat crew commanded by a captain aircraft commander. The AC was unquestionably the "boss" when the crew was assembled on the ground and in the air. Captain John Williams was the Navigator, a quiet spoken young professional who knew most all of the intricate ways to get the aircraft from "point A to Z". He was a bachelor as was Mike. They had become good 'drinking buddies' when off duty.

Dalton and Williams were seated in side-by-side ejection seats on the lower deck of the giant bomber and almost directly beneath the pilots' cockpit. These were unaffectionately called the "suicide seats" because the ejection seat systems jettisoned downward which meant that in an extreme emergency situation where bailing-out of the aircraft was the only option, the bomber would have to be flying at a desired safe altitude of at least a thousand feet or higher. The higher, the better! This concern became seriously amplified during training flights for low-level bomb runs which were conducted at nominal altitudes of three to five hundred feet. These two crew members prayed a lot during those phases of a mission!

The Defensive Team included Lieutenant Jack Mayer, the Defensive Systems Operator, or Emergency Warfare Officer ("EWO" and frequently referred to as "E-Whoa") and Technical Sergeant Charlie Grimes, the Gunner. They both sat in ejection seats ten feet or so to the rear of the pilots and faced to the aft of the bomber. The B-52G was equipped with a number of "black boxes" containing a sophisticated array of defensive and offensive electronic sensors and counter measures systems. Jack Mayer could readily detect the electronic emissions from an enemy ground, or airborne, radar tracking their bomber. He could, in turn, send out electronic signals to jam an enemy fighter, or ground radar, which could be preparing to launch an air-to-air or a surface-to-air missile at the B-52. These electronic counter-measures systems were highly classified and greatly envied by the Soviets.

Grimes, the gunner, sat in the ejection seat next to Mayer and was responsible for operating the remote-controlled cluster of four .50 caliber guns mounted in the tail of the G-model B-52. The remote-controlled gun turret was equipped with a zoom-lensed television camera which the gunner used as a gun sight to lock on an attacking fighter. He also assisted the EWO in monitoring the electronic detection systems. Mike was pleased with his crew. He had enjoyed working with them and molding them into the best combat crew in the squadron.

Apache Two-One, paired with Two-Zero on this day's airborne alert mission, was commanded by Major "Chuck" Lamb, an older command pilot who had bomber flying experience dating back to Korea and B-29's. He was considered one of the "steady heads" in the squadron crew force, not a ball of fire, but one who could get the job done. He had no allusions for fast promotions or more responsibility—just give him a job and he would get it done. His crew, likewise, were all SAC professionals, both young and older, but all highly skilled in their positions. Of course, this was true of all Strategic Air Command combat crew members. They were the "best of the best" during the Cold War. They were the Elite among trained professional war fighters.

The two B-52 crews taxied-out their fully loaded aircraft at maximum gross weight. Each weighed approximately a half million pounds. The bombers were configured with two bomb bays each loaded with a mix of nuclear weapons and decoy missiles. Each nuclear bomb was matched with a pre-planned and designated target in the Soviet Union. Apache Two-Zero was loaded with a cluster of four nuclear bombs in the forward bomb bay and a cluster of four QUAIL missiles in the aft bomb bay.

The GAM-72 QUAIL was the latest technology decoy missile system designed specifically to confuse enemy detection and tracking radars. It replicated the profile of a B-52; that is, when the tiny airplane-like missiles were launched from the bomb bay of the bomber, their short five and a half foot wings unfolded. The General Electric J-85 jet engine automatically started, and the 2000 pound "miniature aircraft" flew pre-programmed flight profiles while emanating electronic emissions very similar to that of a B-52. When launched by the bomber crew en route into enemy territory, the whole purpose of the in-flight QUAILs was to fool the enemy's radars into believing that "five", not just "one", B-52 was inbound.

Additionally, Apache Two-Zero carried two GAM-77 Hound Dog air-to-ground missiles with nuclear warheads. One each was hung on pylons between the fuselage and inboard engine pods of the B-52. The Hound Dog was a sizeable missile at 42 feet long and 12,000 pounds. It was powered by a Pratt & Whitney J-52 jet engine, and the missile contained an inertial guidance system which remained updated by the B-52 navigator throughout the flight and up until launched. After launch from the bomber, the Hound Dog could fly up to 700 miles and destroy its pre-programmed target.

Mike was elated that his mission package included a complete array of weapons systems. His bomber represented virtually every capability in the SAC war fighting bomber arsenal. His pride in his crew and weapons systems was supreme.

Approximately 10,000 pounds of the bomber's fuel was used up during starting engines, taxiing, take-off and acceleration to the programmed climb speed. "SETTOAC" was the acronym for summarizing the take-off and climb-out steps. The expended fuel lightened the aircraft, making it increasingly easier to manage— that is, until after the first aerial refueling, which would add approximately 110,000 pounds back into the "beast". There would be two such refuelings from KC-135 airborne tankers during the mission which would take them across the Atlantic, through the Strait of Gibraltar and up the Mediterranean where APACHE TWO-ZERO would proceed into an area of international airspace over the Tyrranian Sea, off the West coast of Italy. Apache Two-One would proceed to a designated area farther to the West of Two-Zero.

As the earlier events were taking place on the flight line, two men dressed in business suits entered the Wing Headquarters Building and into the office of the commander.

"Can I help you, Gentlemen?" the secretary asked.

"Yes ma'am, I am Special Agent Manuel Flores, FBI; this is Special Agent Brent Collins. Is Colonel Blair in, please?"

"Sir, he is in the Wing Command Post monitoring the take off of our two morning sorties. Would you care to have a seat? He should be returning shortly."

A few minutes later, Colonel Bill Blair, Commander of the 70th Bomb Wing, returned to his office. The two agents stood to greet him.

"Manny! It's good to see you! What brings you to this end of the island? Come in, Gentlemen," Blair greeted as he led the two into his private office. He was in an exceptionally good mood. The airborne alert sorties for the day had gone extremely smooth since the wing was directed to support the crisis actions against the Soviets.

"Well, Manny, you are a long way from home," Blair said as they took seats around the coffee table in his office; "coffee, either of you?"

"No thank you, sir," Flores and his partner each responded.

"Well, what can I do for you?" Blair asked, taking a dark cigar out of the teak wood cedar-lined humidor sitting on the corner of his desk; "cigar, either of you? They aren't Cuban, but they are pretty damned good."

"No, thank you, sir," Flores replied.

Colonel Blair settled back in his overstuffed leather chair and placed the cigar between his lips and proceeded to soften the tip with his tongue.

"Colonel Blair," Flores began. "We are here to visit with one of your officers, a Captain John Michael Scott. We're afraid that he may be in some difficulty."

"Mike Scott!" Blair sat up straight. "What kind of difficulty? Scott is one of the brightest young officers in my wing. What are you talking about?"

"Sir, to put it bluntly, we are here to serve a warrant for his arrest and questioning. We..."

Blair jumped to his feet, almost tumbling his chair behind him.

"Arrest?" Blair shouted. "What th' hell are you talking about? Questioning...about what, for Christ's sake?"

"Colonel," Flores replied, clearing his throat. "We have an arrest warrant issued by the U.S. Attorney in San Juan, citing Captain Scott for suspected fraudulent activities against the United States Government, including cover-up and possibly giving false and misleading statements to a federal agent. And, Sir, it gets worse; there is developing evidence that the allegations may be more serious than that."

"Good Lord," Blair blurted and stormed around the office.

"Manny, you guys are crazy! I have known Mike Scott for two years and his track record here and before coming here, is impeccable. You are barking up the wrong tree."

"Colonel, I can imagine how you must feel," Flores said softly. "I conducted a routine interview with Captain Scott two weeks ago, as well with his squadron commander and I agree with you, he appears to be an unquestionably good and reliable officer. He also speaks well for himself. I did not detect anything untoward when I visited with him, nor did I indicate to him that he was in any suspected difficulty. We are as perplexed as you."

Blair did not respond, he stood starring out his window on to the manicured lawn and palm trees gently swaying in the light breeze.

"Colonel, if we might see him today, with one of your legal counsels present, perhaps we begin to clear up some of our concerns. But, in any case, Colonel Blair, we do have a warrant to detain him for questioning."

"See him?" Blair shouted, still stalking around the room, chewing on the end of his unlit cigar. "You heard those two bombers take off awhile ago? Captain Scott is the aircraft commander in the lead aircraft."

"When will he return?" Flores asked.

"Return?" Blair sneered. "Return? Those guys will be up there for at least twenty-five hours, if we don't go to war with those Goddamn

Soviets. If we do, then you may never see him. Otherwise, Scott and his crew will land about an hour later than this time tomorrow."

Blair took a deep breath, softened his tone and continued, "Manny, are you sure your information is correct? Can you tell me what this is all about?"

"Sir, I can't go into the details of this case," Flores replied. "Except to tell you that the evidence revealed thus far is very serious, unfortunately I cannot compromise the information at this time. I am truly sorry."

"Well, I can appreciate that," Blair softly replied; now resolved to the situation, he returned to his chair behind the desk.

After reaching cruising altitude, Apache Two-Zero and Two One flew in cell formation, roughly three to five miles apart, to a point over the western Atlantic Ocean where they rendezvoused with their respective aerial tankers for their first refueling. It was a clear, beautiful afternoon over the Atlantic Ocean. The refueling tankers had also departed Ramey some twenty minutes before the two B-52's and positioned themselves to intercept the bombers when they arrived at the pre-planned refueling area.

"Apache Two-Zero, this is Clancy Four Four, how do you read, over?" the airborne tanker called as the two B-52's approached the refueling rendezvous area flying at 30 and 32,000 feet, respectively, now with their lightened gross weight.

"Roger, Clancy Four Four this is Apache Two-Zero; read you loud and clear. We're inbound at three-zero thousand feet, over." Bill Self promptly acknowledged.

"Roger, Two-Zero, we're at three-one thousand and have your beacon loud and clear, how about a fill-up?" The co-pilot on Clancy Four Four, acknowledged.

"Roger, we're ready," replied Bill Self. "Guess this isn't a practice mission, is it?"

"Roger that, Twp Zero, this could be as bad as it can get!"

"Okay, you guys knock off the chatter," Mike piped in. "Let's get with it. Four Four are you ready? Do you have us in sight?"

"Roger that, Two-Zero, we have you dead ahead at two four zero degrees, commencing rendezvous."

At this point, the navigators on the tanker and the bomber took charge of the rendezvous procedures and directed the necessary headings for the pilots of each aircraft to fly in order to place them in their respective air refueling positions. The procedure required the KC-135 to fly directly toward the B-52 at an altitude of 1,000 feet above the bomber and then to begin a timed turn so as to arrive in front of and above the bomber heading in the same direction. The procedure positioned the tanker nominally a mile ahead and a thousand feet above the bomber. The KC-135 established a refueling indicated airspeed of approximately 230 knots, and the pilot engaged his auto-pilot in order to stabilize the tanker.

"Four Four, I have you directly ahead," Mike reported to the tanker. "We're coming in."

"Roger, Two-Zero."

"Boomer, he's all yours," the tanker pilot directed his boom operator. The boom operator on the tanker, lying on his belly in the refueling bay, watched the bomber close in to connect with the refueling boom and take on his fuel.

"Sir, I have you at half a'mile and closing, now 2000 yards, 1000 yards, 500, 100, closing slowly...steady...you're making a good approach. Boom coming down."

The boomer lowered the tanker's boom as the bomber slowly moved into position. Mike gently flew his B-52 into the "refueling envelope," a scant thirty feet from the belly of the tanker; the boom operator "stabbed" the bomber's refueling receptacle with the refueling boom, and Bill Self reported: "We're taking on fuel." It was a smooth day for refueling, and Mike had little difficulty holding the B-52 in position for the twenty minutes that it took to take on 109,400 pounds of JP-4.

Bill announced to the boom operator: "That's it, we're topped-off."

The boom operator responded: "Breakaway, breakaway."

At that point the boomer retracted the refueling boom; Mike pulled back the power slightly and allowed the bomber to descend a few hundred feet. The tanker pilot maintained his altitude, made a gentle turn to the West, headed back home with not much fuel of his own to spare and bade the B-52 crew a farewell.

"So long, Twp Zero, good hunting, good luck and a safe trip home!"

Mike responded: "Thanks guys, and we appreciate the fill up."

Meanwhile, the same events were taking place with Apache Two One and a couple dozen or so other B-52's in various parts of the world. The wartime rules of engagement for aerial refueling tankers directed that the tanker crew would off-load as much fuel as a bomber could take, even if it meant that the tanker would run out of fuel before he could make it safely to an airport. These missions were conducted under wartime rules, but fortunately, all of the pre-flight planning up to this point provided both the bombers and the tankers their respective fuel loads to fly their sorties.

For the next several hours, Mike Scott's crew had studied the mission plan and discussed possible contingencies should they encounter Soviet fighters who might venture out to where they were or whatever else might happen.

Mike queried each crew member regarding their respective preparations, concerns and apprehensions: "Well, fellows, we're on our way. This is day four of SAC airborne alert sorties, and so far it appears that we're still at a stand-off with our Soviet friends. We've got awhile before our next refueling, so I want each one of you to quiz each other on your procedures in the event we get our number called and get some rest. After we get on station and in the orbit pattern, it is going to be wide-awake time for everybody; any questions?"

There were no questions. Mike's comments were sobering, but he instilled confidence in each of them. They did not know what was ahead of them, but they were ready. Their training and discipline gave them self-confidence that if worse came to worse; they would still come out okay. No one on the crew really gave serious thought to actually "going in" and dropping their bombs and launching their missiles. It was instinctive for all to believe that "war won't start today," and "we'll get back home."

They chatted casually over the intercom, nibbled on their food stores, drank coffee and took turns resting. The next refueling would take place roughly six hours after the first, over the Mediterranean. The tanker would "pop up" from a staging base in Spain.

"Charlie, wanna come up and sit in my chair for awhile?" Mike called over intercom to the gunner.

Mike got out of his seat, and Charlie Grimes moved forward and got into the pilot's seat. His job would be to keep the copilot company and provide another set of "eyeballs" to monitor cockpit instruments and activities. This was routine and commonly practiced on Chromedome sorties during periods of inactivity with crew members taking turns getting out of their seat, stretching, hunkering around within the sparse maneuvering room inside the bomber and curling up for short cat naps. On this flight, no one could really relax. They could move around some, stretch, relieve themselves and finally climb back into their normal working positions.

Mike was particularly pensive. He couldn't relax or sleep— only think of the events ahead of him and the precision with which he must execute every detail on this day. His thoughts cycled between the mission and requirements in front of him and reflecting back on how he got to be here on this day...

ONE

Sasha

"Ahhh, there you are, Lieutenant! It's a boy! Your wife is fine. Are you awake, Lieutenant?"

Lieutenant Viktor Katsanov was startled by the nurse's words as she came rushing up to him, jolting him out of a restless nap in the uncomfortable chair in the stark waiting room.

"Uh, Uh? Dah, Dah! Spasee'ba! (Thank you!) It's a boy? It **IS** a boy!" Viktor shouted. "Is Tatyana, my wife...is she well?"

"She is fine and so is he, a very handsome young man. What will you name this youngest new Russian?"

"I am not sure. I will have to consult with my wife. When can I see her?"

"You may come with me now and see them both," the nurse beckoned.

Viktor Aleksandrovich Katsanov was born on May 1st, 1930, May Day, in a Soviet military hospital outside Stalinabad, a small city later renamed Dushanbe', the capital of Tadzhikstan, and near the Afghan border. His father was a young officer in the Voyenno-vozdushnyye sily - VVS, Soviet Air Force, at a training base instructing young pilots. The whole of Russia was in turmoil as Josef Stalin orchestrated a reign of terror against his people in an attempt to drive them into a single-minded communist society. The recovery from World War I had left the country devastated, as had the numerous wars before in Russia's checkered history. Military families, such as the Katsanov's, suffered equally with the masses. Food was in short supply. Wages were so poor that they could barely purchase what little was available. Living away from Moscow, though, had some advantages. There was the appearance of more freedom and less oppression, and occasionally more fresh produce was available. It was not a good time, in any event, to bring a child into the world, especially in Russia.

The newborn Katsanov was named after his father, who went by his given name, Viktor, so it was decided that his son would go by his middle name, Aleksandr and would be called Sasha, the Russian equivalent of Bill for William or Dick for Richard. Sasha's mother, Tatyana, was a school teacher in her mid-twenties. She taught English and social studies at a local school of mostly military dependent children. Her added income helped the family to live slightly above most of the others. Sasha was the Katsanov's first born and promptly became his father's idol. Viktor envisioned a great military future for his son. He would grow up strong, intelligent, and become an officer and pilot in the Russian Air Force. He would be a loyal communist and a part of making Russia great again. Viktor knew that growing up as a devoted communist would be necessary in order to fully achieve the military goals he had conjured up for his new son. He had learned well as an officer in the Krasnaya Armiya, Red Army, that one's politics and allegiance came first and were the only route to better positions. To believe otherwise would lead nowhere.

Sasha's father, Viktor, was born shortly after the turn of the century during the reign of the last czar, Nicholas II. His parents and their parents before them were peasant farmers within a rural and very poor village commune south of St. Petersburg. They had known no other life beyond the dictatorship and oppression of the czarist regimes. Tatyana, his mother, was born and raised in Moscow where her father served in the administrative offices of the Czar. Consequently, she had the benefit of more formal education and training as she grew into womanhood than would have, say, the daughter of a serf. There was considerable unrest in the early 1900's in Russia.

Viktor had avoided being conscripted to fight in the Czar's army in World War I against the Germans because he was considered necessary to the communal farm work and producing food for the army. But, he found time to join a secret band of young revolutionaries from his and surrounding villages. On the eve of the showdown with the Czar's army in the streets of Petrograd (formerly St. Petersburg) in March, 1917, he and members of his village revolutionary group made their way to the city and joined up with Lenin's Red Guards to bring the downfall of Nicholas II and the czarist monarchy. In the aftermath and turmoil following the take-over by the communists, Viktor earned recognition for his loyalty and obedience to the revolutionary leaders.

In November of that year, Viktor participated as one of Lenin's soldiers in the final raid to overthrow the Provisional Government set up after Nicholas' abdication. He witnessed the storming of the Czar's Winter Palace by out of control Bolshevik mobs; he joined with the Red Guards in quelling the riot and stopping the looting of the Palace and the murder of the remaining Czarist ministers hiding there. Viktor matured quickly during the several months he served with the Red Guards. He witnessed the brutality of the new Bolshevik government—the mass execution of czar ministers and loyalists, and the disarming and execution on the spot of citizens considered suspects. He remained in Petrograd with the Red Guards, and in July, 1918, he was assigned to a military contingent to escort Czar Nicholas II and his family to an exile location in Ekaterinburg.

The weakened Provisional Government had petitioned Lenin's Bolsheviks to permit the family to relocate safely to England, but instead lower level henchmen decided to take them to a house in the distant city. Lenin agreed and gave his word to the Russian people that the Czar and his family would be safely cared for. The Guards delivered them to a confiscated home in Ekaterinburg known as Ipatiev's House with the understanding that they would be kept there until the unrest in the country settled down. There was another family also staying on the ground floor in the house for security purposes. Their name or status wasn't known to the guards accompanying the Czar.

Viktor was on duty outside Ipatiev's House on July 16th when Pavel Medvedev, the Sergeant of the Guard, came out of the house and collected the revolvers from each of the twelve guards on duty. No one knew why. Medvedev told them that it was for their own protection. He didn't want anyone to mistakenly shoot one of themselves. He also told the guards that if they heard gunfire later during the night, they should ignore it and forget it.

About midnight, the commandant of the Red Guards, a belligerent Bolshevik named Yurovsky, entered the Czar's family quarters. "Sir, I am sorry to wake you in the middle of the night, but I must ask you to get your family up and for all of you to get dressed. We must leave," Yurovsky politely ordered.

After they were all dressed and assembled in the main room, Yurovsky led them downstairs and out of the house into the courtyard, and then back into an entrance which led to the basement. Inside the dimly lit and damp basement, there were three wooden straight back chairs aligned side by side.

Yurovsky pleasantly directed: "Your Excellency, you, the Czarina and your son may sit in these chairs. You girls and the rest of you, come and stand behind the Czar."

The Czar's four daughters, his personal physician, Doctor Botkin, a maid and two servants, all of whom had traveled with the entourage from Petrograd, quietly moved in behind the chairs with their backs against a stone wall. They were all situated as if they were about to pose for a photograph. Suddenly, the basement door swung open and in rushed six Red Guards each holding a Kalashnikov repeating rifle with bayonets fixed in place.

No orders were given, no one spoke. The Guards quickly lined up side by side and commenced firing at the startled and helpless forms before them. They continued firing until all were riddled with bullets and their blood flowing in streams across the floor. The last czar of Russia and all of his potential successors were dead.

Shortly after one a.m., Viktor and the other guards heard several volleys of muffled rifle shots. No one spoke. A short while later, Medvedev ordered Viktor and the guards to come to the basement. None of them could believe what they saw. The bodies of the Czar and his family lay in a bloody heap, sprawled atop one another. Some of them had their eyes fixed in an open stare. Yurovsky and the firing squad were nowhere to be seen. The guards could not be sure who did the grizzly work.

Medvedev broke the silence. "Okay, you men, pick up these bloody wretches and drag them outside."

Still in shock at the sight of the carnage, the Red Guardsmen began to slowly pick up the bodies and half carry, half drag them out of the basement and into the outside yard.

"Bring them this way!" Medvedev, also visibly shaken by the scene, his voice dry, quietly ordered.

The guards carried the bodies, one by one, to an open pit several hundred meters into the nearby forest. Viktor remembered that he had seen peasants digging in the area the day before but paid them no mind.

"Lay them out in a row in the pit," Medvedev directed.

Some of the guards were still retching as they carried out the vile work. After the bodies were in the pit, Medvedev instructed four of the guards to fetch the several bags of lime that were stacked innocuously next to the house.

"Spread the stuff over them," he ordered. "Use up all of it. And throw the bags in as well. Katsanov! Get out of your stupor, and help the others to lay those railway cross ties across that mess."

Viktor was still nauseated from the ordeal and moved slowly with the others to pick up the heavy cross ties which had been pre-positioned nearby. They laid them across the lime-covered bodies.

"Well done, men," Medvedev acknowledged as he viewed the neatly accomplished horror before them. "Now, get those shovels and cover all of this up. Then rake it clean and scatter brush and leaves over the whole area. I want this place to look like no one has ever been here. Make it good, and we'll be gone.

The memory of the bullet-riddled bodies, the streams of blood covering the basement floor and the distorted figures lined up in the pit remained a deeply imbedded secret within Viktor for the rest of his life. The Red Guards detachment at Ekaterinburg was disbanded, and the members dispatched in different directions all over Russia with a warning to forget everything about the events of that bloody night. Viktor was more fortunate than some, he was dispatched to Moscow. He never spoke of the incident at Ekaterinburg to anyone ever, and when on a few occasions he would come face to face with one of the other guards from that ill-fated period, neither would acknowledge the other. He continued to serve as a soldier in the Red Army, and he was later awarded for his loyalty and deeds with an appointment to the revolutionary officers' academy. While he had little formal or substantive education, it didn't matter. Loyalty to the new Communist Party was sufficient to prove his worth.

It was in Moscow that Viktor met Tatyana at a social gathering arranged at the officer candidate school when he was in his third year. She was smitten by his bravado and tall, dark and ruggedly handsome features, as was he by her extraordinary intelligence and beauty. She was tall and thin with light skin texture, and she had penetrating blue eyes. The fact that he was a loyal and devoted communist bothered Tatyana, but she managed to overcome her doubts in favor of love. She was an accomplished student of Russian literature and languages, particular the prose and poetry of Fyodor Dostoevsky, an early day Christian who maintained certain mystical beliefs. The influence of his works upon Tatyana persuaded her that she could move Viktor away from his communist leanings. Sergei Aksakov and Tolstoy also inspired Tatyana's hopes for a new Russia, but her devotion to Alexandr Pushkin's incarnate Russian spirit was perhaps the most influential in her beliefs.

Tatyana's mother, Bonita, a stern woman and bitter survivor of the revolution, had guided Tatyana's learning. She told her daughter that her name had been drawn from Pushkin's, "EUGENE ONEGIN." In the story, Pushkin described one his characters, Tatyana, as an immortal heroine. "She captured beauty, youth, freshness and angelic innocence." Tatyana was a "Madonna", as the story was told. "She was a peerless ruler of sanctity, perfectly self-possessed, proper in all things and faithful to her husband." These things Bonita impressed upon her daughter to indulge. Accordingly, Bonita did not approve of Viktor for Tatyana. He was ruggedly handsome but with a peasant crudeness and complete lack of appreciation for noble finery. Nevertheless, Tatyana allowed herself to be pursued through the next year and married Viktor upon his graduation and commissioning as an officer in the new Soviet Red Army. It would, nonetheless, be her strong influence that cultivated his bearing and military career, although it could not diminish his devotion to the communist cause.

The honeymoon of freedom from czarism was short lived. The provisional government set up by Lenin lasted only eight months. The brief respite from autocratic and totalitarian rule ended as the

Bolshevik Communist leaders promptly reinstituted the secret police, censorship and suppression of all citizen rights. The communists moved quickly to restore order. In doing so, tens of thousands of former soldiers and government officials serving the Czar were rounded up and either sent to detention facilities or executed on the spot. Carrying a weapon was automatic death to the offender. Extremism was always a Russian trait, but the communists went far beyond that because it was necessary to bring the revolutionary chaos under control.

Lenin established the Chrezvychayna Kommisiya, the Cheka, secret police, to enforce his rule. A renewed reign of terror was levied on Russian people, even greater than that during the era of the czars. The Cheka had a free range of authorities extending from arrest, to interrogation, to torture, to prompt execution, if deemed warranted. The Cheka would eventually evolve into the Narodnyy Komisariat Vnutrennikh Del (NKVD) and finally the Komitet Gosudarstvennoy Bezopasnosti (KGB) with off-shoots and collateral agencies all combining to keep the Russian people captive and terrorized.

Lasting Contempt

Viktor's new wife, Tatyana, told him shortly after they were married that when she was fifteen years old, and at the height of the revolution, a knock came at their door in the early hours one morning. Her father was told to get dressed immediately, and he was hustled out by four sinister looking men who identified themselves as police. Tatyana's mother tried for days to make contact with her husband, and then in a week, a dark-suited man came to their door.

"Your husband is fine," he told my mother. "He was being detained for political reasons and would likely be released shortly. However, in the meantime, you must begin now making payments for his care. He requires warm clothes, food and personal necessities. The normal things, you know."

He continued, "The amount payable now is two hundred rubles, and I will continue to come by and collect the same amount each month until he is released."

"But how long will that be?" Bonita asked. "We have no money. Since the revolution my husband has not been paid. He has had to do odd jobs just to feed us. I do not even have two hundred rubles to pay you now."

"Madam that is your problem; perhaps I can arrange to take some jewelry or similar valuable item in exchange for this first payment. I am sure my superiors will understand, but I must return with some representation of your concern for your husband. You do understand, don't you?"

Bonita was frantic. She made quickly back into her bedroom and took a gold and amber broach which had belonged to her mother. It had some obvious monetary value but also great sentimental value to her.

"Here is something to begin with," she said, handing the broach to the grim looking secret policeman. "It is all I can come up with at this moment."

"Dah, dah," he responded, "but you must begin paying in rubles after this, or your husband will have to do without his necessities. I shall be back in one month unless, of course, your husband is released by then. Goodbye!"

Bonita went to the Cheka headquarters numerous times to try to visit her husband only to be told that he was in detention and could not have visitors until the magistrate had ruled on his case. When she petitioned to try and determine what the charges were against him, she was given only vague answers.

"He is charged with continuing allegiance to the Czar," or "He has not shown loyal support to the new revolutionary government, and he is suspected of being a traitor," and, "His case will come before the judges soon."

The days of Tatyana's father's confinement moved into weeks then months, and finally into agonizing years. Still, neither she nor her mother were allowed to visit or talk to him by telephone. She said that they were forced to move into a one bedroom apartment in a government managed complex. Her mother took a job at a food cooperative, distributing rationed produce and meat to authorized patrons. She was barely able to make enough money to pay the required monthly fee to the police authorities as well as take home a meager amount of food to sustain the two of them. Tatyana said that she worked at a small state school where she learned and eventually taught English, mostly to Soviet trade bureaucrats and police agents.

Late one evening, Tatyana and her mother were preparing for bed when there was a knock on the door. Fearing the worst of late night intruders, Tatyana called through the door, "Who is it, please?"

"I am Vitali Kraftsov, I was an acquaintance of your father's," the weak response came. "I promised your father I would visit you to see about your welfare. May I come in for just a brief moment?"

Apprehensively, Tatyana opened the door to the dimly lit hallway and took full view of a tattered looking shell of a man who was likely much younger than his worn-out appearance. He looked harmless, and Tatyana permitted him to come in, quickly re-bolting the door.

"Please sit down. I am Tatyana. You said you had word about my father? But first, may I get you some tea?"

"A glass of warm tea would be fine," he said. "I am not hungry. I apologize for disturbing you so late, but I have been searching for you and your mother for several months. Is your mother well? Is she here?"

Tatyana's mother entered the small sitting room. "I am Bonita Petrovich. Who are you?"

"Madam Petrovich, I am Vitali Krafsov. I promised your late husband, Ivan, that I would bring you his blessings and concerns as soon as I was released from prison and permitted to leave."

The words, "late husband," froze in the minds of Tatyana and her mother. They had begun to expect the worst anytime in the recent years, but now to hear the news came as a shock. They put their arms around each other and began to quietly sob. Finally, Tatyana's composure returned.

"Permit me to get your tea. Please tell us what has happened to my father?"

Vitali looked up a bit surprised as he eyed the two women.

"What do you mean, what happened? Do you not know that your father, Ivan, is dead?"

Bonita could not speak. Tatyana took in her breath as she sat the clear glass cup of tea on a side table.

"When did he die? What happened? Was he ill?"

Vitali still had a look of disbelief. "Did you not know that your father died over four years ago, just three days after he was arrested? Four years ago!"

Tatyana sat next to her mother on the small sofa and held her close. Taking Vitali's words in, Tatyana began to ask question after question while her mother sat and stared at this stranger, tears streaming down her face.

"What, how did he die? How is it possible that he died four years ago? We have been paying a monthly fee to help keep him in clothes and food. Was he ill? Did they kill him? What on earth happened and why?"

Vitali began his story: "I was already a prisoner in a jail cell at Lubyanka Prison when they brought your father in late one night. They literally threw him into my cell. He had been beaten badly and was bleeding from wounds in his head and body. I tried to assist and comfort him as best I could with only rags and a little water. By morning he was conscious, but in such pain from the beatings that he could not move. He told me about the two of you, and he gave me this gold R5 ruble coin which he had hidden in his sock." He handed the gold coin to Bonita. "He said that it was his good luck piece, and you would recognize it as being from him. He said that I should take it and give it to you if something happened to him and I was able to leave the prison."

Vitali continued: "Later that morning, they took him away for the most part of the day, then returned him to the cell that evening. His wounds had been cleaned and bandaged, but the beatings had taken away most of his strength, and whatever they did to him that day had left him dazed and incoherent. Early the next morning the guards came again and took him away. I think they were questioning him and probably torturing him to answer their questions. I don't know. I was never able to talk to him again. On the third day, I think, they took him away for the last time. Later, a guard told me that he had collapsed and died while the interrogators were questioning him. 'Too bad,' the guard said. That is all I know, but I am shocked that you were not informed of his death."

Bonita spoke. In bitter words she told Vitali of the visit by the secret policeman three days after her husband was arrested, how he had demanded a payment for her husband's upkeep while in prison, and how she had continued to give a police officer money once each month when he came by to collect. She said that this had gone on for over four years.

She lamented, "He was probably already dead when that despicable brute first came to our door."

"What can I say?" Vitali asked. "I am truly not surprised by what you tell me. I have heard stories even worse than yours since I was released. I am so sorry that you have had to endure this for so long, and that I am the bearer of such bad news. Forgive me."

Bonita asked, "How is it that you are free? Why did they let you go? You are not some secret policeman yourself, are you?"

"No, no, please." Vitali quickly responded. "I was being held on a charge of petty theft. I took some vegetables and fruit from a market shelf to feed my family and was caught. I spent almost four years in Lubiyanka serving out my time as a janitor and servant to the jail bosses there. I was beaten and humiliated daily. Finally, the prison became so crowded they released me. It could have been worse. Often they killed prisoners for no reason and dispensed with their bodies."

He continued, "While I was in prison all this time, I learned that my wife died, and my two children are nowhere to be found. You know how confusing our city is now, everyone has been displaced, even you; I had a very difficult time finding you."

Bonita apologized, "I am so sorry for you. We thank you for coming and telling us what we had dreaded but already suspected."

Vitali Kraftsov departed after awhile and was never heard from again.

Tatyana told Viktor that her mother went to the Lubiyanka Prison offices following Vitali Krafsov's visit, and after several fruitless attempts she was finally granted entry. She was then passed on to a half dozen petty bureaucrats who denied any knowledge of her husband, much less the collection of monthly payments for his upkeep. Ivan, having been an employee of the Czar's Administration, was a non-person in the eyes and records of the new Soviet Government. She got nowhere and finally gave up her quest.

She said that she and her mother continued to work at their respective jobs and did their best to cope with the turmoil around them. Tatyana was exceptionally bright and continued to study and improve her education status. While she despised and hated her masters, she was forced to play the game and to demonstrate her loyalty in order to make her way. During her courtship with Viktor, she completed the requirements to be certified as a language teacher. This enhanced her citizen status considerably. She had been accepted as a loyal communist and devoted worker. This was a pre-requisite for survival. In her heart, Tatyana maintained intense hatred for the Soviets and everything they espoused. Even as she was courted by Viktor, an avowed communist and officer-to-be in the Red Army, and though she eventually fell in love with him, she retained deep emotional scars and serious doubts regarding the Party.

"So now you see, Viktor, why I have so much distrust and hatred for our government."

Tatyana's story about her father stirred deeply within Viktor. He recalled his own dark memory of the events that took place at Ekaterinburg the night the Czar and his family were executed.

"I do understand, Tatyana," Viktor tried to reassure her. "I have seen many terrible things which the secret police have done. And, I do not approve, but I believe that good will come from all of this. We are recovering from a sad period; many people have been unfairly treated, but in the end order will be restored. I know that it will. We must trust in our leaders."

Viktor knew just how brutal the Bolshevik communists could be. But his secret remained within him, and he never revealed to Tatyana or anyone his involvement in the massacre of the czar and his family.

Class Survival

Tatyana and Viktor continued to live their sparse existence in the military community near the rural Afghan border. They did their best to nourish their son to a healthy start in life, while Russia moved further into turmoil. Viktor was a loyal Red Army officer, and with Tatyana's skillful help, he worked hard to prove his value. Stalin unleashed more repression with the "yezhovshchina" movement, the

Great Purges, named for the head of the dreaded NKVD secret police, Nicolai Yezhov. Stalin eventually also had Yezhov executed when he failed to carry out vengeance quickly enough.

During the period between 1931 and 1937, over 14 million Russians were either executed or rounded up and sent to forced labor camps created all over the country. Those found most dissident were either promptly executed or if they possessed a particular skill, they were sent to the further most camps in Siberia which were under the control of the NKVD. In most cases, these camps were worse than death itself.

In 1937, Stalin fearing a mutiny, eliminated over 500 of his generals and admirals, including the Chief of the Red Army and the Commander-in- Chief of the Red Navy. An estimated 33,000 Russian officers were either executed or sent to labor camps. This both traumatized, and benefited, many younger officers who survived and were suddenly promoted up the chain to take the place of one moved ahead of themselves. Viktor was promoted to major, skipping the grades of senior-lieutenant and captain. He had impressed his superiors with his loyalty and obedience. The promotion, in addition to providing a little more income, brought relocation to Kiev.

Viktor was given command of a Frontal Aviation squadron providing tactical support for the ground forces dispersed around the capital city of Ukraine. Here they moved into a small government-provided apartment near the air base. Tatyana obtained a job as a teacher at a Russian-supervised school.

The assignment to a military post outside Russia was considered a special treat because Soviet officers received additional pay and allowances for Foreign Service. The Russians, however, were unwelcome guests in Ukraine, and they lived in tight knit communities. Fraternization with locals was strictly discouraged. The past deeds of the czars and the communists were not easily forgotten. Consequently, tensions flared frequently when Russian soldiers and airmen ventured into the city.

Tatyana kept close to her community and continued to raise and educate young Sasha. It was apparent from his very early years that he was an exceptionally bright boy. His mother spent endless hours tutoring him as well as insuring that he enjoyed the healthiest food she could find. The mother and son grew extremely close to one another as she introduced him to her same appreciation for literature and languages.

The Russian Air Force was slowly building its aircraft inventory and although had very few aircraft in flyable condition at Viktor's base, several new IL-2 "Sturmovik" armored ground attack fighter-bombers were soon to arrive. During the dull period, Viktor was able to spend much more time with his family than would have been the norm. The majority of his duty time was spent getting his enlisted men out of trouble and disciplining them. This was hardly the job for a fighter pilot eager to participate in the development of Stalin's great fighting force. He was also aware that being stationed in the Kiev Military District, which had a reputation for being "the gateway to power" for aspiring officers, was the place to be. The brilliant careers of many Russian generals, both in the ground and air forces, were forged through a duty tour in the tough Kiev Military District. Viktor's career might have taken a turn for the worse except for the brilliant judgment of Tatyana, a fortuitous accident and a Ukrainian benefactor.

Viktor awakened one night by the loud ringing of the telephone.

"Dah!" he answered.

"Katsanov, a stupid Ukrainian girl has been raped and murdered tonight in Kiev. Two soldiers in your squadron have been identified by others who saw them take the girl away from a drunken party," the voice screamed. "Why were your men in the city, Katsanov? I want you to find them immediately, lock them up and keep them out of sight!"

His commander further told him to keep the situation under control and get the soldiers quickly transported out of Kiev and back to a base in Russia.

The colonel closed with, "I don't want any bad publicity over this, Major Katsanov. Do you understand? It will be your head if this situation gets out of hand! Now, go find them!"

Viktor called his operations officer and the two went to the squadron barracks building to find the two suspects. They were both in the barracks, in their bunks and obviously suffering drunken hangovers. After they rousted them out and threw them into a cold shower, Viktor and his operations officer questioned them. Both denied the incident and the charges, saying that they didn't leave the base the night before. Meanwhile, Viktor's commander summoned him to come to his office immediately.

"Major Katsanov, did you find your soldiers?" The colonel asked.

"Yes Sir, Colonel. We have them isolated in a room in the barracks."

"Good, we must act quickly. The people in Kiev are causing big trouble over this. We could have a riot. The mayor called me to ask what I was going to do, and I told him that we did not know anything about the incident and the girl's murder. Now, understand Katsanov, the mayor is one of us; we don't have to worry about him, but his vice mayor is a very nationalistic Ukrainian dissident. He is smart and has the people behind him. He wants us to turn the two soldiers over to the local police to be charged and tried in their court. I do not want this to happen and the resultant bad publicity I will receive for the acts of these two idiots. You must get rid of them, and now!" the colonel was shouting.

"Yes Sir, Colonel. I will arrange to get them on an airplane or train as soon as possible." Viktor replied and then asked, "but Sir, would it not be better for our reputation and the image of the Soviet Air Force if we turn them over to the Ukrainian authorities and satisfy the locals? We are not well-liked by the Ukrainians, and this might help change their opinion of us."

"Katsanov, this is my command and my reputation at risk. I want this situation closed immediately. If the two soldiers are not here, then nothing happened. Do you understand?" The colonel stood glaring. Viktor saluted smartly and departed.

Viktor told his operations officer to keep the two soldiers locked up, gather their personal effects and be prepared to dispatch them with an armed escort to wherever they could find transportation headed toward Russian territory. He then went by his house to collect his briefcase which he had neglected to take with him in the haste of the early morning phone call. He told Tatyana about the events surrounding the call and the colonel's orders. Tatyana was livid.

"Viktor, you cannot do this! An innocent girl has died, and your animal of a commander wants to let the two murderers go free just to protect his reputation. You are a fool if you go along with him. You will be equally responsible for the murder, if you let them go free. You must not!"

"What else can I do, Tatyana?" He was perplexed.

The phone rang, and it was his operations officer.

"Major, we cannot find any transportation to move these two until at least late tomorrow. Everything is tied up with the war. There is no room for two soldiers and a guard on any movements headed east."

Viktor headed back to the colonel's office, terrified of the prospects of the wrath he was surely going to face. When he arrived, he was told by an aide that the colonel had suddenly been called to Moscow and was at the moment at the flight line preparing to depart. This gave Viktor some breathing room. He had heard both the colonel's orders and Tatyana's plea to not help the murder suspects escape. As he was about to leave the colonel's office, a short stocky man in a dark civilian suit barged in.

"I am Mikola Balatskiy, vice mayor of Kiev. Where is Colonel Zorik?"

The aide responded, "Sir, I am sorry, but Colonel Zorik is away to Moscow. Can I help you?"

The vice mayor was upset with mounting anger.

"Yes! Who can I speak to about the two soldiers who are suspected of murdering a young Ukrainian girl last night?"

"Sir, I do not know what you are talking about," the aide haughtily replied. "We are not aware of any such murder by any of our soldiers. You must be mistaken to come here. How did you get into our base? Who permitted you to come here?"

Balatskiy was livid with the curt response. He began to raise his voice.

"The people of Kiev will not tolerate such acts by you Soviet animals that roam our streets by night. I demand to see someone who is in charge. I will not leave until I have!"

Viktor had heard enough.

"Mr. Balatskiy, may I speak with you?"

He guided the vice mayor to an empty office and closed the door.

"Sir," Viktor began, "I am Major Katsanov. The two men you seek are in my custody. I am so very sorry for what happened, and I am prepared to turn them over to your authorities. If you agree, I will have them escorted outside the air base and release them to the custody of the Kiev police when they are ready to receive them."

Balatskiy looked at Viktor firmly.

"Why have these men not been turned over before this? Why did I have to come here personally to demand their arrest? Has someone been covering up for those two animals?"

"No, Sir," Viktor replied, coloring his story slightly. "I was just here to also see the colonel and to tell him that we have the two suspects under arrest, and I wished to turn them over to the authorities. Where shall I have them delivered?"

Viktor felt both relieved and frightened. He knew that he was doing the right thing, but he also knew that when the colonel returned that he might likely be worse off than the two soldiers.

Tatyana was delighted with Viktor's news. She said that he was a hero for standing up to his tyrannical boss. Viktor was not so sure.

The soldiers were delivered that afternoon to the Kiev police as promised. The following day brought a strange and fortuitous twist. Colonel Zorik's single-engine aircraft crashed on its return trip to Kiev, and he was killed. Viktor was saved.

Later in the week, he received an official looking envelope at his office. It was from the vice mayor's office and contained an invitation for Tatyana and him to attend a dinner at Mr. Balatskiy's apartment the following week. Viktor showed the invitation to Tatyana. They had never been invited to a civilian official's home ever, much less in Ukraine.

"They don't like us, they even despise us," said Viktor. "I believe we should ignore it and stay away. It could be some publicity trap to embarrass us and our government. We need to be careful."

"Viktor, we are going to the dinner. You are being recognized for doing your duty with those murderers. We will go. It is our duty, and we should try to be friends with the people of Kiev. Besides, they believe that Russians are barbarians, and we need to show them that we are not."

Viktor and Tatyana arrived at the vice mayor's apartment on the appointed evening. They were welcomed warmly by Balatskiy who answered the door. He introduced them to his wife, Maria, and four other guests, all Kievans. The apartment was surprisingly small and compact. They had expected a more elegant home for such an important man as the vice mayor. But, in spite of the closeness of furniture, table and chairs, the two hosts and the six guests got off to a pleasant evening. Mr. Balatskiy's generous dispensing of vodka helped to lighten the conversation and engender the new friendships. There were many toasts, and Viktor received his share. The vice mayor extolled Viktor for his quick work; "capturing the murderous scum" and turning them over to the proper authorities.

"I was shocked," he said, "when Major Katsanov told me that we could have the suspects that very day!" And, he chided Viktor for the benefit of his other guests. "Perhaps the Russian guests in our country are not all bad." They all laughed.

Viktor smiled and humbly took the praise. Only he and Tatyana knew how close they all came to facing a potential crisis or maybe even a disaster had his commander not crashed and died. Viktor himself might not even be around this day if events had turned otherwise. The evening was a joy for both Viktor and especially Tatyana. She had great empathy for the Ukrainian people. They had suffered at the hands of the communist tyrants not unlike she and her mother with the tragic death of her father. Kiev was the cradle of the Slavic people and the first capital of Russia. It had endured 1500 years of patchwork history with periods of prosperity followed by years of decline caused by numerous enemy raids by various factions dating back to era of the Mongols. And now, as the Germans were advancing from the west, Russian troops were stationed throughout The Ukraine in an attempt to use the land and the people as a buffer.

As the delightfully prepared dinner came to a close and guests were sipping their hearty Moldavian wine, they were all taken by surprise when Mikola Balatskiy began to sing a Ukrainian love ballad from his place at the head of the narrow table. His voice was strong but softly muted. And as he reached the end of the first stanza, Maria responded to him with an equally delightful retort. Her voice, as well, reflected firmness and resolve. Their voices rose and fell now together, and then in beautiful counterpoint. Viktor and Tatyana, and the other guests, sat transfixed by the extraordinary outpouring of love and devotion between Mikola and Maria. Tatyana could scarcely breathe.

The evening was complete. Viktor was emotionally moved. It was then that he truly understood the passion that Tatyana had for people and the deep wisdom she possessed to influence his actions. They departed feeling as though they had spent a magical evening, deeply immersed in the heart of the Ukrainian soul. It was as if they had been entertained by a czar of the past.

As they walked out the door, Balatskiy smiled. "Thank you, major, and I want to tell you that I have written a personal letter to the chief of staff of your Air Force to thank him for your honesty and integrity, and for what you have done to help the relationships between our peoples."

TWO

The Great Patriotic War

The war in Europe began in earnest for the Russians in June, 1941, when the Germans launched Operation "Barbarosa," viciously attacking Ukraine, Byelorussia and the Baltics. Minsk held out for three days, and Kiev for two more days. Viktor was able to get Tatyana and Sasha safely on a train to Moscow before Kiev was overrun by the German ground forces. He also escaped ahead of the Germans along with several other officers, reaching Moscow several days later. The Soviet government and the military were in chaos. The Germans had destroyed most of the Russian Air Force. Leningrad was under siege, and the Nazi forces moved to within twenty miles of Moscow before grinding to a halt in the worst winter in Russian history.

Viktor reported to Red Army Air Forces Headquarters in Moscow and was assigned as a planning officer. Thereafter, he saw no direct combat during the war, only an occasional visit to units at the Front.

As the Great Patriotic War, the Russians' name for World War II, wore on, Viktor excelled as a planning strategist and had been steadily promoted, becoming a Colonel and serving on the staff of the Minister of Defense in Moscow. He had located a suitable apartment for his family, and Tatyana taught English in a Moscow school. Later, she was selected to teach at Moscow University, where English became a primary subject for Soviet controlled education. A considerable part of her teaching duties were instructing NKVD (later known as the KGB) secret police agents in the English language. As a result of Tatyana's teaching skills, Sasha also became fluent in English. He spoke English easily as a young child, and later as an adult without a trace of Russian accent.

Stalin began a systematic purge of any, and all, who might pose a threat to his aim of a totally controlled society within the bounds of the newly formed Soviet Union. While the Western Allies were completing the task of defeating Japan in the Pacific, Stalin was busily reconstructing Eastern Europe with only passive opposition from the West. The purge of senior political officials and military officers was the second of the Stalin regime. The consequence of the first purge almost lost his war with Germany.

Young Communist

Sasha was fifteen years old when the war came to an end in 1945. His father had escaped the wrath of Stalin's purges by remaining a loyal communist and was now a trusted senior officer and a major general on the Soviet General Staff. Tatyana, on the other hand still did not share her husband's zeal for the "new" Soviet Union, but she understood the reality of the harsh culture to which she had grown accustomed. She had dreamed of a more liberal Russian society after the war, one in which her son could become highly educated and excel in a profession of his choice. But, it became quickly evident that Stalin had far different plans for his Soviet Union. In a matter of two years, he turned his ideological fury on the West and began a systematic program of "fencing-in" the people living within Russia and the Soviet States.

The "Iron Curtain" became the barrier between Eastern and Western Europe—principally to keep Soviet citizens in rather than others out.

Sasha had easily, eagerly for that matter, adapted to the catechism of pro-communist teachings to which he was exposed in the very first years of schooling.

He was enrolled, at the age of eleven, in the Young Pioneers. The program of indoctrination was patterned after the Hitler's Youth organization, which featured weekly military training sessions integrated into the public school curriculum. In addition to the theory and concept of social and communal lifestyle, he was taught basic crafts of the Soviet military, including map reading, marksmanship and first aid. The Pioneers were taken on field trips and participated in modest paramilitary exercises to practice their learned skills. The Young Pioneers were not unlike the Boy Scouts of the West except that "God and Country" were supplanted with "Stalin and Communism." The Pioneer motto was: "Vsegda gotov" - Always ready. Sasha excelled in every phase of the Young Pioneers' indoctrination and training.

He zealously studied the Tovarishch, the Pioneer handbook, which contained a colorful array of Soviet military arsenals, tanks, aircraft, military uniforms and the various rank structures of the military, all intended to entice impressionable young boys.

"I will become an officer in the great Soviet Army," Sasha would boast to his parents.

The Young Pioneers were also heavily immersed in the policies and requirements of the Communist Party and the Soviet Government, especially the enemies of the Party and the Soviet Union. He learned that he must have a strong moral-political belief and bearing if he were going to serve his country as a good soldier and communist. His Pioneer druzhina (brigade) commander lectured the students that too much affection, sentimentality, love and care could produce egotism, laziness and distraction from labor and concentration on important goals.

Tatyana frequently attempted to temper Sasha's zeal and fervor for becoming a devout communist and military war fighter like his father and remained at odds with Viktor on the issue. But Viktor continued to tutor the young Soviet-to-be who absorbed his taught skills and learned them well. The conflict caused considerable stress within the young communist who was very close and devoted to his mother, but the attraction put forth by skilled Soviet education leaders was sufficient to sustain his interest.

Sasha later joined the KOMSOMOL, The Young Communist League, created by Stalin to capture the minds and hearts of young adolescents, to inspire Russian patriotism and to foster antagonism toward all non-communists. The League's program of indoctrination and training was filled with Marxist-Leninist dogma and communist morality designed to entice and motivate young men and women to become soldiers for Mother Russia. A central part of the indoctrination was also intended to prepare young Soviets to meet the district Military Commissariat (voyenkomat—draft board) when they turned eighteen and became eligible for conscription.

Preparing for conscription was not in Sasha's career plans, however. He fully intended to present himself for officer training and then become a pilot in the Soviet Air Force like his father.

As rewards for excellent performance, students were given opportunities to ride in a tank or to take a short ride in an AN-2 trainer plane. There was no doubt after his first plane ride that Sasha was going to follow his dream to be an aviator.

Both the Young Pioneers and the Komsomol were heavily infiltrated by KGB agents, some acting as teachers or instructors, and within Komsomol, even students. The KGB influence, of course, manifested many dark sides. Among them was the encouragement of spying and snooping on family members and neighbors, and they were required to report any suspect activities, overheard conversations or written materials which might be interpreted to reflect anti-government sentiments. This aspect of KOMSOMOL caused Sasha considerable difficulty. He had grown increasingly aware of his mother's sentiments about the post-war Soviet Government and the wrong direction she felt it was taking the people. He tried often to engage her in philosophical discussions about communism, Soviet society and his future goals, but more often than not changed the subject of conversation lest he fall into a trap of deceit and possible compromise of his mother's feelings.

On one occasion he was moved to the verge of talking to one of his counselors about his mother after she had returned from a government sponsored trip to London to participate in a language seminar and to polish her teaching skills. Upon her return, she had been filled with enthusiasm and the spirit of being away from the misery of Moscow and the constant intolerance of human dignity. She flowed with stories of London, the people and their happiness and freedom to do anything and go anywhere they wished without government questioning or intervention.

"No one in England is afraid of the police, or anyone else," she said. "Everyone is happy that the war is over and that their lives are prospering."

Sasha and his father were both distressed by Tatyana's stories and her new feelings. Sasha couldn't sleep comfortably for days or get his mother's attitude out of his thoughts. The Komsomol indoctrinations and daily admonitions by his teachers and trainers haunted him constantly. Eventually he erased from his mind all reflections of his mother's feelings and thoughts and became even deeper involved with the Komsomol and its teachings.

In 1947, at seventeen, Sasha joined the DOSAAF, the Volunteer Society of Cooperation with the Army, Aviation and the Fleet, which had also been created by Stalin as a "defense-patriotic organization." The main purpose of DOSAAF was to continue to strengthen the Soviet military by intensifying the training of young men before they reached the age for conscription. Although the war had been over for two years, DOSAAF continued to enlist older workers and gave them instruction in home defense. There was little doubt of Stalin's goals.

He joined an elite group of others to participate in light aircraft instruction, parachuting, weapons handling and marksmanship. Sasha easily took to the flying instruction, quickly soloed and continued to impress his teachers with his enthusiasm, intelligence and loyalty. He ranked first in virtually every category of training and skills challenges presented in DOSAAF, and he scored equally high in academics. With his mother's encouragement, he continued to use English as much as possible at home. She felt that the future of Russia would rely upon the West and the English language. Sasha was careful, however, not to overdo it with his classmates or teachers.

Conflict

The KGB had first noticed Sasha through one of its agents within the KOMSOMOL. They placed him on their special monitoring program and continued to track his progress in DOSAAF. The secret police were always on the lookout for exceptionally bright students; if they displayed extraordinary loyalty, even better. Sasha was under close surveillance, along with his family, for several years before he was advised of the KGB's future interest in him. During their surveillance, they did not detect any lack of patriotism or loyalty on the part of Tatyana. She, like many Russians with even less personal animosity toward the government, had lost her faith in the communist ideology and the country's future. She retreated into her inner self. She kept her feelings well hidden. She suffered greatly within.

An even deeper secret kept by Tatyana was her participation in an underground intellectual society with whom she met once every two weeks. The kruzhki ("Circle of Devotees") dated back to the mid-1800's and the Tsarist period. It attracted men and women who were willing despite risk of discovery, torture, imprisonment and even death, in an attempt to find some peace through intellectual fellowship with other concerned citizens who had the belief and hope that there was a better Russia to be achieved. The small groups of kruzhki, often less than a dozen within each cell, would meet at pre-designated locations, usually at night in someone's home in an attempt to create a small niche of freedom of thought and ideas.

It was certainly suspected that open dissidents such as Roy Medvedev, Andrei Sakharov and Lev Timofeyev, as well as numerous members of the Writers' Union and the Russian Academy of Science, were among those who met at similar gatherings. Some were discovered, but many were not. Russians who dared risk becoming a member of the kruzhki worked at creating two distinct minds: a day mind to go about their normal lives and work, and a night mind with which to release their frustrations and create dreams and hope for the future of their family and country.

The kruzhkis learned to create a strong discipline in each mind culture, lest one betray the other and cause sure disaster for themselves and their colleagues. At these meetings, Tatyana and her friends would discuss everything from religion, science, literature, philosophy, politics, government policies and the ever-tightening restrictions. They would also discuss daily events, news and the impacts on their lives, and always with a longing and hope for the potential for a better future. She would attend meetings on the pretext that she was tutoring English to weaker students. In the days after the meetings, Tatyana and the other members would go about their daily lives. If they, by chance, met one of their kruzhki colleagues on the street or elsewhere, there would never be an acknowledgement of familiarity. Neither Viktor nor Sasha ever suspected Tatyana's outside activities.

The KGB in its surveillance and background development of Sasha were also neither aware at the time. The ever-present fear among the kruzhki was KGB infiltration and the insertion of an agent within a meeting group. It happened occasionally and the result was always the same; catastrophic for all.

Officer Candidate

Sasha met all the qualifications to become an officer candidate and future aviator. He had performed superbly in the KOMSOMOL and the DOSAAF. His academic grades placed him at the top of his class, and he displayed all of the characteristics of a devout and loyal communist. Sasha also became accomplished at flying small airplanes. He was a fair-haired young Soviet in the eyes of his mentors.

The Soviet Union conducted officer candidate training at 160 Higher Military Training Colleges, Academies and Secondary Schools. Twenty-four of these colleges were run by the Soviet Air Force. Ten of the colleges were for training pilot officer candidates, and the remainder was for training navigators, military engineers, communications officers and maintenance technicians. With his father's influence, his son's proven abilities and the interest of the KGB, Sasha was selected to attend an Air Force Pilot Training College.

Sasha's parents saw him off to the Volgograd (Stalingrad) Higher Military Aviation College for Pilots, located some 600 miles south of Moscow, where he would spend the next four years. If all went well, he would graduate with academic degree and a commission as a lieutenant with pilot wings.

Sasha had strongly desired to follow his father's footsteps, become a fighter pilot and to share the glory of those pilots' daring do, but he was greatly disappointed when he received his orders to report to the bomber pilot training college at Volgograd.

"Volgograd trains bomber pilots, father. I want to become a fighter pilot like you. I want to be a jet fighter pilot," he lamented.

Viktor attempted to influence his son's appointment and was convinced that there would be no problem in getting his son into the school of his choice, but the KGB had other plans for Sasha. They had arranged for his appointment to the Air Force Officers Training College where long-range aviation training took place. Viktor appealed, but the decision had been made "higher up". Sasha would go to Volgograd. Viktor knew the consequences of making any further issue of the decision.

Traditionally, newly inducted cadets spent their first two months in basic military training, after which they would begin to concentrate on an intensive regime of academic study. However, the initial training phase was left up to the school commandant and could continue until he was satisfied that the cadets were well indoctrinated into military life. Initially, the cadets were outfitted in traditional thick khaki uniforms with red and gold shoulder boards with large "CA" (Soviet Army) letters and they were issued calf-high leather boots and rough-cut shoes. Sasha and his classmates looked more like head-shorn, confused convicts than officer cadets. The aviation colleges generally provided adequate, but dull food, quarters and uniforms, and a monthly allowance of 15R (rubles)—about $20. Flight training usually began in the second year. The program continued for the next three years, culminating with graduation, commissioning as an officer, a degree and Soviet Air Force pilot's wings.

Initiation into military life was rigorous from the outset. Military training was conducted by tough and hardened NCO's, who at one time might have been candidates themselves but flunked out for one reason or another. Now they were in a position to try to wash-out others, with severe and often brutal treatment. The routine for Sasha and his classmates usually followed a schedule of alternating between two weeks in the classroom studying military, civil and political theory and two weeks at the training center studying meteorology, basic navigation techniques and the theory of flight. Hazing and brutal punishment were the order of the day and night for Sasha and the other cadets.

The days began with a 6:00 a.m. reveille, fall-out on to the parade ground for physical exercise, dress for breakfast, followed by a usual daily monotonous offering of two slices of black bread, a quarter gram of butter, a bowl of kasha (weak wheat gruel), or some fish or meat stew-like substance of unidentifiable origin and a mug of bitter tea with a lump of sugar. The breakfasts seldom varied. Then they went out to the parade field for roll call formation, dress inspection and close order drill, followed by a long day of classroom instruction.

The nights became a dread. The NCO's worked in shifts with a hazing routine, terrorizing the cadets with false charges of insubordination, lying, stealing and so on. The barracks were generally without heat in the winter which added to the misery. "Games" were conjured-up by the thugs in charge which might include directing a cadet to measure the length of the barracks with a match stick and then report back his findings. The cadet's answer was never correct. On one occasion, Sasha was singled out for a minor infraction. He was ordered to clean the commodes in the latrine with his only issued toothbrush, to work until finished and inspected to the satisfaction of an NCO. The latter was never achieved, he sat up most of the night waiting for the NCO to return, which he didn't, but he wouldn't have passed anyway—rust and residue scale accumulation over the years prevented any semblance of removal or cleaning.

There were other more distasteful games and challenges to the cadet's dignity, such as "The Horse Races" or "Jousting". The cadets would be ordered to strip naked, and the NCO's would take turns "riding" them like horses, beating them on the behind with their heavy belts or sticks until they were bloody and bruised. Many were hospitalized with their injuries, yet the "games' went on with the hazing rules made up by the NCO's. The officers in the school seldom interfered, and only if a serious injury or death occurred, which it occasionally did. Sasha came close only once to becoming a "horse," but his turn was interrupted when an officer came upon the event and stopped the activities.

Finally, at the end of the day and "horseplay," Sasha and his fellow cadets were gathered around the single black and white television in their barracks to watch Soviet TV News, which came on nightly at 9 p.m. The basic training credo of the college was: "Before we can allow you to study and become smart, we must make tough soldiers out of you!" The first two months of officer training was designed to eliminate any independence, or insubordination, which an energetic young man might display. Sasha was shocked by the treatment, which he had not expected, nor had his father alerted him to prepare for.

The cadets' routine was the same every day except Sundays which then brought only slight relief. The difference between Sundays and other days of the week was that reveille was at 0700 instead of six. The extra hour and the lack of intense Sunday interest by the training NCO's, who were, for the most part, nursing hangovers from their Saturday night before, made those mornings seem almost like a holiday. Of course, the requirement to fall out for roll call, exercise and breakfast were the same dull routine. After breakfast the cadets were required to watch the weekly Sunday propaganda program, "I Serve The Soviet Union."

The remainder of their Sundays was different than the weekday routine; they belonged to the zampolits. The college had several assigned, as did all other educational activities in the Soviet Union. This meant that the regular political indoctrination was intensified with special lectures and sports competitions oriented toward exemplifying good Russians pitted against evil perpetrators. No one was exempt from the Sunday games. The lectures followed the traditional communist rhetoric which characterized how bad things were in Russia before the Revolution, how good life is now and how the slaves in America and the West were oppressed by the capitalistic masters. Every unit had a zampolit assigned just as Sasha had experienced in his KOMSOMOL training. They zealously ruled "their day" with the cadets.

Sunday was also movie night, not the traditional movies one might anticipate, but political films about the Revolution, Lenin and Stalin. Sasha had long since become a devotee to communism and the Soviet socialist cause, so the dull indoctrination dreaded and passively rejected by many of his fellow cadets was readily absorbed by him. He became a scholar of Lenin's dialectical social order much to the pleasure of the zampolits and the officers in the college.

Oath of Allegiance

The most important requirement of a Soviet career officer is political reliability and military allegiance. To be successful, an officer candidate is taught that he must, in addition to learning his military skills, be a loyal communist and a member of the Party. As a continuing part of this process, in the fourth week of training, Sasha and his class were assembled for a special political lecture by the zampolits and a military responsibilities lecture by a senior instructor after which each cadet was required to individually repeat the Soviet Military Oath:

"I, a citizen of the Union of the Soviet Socialist Republics, on joining the ranks of the Armed Forces, take the oath and solemnly swear to be an honorable, brave, disciplined and vigilant warrior, to safeguard military and state security strictly and unquestioningly to carry out the military directives and orders of my commanders and superiors.

I promise to study my military duty conscientiously, to protect military and state property and, to my last breath, devotedly to serve my people, the Soviet Homeland and the Soviet Government, I will always be ready, on orders from the Soviet Government to defend my country, the USSR, and as a soldier of its Armed Forces I swear to defend it courageously and skillfully with worthiness and honor, sparing neither my life nor my blood for the attainment of complete victory over our enemies. If I should break this, my solemn oath, then let me suffer the severe penalties of Soviet law and the general detestation and contempt of all workers."

The harsh treatment of basic training went on for two long months after reporting to the college during which the first-year cadets had not been permitted to write letters, much less make telephone calls. The rule was simple: "If there is a problem with you, your parents will be advised." Sasha's earlier bright dreams of wearing the uniform of an officer candidate cadet grew dimmer with time. There were many instances when he was ready to rebel. But, his respect for his parents, and his years of indoctrination in Komsomol and DOSAAF, prevented him from rebelling. Also, there had to be a light at the end of the tunnel. After all, he had grown up in a military family and knew the respect that Soviet officers were given.

Sasha thrived on the thought of reaching that plateau and one day even coming back to this school, or wherever they were, and settling with the NCO thugs. Sasha and the cadets had created a plan to carefully memorize each of their names, and they listened for clues in their conversation about where they were from, or may go next. They documented their "NCO personnel files" and exchanged them with one another. They knew that sooner or later one or more of them would "track down" some of these brutes. Sasha was no fool either. He endured the harsh treatment, catered to the whims of his masters, just sufficiently, to protect himself from bodily harm. They could not break his spirit or his dreams.

Finally, at the end of two and a half months, the cadets remaining in Sasha's first-year class - only 560 out of the original 1000 - were herded into the large meeting hall where they were greeted by the school commandant. From the time of his arrival at the training school, Sasha and the other cadets had been issued over-sized and baggy fatigues and ill-fitting boots. The rank on their shoulder boards was that of a basic soldier. On this day, the commandant congratulated the class on having completed the "boot training" phase of their training and announced that now they would be issued the uniforms of officer candidates, with the velvet shoulder boards denoting their status. But the session with the commandant was also a period assessment.

Vlad

Making close friends or confidants within the training school was discouraged and monitored closely. Classes and barracks assignments were juggled around and students constantly switched about so that there was little opportunity for close friendships to develop. Sasha heard the constant drum beat of his instructors: "Make no friends and trust no one." However, he did make one friend and by an apparent "quirk" in the juggling process, he and Vladimir Yepishev seemed to always end up in the same training sessions.

"Vlad" was several years older than Sasha. He said that he had served three years in the army as a conscript before being selected for aviation officer training. Sasha welcomed the opportunity to place some trust in someone and with whom to share his thoughts. It turned out that Vlad also spoke reasonably good English, but he was vague as to how a foot soldier from a rural farm region could have learned the language so well. Sasha and Vlad became good friends and shared aspects of their lives, but Sasha was careful not to make any mention of his mother's questionable sentiments about the government or the Soviet society.

"I was raised on a collective (farm) near Novograd between Moscow and Kazan," Vlad told Sasha. "My father was the farm manager, but that did help me any. I worked just as hard as everyone else, often harder. My father expected it. I was not fortunate to attend any prep schools like KOMSOMOL or the others, but when I turned eighteen, I met the commissariat committee and was sent off to infantry training. After three years of consistently applying, I was finally accepted for officer training."

Vlad said that he was also shocked at their treatment at the hands of the hardened NCO's. He said that he had been convinced, like Sasha, that officer training meant that they would enjoy a reasonably good life and, certainly civil treatment.

Following the "Day of Assessment" with the commandant, Sasha had begun to receive mail from home, but he was still forbidden to make phone calls. The letters from his mother encouraged him and gave him renewed strength and self-confidence. She never alluded to her true feelings. One day, however, Vlad asked him about his mother and her job teaching English.

"Where did your mother learn to speak and teach English so well?"

"Oh, she has studied English here in our schools since she was very young."

"Has she ever traveled outside of Russia?"

"Yes, she went to London once with an exchange group. She enjoyed it very much."

Then Vlad asked, "Has she ever expressed any feelings about the Soviet government or the Party?"

Sasha quickly responded, "Vlad, my mother and father are true loyalists. As you know, my father is a professional soldier serving in the Ministry of Defense. My mother is equally loyal."

While he was surprised and a bit suspicious of these questions by his friend, Sasha brushed off the concerns, did not reveal any unusual information and chalked it up to the further development of a closer friendship.

Betrayed

The absence of Sasha wore heavy on Tatyana with each painful month and was further aggravated by Viktor's long work days. She immersed herself even more deeply into the krushki. The frequent meetings with her soul family helped to meet her emotional needs and to partially assuage her frustration. She became particularly attracted to one extremely bright and articulate krushki member, Vasili Ershov. Ershov was an engineer. His employment with the Moscow Telephone Company provided him the opportunity to utilize his skills to provide special assistance to krushki members. He could legitimately go to members' apartments and look for suspected surveillance and listening devices which may have been planted by the secret police. In turn, it was relatively simple to render any such devices inoperative without undue suspicion since the telephone system in Moscow was so antiquated and unstable that outages and failures were not unusual.

Tatyana enjoyed discussing political and social reform with Ershov and would occasionally join him for a coffee after a meeting of their krushki cell. Eventually, they became very close friends and confidants. She trusted him completely.

"Tatyana, are you confident that your apartment isn't bugged? You know that the Soviets don't even trust their own, especially their senior military officers. Would you feel better if I came by and conducted a check of your living quarters?"

"Oh, I don't know, Vasili. I don't think that my husband would approve. I believe that he is fully confident his home is not being monitored by anyone. And, I am very careful not to openly express any sentiments to anyone, even to my mother when she visits. I don't think it would be a good idea for you to come to our apartment."

"Well, Tatyana, my dear friend, you know that we can't trust these swine that govern our country, especially the secret police. I would be pleased to take a look if you agree."

"Vasili, if you think that it would be a good idea, then I would be pleased if you would."

"Good! When would be a good time? I will need at least two hours or so to conduct a thorough inspection."

Tatyana felt a bit uneasy with Ershov's proposal, but she agreed.

"Any afternoon during the week will be fine....say, between two and six p.m."

"Fine, Tatyana, I will plan to come by the day after tomorrow around two. Would you like another coffee?"

"No, Vasili, thank you. I should be going. Thank you for being such a good friend. I sincerely enjoy our discussions."

Vasili Ershov arrived at Katsanov apartment sharply at two p.m. on the appointed afternoon.

"Come in, Vasili. It is good to see you. Would you like a tea or coffee?"

Vasili took her hand warmly and buzzed her on each cheek.

"No, thank you, Tatyana; It is good to see you as well. May I begin to look about?"

"Yes, please feel free to do anything you wish. I would ask that you be careful not to leave any evidence of your work. I did not tell Viktor about your coming. He would not approve."

"Not to worry, Tatyana, I am an expert with my work. Nothing will be disturbed."

Ershov carefully removed and replaced every light switch, electrical receptacle, phone jack, dismantled lamps and light fixtures, looked under and into every piece of furniture and appliance in the apartment. When he completed his inspection, he declared her home "bug-free."

"Thank you, Vasili, it was very kind of you to do this for our safety."

Vasili took Tatyana's hand and held it firmly. "Tatyana, I would do anything for you. You are a very intelligent and beautiful woman, and I have come to care for you very much."

He attempted to pull her to him.

Tatyana immediately recoiled. "Vasili, I think you should go now. Thank you for your good work."

"Tatyana," he again attempted to pull her to him. "I would like to have that tea now. May I, as a reward for my work?"

Tatyana was unnerved. She felt trapped. "Yes, please be seated and I will bring tea."

Vasili followed her into the kitchen. When she turned, he took her into his arms and held her tightly. When she tried to resist, he held her and kissed her on the lips.

She gasped and wrenched herself free. When he moved toward her again, she slapped him across the face with full force. She felt a bone in her hand snap.

"Get out!" she hissed. "Get out now! Do not ever come near me again! Ever! Leave now!"

Ershov retreated without speaking, rubbing the side of his face. He left, slamming the door behind him.

Tatyana was devastated. "What have I gotten myself into?"

Sobbing, she made her way to the bathroom and carefully wrapped her bruised and broken hand in a bandage. She would tell Viktor that she tripped and fell on her hand.

After the incident with Vasili, Tatyana did not know what to do about the krushki meetings. Finally deciding that she would not be bullied by Vasili Ershov or anyone else, she went to the next scheduled meeting. When she arrived, she nervously looked around for him, but he was not there and did not come to the meeting. She never saw him again. One of the members said he had heard that Ershov now attends meetings at another cell across the city. She was greatly relieved and still embarrassed at her gullibility.

But Ershov did not take rejection lightly.

The phone rang in the office of a KGB internal security precinct office.

"Comrade, this is a loyal citizen. I cannot tell you my name, but I wish to report that there is dissident in our midst, and she is the wife of a very high ranking military officer."

The next several months saw a general improvement in the cadets' living conditions. Their food improved considerably. The NCO's had let up somewhat on their "night games." They were able to get some sleep and were treated with a little more respect and dignity. It remained important to keep one's guard up, because every cadet was under constant surveillance for conduct and actions. The remainder of their routine remained the same: reveille, physical training, breakfast, academics, drill and more training. It would be another five or six months before they would begin their academic preparations for flight instruction. Sasha looked forward to that even though he would later end up as an M-4 Bison or TU-95 Bear bomber pilot, rather than in one of the future MiG jet fighters. But, importantly, he was still in school. That would make his father proud.

The indoctrination in communist ideology became more intense. Cadets were admonished constantly: "The Communist Party wants to develop unconquerable soldiers and officers, ones that are more dedicated to Leninism than to their families— intellectual athletes of Olympic quality who know their airplanes and weapons better than the designers!" They were drilled and tested daily on the fundamentals from politics to weaponry to aircraft nomenclature to their own moral beliefs in the future of the Soviet Union. The first year of officer school finally came to an end. The great relief, however, was crushed by a disappointing announcement that there would be no summer vacation or leave from their training, due to the "great press for mobilization for fighting men to meet the growing threats from the West." Sasha and his classmates had long since grown used to disappointments in their lives, so they mentally prepared themselves to move on.

Sasha entered his second year at the training college in 1951. He was twenty-one. The Cold War, as it had become known, was well into its fourth year. The animosity toward the West, and the United States in particular, was the topical discussion in virtually every phase of training and communist indoctrination. Teachers and instructors constantly reminded the students that the United States was the sworn enemy of the Russian people and that they must prepare to fight a great war against the aggressors when they eventually attack. Political indoctrination was intensified and became almost equal with academic and flying training requirements.

Viktor was able to visit his son twice during the second year of training. These meetings were not welcomed by the commandant, but Viktor was on the General Staff in Moscow and the commandant yielded to the modest requests to visit his son. The meetings were very brief and held in secret in the commandant's office. Before and afterward, Sasha was always seriously admonished to keep these visits by his father secret, lest he suffer punishment. He was very grateful for the opportunity to see his father, even briefly, but he longed for his mother.

The second year of training college followed a long, hot summer of weeks of intensive, and physically exhausting, soldiering and field training exercises. Soviet military training worked on the theory that young men kept physically and mentally occupied for every waking minute of every day inhibited most idle notions of "escape" or desertion. The summer intensity finally gave way to the beginning of the second year of academic and military training. Sasha eagerly looked forward to the time when pilot training would become an active part of the curriculum. That alone served to motivate him to stay with the program. The Soviet Air Force was enjoying a vast expansion, and Sasha and his fellow cadets were eager to learn to fly and become a part of the Soviet defense against the capitalist aggressors of the United States and the West.

The routines as a second-year cadet were not much different from the first. Each cadet continued to be closely monitored for conduct, personal achievement and consistent loyalty. Infractions continued to be promptly dealt with, incurring severe punishment for the accused. It was not uncommon for punishment to include standing at attention in the center of the parade field, dressed in full training gear, including a fifty-pound back pack in either summer heat or freezing winter cold, standing at attention in the barracks with a stack of books balanced on the head or locked in a cold or hot solitary confinement cell, often for periods of a full day, night and even a week if the infraction warranted. The name of the game was to "stay clean," obey the rules, study hard and demonstrate the attitude of an obedient Soviet.

The second year brought in smaller numbers of cadets housed in the barracks. The first-year cadet barracks housed a hundred students with the NCO's acting as their disciplinary seniors. Now they were in a barracks with only fifty cadets including four seniors and eight third-year students. These upperclassmen had been chosen and assigned based on their demonstrated leadership and officer potential. They were to act as mentors to the younger second-year cadets.

Sasha immersed himself in the pilot training phase of officer training with enthusiasm. He couldn't wait to begin flying in earnest.

Soviet pilot training units were extremely limited in the types and numbers of training aircraft they had available for cadets. The war had claimed most of their flyable aircraft and had decimated their flying training programs. Consequently, cadets were trained to fly in very old, and some acquired, trainers. These ranged from the Russian-built Polikarpov Po-2, 100 horsepower by-plane manufactured originally in 1928, the German manufactured Bucker Bu 131 Jungmann, a four cylinder 100 horsepower by-plane and a few Boeing-Stearman PT-17 Kaydets, a "modern" 1940 7-cylinder, 220 horsepower trainer provided at the end of World War II by the U.S. Government.

That these aircraft were antiquated made little difference to the Soviet cadets. As far as Sasha was concerned, this was the best part of school training to date. Once again he excelled in learning to fly. His instructor told him that he was a natural aviator and would make a great Soviet pilot!

As Sasha came to the end of his second year, he looked forward to the promised two weeks of leave so that he could finally go home, barring another disappointing cancellation, as had been the case the year before. He made extraordinary plans as to how he would spend his time. Mostly he would enjoy his parents, his mother especially, and sleep, eat and sleep in that order. He was homesick! And he became increasingly so as the final days closed.

THREE

Lesson Learned

Within a few weeks of the long year's end, an event occurred that sent chills down his spine and terrified all of the cadets.

One night two of the senior cadets, Ivan Koschkov and Naminski Pavlov, who were bunked in his barracks, as mentors, decided to visit the neighboring village where they had met two girls on a prior weekend senior cadet outing. After lights-out, the two carefully bundled-up clothing and blankets and made their beds look as if they were fast asleep in the event the cadet barracks fire guard or an NCO happened by. They slipped out of the barracks and made their way across the grounds, through the barbed-wire fence and other defenses designed against such "escapes" from the college compound. They were gone no more than three or four hours and carefully made their way back into the barracks building before daybreak and quietly got into their beds. Any cadet who may have witnessed the event was so disciplined to not tattle on any other cadet for fear of their predictable demise and would never do so.

Morning came with reveille, physical exercise, breakfast and then the usual fall out in uniforms for morning formation. Every event of the morning was the same routine until the commandant took the lectern facing the assembled cadets and called for the reading of special orders. Promptly, the adjutant stepped forward to the loudspeaker.

"Senior cadets Ivan Koschkov and Naminski Pavlov, step forward!"

The formation of cadets were all relaxed, thinking that these two were about to be lauded for exceptional performance and made examples for the other students to follow. But, Sasha sensed something terribly awry because he was well aware of the night excursion by the two, and this was "too coincidental!"

As the two nervous cadets moved out from their positions in the ranks and stood rigidly in front of the platform where the commandant and his staff were located, two burly NCO's promptly stepped beside each of them and without a word being spoken, ripped off the two cadets' shoulder boards. Then they grabbed their caps from their heads and tore the buttons from their uniform jackets. While the tortuous humiliation was in progress, the adjutant began the denouncement.

"Comrades, you are witnessing the end of the careers of two of your fellow cadets. They have disgraced each of you, the academy and the Soviet Army. They committed unforgivable crimes against the State by dishonoring their oath of allegiance, desertion, failure to obey orders and disobedience. They will be immediately expelled from your ranks and sent to camp with common conscripts. Perhaps there, they will learn what they refused to do here at this great academy."

This was the severest of object lessons for all to absorb. The adjutant never mentioned the specific violations or crimes committed. To do so would have made a joke out of the long list of allegations and weakened the message. This was a personal disaster for the two senior cadets who in two weeks would have been commissioned as officers in the Soviet Air Force and gone on to advanced pilot training.

In an instant their lives were ruined forever. This event demonstrated with graphic results the requirement for complete and total subordination by Soviet military members. It also clearly reflected the extremes to which military officials would go to make their case for absolute discipline, even to the extent of destroying careers and lives for apparent marginal conduct. The destruction of these cadets' lives was calculated as an exchange for the obedience of hundreds of others.

But the morning's activities weren't over. After Koschkov and Pavlov were escorted away, the adjutant then called out the names of the two cadets who were on duty as barracks fire guards the night before. As they stepped forward, he announced:

"Comrades, before you we now have two additional fellow cadets who are being placed under arrest for dereliction of duty and confinement to solitary cells for two weeks. Perhaps this will serve to sharpen their surveillance and observation skills. Guards, take them away!"

No specific charges were made regarding their infractions. The two were swiftly escorted off the parade ground by security policemen. The commandant stepped back to the loudspeaker and began a lengthy rhetorical speech about discipline and adherence to rules of conduct.

"Young Tovarishtchi (Comrades), one of my important responsibilities to our great nation and to you, is to weed out misfits and unworthy officer candidates. These two, who have shamed our government and our college, would have soon become officers in the Soviet Air Force and your trusted colleagues, had we not found them out! You will be grateful that they have been removed from your presence and will never be in a position to spoil the image of our great service."

He continued, "They must pay for their crimes. We will be more lenient with the two other younger cadets who failed in their responsibilities to inform their superiors of the serious infractions of others. They will be given another opportunity to perform but will be closely monitored for satisfactory conduct."

And, finally: "I hope that each of you have learned a valuable lesson about obedience, conduct and discipline. If so, this has been a good experience and you will all go on to serve the great Soviet Union."

Again, the commandant did not mention the crimes committed, only Sasha and some of his barracks mates were aware of the true misdemeanor. Cadets living in other buildings remained in the dark about the cause of the severe punishments meted out, but they did not fail to grasp the harsh object lessons presented during the chaotic morning.

The formation of cadets stood thunderstruck. It was not unusual for students to be punished, but this was by far the most dramatic any had witnessed during their time in the college. Sasha had heard stories about these types of punitive actions, but to witness one was devastating. As he stood rigidly with the others listening to the commandant's lecture, Sasha wondered "who" in his barracks would have turned in the two. It almost had to be one of his barracks mates, but the cadets had a creed among themselves to protect one another; to turn in two senior cadets. "Wow!" Then in an instant, he glanced to his right and caught a glimpse of Vlad with the faintest smile on his face and a look of apparent satisfaction. He promptly knew the answer!

Suddenly, a multitude of past events and situations came to mind. Other cadets had been punished for infractions, and no one could figure out who told. Neither he nor Vlad had ever been severely reprimanded. Even the toothbrush incident was minor and he was issued another brush the next day. Neither had either of them been subjected to the brutal horseback games. And, neither he or Vlad had ever been challenged or reprimanded for walking about and talking for which numerous others had been punished.

Too much was adding up as he recalled other instances when cadets were punished for infractions which no one could understand how the NCO's found out. Vlad was a snitch, maybe even worse.

But, why, he thought, was he protecting me and turning in others?

Later in the day during a break between classes, Vlad made his way over to Sasha which terrified him. He didn't know what to say, but Vlad was his usual pleasant self.

"Comrade, are you ready for your vacation? Boy, I am! I am ready to get out of this place and head for home. It has been a long time. How about you? You are going directly to Moscow, I presume?"

"Dah," Sasha responded. "I am going directly home. I can't wait to get back into my own bed and try to eat my way through the kitchen."

Vlad didn't mention the morning's events and went on to talk about their forthcoming two week's leave and how happy he would be to get home and to see his family. Sasha went along with the chat and dared not reveal his thoughts. Sasha remained guarded with his conversations with Vlad for the remaining days of the school term.

Home At Last

With much anticipation, coupled with accompanying apprehension that something might happen to prevent their leave, the time finally came on a Saturday morning. With only a few hours notice, the announcement was made that all cadets completing their second and third class years, having no pending punishment, could depart on leave immediately. The college had made arrangements for a troop train to take the cadets to Moscow which would be the central dispersal point for drop-off and later, collection location, for all the cadets going on leave. Those who didn't live in or around Moscow were given up to ten days of additional time off for travel to and from their homes, but they had to make their own uncertain arrangements to get to their destinations and return. Uncertain, because very few of the cadets had money, and would have to rely upon a loosely operated military social service system that operated in train terminals and airports to assist military members in obtaining space-available free travel. Sasha was one of the fortunate—his parents lived in Moscow.

The fourteen-hour train ride from Volgograd to Moscow was miserable. The train seemed to chug along at a snail's pace. Everyone on board was pensive and stressed out that they still might not make it. Sasha almost immediately noticed that Vlad was not on the train. How strange, he thought. Surely Vlad had to go to Moscow to make connections to get to his home. He dismissed the strange circumstance and wrestled with brief naps until the train finally arrived at the Yaroslavski Voksal (terminal). Sasha quickly made his way to the adjacent underground metro stop at the Komsomolskaya Station and across the city to his parent's apartment building on Varsonof Prospekt (street). With no advance notice, he knocked on the door.

FOUR

Enmeshed

Viktor had carefully monitored the activities at the Volgograd Aviation College to determine whether his son would finally be granted his leave. He had not told Tatyana that their son could be coming home within a few days for fear something might suddenly change. Soviet citizens, the military in particular, were always wary of too much anticipation.

When Tatyana opened the door, she was overcome with shock and unable to speak. She put her arms around her son and held on tightly for fear the moment might not be real. Finally, she pushed him back, stared at his face and took in his presence for another full minute before she could utter a word. Then they both burst, with a flood of tears and words, a mixture of Russian and English all jumbled together. This was truly a moment that both had longed for, but neither, in their dream of dreams could imagine when, or if, it would ever happen.

Once past the initial shock of his sudden appearance, Tatyana burst forth with questions.

"Are you alright? Are you healthy? Is it safe for you to come home? Are you hungry?"

The questions, and Sasha's reassurances, went on for an hour while his mother hurried about the small kitchen trying to assemble a dinner worthy of her son's homecoming. Food was scarce, as it had always been, and even Viktor's position as a general officer in the Soviet Air Force and a member of the General Staff did not make the situation much better. Tatyana's daily routine had become one of leaving her apartment just after daylight every morning to literally forage for food, mostly for the scarcest items, meat and bread, before she reported for her teaching job at Moscow University. She had learned though, that food was available if sufficient rubles were in hand to purchase it. These transactions usually took place through the shadowy back doors of the shops that risked black marketing their products. She did not have an abundance of food on this evening of Sasha's return, but she was able to improvise sufficiently. With a few vegetables and a bit of beef and bread she was able to put a dinner together. They talked nonstop while Tatyana carefully prepared the meal, asking questions back and forth.

Sasha put the best light on the college and his training experiences. He did not want to let his mother know in any way, how really bad some things had been. As he talked, the more he reflected positively about where he had been and where he was going. He was a devout communist and Soviet, and his own beliefs were reinforced the more he reflected on his two years as an officer and pilot candidate. Only one day removed from the harsh conditions of the barracks and the NCO's, he felt refreshed and was able to project himself into the future, his perceived life of excitement and service to his government. He had bright visions of how great the Soviet Union would become.

Tatyana listened and felt a chill at her son's enthusiasm for what she knew was not to be, not in her lifetime nor his. This government and social order was fatally flawed and someday doomed, and she knew it. People were not meant to live under such oppression. There is a better life outside the "walls" that kept Russian people captive. Although she was a student of Russian history, Tatyana clearly understood the three hundred years of oppression under the Tsars and the thirty years of false promises of the communists. She continued to believe that some day the Russian people would come into a better life. She had also held out the hope that her son would be a part of a new Russia.

Over the past two years during Sasha's absence, she had actively continued to meet with the kruzhki members. That respite from the daily drudgery of her real world kept her mind alert and her hopes alive. She had continued this meeting practice at the great risk of exposure, the end of Viktor's career and possibly her own demise. But she felt that she had the inner strength and confidence that the potential risk was worth the opportunities to maintain both her mental well-being and fervent hopes for a more humane and decent society.

From an early morning of scouting and walking about Moscow and savoring the respite from the rigors of the training college, Sasha came back to his parents' apartment on his sixth day at home to find two men in dark suits waiting for him. Sudden fear rushed through his body. He felt limp as he surveyed the tiny room that served as both parlor and dining room. Instinctively he knew that they were KGB agents.

But why were they here? Had they discovered something about him? His mother? Was his father in trouble?

His mother looked stricken, not with a look of fright, but of despair. It was apparent that she didn't know why they were there either.

The more important looking one of the two rose from his chair and stepped forward with his hand out when Sasha came into the room. "Hello, Tovarish (Comrade), I am Anatoli Kulikov and this is my colleague Vasiliy Pakilev. We bring greetings from the commandant of your college and from our superiors. We have *good* news for you."

Sasha, still struck by this sudden intrusion, could barely utter what he was trying to say. "Dobriy' ootra, Comrades, I am puzzled by your presence here. What can I do for you?" Sasha finally offered.

"Dobriy' ootra, Comrade Alexandr. It is a good morning, and we have come to personally deliver some special orders for you. You are to accompany Vasiliy and me back to Volgograd immediately, but please, put your mind at rest. You are not in any difficulty. You have been specially selected for a project of the highest priority, and the commandant and our superiors require to meet with you as soon as possible."

Sasha was at once outraged, but tried not to reflect it openly. His discipline kept his feelings and expression in check. "What special assignment?" he responded. "I am on my two weeks leave between classes. I am sure there is some mistake. Are you sure they want me to return so soon? And," he continued, "why was I not informed of this before I left only five days ago? I do not understand. I don't know who you are, or your authority."

The spokesman, Anatoli, reached into this coat pocket and showed Sasha the telltale identification card of a KGB agent. At the same moment Vasiliy presented his identification. "Comrade Alexandr," Anatoli replied, "it is of the greatest importance to you and to our government that you prepare immediately to depart. Please gather your belongings. We have a car waiting, and the train for Volgograd will leave in about two hours time."

Tatyana buried her face in her hands but did not utter a sound. She feared the worst for her son. She felt, instinctively, that she would likely never see him again. Her worst fear was that he was going back to be arrested and perhaps held hostage for her anti-government sentiments. But how could they know? Did they know anything? Were they going to torture him and use him to force her to reveal others of the kruzhki? Her mind was racing to assess what options she had available to deal with this frightening intrusion into their lives. Her own self-discipline kept her emotions intact. She said nothing for fear of saying more than she should. She obediently got up, went to Sasha's room and quietly began to gather his clothes for the return trip.

Sasha thought of a hundred questions to ask but let them linger in his mind. He asked, "May I visit my father before I depart?"

Anatoli quickly responded, "Your father has been informed of the requirement to return to the college." He added with obvious arrogance, "*Because* of his position, he will be allowed to meet with you briefly at the train station." The KGB, for the most part, held the military in contempt and mocked their *superior* status. Anatoli then quickly added, "The sooner you prepare to depart, the more time you will have to spend with your father at the station. And, Comrade, you do not need to bother with wearing your uniform. We want you to be relaxed on the train."

Sasha joined his mother in his room and began to listlessly help her put his things into the canvas bag in which he had brought them. He tried to speak but couldn't. Words wouldn't come, nor tears. He moved about slowly for a few minutes. Then the discipline of training took hold, and he said firmly to his mother, "I must go now. I will write or call after I arrive. I have enjoyed our visit but must now get back to my training. Thank you for a pleasant visit." He was almost business-like in his final few minutes.

Sasha was resigned and ready for what might be ahead of him. His mother hugged him, gave him a kiss on the cheek and told him goodbye. Likewise, the tough Russian discipline within Tatyana made her accept the unraveling traumatic events. As her son departed with the two strangers, she watched as long as she could see them as they descended down the stairwell of the building.

Sasha's parting visit with his father at the Kazanskiy Train Station was brief and revealed nothing with regard to why he was required to leave, or where he was going. Even as a senior general officer in the Ministry of Defense, Viktor had not been informed of the reason for his son's sudden departure nor why he was being escorted by KGB agents. Anatoli broke up the visit politely, but firmly, and hastened Sasha aboard the train where they entered a compartment for the three of them.

Anguish

Viktor returned promptly to his home after the brief visit with Sasha at the train station. He knew that Tatyana would, without a doubt, be in distress. He walked into the apartment to find his wife in the bedroom sobbing uncontrollably. He began to speak to her softly in an attempt to control and quiet her convulsive crying.

Finally, she rose from the bed and stood facing him. "Viktor, I am outraged! I am ashamed of you, and I am ashamed, angry and humiliated by the quagmire in which we live. You have just come from seeing our son taken away by two petty gangsters of our government, and you did nothing! You are a fool! Viktor, do you not remember the story of my father? He was dragged away in the night by two very similar scum as those who took our son. And, Viktor, my father was dead in three days beaten to death unmercifully by the KGB thugs who run this country. Have you no outrage? You stand there and look at me as if I am crazy. Our only son has just been taken away from us for no apparent reason, and you apparently go blithely to the station and tell him goodbye."

Tatyana was screaming now and beating Viktor's chest with her fists. "Where have they taken Sasha? What do you know? Why are you not outraged? Why haven't you done something to stop this insanity? Do your communist roots go so deep that you have become a robot like the rest of your insane colleagues? I do not believe that this is happening!"

Tatyana collapsed back onto the bed in uncontrollable convulsions insane colleagues? I do not believe that this is happening!"

"Tatyana, please," Viktor pleaded. "Please do not do this. You will be ill. Please stop crying. Please!" He tried to touch and console her, but she shoved his hand away roughly.

Bewildered, Viktor went to the kitchen and began to heat water for tea. He was at a loss as to how to get Tatyana to come around. He thought about calling her mother, Bonita, but then thought better of that notion. Bonita would likely unleash a similar barrage at him and everything else as well. As he watched the pot of water heat, he recalled his darkest secret about the night Czar Nicholas and his family were gunned-down, murdered by the same kind of people that killed Tatyana's father. And now, his son was in the hands of the same ignorant and arrogant secret police thugs. But, somehow in his own mind, he felt that Sasha was safe from harm.

He had been called by a colonel in the GRU chief's office and told that Sasha had been selected for a special training program, and that he should not worry. But that was all that he was told—nothing more, no details. That was the way of the secret police, be they KGB or GRU. Even senior military officers such as he did not question motives or details. That was simply forbidden.

As Viktor was finishing the preparation of the tea, Tatyana walked into the kitchen. He handed her a mug of steaming tea. She did not look at him and made no comment. She took the mug and walked slowly into the living room and sat down in an overstuffed chair. Viktor cautiously followed her, not saying anything. She sipped the tea, staring out through the window. Finally, she turned her gaze toward Viktor who had seated himself on the sofa.

"Viktor, I am in control of my emotions now," Tatyana began. "You know that it is not my nature to lose control. This has been a very emotional period for me. Sasha left us almost two years ago and we have not seen him until he arrived six days ago for supposedly a two week visit; and, tonight he is gone to no telling where in the company of secret police. Can you tell me what he has done? You spoke with someone who told you that he was going to be picked up. What did they say? Tell me! Please tell me!" She almost erupted into a scream but managed to keep her balance.

Viktor paused. "Tatyana, I was told just this morning by a colonel in one of the agency offices, I cannot tell you which one, that Sasha has been selected for a special assignment. He would not tell me anything about it but assured me that Sasha was in good hands. He said the assignment was a reward for his good work at the academy. Tatyana, I believe that all is well with Sasha. They will take good care of him, and we will soon know what he is doing."

She looked at Viktor with stone, cold eyes. "Viktor, I think you are a fool. You are so immersed in this sewer of a government and military that you cannot see beyond your nose. You believe any and everything they tell you. You call yourself a general, but you are a puppet. That murderer, Stalin, and his bastard henchmen have you by the nape of the neck just as they have everyone else. Viktor, this country is doomed. There is another world outside the walls of Russia. I have had just a glimpse of it, but I know that there is more than we could ever dream of here. Someday, the Western nations will see us all die from the oppression of our own government leaders. They will come to find the truth about Russia, that we are a facade, a fake, and our leaders are the same."

Tatyana took a deep breath and Viktor did not dare to interrupt her. "Viktor, we are doomed to die in this hell. We are in a swirling brew of hate and anger. Our leaders dangle us on a string like spineless puppets. My mother and I suffered and sacrificed greatly under the boots of these tyrants, and I will not have my son taken from me in the same way!" Keeping her voice even and not shouting, she continued with a barrage of words and expressions that shocked Viktor. "We are slowly suffocating, Viktor. You cannot see it, but we are. Sasha's departure today should be a message to you. We are dying, day by day. Each time we hope for the better, it gets worse. And, my husband, we are so much better off than most. I do not have to beg on the streets because of your position, but even so, we are not protected from the wrath of the devil in this country. A knock can come to our door at any time, just as it did today, and suddenly our world is crushed. Our own son, the son of a mighty general of the Kremlin, is snatched away. Viktor, do you hear me? Do you know what I am saying?" She stopped and took a deep breath.

Viktor was frozen. He had never heard his wife speak with such hate and fatal conviction. He tried to speak and give her some reassurance, but he couldn't at the moment. He sat and looked at her helplessly.

"Viktor," Tatyana began quietly this time. "I must confess something to you. It may be my fault that has caused us such misery this day." Her demeanor had changed completely. She was now almost pitifully compliant. "Viktor, I have for some time, several years to be clear about it, attended meetings with people who seek a better Russia than we now have. These people, although many are old in age, are new in spirit. They seek to find a way out of this abyss in which we have fallen. We are not dissident nor are we traitors; we simply seek to exchange ideas and thoughts for a better tomorrow. Viktor, some study group members have been arrested, terrified and some tortured. But none have told about the others. I fear now that Sasha's sudden disappearance with the police may be my doing." Tears were slowly running down her face.

Viktor sat wild-eyed. He couldn't believe what he was hearing. "Tatyana, stop! Stop now! These walls have ears. Do not speak further. You are ill. You do not know what you are saying. Come, you must lie down and rest." He was terrified, not only at what his wife had just said to him, but that his apartment may be tapped with listening devices. No one, even of his senior grade, was safe. And, he knew it.

"No Viktor," she whispered. "Our house is safe. I have had it thoroughly checked by an expert. I have had it checked several times over the years. No one has a listening device in here. Trust me. I have also been worried about that, especially with my mother visiting here. She is too outspoken. And now Viktor, I am the outspoken one. Now you know all about me. But I am assured that our apartment is not fixed with listening devices." And then, cynically, she added, "That means they trust you, Viktor."

Viktor still could not fully comprehend what she had said. He slowly took her by the arm and led her into the bedroom. He turned on the radio and moved the volume up sufficiently to drown out quiet conversation. "Tatyana, are you sure? Who did you have check this apartment? Was he trustworthy? Tatyana, that was a very dangerous thing to do. What if you found something? They would know immediately that it had been tampered with. Are you sure there is nothing here? Why didn't you tell me?" Viktor was visibly frightened.

"Viktor, the people I know are experts in doing these things." She patted his arm. "Do not worry. Now, I must tell you that I am sorry I told you everything. You cannot trust me now, either. But, Viktor, what of Sasha? What are they going to do to him? He could be dead already."

Viktor tried to reassure his wife. "Tatyana, please believe me when I tell you. If there were any reason to take Sasha for any faults of yours or mine, they would not have escorted him back to Volgograd. They would have arrested all of us right here. I am confident that he has been selected, as I was told, for a special assignment. I cannot explain it, but I have confidence in the colonel who called me. He called me on behalf of General Tushenskiy, a rare and unique officer in the Soviet Army. I do not know him well, but I am told that if Tushenskiy says something is to be, then, it is the truth. So, please, Tatyana, try to have faith this one time. I know that you were betrayed by our government when your father was taken from you, and that you harbor ill feelings toward our leaders. But you must understand that it is dangerous to do so. It not only endangers you but your family as well. I beg you to not attend any more meetings of your intellectual group. Believe me, it is very dangerous. We are all being watched. Someday it will be different, but in the meantime, none of us have a choice. We are destined to be who we are and where we are. I am so sorry, but I do not know any other way. I am a professional soldier and you have truly made me what I am. I was a crude and an uneducated peasant until you came along and taught me how to learn and how to conduct myself. And, you have made Sasha what he is, an exceptionally intelligent and physically fit young man. He will be a great man one day. Please try to have faith this time that our son is going to be alright. I will do everything I can to monitor his whereabouts and what he is doing."

Tatyana, now devoid of strength and emotion, nodded with a weak smile.

Knish

There was very little exchange of conversation during the trip back to Volgograd. The two agents were cordial enough, offering to call for tea or food, neither of which interested Sasha. Anatoli attempted to discuss Sasha's college training experience, but after receiving only short, non-substantive responses, finally settled back to drinking tea. He eventually drifted off to sleep in his berth. Vasiliy occupied the berth above Anatoli, which gave them both a clear view of Sasha in his lower berth, on the opposite side of the compartment. Vasiliy insured that the compartment door was locked with his own inside special key. There was no doubt that this was a train compartment specifically designated for KGB use.

Sasha had ridden on hundreds of trains in his lifetime, but he had never seen a compartment outfitted like this one. It had a wall-mounted telephone, an inside door lock, peculiar signal lights and other switches and buttons which he couldn't identify. The KGB left nothing to chance. They trusted no one and had complete authority and control over their charges and their environment. It was very doubtful that these two knew why they were escorting Sasha back to Volgograd. The secret police compartmented everything including all of their information and activities. Every agent, however, would have one to believe that he *knew* everything about the case and the individuals involved.

Sasha, on the other hand, had learned enough and had heard sufficient stories about them, that he had already "chalked-up" these two as no more than run-of-the-mill secret agents who knew little, and were self-importantly carrying out their duties. When he began to observe them more closely, he took note of their ill-fitting suits, scuffed shoes and overall crude demeanor. He had observed other agents similarly dressed and acting with ignorant self-importance during his KOMSOMOL training and at the college. The more important agents were much sharper in appearance and conduct.

The observation of these two heightened his concern that he could very likely be going back to Volgograd to be arrested on some charge or allegation. He intuitively suspected that Vlad was likely somehow involved. He could easily have trumped up a serious charge against him and turned him in for a reward or some special favor. After all, for some strange reason, Vlad wasn't on the train when it left Volgograd for Moscow.

The Soviets did not provide its citizens information on governmental organizations or activities, but Sasha was well aware from his experiences dating back to the Young Pioneers and the KOMSOMOL, that the KGB was a far-reaching security and police arm of the Soviet Government that held supreme rights over everyone. He knew that it was a highly efficient, and dreaded, apparatus, and Sasha did not question its authority and jurisdiction. Now here he was, a victim of that very organization of which everyone in Russia was terrified. This was as close to real fear as Sasha had ever been. The harassment and hazing at the academy was superficial and carried out by ignorant goons. He knew that the KGB was greatly responsible for the surveillance of crimes against the government and closely monitored all Soviet citizens for any evidence of political disloyalty, illegal communication with foreigners, spying and so on.

His stomach churned as he tried to envision the potential prospects which might lay ahead. He recalled his first thought, and one that had haunted him from the time he walked back into the apartment—the fear that his mother had been found to be disloyal. But, they took him instead. He thought further that he could be a hostage to get his mother to confess to some crime. After all, she had traveled to London once and came back enthusiastic about what she witnessed there. There was no doubt that the KGB had closely watched her during that visit. They had agents all over the world and paid special attention to Soviet citizens traveling abroad. They trusted no one. Even though he had concluded that these two agents were not very high up the chain of authority, he wasn't about to challenge them. He was for all practical purposes their prisoner. But why?

The trip back to Volgograd was aboard an express train which made only one stop on the long journey. As he finally drifted off to a restless half-sleep, Sasha pictured himself as a 'knish', a ball of dough stuffed with meat. He wondered who would be the one to devour him at his destination. Twelve hours later, they arrived at the Volgograd Station just after midnight. A black sedan was waiting for Sasha and his escorts. They got in with few words spoken. The driver headed swiftly toward the aviation college. Once inside the college grounds, the driver pulled the car up to a building unfamiliar to Sasha.

An NCO quickly opened the door while another collected their baggage and carried it into the building. Sasha was politely shown to a private room which was far above anything he could have imagined existing on the campus of the college. This was obviously a VIP apartment building. The accommodations heightened, even more, his concerns as to what was going on. He knew that the KGB had many tactics, one of which was "softening-up" a prisoner before they interrogated him in hopes of making the process easier. But interrogate him for what? If it were for his mother's potentially suspected sentiments, they could have done that in Moscow. They could have put the entire family in jail and gotten what they wanted. Another very polite NCO knocked on his door with a mug of tea, asked for his uniform and shoes and said he would put them in good order for the next day. Sasha was astonished. He couldn't believe that there were *any* NCO's around the college that conducted themselves like these fellas. They were actually clean, well-groomed and extremely civil and polite. They were nothing like the thugs that made life miserable for the cadets. He had never heard a "yes sir" or "no sir" from any of them in the barracks, even when they were addressing the officers, and now he was being treated like a VIP.

These events were too strange. Surely, he was being set up for something! The NCO also told Sasha that he would return with his uniform and a breakfast tray at 0800 and that he should be dressed and ready to depart at 0930. Depart for where? He presumed that his two escorts had taken rooms very near his with the intent of insuring that he did not venture away. He was right. The two agents were lodged on either side of Sasha and several NCO's were obviously present within the building during the night.

When he finally lay down, his mind and body were totally exhausted. He couldn't relax or think about sleep. He had been awake for almost 24 hours. A multitude of crazy thoughts and possibilities kept him suspended in anxiety.

The loud knock on the door jarred Sasha out of a sound sleep. He was completely disoriented and so groggy that he had no idea where he was or what time it was, or even what day it was. The NCO at the door said, "Sir, it is 0800. May I come in with your tea and your uniform?"

Sasha replied, "Dah, Dah, come in. I am awake." The NCO came in with a tall glass mug of tea and his uniform neatly pressed and hanging on a rack along with his shined shoes.

Sasha thought he must be dreaming but knew he wasn't. Then he thought about the two senior cadets who were called before the formation just before they were to graduate, with most thinking that they were going to be honored for some act or deed, only to have their careers dashed before everyone's eyes. He had already tried to think of every and any possible thing he might have done to warrant severe punishment. He could come up with nothing. He thanked the NCO as he departed and began to sip the hot tea while pondering what lay ahead this day.

The NCO returned shortly with a breakfast tray that looked every bit like a meal for the czar instead of himself. He nibbled at the food while he washed up, shaved and got dressed. His uniform had never looked better. He really liked the look of himself in the full-length mirror on the closet door. He had never seen himself before, head to foot in uniform. There were no mirrors in the barracks except the small scratched pieces of glass for shaving in the latrines. It was 0915, and he was ready.

At 0920, Anatoli knocked on his door. "May I come in, Comrade Alexandr?"

Sasha feeling refreshed from the tea and a little food, responded in a clear voice: "Dah, Dah, please come in."

"Did you rest well, Comrade?" asked Antoli. Sasha responded that he had, although it wasn't altogether true. He had literally passed out from anxiety and physical exhaustion, and he was actually more fatigued than when he went to bed. Anatoli said, "Good. The driver is here with the car, so we can depart for the commandant's office." This was the first indication as to where they were going, although he had suspected that must be the case. He was about to face his accuser, and surely his demise.

The two agents walked on either side of Sasha as they proceeded up the long sidewalk to the commandant's office. He had been here twice before when he met with his father during those brief opportunities in the previous school year. He did not feel exactly like a prisoner, but the presence of Anatoli and Vasiliy on either side made him uneasy. He had not been that close to real KGB agents before, only classroom political agents and instructors. He felt good in his pressed uniform, and it gave him a certain degree of self-confidence. At this point, he had taken so many deep breaths to calm his nerves that he was actually on a low grade high.

An Air Force major outside the commandant's office stood and greeted Sasha and the two agents and nodded toward the door to the inner office. When they entered the room, Sasha immediately snapped to attention and reported to the commandant: "Sir, cadet Alexandr Katsanov reporting as ordered." The commandant nodded and told him to stand at ease. Sasha looked around at the others in the room. There were three men in dark civilian suits. When he focused on their faces, he froze at the sight of Vladimir, his classmate and dubious "friend," Vlad made eye contact with Sasha and gave him his usual approving smile.

Sasha was unnerved. His mind raced. What on earth could Vlad have conjured up to turn me in for? Why is he in civilian clothes? He looked just like a KGB agent as did the other two.

The apparent senior agent excused Antoli and Vasiliy, thanked them for a job well done and told them that they could return to their office. Anatoli looked crestfallen at his dismissal. He obviously wanted to stay for the action or at least learn why they had gone to all the trouble to escort this cadet all the way from Moscow. They nodded and left.

The commandant spoke first, not bothering to introduce the other three in the room. "Let's be seated. Comrade Alexandr, I have been informed that you have been selected for a very special and highly classified project. The intelligence police, and we here at the academy, have closely monitored your performance, dedication and loyalty. And, for several years, even before you reported to the college, you have been closely observed. I can give you only the smallest of details at this point, and you will be briefed in increments of more detail as your project and you progress."

It became increasingly apparent to Sasha that the commandant wanted to appear fully in charge of this discussion, and to assert himself properly, but also that there was a higher level dictating whatever was going on. He continued, "I am at liberty to tell you that first, you will remain a member of the Soviet Air Force. Second, you will be on a special detached mission to the KGB and the GRU agencies for intensive training. Third, you will not reveal any information about your status or your project to anyone, not even your father. You will take a special oath of secrecy to protect your activities."

The commandant alluded to the fact that he also had certain authorities in this situation. "You will be removed from training here at the college effective immediately, and your classmates will be told you dropped out due to an illness. Your parents will be advised you are on a special detail of great importance and that they should not worry. Eventually, you will be able to visit them on brief occasions, those special arrangements when the time comes. In the meantime, you may not contact either them, or anyone else, without the express permission of your assigned special agent. Do you understand these instructions up to this point?"

Sasha could hardly utter a word, but finally, croaked out, "Yes, Sir."

The commandant quickly responded, "Good, there will be time for questions later. Please allow what I have said to this point to settle within you."

Again Sasha said, "Yes, Sir." His mind was numb. He had heard every word but really understood little that had been said. He couldn't focus his vision or his thoughts. He might have passed out had he been standing. He reached for a glass of water on the side table beside his chair and drank it down.

The commandant then softened his tone, "I wish to congratulate you, Comrade Alexandr. I am always delighted to have one of my students singled out for special duties. I wish you great success in the project ahead and your future." He reminded Sasha that while he would be under the jurisdiction of the *agencies*, he was still a member of the Soviet Armed Forces and would be subject to military law in every respect. "Someday, I hope to welcome you back to continue your Air Force service."

Sasha remained as confused as ever. He could make no rational sense of the commandant's words, which seemed to allude to something, but about which he couldn't relate.

The senior of the three in civilian clothes then spoke: "Comrade Alexandr, I am Major General Dmitriy Tushenskiy of the GRU, and my two colleagues are Colonel Sergiy Sokolov, also from the GRU and Captain Vladimir Yepishev from the KGB. I believe you know Comrade Vladimir."

Sasha glanced again at Vlad and took note immediately of his self-congratulatory look and telltale smile. He acknowledged the General's introductions by nodding but said nothing.

He waited for General Tushenskiy to speak further: "Comrade Alexandr, we are here as the Commandant has said, to inform you of a very special project for which you have been chosen to participate. We will be leaving shortly to return to Moscow. Your personal belongings have been gathered up, as have those of Captain Yepishev. Any records of your having been a student at the college have been removed. Do you have any questions?"

Sasha thought for a moment, his throat was very dry but he found his voice, "General, Sir, I am badly confused by all of these events. I still do not know why I am back here at the college with you, and why I now must leave what has been my lifetime dream. With all due respect, Sir, I do not have a desire to participate in your proposed project, although I do not know what it is. I wish only to remain here and to complete my training and to become an officer in the Soviet Air Force. I am grateful for your consideration of me, and all of the fine treatment which you have accorded me, but I must respectfully decline your invitation and request to remain in the college."

With that General Tushenskiy smiled and nodded to Vlad, who stood up and looked at Sasha. "Sasha, come with me, please."

Vlad stepped over to Sasha who got up immediately, snapped to attention, nodded to the Commandant and the General and followed Vlad through the door.

The Obedient Servant

Vlad led Sasha to an adjoining office, closed the door behind them and instructed Sasha in a friendly, but firm tone of voice to please sit down. His manner was formal, and he acted as if they had just met.

"Sasha", he began, "you are a most unique and special young Soviet. You have proven your devotion to your government. You have studied diligently to prepare yourself for a great future. Special people have been carefully observing you for several years, and the Soviet leadership is very proud of you. You and I have become trusted friends which makes me even more proud that our leadership has decided to appoint you to such a challenging task. We take great pride in selecting the best candidates in all of Russia to participate in projects of importance to the future of our grand social order."

Vlad continued, "So, Comrade, it is of the greatest importance that you enthusiastically accept General Tushenskiy's thoughtful appointment and without any reservations."

Sasha felt a rush of renewed strength and confidence, and responded, "Vlad, I don't know what this is all about. I am completely confused by all of the words of the Commandant, the General and you. All of you are speaking in riddles. I am overwhelmed by even being back here at the college and being catered to in this manner. You are a captain in the KGB -- not a cadet! You befriended me to spy on me, and I know that you turned in other cadets for infractions and watched them suffer punishment. What am I to make of all of this? I am not so sure that you are my friend, or the friend of anyone!"

Sasha grew more confident in his position and statements. "Who are you, anyway? What do I mean to you? Are you really with the secret police? What do they really want of me?"

Sasha was about to continue when Vlad stood up and walked over to where he was sitting. Standing directly in front of Sasha, Vlad quietly began, "Comrade Alexandr, you are about to make a fool of yourself. I was sent in here to talk to you in order to prevent such a terrible mistake. You are very fortunate that General Tushenskiy is a considerate officer. Let me tell you straight away." At this point Vlad's voice was stern and he looked Sasha directly into his eyes as he continued, "We know all about your mother. We know that she is a very active krushki, and that she has very strong anti-government sentiments, bordering on treason. We could arrest her anytime we wish, and you know the consequences of citizens committing treason against the government."

Sasha turned pale and was on the brink of collapse, when Vlad grabbed him by his uniform lapels with both hands and jerked him to his feet. "My comrade friend, you are in no position to tell me, or my superiors, what you want or don't want! Do you know what I am saying?" Sasha stood before Vlad and looked at him, bewildered. Vlad continued with a barrage of additional revelations about his mother, cursing her for her disloyalty.

Finally, he said, "Comrade Alexandr, you hold the fate of your mother, your father and yourself in your hands. We can arrest your mother this very day. Your father will be promptly relieved from his position and may even be implicated with her, and her disloyal friends, in a plot against the Soviet Government. And you, my friend, will be dismissed from this officer training college, sent to the army as a conscript, and never heard from again. You hold more power at this moment over your family, and yourself, than even God!" It was very unusual for a devout communist to use the term "God" except to make an indelible impression. He did.

Sasha stood staring at Vlad who was still in his face. He had lost all his strength and felt drained, but he locked his knees in place until he finally relaxed and let himself ease back into the chair behind him.

Vlad allowed him to sit down and stepped back to the center of the small office. "Well, Comrade?"

After a brief pause, Sasha took a deep breath, looked up at Vlad and replied, "Captain, I will do whatever I am asked to do. May I ask what will become of my mother?"

Vlad responded, "Your stupid mother and her friends are our toys. We can arrest them and do away with them at our pleasure, but, in your case, Comrade, because of your loyalty, we will continue to allow her to play her silly games. She will not be harmed, nor will your father be compromised. We are completely convinced that neither he, nor you, have any knowledge of her disloyal activities. So, let me say in closing, that as long as you remain the same loyal communist and soldier that you have proven to be, your family will be secure. I believe that I do not need to speak further on that subject."

Vlad led Sasha out of the room and back into the Commandant's office. General Tushenskiy and Colonel Sokolov were talking quietly and drinking coffee. The Commandant was no longer in the room. When they entered the office, the General rose to his feet, held out his hand to Sasha. With a knowing smile, he said, "Congratulations, Comrade! You are about to embark on a journey that could change the course of history."

Sasha nodded with a weak smile and replied, "Yes Sir, I am ready."

"Good, Good!" responded General Tushenskiy. "Our aircraft is waiting, so let's be off. Your personal belongings have been collected and will be aboard when we arrive."

Once they were airborne, the steward entered the compartment with tea, coffee and sweet cakes. After he completed his attendant duties, the general excused the steward and locked the compartment door from the inside.

"The compartment is secure so we may now proceed to discuss the preliminaries of what is ahead for you," he said, looking at a pale and exhausted Sasha.

"Yes, Sir," replied Sasha, who would have preferred to close his eyes, block out the agents' presence and reflect on all that had happened in the previous twenty-four hours. They had not allowed him to slow down and collect his thoughts since he left his parents' home in Moscow. He needed to think; he needed to put all of the events and revelations into some perspective, if he could. But that was not to be during the flight back to Moscow.

While the steward was completing his serving duties, Sasha had looked about the compartment of the aircraft. He was hurried aboard so quickly that he didn't even notice what type aircraft in which they were about to fly. He was seated by a window with Vlad on his left and General Tushenskiy and the colonel sitting opposite and facing them across a small table. It occurred to him that he had never flown aboard a passenger plane before, but, he also knew that this was not an ordinary transport plane. The compartment in which they were seated was well insulated and very quiet. There were seats for only eight people—four on his side and the same configuration across the narrow aisle. His outside window was shuttered so he couldn't see outside, and he dared not attempt to open the closure, since all of the windows in the compartment were shuttered closed. He could tell he was in a multi-engine airplane, and most likely a twin engine, but beyond the drone of the engines and his immediate surroundings, he might as well have been confined in a room anywhere.

His brief observations were soon interrupted by General Tushenskiy. He began, "We will be landing at Khodinka Field in about three hours. That will be your home and place of instruction for some time to come. Colonel Sokolov will be your immediate reporting senior from here on. Captain Yepishev will be your mentor. The GRU and the KGB work very closely on many projects, and in your special case, both agencies will be deeply involved.

Sasha had heard stories about the GRU and their headquarters located at Khodynskoye Field. It was the old Moscow Central Airport, simply called Khodinka Airfield, and it was tucked within the environs of Moscow a few kilometers northwest of the Outer Ring. The GRU and Khodinka were even more mysterious to Soviet citizens—Muscovites, in particular—than was the dreaded Lubiyanka Prison which housed the headquarters of the KGB in the heart of Moscow. In contrast to the KGB, the GRU, or 'Razvedupr', is the intelligence, razvedka, organ of the Soviet Government. Its fundamental mission was to prevent the collapse of the Soviet Union from the outside, as contrasted with the KGB whose principal responsibilities had to do with internal stability.

The GRU employed extreme measures against the West to collect technical intelligence on weapon systems and military hardware for exploitation. In the closing months of World War II, the Soviets diligently pursued U.S. technology to apply to their own aircraft and armored systems development. The Tu-4, copycat version of the U.S. B-29 bomber, was an excellent example of Soviet aircraft designers' lazy, but expedient work, to develop war fighting capabilities.

There was a distinct overlap in the respective charters of the KGB and the GRU which reflected that the whole of the Soviet Empire depended on duplication and depth of effort. While these competitive organs had the appearance of mutual respect and support they were, in fact, vicious enemies and constantly attempted to upstage one another. Sasha suddenly found himself in the grip of "both" of these security agencies.

"Beginning now, you will communicate in the English language with everyone who speaks English around you. We want English to become your primary language, American English, if you will."

General Tushenskiy continued. "You will have special tutors in American versions of the language, slang and their colloquialisms. Ha!" he continued, "It is a pity that we cannot use your mother to tutor you! But, I am afraid that would be impossible." He chuckled at his own wit and continued, "I am not permitted at this time to reveal everything about your special training, except to say that you will likely remain at Khodinka for two years or so. During this period you will be required to not only learn and speak perfect English, but you will be taught American history, geography, localized cultures and customs, and trivia of every kind. This phase of your training will continue and transcend the entire period of your stay. You will also study the American Air Force, its history and traditions, and its organizations and aircraft in use. A very special highlight of your training will include a continuation of your pilot training by the most skilled instructors in the Soviet Air Force."

Tushenskiy paused, and then said, "Lastly, I want to caution you. I will warn you that you are participating in a very specialized program tailored expressly for you. It is an experiment of the type we have not tried before. As the project and your training progresses, and you learn more about where you are headed, the greater the requirement for security. We have many nosy and curious people around us, even within the midst of Khodinka, who may attempt to draw you out regarding who you are and what you are preparing for. Ignore them. We will provide you a cover story for use at such times as necessary. We will not reveal to you too many facts along the way so as to relieve you of the undue stress of explaining things to other people."

The general continued, "All of this sounds very strange to you at this moment, and as time goes on you will have many questions. But any questions not directly related to a particular area which you may be studying at the time will be kept strictly to discussions with Captain Yepishev. Do you understand all that I have said to you at this point?"

"Yes, Sir." Sasha responded.

"Do you have any questions of me at this time?"

Sasha had a million questions but was not prepared to ask any in his present state of mind. "No, Sir," he responded, and then quickly so as not to display any indifference to the seriousness of his situation, added, "I am afraid that I am too dull at this moment to ask any intelligible questions. Please forgive me."

"I understand," General Tushenskiy responded. "I know that you are very tired and confused, but, some rest and reflection will soon make you fit again!"

The general then asked Colonel Sokolov if he had any questions or comments. In flawless English, he responded, "No General, thank you. I eagerly look forward to working with Sasha and our exciting days ahead. I think he needs rest for now."

"How about you, Captain Yepishev?" the general asked.

Also in perfect and relaxed English, Vlad responded, "No, Sir, General. I have known Comrade Sasha for two years now, and I look forward to our continued friendship and work on this important project."

No one else spoke. Sasha gradually allowed his eyes to close, and he drifted into half thoughts and half sleep as the engines of the airplane droned on toward Moscow.

FIVE

Khodinka

The German-built Junker J-12 tri-motor transport touched down at Khodinka airfield at 1640 hours on a sunny June afternoon. Sasha had dozed off and slept for at least an hour of the journey. He was still groggy when the aircraft came to a stop. The general and the others got up from their seats and gathered their suit coats and briefcases. Sasha was still in his cadet uniform and felt uncomfortable walking along with the three agents. He felt more like a prisoner than one who been 'specially selected' for an important project.

Sasha and the three proceeded into the operations building a few yards from the tarmac parking ramp. Once inside, General Tushenskiy advised that he would be departing and excused himself, indicating that Colonel Sokolov would now be in charge of project activities. He shook hands with each and wished Sasha well in his forthcoming assignment.

After the general departed, Colonel Sokolov advised Sasha that the following day would be a day of rest and relaxation for him in order to prepare himself for training. He also directed Vlad to take Sasha to a nearby clothier and outfit him in several varieties of civilian clothes. Sasha almost protested to say that he had ample civilian clothes at his parents apartment only a few kilometers away, but he held his tongue. He remembered the rules that had been imposed by General Tushenskiy. Colonel Sokolov said goodnight and departed.

Vlad led Sasha to his quarters. Surprisingly, he had a private room with a small bath located in one of the buildings within the

Khodinka compound. This would be his home for the next phase of his life. His 'companion, mentor and shadow,' Vlad, was in the room next door. Vlad told Sasha to freshen up, wear his cadet uniform for the present and that he would knock on his door in a half hour to go to dinner.

Sasha quickly looked around his room. It was very sparse, but, by far, more luxurious than he might have expected. He inspected the desk, dresser, lamps and the small bathroom, and couldn't find any obvious listening apparatus. In addition to a narrow bed, the room contained an over-stuffed lounge chair, a desk and chair and a floor lamp. By any standard, this was upscale living conditions for a former aviation cadet from the college. He looked through the canvas bag that was delivered to him with his belongings from Volgograd and discovered that he really didn't own anything besides one additional wrinkled uniform, a pair of green coveralls and a pair of boots, along with a few toiletries.

He sat in the lounge chair and tried to recount the past thirty-six hours. Although all of this began only yesterday morning, it seemed like 'forever ago!' He also tried to remember carefully everything that was said to him by the commandant and General Tushenskiy. He had no difficulty remembering the side-meeting with Vlad. He was still shocked and haunted by the revelations about his mother and the thin balance of her situation and his father's, as well as his!

He wondered if he had convinced Vlad that he would do whatever was necessary to protect his family. "I must have," he thought. "Otherwise General Tuskenskiy would have promptly terminated our meeting." He recalled the General's affirmative nod to Vlad when they re-entered the commandant's office following their fateful meeting. It was then apparent to the general he was well aware of his situation and would fully cooperate. But he was still confused and overwhelmed by the escalation of events that had turned his life upside-down overnight.

The knock on the door startled him, and he instinctively jumped to his feet and responded, "Dah, dah, come in!" Sasha opened the door and Vlad greeted him.

"Comrade Alexandr, we speak English here!" Vlad admonished him curtly. "No more Russian except when the other party does not understand. Do you understand?"

"Yes, I am sorry," Sasha responded timidly. "I forgot, it will not happen again, Comrade." Vlad then patted him on the shoulder, "Relax, I am your friend and confidant. I will work with you, and we will work together. Let's go to dinner."

They departed the building and Vlad led the way down a pathway to another building, several removed from the one in which they were housed. Within this facility they walked into a very well-appointed dining room, the likes of which Sasha had not seen since leaving Moscow for the academy. After they were greeted by an attractive hostess, they were seated at a table covered with a cloth, complete with napkins and silverware. Even though Sasha was wearing his cadet uniform, few paid any attention to him. There was a smattering of men and women in uniforms of various services and an equal number in civilian attire. They ordered from a menu, and Vlad was very animated and talkative during the meal.

He congratulated and praised Sasha for his selection to come to Khodinka to participate in a project of such great importance to the government. But he did not in any way reveal any clues regarding the type of "project" that Sasha was destined for. He spoke in general about how fortunate he was to be sent to Khodinka for training. "The best scholars and instructors in every specialty reside here at Khodinka," he said. "When you complete your special training you will be prepared to carry out any mission that is asked of you."

Sasha reluctantly asked if it would soon be possible for him to visit his parents and let them know that he was alright. Vlad told him that it would be possible in due time, but for the present, his father had been given full assurance that he was okay and would be participating in a very special training program. In a whispered voice, Vlad further reassured him that his mother would continue to be secure. Nothing would happen to her, so long as she did not provoke an incident, and as long as he, Sasha, progressed satisfactorily in his training. Sasha felt some relief at the positive tone and confidence demonstrated by Vlad. He was actually feeling more comfortable with Vlad in this new relationship. After all, he had known him for two years, and he had become his only reliable confidant during that period, albeit a spy and betrayer.

After finishing their dinner, they walked back to their quarters. It was still broad daylight on this June evening, as darkness did not come in Moscow until around 10:00 pm this time of the year.

Sasha had passed by Khodinka numerous times over the years in a city bus and had been through the nearby Dinamo Metro station a few times. But, he knew very little about the old Central Airport other than through the rumors that circulated about the GRU and its mysterious activities allegedly carried out there. As they walked along, he began to take note of the many buildings within the airport grounds, and it even seemed stranger that a landing strip still existed within the confines of the complex. Even more odd was the fact that the airfield was literally contained within a *valley* of buildings. He took note of the fact that all sides of the huge complex were surrounded by tall buildings and at least one was fifteen stories high. All of the buildings appeared to be interconnected with no open spaces in between.

Vlad walked him back to his dormitory room and bade him goodnight. Sasha slept reasonably well that night. His nerves had settled considerably, and his confidence had been rapidly restored by the extraordinary treatment of the general, Colonel Sokolov and Vlad. They actually treated him as an equal and colleague. He was dressed and ready for the day when Vlad knocked on his door. They returned to the same dining room for breakfast. With such a variety of food items, Sasha couldn't believe his eyes. Although he was still deeply curious as to why he was here, Sasha was beginning to relax and enjoy this odd turn of events.

During breakfast, Vlad said their first order of business was to visit the clothier within the compound and outfit him in civilian clothes. He also told him there should never be a reason to leave Khodinka, unless he was directed to do so, and then with proper escort. Vlad also told Sasha internal security of the compound was absolute. No one entered or departed Khodinka without proper credentials, special passwords and codes. He was told many of the buildings he would be working within permitted no metal objects to be carried in, including belt buckles, cigarette lighters or mechanical pen and pencils. Everything he needed to work with would be provided within the particular facility. Neither would he be permitted to take any materials out of certain facilities. If he had homework or study materials to deal with, they would be delivered to his room after he departed the area. Sasha was beginning to feel a tightness in his nerves again.

He was a prisoner here. Vlad, sensing his friend's facial expression, attempted to lighten up the conversation by telling him there was everything to occupy his free time. Within Khodinka there was a very good movie theatre, and musicals and operettas were presented frequently. Kiosks were stocked with most every item to sell, and there was a complete physical fitness center open 24-hours a day. Vlad then indicated they needed to move on to the clothier shop.

Back in his room with a full wardrobe of new and comfortable clothes—slacks, sweaters, jackets and two suits along with two pairs of shoes—Sasha felt renewed once again. But he noticed immediately at the clothing shop the clothes selected for him were not Russian, but more like Western, including the shoes. He had never owned such clothing. He wondered why, but as he had never been treated so well, the apprehension about his situation seemed to abate. At least at the college, he knew what to expect from the NCO's. They were predictable. Here, he perceived, was going to be a battle of intellectual exchange. He continued to feel that he was well in over his head. Then he would remind himself of the words of confidence by General Tushenskiy, about how he was specially selected for this mission (whatever it was). After a while, Vlad knocked on his door and asked if he wished to rest further or would he like to hear more about where he was and what he might expect next.

Sasha promptly responded, "I am eager to have you tell me everything that you are permitted to tell."

Vlad smiled, "I will confide in you only what I am allowed to do, at this point. You will grow with this project and information will be provided to you as each phase escalates to the next. Today, I will give you your initial schedule, a few tips and more security safeguards by which you must abide. First, a little about Khodinka. You have already noticed that the complex is completely surrounded by buildings. There are special exit and entry corridors which are manned by guards around the clock. All of your work will be conducted within the buildings of the complex. You saw the runway and the hangar facilities when we landed last night. There are actually two runways here within the confines. They are roughly oriented Northeast and Southwest, and North and South, with smaller buildings at the ends to accommodate take-offs and landings of aircraft. Most aircraft will arrive and depart after darkness for security purposes. Again, you must abide by the security rules at all times. If you have a question, ask me now."

"No, no question," Sasha replied.

"Okay, back to the security elements," Vlad continued, "There are very few telephones within Khodinka, and they are all controlled access. If you are ever permitted to use a telephone, remember that you are being monitored, and your conversation is being recorded. Do not say anything about where you are, and do not ask any questions which could compromise your position. You are living in a completely controlled environment. At first, you will be aware that you are under constant surveillance, but after awhile, you will get into the swing of things, and everything will become normal to you."

"You will not attempt to visit any facility or building unless you have specific directions to do so. Then you will be given the proper passes to permit you to go in. There are many people working on many projects within Khodinka. Do not ask or question anyone about his or her work. That is a forbidden act. Likewise, do not reveal to anyone, except those known personally to you as a part of your project, any information about your presence here, what you are studying or working on. In that regard, you will likely be tested, time and time again, by innocent looking and friendly people who may inquire where you are from, what is your background, where did you go to school, what is your job, who do you report to. Every conceivable innocent sounding question may be posed to you. Your response is to be polite and cordial.

We are all civil here, but move on to innocuous conversation and do not attempt to answer, be cute or give misleading responses in any of your conversations with those whom you do not know completely and are not within your working domain.

"One special caution," Vlad continued. "The waitresses and table servants in the restaurant, or anyone working in one of the kiosks, or in any service facility may also be an intelligence agent. So beware of any casual questions or conversation." He then asked, "Have I given you sufficient safeguards to work with?"

Sasha had heard everything and had absorbed it all. He was surprised at the complexity of it all, but he was not overwhelmed by the prospects of being able to comply with this part of his responsibilities. He had been taught and learned early in the Young Pioneers and KOMSOMOL that security within one's personal life and activities was paramount. He was well-versed in the "Big Brother" syndrome that pervaded the Soviet society. After a studied moment, he responded, "Yes, I understand everything, and I will have no difficulty complying with all of the security requirements."

"Good," replied Vlad. "Let's move on. I am not permitted to go into any details about your project assignment. For that matter, I am not privy to very many details other than you will become an 'American Student.' That is, you are going into a regimen of teaching and instruction about America, our arch Western enemy, and I envy you. I wish that I could be trained to know our enemy better. Following the Great Patriotic War, the Americans and the British took the position that they owned Russia. They tried every ploy to steal our sovereignty, but thanks to the great leadership of Stalin, he outwitted them. Now, we are the greatest and most powerful union of nations in the world. Communism has triumphed, and we will continue to march until we dominate the weaklings in the West."

Vlad's lecture over, Sasha asked, "For what purpose do you believe that am I being taught about America?"

"I don't know the details, but I am sure that is a part of the great plan to better understand and to undermine the west," Vlad replied. "Perhaps we will learn much together, since I am your guardian. Tomorrow you will be given more details and perhaps a schedule of instruction. You may also be warned to not even tell me about some of the details of your project, but do not worry. I will understand and not question you."

"I can tell you that when you return to your room tomorrow after your first indoctrination, your quarters will be completely renovated to include a television monitor, a stereo system which will be operated from a central control center as will special television programs directed for you to watch. You probably have noted that the clothes selected for you are American through and through, not reproductions. Our embassy people do excellent shopping for us. You will wear them from now on, and even when questioned about them, as I said before, ignore the questions and comments. Speak English always, except when the other party cannot. You will be subjected to endless American television programs, current news broadcasts, sporting events and weather forecasts. You will be quizzed constantly about what you have seen and heard. You will be asked to comment on political issues and situations in America and perspectives of their so-called *Cold War* with the Soviet Union. Each evening, you will find a growing collection of reading material, novels, history books, sports magazines, fashion magazines, weekly news magazines and daily newspapers from major U.S. cities. And, when you run out of things to do, your television monitor will broadcast American movies, mostly old classics, but a variety of others to acquaint you with the culture, both good and bad."

Sasha was becoming overwhelmed and feeling very queasy again about all that he was being told. "Are you telling me the truth or are you simply trying to frighten me?" he asked.

"Both!" Vlad snapped! "You must remain on the edge of fright as you are challenged with the elements of your training. The last thing that I am at liberty to tell you is that at some eventual time along the way of your training, depending on your progress, you will transfer to a dacha or *safe house* to continue your education. That may be in six months or a year, depending on your development and the schedule," he continued. "At the dacha, you will live with *Americanized* Soviet teachers who will focus your attention on the minutest of details of your orientation. What I have not commented on in this brief overview is the technical training that you will receive. I know you will greatly enjoy that part because it will deal mostly with the United States Air Force and their operating aircraft. What you may not like so much is that most of that focus will be on U.S. strategic aircraft and ballistic missiles. They have a new heavy bomber soon to be in production—the B-52. We have much information already on its performance and capabilities, as we do on the older bombers—the B-36 and their B-47's, but the GRU Aviation Directorate is always eager to learn more about how the Americans engineer and build their aircraft. Well, my friend I can see that you are becoming very weary with all of this. My watch says that if we do not hurry, we will miss the lunch hour. Are you hungry?"

Sasha looked at Vlad and said, "No, I have already eaten enough in the past twenty hours to last me a month. Why don't you go eat, and I will rest for awhile and think about all that you have told me."

"Very well," said Vlad, "I will knock on your door at 1830 for dinner. Should you become hungry before then, there is a kiosk canteen in the basement of this building. Just sign your name and room number for whatever you want, but save room for dinner this evening! By the way, you will be paid while you are in our program. I will see to it that you are provided with an advance of some rubles tomorrow, a minor detail." With that, Vlad left the room.

Sasha napped and tried to absorb everything that he had been told by the commandant, General Tushenskiy and Vlad.

Vlad returned at 1830 sharp. He was always on time to the second. They enjoyed a pleasant dinner with mostly small talk about the beautiful Moscow summers, a forthcoming visit to Khodinka by the Moscow Circus, which would be a treat, but they did not discuss further any of the previous subjects. Of course, the cafeteria was hardly the place to bring up any of those topics.

In an occasional relaxed mood, Sasha would think about inquiring into Vlad's "real" background. Was he really from a collective farm? How old was he really? How long had he been in the GRU or the KGB or wherever he was assigned? Just what was his real job? These were among many questions that Sasha wanted ask, but he thought better of it. He had listened carefully to all of the warnings about being too inquisitive. With dinner over, the two headed back to their rooms.

Along the way, Vlad asked Sasha if he would like to take in the movie, but he declined, saying that he really needed to rest his mind and to prepare himself for tomorrow. Then he thought, "Whatever preparations might I make?" In any event, he really wanted to get away from Vlad for awhile. He needed some space from the constant shadowing. When he entered his room, he immediately looked around for signs of anyone having been there while he was away. Sure enough, he had carefully placed a thread between layers of his underwear in one of his dresser drawers. It was obvious that the garments had been disturbed, very carefully, but nevertheless, someone had pilfered through his room and his belongings. He instinctively knew that this would be the expected norm from now on. He had heard a lot about KGB tactics, and he presumed that the GRU operated the same. He also wondered if they could also "pilfer through his brain," or that they might attempt to do so. He presumed that the GRU used the same tactics. Exhausted, he finally went to bed, wondering what the next day would bring.

The Candidate

Vlad knocked on Sasha's door promptly at 0630 as he had said he would the evening before.

"Ready for breakfast?" Vlad asked.

"Yes, I am ready. Come in," Sasha answered. "What should I wear today? I forgot to ask last evening."

Vlad looked at him and said, "You look fine. A comfortable shirt and trousers will be all that you will need on this warm day. We dress very casually around here most of the time and only dress up for special dignitaries or events. You will be advised of those times."

They enjoyed another very pleasant breakfast and small talk. If nothing else, Sasha was very much enjoying the pleasure of eating since he had arrived at Khodinka. He did reflect often on his classmates back at the college and wondered about their welfare. Vlad did not provide any information about the forthcoming day's agenda, and when they were finished, he said they must report to Colonel Sokolov at 0730.

Vlad escorted Sasha through several security check points within the building they entered. The tough-looking security guards observed him closely and suspiciously. Twice Vlad was asked to step away to the protection of the guards, vouch that he was not under duress, and that Sasha was an official visitor. Once through the security checks, they entered a very pleasant outer office with an officious-looking secretary and a male administrator. They were both in civilian clothes, very cordial and spoke in English. After a minute's wait, they were escorted into a spacious office. Several people were in the room, and Sasha spotted Colonel Sokolov behind a desk. Again in near-perfect English, the colonel said, "Good Morning and come in Sasha, Captain Yepishev. Sasha, have you rested well since your arrival?"

"Yessir, I have, Colonel, thank you," Sasha responded.

Colonel Sokolov continued, "You look very fit and fine in your new clothes. Now permit me to introduce some of our staff to you. First, this is Dr. Gennadi Ermakov. Dr. Ermakov is the Director of our American Culture Sector. You will be spending much of your time with him and his very capable staff. Next, I wish to introduce Colonel Sergei Lavrov who is in charge of security in this division. He will brief you on the many requirements attendant to your project and security awareness. He will also arrange for your security badges, etc. Next, this is Irina Denisov, our senior American English language professor."

As Colonel Sokolov continued to the next person, Sasha felt a pang of nervousness as he thought of his mother and her English language teaching. He wondered if she knew his mother.

"This is Nikolai Kozlov, our Director of American Systems Technologies. Also with him this morning is Lt. Colonel Boris Sidorov, an expert in American strategic bomber systems. Last, an Air Force officer with whom you will find pleasure working with, Major Mikolai Rozhko, a flight instructor of the highest qualifications. Sasha, there will be some fun associated with your serious work here," the Colonel chuckled. "Although you are quite a ways from continuing your flight instruction, I wanted you to know it will be an important part of your training."

Sasha noticed throughout the introductions that each spoke reasonably good English, not with the British crispness, but fairly casual.

Colonel Sokolov then excused Lt. Colonel Sidorov and Major Rozhko and thanked them for coming. Vlad remained while the two acknowledged and left the room. Sasha felt relieved that Vlad was allowed to remain and would be involved in the indoctrination of his activities. Colonel Sokolov began in a very casual and conversational manner. He was very much at ease with himself and appeared to instill confidence in everyone in the room.

"Sasha," he began, "or do you prefer to be called Aleksandr?"

Sasha responded, "Sasha is fine with me, if it is with you."

"Fine. Sasha, it is," The Colonel responded.

"Sasha, Captain Yepishev has provided you with a preliminary and informal indoctrination of the security requirements here at Khodinka. You will receive much more in detail from Colonel Lavrov and his staff as you proceed into the project. Incidentally, we have selected 'Mackarova' as the name of your project. We believe that the Masquerade will properly characterize what you will be doing, and it will become increasingly clearer to you as we proceed."

Several in the room chuckled quietly.

Sasha had no idea what he was talking about. He tried hard to pick up on the nuances of everyone's comments and to interpret their expressions and smiles. There was obviously a considerable amount of inside jokes about all of this, and he was completely in the dark.

"Sasha, as General Tushenskiy informed you," Colonel Sokolov continued, "you have been very specially selected from hundreds of other candidates to participate in a very important and very daring project. I excused the other officers because it is important we do not reveal every part of the project to everyone involved. Captain Yepishev will be informed of most of the elements, but not all. It will be important that you keep to yourself any, and all, aspects of this project to which you are exposed." He continued, "I know that this may seem very complicated at this time, but as we progress, you will become more comfortable with the mosaic that we are developing. Do you follow me, thus far?" he asked.

"Yessir, I believe that I do," Sasha responded.

"Good, let's continue. You are likely the youngest agent operative that has ever been approved for selection by the senior officials of the KGB and the GRU. You were selected at your early age for several reasons. First, we need a bright young candidate like you that has the time before him to accomplish all that needs to be done in preparing for, and executing, this project. We routinely select operative candidates no younger than in their late twenties or early thirties, married and accomplished in some specialty or technology. You are obviously none of these, which is good for this project. But you have excelled in every challenge put before you, and we have been carefully monitoring you for several years. What you are about to enter is an extremely important and challenging program to make you an American."

Sasha was stunned and confused by the statement, but after all that he had been through, he didn't react or even acknowledge the Colonel's words.

"You will become a typical young American in his early twenties, with an American name," Sokolov said. "A family with an established background; that is all I am going to say at this point, but you need to know that much because it will assist you in accepting the instruction and training which we have planned for you. As Captain Yepishev told you, your dress will be that of an American. You will listen to American radio broadcasts, watch television programs and movies and read current American magazines and newspapers. This will become your daily regimen, in addition to a very ambitious instructional program covering the breadth and depth of everything you will require to become the person we want you to be." Concluding, the Colonel said, "But you will not forget, nor will we permit you to forget, that you are first, and foremost, a loyal communist and member of the great Soviet Society. We will teach you to role play, how to look, act and react like an American, in this case, but you must always be prepared to become yourself when required." And, finally, "We will work with you on all of these things together."

"Dr. Ermakov, would you please outline your program for Sasha?" Colonel Sokolov concluded. "Captain Yepishev and I will leave now and see you later."

Colonel Sokolov and Vlad left the room, and for the next hour and a half, Dr. Ermakov and each of those in the room, addressed the various phases of "Sasha's Education" for which they would be responsible. Ermakov described a curriculum that would include courses in American history, geography, political system, culture, English language, religions, laws, sports as well as basic courses in mathematics, economics and sciences. Sasha was also given an overview of the technical instruction he would receive. He would learn the history of the U.S. Department of Defense, the Armed Services, and the U.S. Air Force—in particular, its culture, missions and operating equipment. Sasha's head was spinning when the session was over. Dr. Ermakov and the others were polite enough and seemed eager to teach and work with him, but he was overwhelmed with the magnitude of all that was being heaped upon him. For the first time he could ever remember, he had a sick feeling he might not be capable of meeting and completing a challenge.

After the session with the instructors, Sasha was escorted to another building in the complex to meet with Colonel Lavrov, the security officer he had been introduced to earlier. Vlad was waiting in the outer office. "How did it go?" he asked.

Sasha looked at him and with a weak smile and said, "I don't feel very good about this. There may be too much for me to learn. I may not be successful. I think you should inform Colonel Sokolov that I am deeply concerned about this program, and I do not think that I am the right person to be chosen to participate. Right now, I just want to get away from here."

Vlad looked at him and calmly said, "Look, my friend, I suffered through two damn years of boot camp and college with you, something I didn't need in my life. But I was directed to do it in order to monitor you, see you tested, and to validate that I thought you were the right candidate for *any* assignment that our government wanted you to do. So don't tell me that you want out. You *are in,* and you are here to stay and finish! Now pull yourself together!" he hissed. "We are going to meet with Colonel Lavrov, and I don't want any of your sniveling in front of him. He is tough and a no nonsense officer; he might just knock your head off for showing this weakness." Vlad finished in a loud whisper, "Got it?"

The door opened and Colonel Lavrov stepped out and nodded for the two of them to come into his office. Vlad signaled for Sasha to precede him into the room. Once inside and seated, Sasha began to feel some of his strength returning and he listened as the security officer began his talk.

"When we finish here," Lavrov began, "Captain Yepishev will escort you to complete your security in-processing, fingerprinting, photographs, some signatures and obtain your security badges." He continued, "At this time I want to follow-up with the informal security overview Captain Yepishev gave you after your arrival here. Khodinka is a unique complex of facilities and special training activities. You are in the center of the GRU Headquarters, the Intelligence Directorate of the General Staff. The main thrust of the GRU is to assess military capabilities of foreign countries outside the sphere of the Soviet Union. You are here to be trained as an agent of the GRU."

Lavrov paused and added, "The KGB will also play a major role in the management of your training program and thereafter, when you leave Khodinka. Just to advise you, both agencies have an interest in your progression and performance. For that matter, when you leave Khodinka, you will be directly under the supervision of the KGB. Any questions?"

The words startled Sasha. He had not heard anyone say anything so direct to him since he began this odyssey. "No, Sir," he responded.

Lavrov then continued, "I suppose that you have been told we normally do not train agents of your age, I personally do not agree with the plan to expose you to this type of training and responsibility because I do not believe you possess the necessary experience or maturity to grasp what we are about. But, I am not completely in charge. So be it." He went on, "You will be trained as an *"Illegal,"* that is okay an agent specially trained to serve outside the Soviet Union and in a foreign country. In your case, you will be serving in the United States of America."

Sasha sucked in his breath and felt his face flush, but he tried not to display any physical reaction to the Colonel's disclosure.

Colonel Lavrov proceeded to discuss the role that Sasha would be trained to play. "An Illegal is best described as a Soviet military officer dispatched to a foreign country to pass himself off as a citizen of that country. You will have a specific mission, for which we will train you here. While in the United States, you will be provided a system of contact officers who are agents of the Soviet Union and to whom you will report as instructed. The details of all of this will be provided you at the appropriate time, but the important thing is that you will never be without someone to contact for assistance, information or in an emergency while you are in the operative country. As I said earlier, my concern with you is your youth and inexperience. I have been informed that your mission requires someone who has sufficient youth to undergo the training here, be placed in the foreign operating location and spend sufficient time there to complete the mission. The average age of our Illegal recruits is between twenty-seven and thirty years. But, all the necessary training we have planned for you will take years to accomplish, so we must begin with someone of your age. Undermining and exploiting the enemy camp is one of our major mission responsibilities. That will be your sole objective. We will train you to become an expert in every skill you need carry out your mission. In the end, the investment in you and your mission performance, if you succeed, will pay great dividends to the Soviet Union."

"Most of your training will be over the next two years," Larov continued, "and will take place here at Khodinka, but periodically you will be sent to other special facilities to work on the unique details of your project. Again, with regard to security, Captain Yepishev has impressed upon you the grave seriousness as I will do so at this point and continue as you enter various phases of training. You will not discuss any, I repeat any, details of your mission to anyone except those who have complete knowledge of your project. Those individuals who will have complete knowledge of your assignment include: General Tushenskiy, Colonel Sokolov, and now we are introducing Captain Yepishev into the project, along with myself, of course. No one else will know of the complete details of this project. Of course, you will have discussions with your instructors about the various incremental segments of your training, but none of your instructors will have knowledge of your overall project. They will not petition you for details. Their task is to teach, train and indoctrinate within their specialties. Is all of this clear?"

"Yes, sir," replied Sasha. He also felt some relief that now, at least, he could talk more freely with Vlad about his activities.

Lavrov proceeded, "I mean *no one*! Each of your training phases will be compartmentalized and taught by the most competent teachers and instructors. But it will be up to you, and you only, to assimilate the training into the single mission of your project. Of course, those I have mentioned as being across the entire spectrum of the program will be available to assist you in understanding and interpreting your studying and training when required. Now, allow me to give you a brief further overview of what you may expect during your training as you proceed, in order to minimize possible confusion."

Lavrov continued his monologue, it seemed, without his taking in a breath. "As your training progresses, you will gradually transition into your new identity. You will be given an American name, birth place, family background and all the necessary vital statistics documentation to support your identification. You will become someone else entirely. You will be tested constantly on your identification, personal background, events in your life, everything to the minutest detail. During your training, we will frequently surprise you with off-the-wall questions about yourself. You must learn to think quickly to respond and to give proper answers, even when we haven't provided you any details with which to respond. You will be judged severely on your ability to respond to impromptu questions and challenges, about any and everything in your new identity. Every answer you give must be above anyone's suspicion. I am told that you are very bright and a quick thinker, so this will be an opportunity for you to put into practice your creativity blended with the required information we provide you. Always be on your toes and never let your guard down. Trust no one. Be suspicious of everyone! After you are well into your training and preparation, you will be informed of the mission requirements and details. That is what we will expect of you when you relocate to your new country. Okay, Comrade Alexandr, we are finished for now," Colonel Lavrov concluded and Sasha noted that he finally took in a deep breath. There was no doubt that he had given this lecture hundreds of times. "Captain Yepishev will escort you to the appropriate offices to complete the security administrative requirements. I will be meeting with you again, periodically, as you proceed. Do you have any questions?"

Sasha had dozens of questions but decided to wait until he felt more secure in asking them. "No, Sir, not at this time. Thank you for this discussion and enlightening me further about my assignment."

As Sasha and Vlad departed Colonel Lavrov's office, he was revisited by the same pangs of insecurity and helplessness. He felt he was on a slippery slide without anything or anyone to cling to. Not even having Vlad to confide in bolstered his feelings. Events were happening so fast that he had difficulty even remembering how he got to be here. His thoughts were jumbled confusion.

Vlad guided him downstairs to the security processing area where he was fingerprinted, photographed, signed several documents certifying his status and issued a laminated security badge with his picture, an identification number and thumb print on the back. The security office personnel briefed him on where the badge would grant him access and where it would not. He was advised that the badge would not permit him to leave the Khodinka complex. He would be issued a special badge along with "exit" and "re-entry" passwords whenever he was given permission to go outside the complex.

After they departed the security processing office and strolled along toward the dining facility, Vlad tried to bolster Sasha by telling him he would likely be given permission within a few days to go visit his parents. Vlad would accompany him. They would probably go on a weekend for a brief visit to reassure his mother and father that he was okay, in good health and working very hard on a special project. Vlad also advised him that he would be present during the visit. This latter condition, for a possible opportunity to visit his parents, didn't particularly bother Sasha. He was so elated at the prospect of seeing them again soon that he would agree to anything.

The two spoke very little during lunch, and neither mentioned the morning's events. Afterward, Sasha returned to his room to begin his preparations and studies to assume his *new* identity.

SIX

Mackye

Sasha was startled when he entered his room. A small speaker on his desk was softly broadcasting an American news information program. He easily distinguished the language from the more familiar British accent he was used to hearing. Just as Vlad had told him, his room had been transformed into a communications center—complete with a television monitor, radio speaker and a telephone. There was also a reel-to-reel tape player. The radio had a volume control, but it could not be turned off, only the volume turned down. He inspected the TV and found that it was a controlled receiver with the channel choices selected from somewhere else.

He also observed a stack of books on American history, culture, politics, sports and economics as well as American magazines and newspapers. The telephone had been placed on the desk. Before he reached for the hand piece, he instinctively knew that it was a controlled phone system and that he could not use it to call out. Sure enough, there was no dial tone.

"Oh well," he thought, "even if I could make a telephone call, it would be monitored, and I couldn't say anything to anybody about anything anyway." In any event, he wouldn't be bored during his off duty and out of the classroom time with all this material left for him to study.

He then inspected his undergarments in the dresser drawer and sure enough, the colored thread that he had moved to another location had definitely been disturbed.

"These GRU or KGB types must not be the first team," he thought to himself, "since they had once again overlooked my thread intrusion detector."

He considered playing some "games" with those who came into his room while he was out but quickly thought better of it. No point in getting "killed" this early!

As he sat to begin thumbing through some of the materials, the telephone rang, startling him. He had not heard a phone ring in so long, much less talk on one, that he was hesitant at first to answer it.

"Comrade Sasha, how do you like your new quarters? And, how about your new telephone?"

"Well, Vlad, they sure outfitted my room with sufficient equipment and study materials. I won't get bored."

"Unfortunately, you will not be able to use your telephone to call out. It is for internal use only, so that any of the staff or myself may call you when necessary. I should add, it is monitored so you must not discuss any sensitive information. By the way, I will be by at 1800 for dinner, if you will be ready."

Vlad didn't issue invitations, he simply stated when and where.

"I will be ready," Sasha responded. "See you then."

The Mackarova Project routine began with intensity the day after Sasha's first meeting with Colonel Sokolov and the training directors. His first meeting was with Dr. Ermakov, director of the American Culture Sector. He was introduced to the other instructors by Ermakov, including Mackye Evanov Bolschekovsky, a young woman who had just arrived at Khodinka following graduation from Moscow University. She introduced herself as Mackye, *"Mock'ee,"* she emphasized the pronunciation with a smile and said she was in Ermakov's classroom to observe teaching procedures and techniques. When Sasha looked at her, he was immediately taken with her striking blonde hair; flawless skin texture and piercing blue eyes. She greeted him with a warm, confident smile. Their eyes engaged for a lingering moment as they shook hands. Ermakov gave him a syllabus of instruction that would take him through the next six months.

First, he would be trained in American English language concepts and vernacular. The emphasis would be on the colloquialisms of the upper Midwest United States—Ohio and Illinois—in particular. He would also concentrate on the cultures of the Chicago and Cleveland areas, urban centers where European accents are not too unusual. Therefore, if his Russian accent "filtered" through at some point, then it would not be as apparent as it might be if he claimed the South, Southwest or the West as his home. American English would become his "*native*" tongue hereafter with most all classroom instruction taught in his new language. He was surprised by the number of instructors who were very fluent in English. Concurrent with his study of conversational English, he would also enter instruction in American history, culture, laws and religion.

The basic and instinctive activities of his cultural area of study would not only have to be learned but become second nature to his conduct and reactions. His language training was difficult at first, but eventually he began to pick up the terms and slang. Listening to the nightly radio news broadcasts and mimicking the words helped a great deal. The radio also gave him insight into what was important in the American news. His initial routine became spending four hours in the classroom each morning with courses of instruction in various phases of American culture, history and life.

After a two-hour break for lunch, he then had another four-hour session of practical language application through discussions with teachers on a wide range of American topics: history, politics, sports, movies and ordinary subjects about the kinds of food, drinks and other innocuous activities. All must be mastered and integrated into his new identity.

He was very pleased that his new acquaintance, Mackye, sat in on many of his classroom lectures. She was near the same age and in a somewhat similar situation. As he was a student, and she, an instructor understudy, they easily became friends. He enjoyed his new role and, especially, this new and exciting friendship. They began a routine of meeting in the warm August evenings, usually after he was free from Vlad's daily *chaperone*. They would walk about the complex, talk and occasionally study together in the Library Hall. Mackye spoke reasonably good English with a distinct Russian accent. They had fun practicing and developing their *new* language. At first, the ever-observant Vlad didn't seem to mind Sasha's interest in Mackye since she was considered a faculty member and did not represent a threat. He did, however, issue a caution to Sasha not to discuss, in any way, his training other than the academic courses.

"Everyone is watching everyone else here," he cautioned.

"I know," she nodded knowingly.

Sasha learned that Mackye was born in Paris where her father, Sergei, an apparatchik, Party Bureaucrat, was posted in the Soviet Embassy.

"My mother, Tiina, died three years ago," she said, "following a lengthy illness and my father continues to serve the government in Moscow."

"I seldom see him," she added. "We have never been very close and even less since my mother died."

One evening after Mackye and Sasha had shared many experiences about their lives, she confided in him further.

"Two days before my mother died," Mackye said, "she told me that Sergei was not my natural father. She said that she and Sergei had been married for many years and that while he wanted children, they had not been successful in having any. When they lived in Paris my mother first casually met, and after a time, fell in love with Jean-Francois E'van Guirand, a noted poet, satirist and politician. He was also a communist and moved with ease between his own people and the Soviets. My mother said that she conceived his child, and that I am the daughter of Jean-Francois E'van Guirand."

Mackye took a deep breath, and calmly continued. "My father, Sergei, knew all about the affair and me, but did not reject my mother; rather, he seemed to relish holding the weight of guilt over her for the rest of her life."

Mackye said she had not told anyone this story until now, but because she felt so much at ease with Sasha that she wanted to talk about it—tell someone she trusted. She also said she had only now come to realize why her father had virtually rejected her all of her life. He had never shown any affection toward her or, for that matter, her mother.

Mackye was very strong, determined and showed little emotion as she revealed the story to Sasha. She laughingly said, "My mother told me my father wanted to name me Olga, after his mother, but my mother held forth and succeeded in naming me Mackye." As she told the story, she smiled and said there was a bitter and lingering disagreement about her name.

"Sergei, my father had argued that Mackye was not a fit Russian name. I kept it anyway," she smiled. "Before she died, my mother gave me a folder containing several love letters and poems written by Guirand. I have read them over and over. And, it was then I realized why my mother coached me all of my life to have an appreciation for the literary arts and languages."

"My mother said Jean-Francois was loved by many women and that she knew she wasn't the only one in his life," she lamented tearfully. "She did love him at the time, and I was the product of that love. My name, 'Mackye', was drawn from my mother's love for reading many and varied prose. She said she discovered the unique name years before I was born; was taken by it and savored it for the time she might have a daughter."

Sasha was touched by Mackye's story. Much of the description of her mother was analogous to that of his own mother, Tatyana, and her deep appreciation for literature and the Russian arts, but, he had by no means experienced the personal emotion in his life, such as that revealed by her. His main concern was for his mother's dissenting political feelings and the risks she took in that regard. Mackye's story brought the two of them much closer together. She brought the folder of letters and poems one evening, and they sat on a bench in the park as she read them to Sasha. He was deeply moved by the poems. They stirred feelings in him he had never felt before. He was grateful to her for sharing her story and the poems, and his admiration for her beauty, strength and soul grew as they saw even more of one another.

Sasha was particularly intrigued by the history of the United States and the fact that the Americans won their independence through a revolutionary process not unlike the communists did under Lenin. His instructors, however, did not attempt to color the vast differences between Soviet Russian lifestyles and that in the U.S. The remarkable freedom enjoyed by Americans was difficult for him to grasp. Although his mother had characterized the openness she observed when she visited London, he still could not fully comprehend that Americans had considerable freedom to move about, travel and relocate without government restrictions or boundaries. It must have also been difficult for his instructors, several of whom said that they had served with the Soviet Embassy or consulates in the United States, to share their observations and perspectives on these freedoms.

Vlad, in his role as mentor, and avowed Soviet secret police agent, would often remind Sasha that while these appearances of a kinder and pleasant lifestyle in the U.S. were appealing, they were mostly a facade and the false pretenses of stupid democracies. Mackye reinforced this view.

"Sasha, once you get into the depth and soul of the superficial processes of the United States and all democratic societies, you will understand that it is built solely upon idealism. They pretend to freely elect their officials, but they don't. All of their so-called elections are shams and are fixed to benefit the wealthy bureaucrats. They pretend to worship their God, but in truth, narcotics and alcohol are at the center of their greed and depravity."

Mackye was a loyal communist and ideologue, and she rejected any notions that the United States or any place in the West was superior to the Soviet Union. Sasha, however, was intrigued by the United States and how it had evolved over its history. While he had not been there to see it firsthand, he was fascinated by the apparent ambiance of the culture and the unheard of material abundance. As his training progressed, his interest steadily increased with every facet of the instruction process. He became so engrossed in learning about the different life ahead he gave little thought as to what his mission might be. He did occasionally ask Vlad about what he might be expected to do when he transferred to the U.S. But Vlad either didn't know or would not divulge any information, except that it would be an extremely important mission. The results would greatly increase the importance of the Soviet Union and hasten the downfall of the American imperialists.

Vlad constantly lectured Sasha during their lunch and dinner breaks. "Soviet national power and prestige are supported by our strong ideology. We are in a constant struggle with the forces of the West, and our struggle is a necessary part of the forward movement of history. Sasha, the force of communism is more progressive than the forces of the West and will inevitably triumph over capitalism. There is no acceptance in our government that maintaining status quo or international stability are options to ending the ideological struggle."

It was apparent that Vlad's role was as much to insure that he did not forget his allegiance to his government as it was to monitor his training attitude. The Soviets frequently risked losing agents to Western influence once they were exposed to the life outside Russia. To minimize such defections, there were always layers of handlers and monitors watching over each other. And, when the KGB recovered a defector, which they often did, the results of his deeds and punishment were well-circulated amongst other agents.

After the first month's training, it became apparent to his supervisors that Sasha had settled reasonably well into his new environment. With that reinforcement, Vlad told him over dinner one evening that he would be permitted to leave Khodinka and visit his parents briefly, for a few hours, the following Sunday afternoon. Sasha was elated. This was Wednesday, so he had only three days before he could step outside the complex, see the streets of Moscow and, best of all, see his mother and father. Neither did he let up in his study endeavors. He was motivated anew by the prospects of visiting his parents.

Mackye shared in his joy. "Sasha, I have not fully appreciated how difficult it is for you not to be able to leave the training center. It is a freedom that I have taken for granted. I wish for you a good visit with your parents."

Vlad told him that they would leave the Khodinka compound after lunch on Sunday and would have to return by 1800 hours. They would be driven by civilian automobile and dropped off a block or so from his parent's apartment building.

Homecoming

Sunday noon finally came. On the Saturday evening before the planned visit, Sasha and Mackye studied late in the library and then took a walk in the brisk evening. Mackye became chilled, and Sasha suggested that they stop by his room which was near by so she could warm before returning to her quarters some distance away in complex. The occasion of their few private minutes alone in Sasha's room predictably resulted in the inevitable. Sasha and Mackye were in love, and they fulfilled their expressions during that evening.

Sasha, preoccupied with the lingering thoughts of Mackye and the opportunity to finally leave his captive environment to visit his parents, tried to study all morning but with little success. Vlad finally rapped on his door at 12 o'clock sharp and they departed for the dining facility. Vlad was very animated over their lunch, while Sasha remained tense and played with his food until they could leave. The two departed the dining room and Vlad led them to the appropriate exit hall. This was the first opportunity that Sasha had to exercise the "one-time" departure pass and exit password procedures. They "worked" and he was out on the street! He breathed in deeply the musky Moscow air as if it were fresh from a new found source. A nondescript black Lada sedan was parked at the curb side.

"Come along," said Vlad. "Let's go."

Sasha looked around for familiar sites and then followed Vlad into the rear seat of the sedan. As they moved through the light Sunday afternoon traffic, Sasha felt a rush of uplifting. Being driven through Moscow in a chauffeur driven sedan, he had a feeling of freedom and importance! If only the cadets back at the college could see him now!

He thought, "This is too unreal to be true."

The past month had been traumatic and grueling. Only meeting Mackye had helped him maintain his balance of reasoning. What a change in his entire life!

"How on earth did this happen to me?" he wondered now, as he had many other times since arriving at Khodinka.

It seemed as though an eternity had passed, and yet, he was only beginning. His relief was short-lived.

"Comrade Sasha, I need to caution you about personal involvement with individuals during your training at Khodinka. My purpose in raising this subject with you is that it has been duly noticed that you and Comrade Bolschekovsky have been spending considerable time together, perhaps more than two professional people should in your positions. Let me caution you, great trust has been placed in you. You are expected to conduct yourself accordingly. For that matter, Comrade Bolshekovsky also needs to exercise restraint. You do understand, do you not?"

"Vlad, I appreciate what you are telling me, but Mackye Bolshekovsky is a very professional lady, and my relationship with her is proper in every way. We enjoy studying together and exchanging thoughts, nothing more. You need not be concerned. I understand my responsibilities completely."

"Comrade Sasha, you are not getting my point. Your Comrade Bolshekovsky is never to enter your private quarters again! Now do you get it?" Vlad breathed the fiery words under his breath to keep the driver from hearing everything.

Sasha was furious. "I get it, Comrade! Say no more to me on that subject."

He breathed deeply, paused for a moment and then calmly asked, "What am I allowed to discuss with my parents?"

Vlad quickly restored his own calm. "Only that you are in special training near Moscow, super secret and important training to make use of your skills for the good of the government. Tell them that you are still a student in officers' training. The special school you are now attending has taken precedence over the college courses in Volgograd, but you are still in training to be an officer and pilot in the Soviet Air Force. That will be sufficient to tell them. Your father will understand state secrets are taken as they are given and your mother will likely not ask further questions. After that issue is cleared up you may discuss your health and well-being, and that I am a good friend whom you asked to come along today." Vlad continued. "We will stay for two or three hours, then you will excuse us to leave. Do not force me to urge our departure. If this visit goes well, I will recommend that you be permitted to visit again soon, that is, if you also heed my admonitions about Comrade Bolshekovsky. Now, I believe that these visits are good for your morale and that of your parents. Is this all agreeable with you?"

"I understand everything, Comrade," Sasha responded sharply. And, then almost solicitous, "I want to thank you for supporting this visit. I will be obedient to the rules. Thank you."

The sedan came to a halt at curb side and Vlad opened the door to let them out onto the sidewalk. He nodded to the driver without giving any instructions.

Once again, Sasha was reminded he was in the hands of professionals. Every detail was executed with clockwork precision. They walked casually up the street. Neither was leading. It was obvious that Vlad knew as well as he the proper direction to take to the entrance to the apartment building on Varsonof Prospekt.

"I presume that my parents are aware we are coming and they will be waiting?" Sasha asked as they walked along.

Vlad smiled and patted him on the shoulder. "Sasha, Comrade, do you think I would take you on a wild goose chase on this special afternoon? Everything will be fine. Enjoy your visit. I look forward to meeting your distinguished father, the general, and your mother, the intellectual one."

There was a tone of condescension in Vlad's latter reference to Tatyana.

Arriving at the entrance to the apartment building, Sasha lead the way up the stairway to the third floor and his parent's apartment. He rapped on the door, and it was promptly opened by his mother. She gave him a huge hug and beckoned the two of them into the small parlor. Viktor also was waiting to hug his son and warmly greet him home.

"This is my good friend, Vladimir. Vlad, I want you to meet my parents," Sasha began.

Vlad was greeted warmly by Tatyana and Viktor. "Only that you are in special training near Moscow, super secret and important training to make use of your skills for the good of the government. Tell them that you are still a student in officers' training. The special school you are now attending has taken precedence over the college courses in Volgograd, but you are still in training to be an officer and pilot in the Soviet Air Force. That will be sufficient to tell them. Your father will understand state secrets are taken as they are given and your mother will likely not ask further questions. After that issue is cleared up you may discuss your health and well-being, and that I am a good friend whom you asked to come along today." Vlad continued. "We will stay for two or three hours, then you will excuse us to leave.

Do not force me to urge our departure. If this visit goes well, I will recommend that you be permitted to visit again soon. That is, if you also heed my admonitions about Comrade Bolshekovsky. Now, I believe that these visits are good for your morale and that of your parents. Is this all agreeable with you?"

"I have tea and sweets prepared and ready," said Tatyana. "Please be seated and I will be right back."

"It is great to have you home again, Sasha, and, so soon!" his father offered. "I have been informed you are now in a special training program and not attending the college at Volgograd."

"That is true, Father. When I was summoned back to Volgograd, I was informed I was being reassigned to a special training program, in lieu of the Volgograd officers' training college."

Vlad interrupted, "Yes, General, Sasha and I both were honored to be selected for special training. In the end, the officer's commissions will come as well as pilot training. Meanwhile, we are specializing in a very important project. I am sure that you have been informed, at the minimum, that the new assignment is of great importance, and that Sasha's selection is a special feather in his cap."

"Yes," Viktor agreed. "I have been given some assurance that all is well with our son, and the authorities are positioning him properly for very important duties."

Tatyana entered the parlor with a tray of tea cups and a plate of sweet cakes. She was nervous but displayed great control over her emotions. It had been only a few scant weeks since Sasha's leave had been interrupted by the appearance of the two KGB agents who had whisked him away without explanation. She had lingering memories of her father's arrest in the middle of the night and his ultimate fate. It was only within the last few days that Viktor had been informed that Sasha would be visiting on this Sunday.

"Hot tea and sweets," Tatyana announced.

"Sasha, we are so pleased to have you back home and so soon! Are you well?" she had to ask, even after having been alerted by Viktor that Sasha would, in all likelihood, be escorted during his visit by a secret police agent.

"I am fine, Mother," Sasha put on his best face. "As father has been advised, I have been selected for specialized training and will not be returning to the Volgograd College, at least for the present. Everything is going very well. I am very happy with my new assignment."

The remainder of the visit consisted of small talk and of little substance. Vlad interjected various observations regarding innocuous and non-substantive subjects: the weather, how well the Soviets were governing the country, rumors their great leader, Stalin, may be ill, and who might replace him. But no one really concentrated, or was serious, during the casual small talk. Tatyana was very frustrated by the false pretense of it all, but she maintained her discipline and restrained herself regarding the serious concern for her son, although she did take comfort in the apparent fact that he looked very well. He was nicely groomed and his clothes were extremely fashionable. She felt somewhat comforted that at least he wasn't in trouble or under duress although she had learned never to trust the KGB or any government agents. Although Sasha's friend did not look like a secret police agent, she wasn't comfortable with him.

Finally, Vlad, growing impatient, spoke to Sasha.

"Well, Comrade, we must go 'lest we be late to catch the metro train."

"Dah, we must go. It has been a very pleasant afternoon, Mother, Father. I hope that my work will permit me to visit again soon. In the meantime, please do not worry about me. I am fine. As you can see, I am healthy and enjoying my work very much."

The brief meeting was far too formal and businesslike for her, but Tatyana dealt with it for fear that if she did not, only the worst could happen. Viktor had sternly cautioned her not to conduct herself otherwise, particularly if Sasha were accompanied by a stranger, which he was. After the visit, she felt nothing but despair. Sasha's absence for two long years had been painful. When he finally came home, her hopes were renewed for a son that she felt was destined to become great. Even if his success was but to be a Soviet officer, she felt that she had done everything within the system to teach, support and encourage him. After he was all but kidnapped by the secret police, only six days into his leave, and then disappeared again for over a month without a word, she felt completely betrayed. Even Viktor, in his position as a Soviet general, could not learn of their son's fate. Although he appeared relaxed and confident during his earlier leave from officers' college and even more so during this brief afternoon's visit, she felt fear for his well-being and safety.

Viktor could neither enlighten her about Sasha's activities nor relieve her anxiety. She was certain of one thing—her son was undergoing a profound behavioral change in his character, appearance and conduct—a metamorphosis.

He was not the Sasha who left home two years before to attend the academy. In fact, he had changed dramatically in just the short month since he came home on his first leave. He talked differently and acted very stiff. He was not her same Sasha. She thought that it possibly could have been the stress of having his "friend" with him, closely monitoring every word of their conversation. Tatyana had spent enough time around the KGB agents in her teaching classes to recognize that Vlad was not an ordinary friend as he was introduced. He was carefully managing Sasha's every move. The visit left Tatyana more depressed than ever.

"You conducted yourself very well, Sasha," Vlad told him as they strode down the sidewalk after the visit. "I will insure that you have other opportunities to visit with your parents. I think it served both you, and them, very well. After all, we want you to be relaxed and happy in your work."

"Thank you for arranging for the visit, Vlad. I think that it helped relieve my mother of some anxiety, but I don't know how much. She is puzzled and very troubled about where I may be and what I may be doing. It is very mysterious to her. As you could see, my father is unable to assist in relieving her concerns."

Sasha knew that he was being forced to grovel for Vlad's support, but that was the system. He knew that if he walked the line and operated within the rules, he would be rewarded.

"I was very impressed with your mother, Comrade Sasha. It is apparent that she is a very intelligent person. It is too bad that she does not believe in her government and her country," Vlad retorted. "She hates us."

Sasha wanted very much to challenge Vlad, but he knew that no matter what he said it would lead to a confrontation, and he did not need that. He responded calmly. "She is a very intelligent lady and has great affection for my father and me."

The sedan was waiting at the appointed place at curb side and the two got in. Without a word being spoken, the driver eased off toward Khodinka, making several irregular turns down side streets to insure that he wasn't being followed. Agents left nothing to chance.

Summer moved into fall, and Sasha continued with his intense training and study. The areas of instruction totally absorbed his interest. He could not believe that a country like the United States could be so multifaceted: politics, economics, technology, entertainment, sports, food; the breadth of learning seemed never-ending. He enjoyed every aspect while attempting not to dwell too heavily on comparisons with the state of the same elements within the USSR. In reality, he could not wait for the day to come when he could see for himself if all these things about the avowed enemy of the Soviet people were true.

Recalling his instruction and indoctrination dating back to the Young Pioneers, KOMSOMOL, DOSAAF and the teachings of the zampolits, all emphasized the pitiful state of affairs in the West, and the United States, in particular. They all went to great lengths to denigrate the progress of the democratic process and the poor conditions of the "downtrodden" people outside the Soviet Union. He was amazed at the almost completely opposite depictions which were being introduced to him in preparation to actually go to the U.S. He spent sleepless hours wrestling with these dichotomies, but agent handlers, Vlad in particular, constantly reminded him of his role and responsibilities as well as his allegiance to the Soviet cause. He must never allow himself to be duped by the veneer-thin facades of the West, not now, nor when he was actually in "the belly of the beast."

Sasha continued to see Mackye. Their friendship blossomed into a serious romance. Neither wanted to offend the officials at Khodinka, but their relationship eventually became an inevitable issue, and the system stepped in. She sent him a note to meet her on an October evening at the library. He promptly recognized that she was visibly upset.

"Sasha, I will be leaving Khodinka tomorrow. I have been issued orders to report to the university for advanced studies. Originally, I was supposed to spend one year here as an understudy, but today I was advised that I am to continue my formal education immediately."

Sasha was stunned. "Mackye, NO! This is terrible! It is unfair! Do you believe that this is a routine change in your program or do you think someone is behind your sudden move?"

"I am not sure, Sasha, I don't want to sound paranoid, but I am suspicious that someone has decided to put a stop on our seeing each other."

Sasha didn't voice his opinion, but Vlad's devious influence had already entered his thoughts. "Let's take a walk, Sasha. I want to get out of this dreary library."

They strolled out of the library just at dusk and walked about the complex for a while before going to Sasha's room. Both realized the risk, but neither spoke of it. Mackye would leave Khodinka the next day.

Sasha, along with Vlad in tow, visited his parents again on the occasion of a holiday, November 7th, Communist Revolution Day. The visit routine was as structured and stilted as the first. The presence of Vlad during their conversation left both Sasha and his parents more frustrated than before. However, Tatyana maintained her cool presence and did not lose her control, which was Viktor's greatest concern. He continued to impress upon her that she must not question any aspect of Sasha's work or whereabouts. If she did, without a doubt, the visit privileges would be lost. But she couldn't resist asking about Christmas time.

"Sasha, will you be privileged to be home for Christmas?"

Vlad quickly interjected. "Dah, Madam, I am sure that we will be able to come for a few hours on that holiday. We will request to do so." Christmas was not widely celebrated in the urban areas—Moscow, in particular, but there was a general Soviet tolerance of the Russian Orthodox celebration of the Christmas holiday period.

The training activities continued. Day after day, Sasha studied and applied himself with an ever-expanding vision of his next life to be. He was now fully conversant in American history and had about sorted out the political process in the United States. However, he remained confused by the notion that elections for president and the congressional bodies took place so frequently and that the people could actually cast votes to keep, or reject, individuals in the governing bodies. He had difficulty understanding how a government could remain stable with so much turmoil of leaders coming and going.

Josef Stalin had been the supreme leader of the Soviet Union during all of his life, and seldom did anyone discuss a possible successor. Although there were whispered rumors of Stalin's illness from time to time, and that someone else might assume the leadership, such a change would never be left to the people to decide. Sasha often wished that he could discuss these and other issues with his father or his mother, who had great knowledge about the Soviet Union, and the world, for that matter. But, his brief visits were always chaperoned by the ever present Vlad and very little of substance could be discussed. He often felt that he was trapped within a vacuum tube with little or no opportunity to breathe anything other than the air provided him.

The ever-political Vlad, however, kept Sasha dangling. When he would catch him at a low ebb, he would sweeten the dinner conversation with a carrot.

"Sasha, I have good news. The Christmas Day outing is all arranged. We will be free to depart the compound early on that morning and spend an entire leisurely day with your parents."

Sasha had mixed emotions about the whole process. He was both grateful to, and despised, this character in his life. He was fully dependent on Vlad's manipulative control.

Sasha worked at remaining motivated, however, to learn and to be exposed to new information about the imperial enemy, the United States. The terms Cold War and Iron Curtain, in reference to Western terms describing the impasse between the West and the Soviet Union, and the so-called "shield" around Russia and the Soviet States, captured his attention.

"How could anyone outside the Soviet Union describe our sovereign borders as an 'iron curtain'"? he asked.

"The West is extremely jealous of the great fortress of strength represented by Russia and the non-Soviet Warsaw Pact countries. We are united to protect ourselves from encroachment and domination by the aggressors such as the United Kingdom and the United States.

Those imperialist governments suck blood from smaller, weaker countries, taking their wealth and leaving them helpless in return."

The party line was consistent and firm.

"The battle for sovereignty that rages in Korea is a good example of the United States, Britain and a few other radical tyrants' attempt to overthrow a legitimate communist government and to strip them of their identity. The Soviet Union and China will go to great lengths to prevent such encroachments by providing war-fighting equipment and troops if necessary to the loyal North Koreans. Besides, the event in Korea provides the Soviet Union an excellent training and testing place for both our ground equipment and our new MiG fighters. Our fighter pilots are becoming great heroes in the air, defeating the American F-80's and F-86's as well as their antiquated B-29 bombers."

Sasha was impressed that Soviet pilots were fighting in combat and half way around the world in Korea.

With the daily indoctrination and reinforcement of thought, Sasha became more consumed by his training. Although he had no idea where it would eventually take him, he did feel that he was playing an important role in the defense of his country. This was so far ahead of the modest indoctrination in the DOSAAF and KOMSOMOL received earlier in his youth. Most of that training had been spent on ideology and allegiance to communism only touching briefly on the growing threat of a confrontation with the United States and its aggressive Allies. He often wished that he could discuss these issues and events with Mackye. He missed her insight and logical analyses of history and Soviet objectives, but mostly, he just missed her!

While all of his training was extremely interesting, his classroom instructors mostly just mouthed their political rhetoric out of printed texts and did not venture into discussion or debate. He had already determined that Vlad had no real ideas or thoughts either, beyond the party line.

Moscow Christmas

As time passed, the irritation of Vlad' shadowing bothered him less and less. He felt a growing superiority over Vlad. He, Sasha, was the principal in this program, not this petty agent, who was assigned to tattle on him if he stepped out of bounds.

Christmas Day finally arrived, and while it came on a Thursday and was not an official Holiday, Vlad had arranged for Sasha to have the entire day off to visit his parents. It was a cold, bitter and wintry day in Moscow as they departed the Khodinka compound. The luxury of riding in a warm sedan to within a couple of blocks of his parent's apartment building was welcome. He had purchased some small gifts at one of the compound's kiosks: a pair of fur-lined gloves for his mother, a hand carved wooden smoking pipe for his father and a hand-woven wool scarf and mittens for his grandmother, Bonita, whom he expected to also be there. He had not seen Bonita in over two years, since the summer he left for Volgograd. He wondered if she was as outspoken and "charged-up" as ever. Hopefully, he thought, his father had given her a stern caution not to get carried away with her anti-government sentiments in the presence of Vlad.

By this time, Sasha had assumed that his father was well aware of Vlad's status and had cautioned his mother and anyone else who might be present when he visited.

An aromatic mixture of baking and cooking swept into the hallway when Viktor opened the door to let Sasha and Vlad come in. Sasha greeted his father warmly with a handshake and bear hug. He was truly glad to be home. Tatyana rushed into the small parlor when she heard Viktor greeting the young men. She wrapped her arms around her son and kissed him on both cheeks.

"Welcome home, Sasha! You too, Vladimir. We are so pleased to see you both. Merry Christmas!"

The weeks between Sasha's visits always seemed like months to her. She couldn't understand why they couldn't at least talk by telephone during his absences. But this was Christmas and he was home!

While the greetings were being exchanged, Bonita slipped quietly into the room and observed the happy event. When Sasha saw his grandmother, he warmly greeted her and gave her a hug. Bonita was not a very warm or expressive person, and Sasha knew that a brief hug and peck on the cheek would do.

"How are you, Grandmother? It has been so long since I saw you last, almost two and a half years, as a matter of fact. You look great!"

Sasha smiled upon the small, but regal lady whom he had known all of his life. He had never been close to her, nor she to him. Their relationship had been more through Tatyana's allegiance and respect for her mother's difficult and sad life, than one of a feeling of love and devotion for a grandmother.

Bonita accepted Sasha's greeting, and promptly eyed Vlad.

"Who are you?"

"This is my friend, Vlad, Grandmother. Vlad, this is my grandmother."

Vlad held out his hand which she briefly shook.

"What do you do?" Bonita asked.

"I am a good friend of Sasha's. We are in training together," Vlad responded.

"Where are you from?" She probed further. "You look much older than Sasha. Did you get a late start in life?"

"I am from a collective farm near Sverdlovsk. I worked on the farm until I was conscripted and eventually selected to go to specialized training. That is where I met Sasha."

Vlad then turned his attention to Viktor and Tatyana.

"I want to thank you, General, and you, Madam Katsanov, for permitting me to join you here on this special day."

"You are quite welcome, Vlad," Tatyana acknowledged. "You are a friend of Sasha's, and you are always welcome."

Viktor nodded to Vlad, and exclaimed, "Well, this is a very special day and a special occasion with our family together!"

Then he stepped over to a cabinet and took out a bottle of cognac. He removed the seal and cap from the unopened bottle as he began to pour the smooth liquor into the five glasses on the coffee table.

"I want to propose a toast to each of us, to our well-being and to our great leaders on this good day."

They each took a glass and Sasha and Vlad responded in unison, "Hear, Hear!" as they sipped the strong contents.

Tatyana took only a small sip and Bonita set her glass back on the table without drinking any. She stood quiet for a moment while the men savored the alcohol and then blurted, "Viktor, we have nothing to be grateful for from our Great Leaders, as you call them—unless you believe that the misery we are forced to live in is something to be thankful for. We are no better than serfs and slaves under the thumb of Stalin and his murderers."

"Mother!" Tatyana gasped in a low voice. "Come, let's get to the kitchen and finish the dinner preparations."

She took her mother by the arm and guided her out of the room.

Bonita looked back at the men as she and Tatyana left the room. "Death kills fewer people than fear!" she exclaimed.

Viktor, looking at Vlad, said quietly, "You will please forgive Bonita. She has had a very difficult life since her husband died."

"How did he die?" Vlad was forced to ask.

"We are not sure. He was arrested and apparently died while he was awaiting the disposition of his case. That was years ago."

"Why was he arrested?" Vlad persisted.

"We are not sure," Viktor responded. "Tatyana was still a young girl, and it was during the difficult times after the revolution. Many mistakes were made by the police at the time, and Bonita was never given a full explanation of why he was arrested or how he died. That accounts in great part for her bitterness."

"Here, allow me to recharge your glasses. We must celebrate this day and reunion with Sasha and you, Vlad."

Vlad did not pursue the subject further, but being a member of the secret police, he was instinctively inquisitive. He also concluded that this issue was likely the reason for Sasha's mother's dissident attitude. He obviously filed away the sketchy information in his mind for further research later. Vlad's questions were not lost on Sasha. He listened carefully to the brief interrogation and could almost read Vlad's mind as he absorbed the small details.

"Here's to our great Union!" offered Viktor.

The three hoisted their glasses to one another and finished off the cognac.

"Gentlemen, we are ready for dinner," Tatyana announced as she entered the room.

The three followed her into the small dining room, which also served as a combination living room and library of sorts. One wall supported book shelves filled with books, several family photographs, a few military artifacts and a phonograph turn table. A soft Tchaikovsky rhythm drifted through the room from the speaker. A sofa was pushed against the opposite wall to make room for the table which was designed to unfold and extend to accommodate up to two chairs on either side and one on each end. An apartment typical for Soviet families, even senior officers, usually consisted of two or three small bedrooms and a kitchen in addition to the entrance parlor and the combination living room/dining room/library. If the tenant were fortunate, there might be a narrow balcony off one of the rooms on which potted plants could grow in the warm months.

A perk for senior military officers and government bureaucrats sometimes included the ownership of a small dacha, usually somewhere outside the urban area. It afforded the opportunity for the official and his family to get away from the cramped apartments and crowded density of the city. Viktor and Tatyana had such a dacha but seldom visited it because of the demands of Viktor's position in the Defense Ministry. There was also the paranoia common amongst generals and government bureaucrats to never leave their work places for very long periods for any reason, especially for pleasure, for fear of returning to find themselves replaced by a zealous interloper.

"Life in the Soviet Union is harsh. Serving in the Government is difficult and challenging, but what are our other choices?" Tatyana often asked herself.

She had continued to hold out hope for Sasha's future. But as she watched him grow older and life about her grow even more tense with evermore onerous government controls, her dreams for a better future dimmed. She resolved to make the best of the situation. She would love and support Viktor and cling to every opportunity to be with her son. In order to maintain her equilibrium of sanity, she continued at the risk of losing everything, even Sasha and Viktor, to attend secret meetings of the kruzki.

Tatyana beckoned the three men and her mother to take their seats around the table—Viktor at the head, Sasha and Vlad on one side, Bonita on the other—while she stood and surveyed with pride the enormous spread that she and Bonita had prepared. After the others were seated, she went back into the kitchen and returned with a huge platter holding an oversized goose, baked to perfection. She placed it before Viktor.

"Now, I wish each of us to hold hands." As each one obeyed, she quickly began, "Our Father, how thankful we are for You and for this day, this family and this friend gathered here. Bless each and everyone to Thy name, and bless this food to the good of our bodies."

Vlad was aghast and would have quickly recoiled from the situation had he not been holding Viktor's hand, which was in a firm grip.

In an instant, the prayer was over with the two women murmuring an "Amen," while the three men remained quiet.

Vlad was unnerved. He could not believe that a senior Soviet officer would allow himself to participate in a religious prayer!

Tatyana quickly broke the brief silence. "Viktor, you have the honor of slicing our beautiful bird. Please, everyone, let's enjoy this special day and this food."

Everyone began to serve themselves and eat heartily. One after the other complemented Tatyana and Bonita for their cooking skills and the sumptuous food. Even Vlad warmed up to the conversation after overcoming his shock of participation in Tatyana's prayer blessing. Tatyana had obviously foraged for the meal ingredients for weeks, maybe even a month or more, in food-scarce Moscow in order to prepare such an offering. In addition to the fine goose, she had prepared as many of Sasha's favorites as she could find: cabbage and beet borsch, baked ham, fried fish fillets, canned jellied fish, omul (smoked salmon from Siberia, rarely found in Moscow markets) knish (beef in a roll), and fresh greens—ice cream would come later.

Bonita remained quiet, eating and listening to the banter. Finally, she looked at Sasha, catching his eye. "Do you have a girlfriend yet, Sasha?"

"No, I am afraid not, Grandmother. I remain too busy to have time for girls."

"Too bad," she said. "You should take time for a girl friend. She would be good for you. What about you?" she inquired, looking at Vlad.

"No," Vlad answered. "I have a wife to be responsible for."

Sasha all but choked on his food. He stopped eating, took in a deep breath and sat staring at the table.

He thought to himself, "Boy, this is something. This bastard is full of surprises. I have known him for almost three years, and never has he even intimated that he was married. In fact, he has never talked about girls at all for that matter. This is unbelievable!"

Bonita continued, "Why are you not with your wife today?"

The ever-quick Vlad responded, "She is with her parents in Vladimir while I am undergoing our training."

"Do you have children?" She pursued.

"No," he replied. "My wife is working while she stays with her parents. There will be time for children later should we so decide."

The remainder of the conversation during dinner was mostly about the fine food, how Tatyana must have planned so far in advance, and how fortunate she was to find the various offerings. Sasha concluded in his thoughts that the cognac must have loosened Vlad's innermost guarded confidences, and it allowed him to share some of his personal life.

After dinner there was the exchange of gifts with Sasha distributing those that he brought and Tatyana presenting to both Sasha and Vlad colorful wool scarves she had purchased for the occasion. The day came to a close, all too soon, for Tatyana and Sasha. But by now, both had concluded that there would be other such visits, and they would continue to savor each for as long as they could. Sasha and Vlad departed and returned to Khodinka.

SEVEN

Another Lesson Learned

Sasha's training routine moved on into the spring. It had been over six months since Mackye had departed, and he had heard nothing from her. He longed for her companionship. He missed her sprite and upbeat spirit, her warm smile and her intellectual and thoughtful insights. She was so well-informed on the workings of the Khodinka Center, the Soviet Union and life in general. He had come to depend more heavily on her each day. She had really provided him the motivation he needed to take each new challenge in his program with welcome interest. He also missed their brief, but intense physical relationship. Often, at night, when he was alone with his thoughts, he could remember so vividly the touch and scent of the beautiful woman he had known. It was impossible for him to try to telephone her, even if he knew where she was. Sending and receiving mail was not permitted at the center. He brooded for quite awhile and then immersed himself deeply in his studies.

Over a period of months, as the long, cold and dreary winter came and then began to recede, he noticed and began to exchange greetings and pleasantries with an usually attractive blonde, blue-eyed girl of about twenty who worked as the hostess in the Khodinka Officers' Dining Room. If Vlad happened not to be with him, he would stop and chat with her when she wasn't busy. Her name was Galina Pakilov, and she was a native Muscovite who had worked in the dining room for three years. Girls had not been a part of Sasha's life before Mackye.

After a period of working up his courage, he decided to ask Galina if she would attend an operetta at the theater that was to be presented by a gypsy group on a forthcoming Sunday evening. She agreed, and the arrangements were made to meet at the employee entrance to the compound at five p.m. on the appointed Sunday. Sasha was excited. He had buried himself completely in his studies ever since Mackye departed. He carefully planned the rendezvous and felt that he must tell Vlad of his plans, otherwise he might be again cited for questionable conduct.

"Besides," he thought, Vlad usually has other activities or isn't even around on Sundays unless there is a special requirement.

Vlad listened as Sasha told him that he had invited the young lady from the club dining room to attend the theater. Vlad responded by cautioning him once again that he must be very careful who he consorted with; there were observers everywhere, and he should not do anything to cause himself a problem.

Finally, he warned, "Do not do anything stupid or have any discussions about your work or who you are. Also, keep in mind that we must always be alert to a provokatsiya (KGB-laid traps)!"

Sasha was once again put off by Vlad's admonitions, but at least he didn't tell him not to see the girl. He felt confident as he proceeded to think about the forthcoming social evening with Galina. Although he was fully aware of his confinement within the compound, he was confident they could have an enjoyable evening and perhaps develop a friendship. After all, she was apparently attracted to him and they had enjoyed a few bits of conversation and some humor.

The Sunday evening finally arrived. Sasha dressed warmly in his Western style slacks, sweater and leather top coat. He felt very dapper and confident as he walked down the sidewalk, still lined with patches of snow from the lingering winter, to the agreed-upon meeting place at one of the entrances to the compound. Five o'clock came and Galina did not arrive, then five-thirty and finally six p.m. He grew very chilled, and agitated, as he paced back and forth near the compound entrance. He finally entered the "sterile zone" alcove, where authorized individuals are cleared through, and asked the security guard on duty if a young woman had possibly tried to enter or had left a message.

"Nyet!" The guard replied, "You have no business here. Leave now!"

The operetta was to begin at 6:30, and if they didn't get there soon, all of the seats would be taken. But six-thirty came and went. Still Galina did not appear. Sasha became extremely concerned.

"Could she have been involved in an accident?" he wondered.

But there was no way he could contact her, nor could she contact him. They had not made any contingency plans, assuming that everything would go as planned. Finally, he trudged back to his room. It was now after seven p.m. He changed his clothes and turned on the T.V. monitor to view whichever U.S. movie was on the agenda for the evening.

Finally, he went to bed with great disappointment and entered a restless night. He made his way to the dining room very early the next morning, well before Vlad came by to walk him over to breakfast. He entered the room expecting to see Galina, only to be greeted by a hostess he had never seen before. "Where is Galina? Why is she not working this morning?"

The hostess responded, "I do not know Galina. Who is she?"

He raised his voice. "Galina is the principal hostess who is here every day. Do you know if she is ill or what?"

"I cannot answer your question, Sir. Perhaps you should ask the manager."

Sasha promptly went to the dining room manager's office and without knocking went in. He had met the manager only casually, but they knew each other.

"Where is Galina, the dining room hostess?"

"Galina does not work here any longer," the manager answered.

Sasha was perplexed. "What happened? She was here on Saturday and her day off was yesterday. How could it be that she is not at work today? What do you mean, she does not work here anymore?"

The manager, obviously irritated, looked directly at Sasha and spat a response. "I told you, Comrade. That lady does not work in this facility any longer. That is all I know. Now, please, leave me to my work. Good day!"

Sasha went back into the dining room and took a seat at the familiar table where he always sat, just as Vlad came in and joined him.

"I came by your room, Sasha, but you obviously had already departed. Why are you up so early this morning? Could you not sleep?"

Sasha was deep in his thoughts after the encounter with the dining room manager. Finally he looked up at Vlad.

"No, I couldn't sleep, Comrade. I had a very bad night."

"Is there any particular reason for your bad night, Comrade?"

"**Yes**, there was a particular reason!" Sasha spewed back.

"Wow, sorry I asked." Vlad responded. "What's up, have you encountered problems in your work or with someone? Can I help? That is my job, you know, to insure that everything goes smoothly for you."

Sasha sipped his tea. He was still seething, and then he looked directly into his eyes.

"Well, my friend. Permit me to tell you that I think you and the other bastards here are working very hard to make my life as difficult as possible. You work very diligently to insure that I am completely isolated from the rest of the world. You have made me a prisoner within this Godforsaken place and denied me contact with everyone, even my family. Even when I see them, you carefully monitor and measure every word spoken between us. I had a social engagement last evening with Galina, the lady who was the hostess in this dining room. But it seems that because of the meeting I was supposed to have with her, she has been terminated from her position. For all I know, **you** and these other spooks may have had her exterminated!"

As he spoke, furious anger erupted in him for the first time since he arrived at Khodinka. "I don't know what all is going on, Comrade Vladimir, but I am not stupid. I am also not a puppet. All of you give me high marks for intelligence and great character for this project for which I have been specially selected. Yet, you are treating me no better than a country dolt or a stupid peasant! Why? Why? Tell me what's going on here! This is the second time that you have interfered with my acquaintance with a female! I will not tolerate anymore from you!"

The Russians hate besporyadok (disorder). The persistent fear of being set upon by the police or secret agents even causes agents themselves to shun public outbursts.

Vlad waited for a brief moment and then quietly and firmly, "Lower your voice and shut up! This room is full of ears who are listening to you, just waiting to file a report for any reason."

He waited another few seconds, then, in a biting whisper, "Do you wish to have breakfast? If not, let's get out of here!"

They departed the dining room and Vlad led him to a bench located in an open hallway where they could talk without the likelihood of being overheard or monitored.

"Sit down!" Vlad instructed. "My friend, once again you are conducting yourself on the edge. Now, I don't know what your problem is today, but stupid outbursts such as you just demonstrated in that dining room with dozens of people within earshot is out of bounds. I will not bother to warn you again. I will be required to report your conduct to Colonel Sokolov and let the chips fall where they may. And," he gently added, I can promise you that whatever the outcome, it will not be pleasant for you.... or your family." Vlad didn't let up. "Now, whatever happened to your friend who worked in the food service operation here is of no concern to you. For whatever reason she has apparently been relieved of her duties, or reassigned elsewhere. Byvaet! (It happens!) In any event, yours is not to question the disposition of employees here in this complex for any reason. At this moment, you are approaching being late for your morning class. I suggest that you get your head together and get moving."

Sasha stared at the floor during Vlad's lecture. He finally took a deep breath, got to his feet and walked away without responding. As he reflected on Galina's unexplained failure to meet him on the evening before and her sudden disappearance from a job where she was apparently a very trusted employee, Sasha couldn't shake the suspicion that Vlad was involved with the entire escapade just as he was sure that he had been involved in Mackye's sudden departure.

He remembered all too well the incident back at the college when the two senior cadets were turned in for leaving the barracks after hours, dishonored and denied graduation and their commissions. He knew that Vlad was unquestionably the perpetrator then. He just hoped that Galina was all right, and he deeply regretted that he had caused the whole thing. The remainder of the day did not sit well. He was caught on the horns of a dilemma. He had no choice but to maintain a civil relationship with Vlad, his only conduit "through the system," and to his parents. He wrestled with his conscience, his emotions and his judgment, as how to best move on without further turmoil.

Promptly at 1800 hours that evening, the usual rap on the door indicated that Vlad was there to go to dinner. Working up his courage and best front, Sasha opened the door.

"Hey, how did it go today?" Vlad began in his usual jovial manner. "I continue to receive very good reports on how well you are progressing. The rumors are that you are by far the brightest trainee to come along in a great while. Congratulations!"

"Thank you, Vlad. Come in."

And, that was it. Just as it was after the senior cadets' incident at Volgograd, after Mackye suddenly departed, and now after the incident with Galina, Vlad had a remarkable ability to turn it on and turn it off. He moved on as if everything were perfect. And, it was, as long as everything went his way. They proceeded on to dinner, and the subject of the morning was never mentioned again.

FIVE

New Identity

Sasha continued his rigorous training, taking each block of instruction in stride. He impressed his trainers and teachers with his quickness to grasp the many complex subjects and features describing the history, culture and the great military strength of the United States, the arch enemy of the Soviet people. He also had begun to adopt his "new" identity and could respond to questions about virtually everything within and about the U.S. He was given a new name which would become his identification, and family heritage, when he departed for his assignment.

John Michael Scott was born in Cleveland, Ohio, on July 30, 1930. His parents had both been killed in an automobile accident when he was ten years old. He was raised for a time by his grandmother before she died. Thereafter, he was shifted from one relative to another living in and around Cleveland, and for a time in the suburbs of Chicago. John Scott was killed in a fight in a South Side Chicago bar when he was eighteen. His body lay unclaimed for several days until it was "identified" by a man who said that he was the youth's uncle. The "uncle", Igor Zotov, assigned to the Soviet Consulate in Chicago, had the body of Scott buried in a pauper's cemetery, then set about reestablishing the boy's identity for later use. With the number of deaths of nondescript people in the Chicago area, Scott's went unnoticed except by those who were in the business of making use of lost identities to reestablish the same for their own purposes. Zotov researched and developed a comprehensive file on

John Michael Scott, adjusting his physical description to match those of the candidate *illegal*, Viktor Alexandrovich Katsanov, in training in the Soviet Union.

The "reconstructed" file contained a birth certificate, social security card, elementary and high school records, driver's license, inoculation records, his parents' death certificates and an "open" transcript from Milner College to be updated and completed at the time John Michael Scott is *reincarnated*. The file was hand-delivered to the Soviet Embassy in Washington for storage until implementation and copies further delivered by secure diplomatic pouch to KGB Headquarters at Lubiyanka in Moscow and the GRU training facility at Khodinka.

The month of March usually indicated a break with winter. Once again, Vlad arranged for Sasha to leave the compound to visit his parents. The visits permitted by his handlers had a two-fold purpose. First, they provided a means of motivating Sasha and instilling in him greater confidence in the project he was undertaking. Second, they created a feeling of goodwill with his parents. These intangible *perks* were an important part of the KGB's and GRU's methods of developing loyal and trusting agents. It was a bright March afternoon when Vlad and Sasha departed Khodinka. Sasha was in particularly good spirits. Not only was he being permitted to leave his confines to visit his parents, but he had been informed that on the next Monday, he would again take up flying instruction.

It was a good day. The training and testing had gone well. Vlad did not seem to be the nuisance and nag that he had previously been, and he was going to be permitted to have some relief from the classroom by getting to fly again. The same routine as his previous respites from Khodinka were followed. Accompanied by Vlad, he exited through tight security checks and onto the street for a short walk to a waiting car and driver. Along the way, in good spirits, he was very animated in his conversation with Vlad, who had to "shush" him with a finger to his lips a couple of times, lest the driver hear something which he shouldn't.

Viktor had taken the afternoon off from his duties to be home when Sasha arrived. The warm greeting from his mother was the same. She savored these visits, even as brief and impersonal as they were. As always, special delicacies and tea were ready to serve the two guests. She had grown used to the almost business-like visits, and how quickly the time passed when Sasha was there. This day was little different. There was an exchange of greetings, questions about the well-being of each other and Bonita.

In awhile, the telephone rang. Viktor promptly left the parlor to answer it. They could hear Viktor's muffled voice coming from the bedroom, then there was a long silence before he stepped back into where the three were sitting.

Viktor stood for a moment in the doorway and Tatyana instantly read something very disturbing in his face. He finally said, "Our great leader, Stalin, is dead."

Tatyana sighed deeply and whispered to herself, "Thank God!" And then, she murmured an old Russian proverb, "Every bastard meets his master."

Sasha took a deep breath, attempting to mentally assess what the passing meant and remained quiet.

Vlad, shocked by the announcement, promptly asked, "What did they say about his successor?"

"Nothing at this time; of course, it's too soon to consider that," Viktor responded in return. "There are many tasks to be accomplished at this moment before anyone begins to consider who will lead our government." Viktor gave Vlad a stern look, "His body isn't even cold, and you asked that question." He was visibly angry. "Our nation is strong and great. We don't need to worry unnecessarily about leadership. We are abound with leaders." Then, in a courteous retort to Vlad, with full awareness that he was addressing a secret police agent, he said, "I apologize, Vlad, for snapping at you. We will go through a period of mourning of the greatest leader in the world. Then there will be an orderly transition to a new leader of the Soviet people."

Vlad responded, "Sir, please do not apologize to me. I was merely thinking out loud. It was not proper for me to even voice such a stupid question. Forgive me."

"That's okay, Vlad. We are all a bit emotional at this moment. Well, I must leave immediately and return to my office." Viktor proceeded to get his uniform cap and shake hands with Sasha and Vlad. He gave Tatyana a kiss and bid them all goodbye.

Sasha and Vlad departed shortly thereafter with goodbyes and expressions of hope to see each other again soon. Back in the sedan, it was Vlad that was elated with the prospects of new excitement in the lives of the Soviet people. Even with the only leader he had ever known, dead, he felt a strange exhilaration. He couldn't help expressing his feelings, not so much about the death of Stalin but more on who might succeed him. He whispered to Sasha, "Beria will be our next great leader. We are all sure that Stalin had already chosen him as his successor. He will be a no nonsense leader of the people."

Lavrenti Beria was Stalin's long time head of the KGB. He was feared by all those around him. He earned the respect of only the petty functionaries such as Vlad, because they knew no better. The other *disciples* closely surrounding Stalin, *jockeying for position* during his last days, included Nikita Khrushchev, Vyacheslav Molotov, Georgi Malenkov and Nicholai Bulganin. Of the five, Beria was the most feared by the others to rise to any position beyond where he was. Not only did he control the KGB, he also had close ties with the Red Army General Staff and their military intelligence arm, the GRU.

Within days of Stalin's death, however, Beria was lured into a room in the Kremlin by the other three to discuss the division of power. It was never made clear who fired the bullet into Beria's head, but the threat of his consolidating too much power ended that day. Khrushchev and Malenkov hustled Molotov and Bulganin off to bureaucratic positions away from Moscow, and for a time they put on a front of *joint* leadership of the Soviet Union. Eventually, of course, Nikita Khrushchev politically disposed of Malenkov and assumed the chairmanship of the Central Committee. In spite of the turmoil and the political battles for position at the upper *apparatchik* level, in the aftermath of Stalin's death, there was not a ripple in the central direction of the Soviet machine.

The Russian people were never aware of any significant change in their lives. Their personal struggles went on as before. The same was true with the objectives of the KGB, GRU and the Soviet Military. Their indoctrinated discipline and direction was absolute. The casual posting announcing that Lavrenti Beria, loyal and dedicated servant of the Soviet people, had died suddenly, essentially went unnoticed by most. Even young and aspiring zealots such as Vlad and his superiors took the news in stride with a shrug.

The next several days and weeks found Moscow in various stages of official mourning. However, the activities at the training center within Khodinka continued on schedule.

The following Monday morning, after the visit with Viktor and Tatyana, Sasha had reported as scheduled to the flight operations office near the runway that cut through the center of Khodinka. Vlad didn't accompany him on this visit to the new block of instruction. It appeared that, more and more, he was being granted independence of movement around the complex. Sasha was greeted inside by Major Mikolai Rozhko whom he had met earlier during his initial orientation.

Aspiring Aviator

"Good morning, Sasha," Major Rozhko offered, holding out his hand. "Good to see you again." He spoke reasonably good English.

"Good morning, Major," Sasha responded.

Major Rozhko guided Sasha into one of the several offices along a hallway. "Come in and take a seat. Let's talk about what we are going to do for the next several weeks. First, our schedule for this morning will include getting you outfitted in a flight suit, a discussion about your instruction and a walk around the aircraft we're going to be flying. So, I think I would like to do the morning in reverse order. Let's talk about the flight instruction first."

He continued, "Over the next few weeks, we will log about twenty hours of flying. That is, if the weather cooperates. Now, I understand that you have had some flying experience over the past several years. Is that correct?"

"Yessir," Sasha answered. "I received flight instruction within the DOSAAF and also at the Volgograd College, probably twenty-five hours total, and I soloed in both programs."

"Good, that will us put far ahead in what we want to do here," Rozhko acknowledged.

"In my instruction program, I am not going to spend extensive time in going over theory of flight. Airplanes are built to fly. That's it. We learn to fly them, and the theory comes with learning the maneuvers. Also, you will learn about this particular trainer aircraft that we have been given to fly as we go along. Today we will do a brief walk-around, take a quick look in the cockpit and tomorrow we will go through start-up, taxi and ground handling. We may even fly a bit, if you become comfortable and the weather is good. Our program together will be free flowing and open-ended, no set schedule to meet, except to bring you up to a reasonable proficiency level within a month. Do you have any questions?"

"No, Sir. I don't at this time." Sasha replied. "I am looking forward to the flight instruction and everything you can teach me."

"Good, let's go get you suited up with some coveralls and go into the hangar," Rozhko responded as he got up and led Sasha out of the office.

Major Rozhko took him to a supply room in the building and instructed the civilian behind a counter to issue Sasha a pair of flight coveralls, a jacket, a pair of boots and some gloves. Sasha took the flight suit and slipped it on over his street clothes to insure that it fit properly. He gave the clerk his shoe size and was handed a pair of calf-high leather boots and some heavy socks. They all fit satisfactorily. Major Rozhko told him to leave the flight suit on, and they would go to the hangar and inspect the trainer aircraft.

They proceeded to the hangar building, processed through a security guard station and into a cavernous area filled with parked aircraft. Sasha was not aware there was such a large hangar located within the Khodinka complex. He was very surprised to see at least a dozen different types of aircraft parked inside the huge building. Some of them were covered with large canvass shrouds. As Sasha looked around, he was also aware he was not familiar with any of the airplanes which he could see with the exception of one Russian-built Sukhoi SU-2. The remainder were certain to be from other countries. Rozhko took note of his expression and told Sasha, "The Army Aviation Armaments Division is very interested in foreign aviation technology. This is where much of the exploitation of other country's aircraft takes place. The aircraft are kept in the hangar, with some under cover, for security reasons."

Rozhko led him over to a bright yellow single engine low-wing plane with a covered canopy tandem cockpit. Sasha looked at the sleek airplane and walked around, admiring it.

"This, my friend, is one of our latest acquisitions. An American Air Force trainer, which they designate as the AT-6. They call it the 'Texan'. I suppose they named it that because they conduct a lot of their pilot training in their state of Texas. I have been flying it now for about three months out of one of our auxiliary airfields to evaluate its performance and characteristics. I have also been flying it in order to prepare myself to give you flight instruction in it. What do you think?"

Sasha continued to admire the airplane. Compared to the antiquated machines he had been exposed to in his earlier training, this one looked like a modern day marvel. "It is a beauty," he replied. "Am I really to take flight instruction in this?"

"Yes, you are," Rozhko replied. "My orders are to insure that you become familiar with the American trainer and to be reasonably proficient in learning to fly it. You will not be permitted to fly solo, unfortunately, even though you may demonstrate that you could. It is too valuable a resource to risk damage or loss." Rozhko continued, "It is a reasonably high-powered aircraft for a primary trainer. We do not have anything like it. It has a 450 horsepower radial engine with a variable pitch propeller, a very functional hydraulic system, good electrical systems and a retractable landing gear. If you master this airplane, you can be very proud of your flying abilities."

"Do I understand correctly that the Americans use this aircraft as an initial trainer for student pilots?" Sasha asked.

"Yes, our information is that they do." Rozhko replied. "I am told they have hundreds of them at numerous training bases. Originally, it was designed for advanced pilot training; that's the "A T" designation, *Advanced Trainer*. But in recent years, both their air force and navy decided to make it their primary trainer and do away with some older and much lighter-weight machines. We have been fortunate to acquire two of them—this one, and one other that is undergoing engineering and mechanical research. This particular aircraft is identical in every respect to the ones being used in the United States for their initial pilot training, down to the yellow paint. The only exception is our red star on the fuselage and the wings."

Major Rozhko led Sasha around the AT-6, pointing out the various features and how to pre-flight the aircraft before flying it. He then instructed him to climb up on the wing and inspect the cockpit and controls. Sasha was overwhelmed with the prospects of flying this "super" aircraft. He thought to himself, "I might become a fighter pilot after all."

After a thorough inspection of the trainer aircraft, Major Rozhko led him back into the office. They spent the remainder of the morning discussing the fundamentals of the AT-6 and the scheduled instruction prospectus. Sasha would begin first thing tomorrow, and they would attempt to get in two or so hours of flying each day. The flight instruction would include basic flying proficiency: taxi, take-offs and landings, aerial maneuvers and safe flying techniques. After his proficiency is assured to the satisfaction of the instructor, he would then take up some basic aerobatics, instrument flying and navigation. This all sounded great to Sasha. He still couldn't imagine that all of this was happening to him. Rozhko showed Sasha to a locker room where he could store his flight clothes and boots and told him to report back the next morning at 0730 sharp.

As he left Major Rozhko's office, Sasha made his way down the hallway toward the exit and suddenly found himself face to face with one of the training NCO's from the Volgograd College. Sasha unmistakably recognized this one; he remembered him as Igor, one of the more brutal hazers and "horse back" riders back in his barracks. For a brief moment he inadvertently blocked the way of the soldier in the hallway and there was no doubt that he was the one and same. As they stared briefly at one another, the NCO gave no sign of recognition. Since Sasha was in civilian clothes, neither did he make an effort to show courtesy. He acted almost as if he were a robot, stood still for a moment facing Sasha, then stepped aside mechanically and moved on down the hallway. Sasha returned to his room and prepared for his afternoon academic schedule. That evening over dinner, Sasha asked Vlad if he remembered the NCO at Volgograd College named Igor.

"Yes, I believe I do. Wasn't he the over-sized brute who worked over some of our friends pretty good?" Vlad replied.

"Yes, that's him and further more, he is here at Khodinka, either working or at least hanging around the flight operations area," Sasha responded. "I am amazed that he would be assigned here. He is a stupid dolt, unworthy of wearing the uniform of the Soviet Army."

"Where, and when, did you see him?" Vlad asked.

"This morning at the flight operations building, walking down a hallway," Sasha answered.

"I will look into it," Vlad responded, and proceeded to ask Sasha how his flight instruction was going.

The next morning Sasha went back to the flight operations building. He entered the locker room, changed into his flight suit and boots and on to Major Rozhko's office. Rozhko was there and dressed in flight clothes, ready to proceed. "Good morning, Sasha. Did you rest well? Ready to go?"

"Yessir, I did, and I am ready when you are," Sasha responded. Then he asked, "Sir, are you familiar with the NCO here in the building who's name is Igor? I don't know his last name."

Rozhko responded, "It is interesting that you ask about Sergeant Butakov. He was assigned to us to do administrative work two or three months ago. Just last night I was informed that the security police had arrested him for some infraction. How is it that you know him?"

Sasha was caught off guard. Obviously *the system* was already at work. He thought quickly, "Oh, I saw him in the hallway here yesterday and thought I recognized him from when I was in college. Last night it occurred to me that his name was Igor."

"Well, whatever the reason, he is no longer here. We are once again shorthanded in our office to keep up with the paper work and files." Major Ruzhko concluded, "Well, let's go to work." He led Sasha out of his office and toward the hangar entrance. The ground crew had moved the bright yellow AT-6 out onto the ramp in front of the hangar. The weather was clear and chilly. As they walked to the aircraft, Sasha couldn't shake the NCO, Igor, from his mind. But, he was gone, so on to the work ahead. The apparent *disposal* of Igor was once again evidence that his handlers at Khodinka did not want any distractions to affect the training and preparations of one of its prize students.

Ruzhko handed Sasha a checklist booklet and instructed him to conduct a preflight walk around the trainer aircraft. Upon completion of the inspection of the trainer, Ruzhko directed Sasha to climb into the front cockpit. After he was comfortably seated, the instructor demonstrated how he should strap into the parachute and the seat. They proceeded to go through the checklist items of engine pre-start, start, taxi and so forth. He instructed him in starting the aircraft's engine. Once it was idling smoothly, Ruzhko, satisfied that he had a very bright and quick-to-learn student, climbed into the rear cockpit.

Major Ruzhko called the tower on the radio and requested permission to taxi around the small airdrome. It did not take Sasha long to master the taxi techniques of the trainer, and Major Ruzhko demonstrated the first take-off. After airborne, they climbed out over Moscow and took the most direct route to an unpopulated area where the aircraft wouldn't be too noticeable, and the air work began. The flight instruction re-invigorated Sasha. It provided him a welcome diversion and an opportunity to clear his mind of the multitude of study and retention requirements that had been thrust upon him since he arrived at Khodinka.

As was expected, Sasha excelled in his flying skills. He was a little rough on the controls at first. But, he noticed immediately that the AT-6 required much less control movement than did the older Russian trainers that Sasha had previously experienced.

Rozhko coached him through several routine maneuvers. "Sasha, think of this airplane as a very beautiful woman. You must gently touch the controls and carefully guide her in the direction you wish. Think of the maneuver you want the airplane to perform as you would in gently coaxing your girl in the direction you wish. Do not rush or be in a hurry, just ease her along." Rozhko smiled as he watched the back of Sasha's head in the forward cockpit and felt him move the controls much more positively and smoothly. Sasha could easily have soloed the trainer after a dozen hours, but that was not a part of the program.

Concurrent with his flying, Sasha continued with his other work, most of which centered around assuming his new identity. He was also reintroduced to driving an automobile which he had not done since before he left for Volgograd over two years before. Vlad had surprised him one Saturday morning by escorting him to one of the large garage-type buildings in the complex and told him that they were going to practice driving for a few hours. In the garage were several Russian and other Eastern European-built automobiles along with a late model Volvo, an older French-built Citreon and a couple of vehicles that Sasha did not recognize. Vlad guided him to one of the unfamiliar models, an American-built FORD sedan. Sasha was rusty at first but caught on fairly quick after a few jerky attempts. They repeated the driving exercise several more times, until Vlad was satisfied that he could fairly well manage an automobile.

In late April, during the last week of his scheduled flight training, Sasha was summoned to come to Colonel Sokolov's office. He had seen Sokolov several times over the months during his training, but he had not met with him formally since he arrived at Khodinka. Vlad had told him that this was a good sign. If a student continues to do well, he will likely not be given added stress by meetings with the senior officials. But now he was being called to a meeting. Suffering with traditional Russian *paranoia*, he worried all of the night before about what he might have done, or, not done, to prompt this meeting.

EIGHT

Reward

Vlad knocked on his door at 1300 hours. He barely had time to shower and get dressed for the meeting. "Come in!" Sasha shouted. Vlad entered the room. "I'm almost ready. What's this all about anyway?" Sasha asked.

"I don't know," replied Vlad. "It could just be a routine meeting to calibrate your progress and well-being, a change of plans or anything. I have no idea. You aren't in any trouble are you? You haven't violated any of the rules, have you?"

"Hell, no! I have been too busy to do anything but work," Sasha shot back. Then, in an instant he thought about the NCO, Igor. What could he have to do with this? Sasha was an exceptionally disciplined and loyal Soviet and communist, and he had worked hard to excel, but his culture never evaded him. Russian people were always made to feel guilty. No matter how good or bad their work and lives were going, "the system" was ever present to cause self-doubt and guilt, even when there was no cause.

"Let's go," Vlad said. "We have to be at Colonel Sokolov's office by 1330."

They arrived in Sokolov's outer office on time and were greeted by a major who asked them to be seated. In a moment, a buzzer sounded, and the major motioned for them to follow him.

Vlad maneuvered Sasha ahead of him into the office. As they entered, Sasha immediately recognized General Tushenskiy in addition to Colonel Sokolov. He was too uptight to conjure up anymore ill thoughts at this point. "Come in Sasha, Captain. Please sit down. Tea, anyone?" Sokolov asked. "You remember General Tushenskiy?" he asked.

"Yessir," Sasha acknowledged as both he and Vlad stepped forward and shook hands with the general. Sasha said, "No tea for me, Sir." Vlad also declined.

General Tushenskiy spoke first. "Well, how is it going with you, Sasha?" Before he could respond, Tushenskiy continued, "I hear nothing but good things about you, your performance and your demeanor. I am personally very proud of you. I have no doubts now that our decision to select you was a good decision. I wish also to commend Captain Yepishev for his excellent investigation, recommendation and his mentoring during your program."

They both acknowledged the general's remarks with smiles and "Thank you's."

"I am told that you have essentially completed most of the academic instruction which was developed for you, and you will also complete the flying training block of instruction this week," Tushenskiy continued. "So, we have decided, in the interest of time and priorities, to move quickly to the next phase. That is to transfer you to a *dacha* for what we call "practical application" training. You will transfer over the weekend to one of our training dachas here in Moscow where you will spend the next two months applying your learned skills. The major part of your experience at the dacha will be the assumption of your new identity and to live as an American. You will find that we can duplicate almost completely an environment very closely resembling that which you will find in the United States. Now," he added, "we have a small surprise for you. It is partially as a reward for your hard work and good results but also to provide you with official status."

Sasha was feeling very good about himself, completely relaxed and absorbing the glowing praise being heaped upon him. "What now?" he wondered.

"Today, I have been given the authority to commission you as an officer in the Soviet Air Force with the grade of Junior Lieutenant," Tushenskiy said smiling. "This will make you an officer and additionally provide you with a career developing status for the future. Colonel Sokolov will administer the oath of office," he continued, "and Captain Yepishev and I will be witnesses."

Sasha was stunned by the general's announcement, but he readily acknowledged the news and expressed his appreciation. Colonel Sokolov stood and requested Sasha to stand before him and to raise his right hand. Sokolov began to administer the oath of commission, "Please repeat after me, stating your full name...."

"I," Viktor Alexandr Katsanov, "do solemnly swear ...."

At the conclusion of the oath, General Tushenskiy, the colonel and Vlad in turn shook hands with Sasha, each offering their congratulations. "Well, continued wishes for success, Sasha," Tushenskiy added. "I regret that your father could not attend this important event. But I did advise him of the good news, and he sends his congratulations. Hopefully, you can visit him soon. In the meantime, Colonel Sokolov will provide you with your next instructions and schedule. Good luck."

General Tushenskiy departed and Colonel Sokolov took over the meeting. "I want you to pack your clothes and personal effects and be prepared to depart for the dacha Sunday afternoon. Captain Yepishev will provide you the exact departure time. It is doubtful that you will return here to Khodinka, so be sure that you take with you the essentials that you will require to live away from here. Don't worry about too many personal effects. Anything you require hereafter will be provided. At the dacha, you will be in the instructional care of three of our very best cultural instructors. You will be introduced to them by your new identity name and background, and you will not be called by, nor referred to thereafter, by your native name. This is extremely important and very serious. You are entering the final transition to your new life. After we are satisfied that you are ready to move on, I will come to the dacha and give you your final instructions and schedule. Do you have any questions for now?"

Sasha wanted to ask several things including when he would be permitted to again visit his parents, but he elected not to venture beyond what he had been told. "No, Sir, I don't have any questions at this time. I will be ready on Sunday to depart."

"Good, Mr. Scott, Mike, I believe you prefer to be called. I look forward to visiting you at the dacha in a month or so. By the way, a small detail, your military pay and allowances will be deposited for you in a special bank account until such time as you may need it. In the meantime, all of your expenses will be taken care of by your managing agents along the way. You can enjoy the "double dipping" in the interim. Goodbye and good luck."

Vlad escorted Sasha back to his room where they chatted for awhile. "Well, that wasn't so bad, was it, Lieutenant?" Vlad offered.

"No, it wasn't, and I owe you an apology for being the ass that I have been, too many times." Sasha replied.

"Not a problem, Comrade, I am used to this. After all, I was a candidate once myself and probably a bigger ass than you at times," Vlad laughed. "I know that all of this has been very difficult for you, but you have handled it well, and you will continue to do so. I will likely not see you again until you complete the work at the dacha but, hopefully, I will at that time. In the meantime, I will work to arrange a visit to your parents when you are finished there, before you depart for your assignment. By the way, I suspect your assignment will come immediately after the work at the dacha." Vlad continued, "I don't know for sure, but the dacha work is usually the last step before the execution of a project. In any event, a case officer will visit you there during the course of training along with Colonel Sokolov to provide you with details. Gotta run, I won't be by to go to dinner with you. Keep up the good work, and I will see you Sunday for lunch and out of the compound."

It was obvious that Vlad was transitioning himself from being Sasha's nursemaid and moving on to another task. Sasha completed his last flight in the AT-6 on Friday morning and thought to himself: "What a great experience this has been!" He said goodbye to Major Rozhko and thanked him for all of his support and good instruction. When he completed his afternoon academic classes, he waited for the signal from his instructors to say goodbye or indicate that he would not be back, but none came. So, he departed his last class as if he would be back on Monday, as did they. That was the way the system worked: impersonal and indifferent, and for the most part, no attachments.

Sasha spent Saturday putting his clothes and personal effects together. He had been given only one medium-sized suitcase in which he was instructed to put everything he "needed." Sunday arrived and Vlad came by his room at 12:00 noon to walk over to the dining room with him. They had a final lunch with mostly small talk; the passing of Stalin and the rumors about who might evolve as their new leader, but nothing about Sasha's next step nor what Vlad would do thereafter. Sasha had long since learned not to press for information not offered. They finished lunch and went back to Sasha's room where they were met by a "new member" to enter his life.

The Dacha

"Hello, Mike, I am Ted Williams, here to escort you to your new home," the stranger said extending his hand.

Vlad shook hands with Sasha, wished him well, said a quick goodbye and was gone.

Mike collected his suitcase, his small personal kit and followed Ted out to the exit corridor. A security officer, waiting in the exit hall, collected Sasha's security badge. They walked out onto the sidewalk to a sedan that was parked along side the curb. There was no driver in the car. Ted motioned for Sasha to put his suitcase and small kit in the back seat, and then got into the car behind the wheel. Sasha got in the right front seat beside him. Ted drove off toward Northeast Moscow. "Well, Mike," Ted began, "we're going to be together for the next couple of months at one of our dachas in the suburbs. My wife, Ann, will be there with us. We have both served in the United States and will be able, we believe, to assist you in your preparations for your assignment there. Our dacha has been transformed into a typical American home. It may not be exact but comes very close to the real thing right down to the furniture and the food. Ann will prepare all of our meals. They, too, will be very much like you will find in the USA. You might as well forget your native name as of today. From now on, you will become John Michael Scott—Mike, for short; we will work with you day and night to assume your new identity. From time to time, other agent trainers will come in to both instruct and test your progress. I have been instructed to put you on a fast track and to evaluate how quickly you can assimilate all that we are going to throw at you. I have reviewed all of your training reports and, I must say, they are indeed impressive. You are a quick study, in spite of your young age. So, that is the program. We will have much more to discuss after you get settled in. Have you given much thought to your new identity?"

"No, I haven't really," Mike responded. "I am well aware of what I must do to become who I will be, but I also will need your assistance in coaching me." He was once again a little bewildered by this sudden change of direction.

Ted drove on for the better part of an hour and finally pulled to the curbside along a typical Moscow street lined with apartment buildings. Moscow has very few private homes, at least visible to the ordinary observer. Ted got out of the car and Mike followed suit, retrieving his bags from the rear seat. He followed his new acquaintance through an archway in one of the building entrances and into a courtyard, then to another archway entrance with a solid door blocking the opening. Ted took a key from his pocket and unlocked the door. The entrance past the door led to another, smaller, outside courtyard. Mike had never seen anything like this in all of Moscow. There in the middle of the courtyard sat a single unit house surrounded by the tall apartment buildings on all four sides. There were no windows in the apartments facing the courtyard. This was a miniature version of Khodinka. He wondered how many other such facilities existed in this mysterious city where he had lived most all of his life. Ted rapped on the door, and it was promptly opened by a very attractive blond lady Mike judged to be in her mid-thirties.

"Come in, Mike," she greeted. "Welcome to our home."

Ted gave his wife, Ann, a peck on the cheek and introduced Mike. Then he led him into a well furnished living room.

"Come on, Mike, I'll show you to your room," Ted motioned.

Mike followed him down a hallway to a good-sized bedroom fully furnished with a double bed, large overstuffed chair, a desk and lamps. Ted showed him the door leading to his own bathroom. Mike had never seen such a house. The bathroom gleamed with a wash basin, bath tub, separate shower stall and a most amazing large and bright commode.

"Welcome to America, Mike," he said.

"Thank you," Mike replied. "This is incredible."

"Take a few minutes to put your things away, and then come on in for tea," Ted smiled, as he left the room.

Mike inspected the bedroom and took note of the New York Times, Chicago Tribune and Cleveland Plain Dealer newspapers along with LIFE, LOOK, Readers Digest and Newsweek magazines placed neatly on a side table. There was a small radio receiver on the bedside table with the volume turned down low transmitting a news broadcast in English. He put his clothes away, re-inspected the fanciest bathroom he had ever seen and found almost every conceivable toiletry item in the cabinet over the lavatory: tooth brushes, tooth paste, shaving cream, razor, after shave lotion, shampoo and several different soap bars in various wrappers. All of the items were American-made brands. He thought to himself, "Boy, this is living! *I* have never seen anything like this before. The facilities at Khodinka were very comfortable. This is incredible! How can it possibly be? My parents' apartment cannot even compare with such luxury as this. I can't believe Americans live this way!"

After the brief survey of his new quarters, he walked back into the living room where Ted and Ann were sitting in two comfortable chairs with a small tea tray before them on a table.

"Please join us, Mike, for tea and cakes." Ann said, as he entered the room. "Are you settled in?" she asked.

"Yes, I am." Mike replied. "As you probably noticed, I was limited in what I was allowed to bring in the one suitcase. I was told that I could get additional clothes as I needed them. I left several items back at the Training Center."

"That's quite alright," said Ted. "We want you to be able to travel light, for the present, anyway. In a day or so, the remainder of your clothes from Khodinka will be delivered here. If you need more, we can get them. Sit down, and I will go over our program here." He sat in a chair opposite the couple while Ann poured him a cup of tea.

Ted began a lengthy description of the *dacha* concept. "This is one of eight or so that are in the Moscow urban area. There are numerous others outside the city, and probably a few in Leningrad. Each dacha is specially configured for a particular targeted country. Each one replicates, as closely as we can, the type of living environment which one might find in the particular country. Not exactly, of course, because regions within countries differ."

He went on to describe how the dachas within the city of Moscow were almost always built within the "well" of an apartment complex. The interior windows of the apartments facing inward to the dacha, which is almost always a single-story house sitting at ground level within the "well", are sealed closed so that the apartment occupants usually have no idea that the dacha exists.

He said, "The entrance from the street level is usually through an open archway or door leading to a second secured entry, through which no one on the outside can see the dacha facility on the inside. The secured entry door is alarmed, should anyone attempt to try to gain unauthorized access. There are no visible security guards or police. But always present, out on the street, is our own security force. They are older men, some women, who look non-descript, but who are entrusted to watch over the entrance way and the immediate area, and to notify the authorities immediately if someone suspicious begins to nose around. You will notice them there, sitting on a bench or strolling around, twenty-four hours a day, always alert to comings and goings. Of course, they are compensated for their loyalty," Ted continued as Sasha marveled at what was being described.

"Some of the dachas are centrally located within government building complexes and are, as a result, easier to conceal and secure. While training within a dacha, the candidate agent wears the clothes and shoes of the targeted country, eats virtually every variety of that country's food during his or her stay, speaks only that country's language, reads all of the newspapers and magazines that can be acquired from the targeted country and listens to taped broadcasts of news reports originating in the country of interest. The instructors assigned to the dachas are usually all former illegals and all have spent time in the targeted country either as an agent or with the embassy. Often they are a husband and wife team, just as Ann and me. Their job is to supervise training tailor-made for the candidate agent, immersing him completely into his future new culture. They conduct exhausting instruction on every conceivable subject associated with the country, region and city where the candidate will likely be assigned. They also subject the candidate to constant and difficult verbal, and often written, quizzes regarding every imaginable aspect of what he has been lectured about, read or heard."

Sasha listened intently, trying not to miss a word of his description, as Ted continued. "He or she will be expected to know on the spot: the names and reputation of restaurants in his targeted city and famous restaurants elsewhere, the name, composition and records of notable college and professional football, basketball and baseball teams around the country, weather patterns in the country, transportation systems, and current political issues and other important events.

"*Illegals* are usually teamed in pairs, mostly husband and wife teams," Ted said, "but there are situations where an individual is specially trained to conduct a highly sophisticated mission."

Mike was amazed. He felt as though he had learned more in the hour over tea with Ted and Ann about "the process" than he had since he began this venture.

His first evening began with a "welcome" dinner of sorts. Ann prepared a sumptuous meal of roast beef, mashed potatoes, asparagus and a lettuce and tomato salad. She served chocolate pie and coffee for dessert. Mike enjoyed the dinner immensely. It was seasoned much different than he was used to, but overall, he thought it was quite good. He asked Ann if this were the norm he might expect at every meal in the United States. "You can bet on it," she said, and they all laughed.

After dinner, Ted continued his discussion in a more general sense regarding what they would expect of him during his stay. Ted also informed Mike that there was a requirement for him to provide Colonel Sokolov periodic progress reports on his performance, but that he would not "sandbag" him. If there were any deficient areas, he would give Mike the first opportunity to explain or correct the situation before he made a formal report. After an exhausting afternoon and evening of "listening," Mike was finally permitted to return to his room to catch up on the reading and radio news waiting for him. He finally went to bed around midnight, tired, but exhilarated with the day's discussions and the positive prospects of this new phase with Ted and Ann. They had put him at ease, and he felt completely comfortable with both of them. There was no doubt they were professional no-nonsense secret agents, but he could deal with that, as long as they were even-handed, and he was convinced they were. But he had a difficult time believing that they were really Russian!

His first full day at the dacha began with a breakfast of fried eggs, bacon, toast, butter, jelly, coffee and *Kellogg* breakfast cereal. He hadn't eaten a breakfast prepared quite like this before. It was different but very tasty. After the large meal, Ted outlined the coming week. They would concentrate on current affairs in the United States: attitudes toward the Soviet Union; American perceptions about the Cold War; financial news and opinions; sports personalities in all walks of American life (political and military leaders, sports figures, Hollywood stars, newscasters and news makers); and any other events, past or present, that would be important to know. He would be given ample free time to read and listen to the taped radio broadcasts. When time permitted they would play a few card games along with checkers and chess. He was not expected to become proficient at any of these, but he needed to understand the fundamentals. Ted told him that they would occasionally go outside to a nearby government physical fitness center to work out and play a few rounds of tennis. He would not be bored.

The first few days suddenly turned into a few weeks, and Mike was moving easily into the routine and his new identity. He was very comfortable with these two new friends. They did not reveal much about their personal life or about their assignment in the United States, except where they could make reference to something he may encounter when he arrived there. Ann did tell him that they had two children, a boy and a girl, and they were in a boarding school in Moscow. They visited them, usually separately, on weekends. Neither of them gave him a clue as to what his assignment would be or where he would be going when he arrived there, much less when he would be going. He concluded that they probably did not know what his assignment would be, only that he would likely be positioned somewhere in the upper Midwest United States.

Mike would continue to learn that compartmentalization was the nature and the order of the system. Agents conveyed and shared information with another agent or to someone else in the system, only on what was considered "need to know" basis. They lived a double life in all of their actions and deeds. The most desirable manner in which the KGB and GRU posted trained agents in a foreign country was to send them as husband and wife teams. If there were children involved, they would in most cases, if old enough, be left behind in Russia to attend a boarding school.

This policy in effect made the children ideal hostages should an agent team considered defecting. If there were no children to be considered, the agencies always had a file on the closest relatives of their posted agents. In Mike's, nee Sasha's, case, his mother made the ideal hostage candidate should the requirement become necessary. Neither the KGB or the GRU were inclined to send unmarried agents to a foreign posting because there was too much opportunity for compromise should they become romantically involved with a foreigner. If an agent was single, and it was deemed important that he or she be posted anyway, a marriage of convenience between two agents would be encouraged in order to carry out the planned mission. In Mike's situation, his new identity and mission project required him to be a single male.

Agency Operations

On Monday of the fourth week at the dacha, an agent instructor introduced only as Sergei showed up. His task, Ted told Sasha, was to introduce Mike to the network of agency support that he could rely on in the U.S. and the code word system that would be used when he relocated to the United States. The KGB and the GRU each maintained agents in the United States with most of the KGB operatives assigned to various jobs in the Soviet Embassy. The GRU mostly operated out of undercover residencies and safe houses. The joint agency which served as the "clearing house," or coordinating body, between the KGB and the GRU was the GKNIIR.

The GKNIIR's main purpose was to coordinate scientific and technical intelligence gathering by the two agencies. There were always *turf* battles between the two competitive secret agencies, but in the end they worked cooperatively for the good of the cause. Mike would receive his directions from the GKNIIR acting on behalf of both agencies. He was told that the GRU underground organization in New York City alone had a varying number of agents, usually seventy, or more, with different specialties to assist in most any project. Other large cities had undercover residences that were also sufficiently staffed to do the same. Likewise, the Soviet Embassy in Washington had more than a necessary number of skilled KGB agents to provide support. The various consulates and trade missions scattered throughout U.S. cities were also manned by competent agents.

Sergei revealed that the centerpiece of all of their U.S. activities was "the most sophisticated and elaborate" communications system in the world. All assigned agents could easily locate, and communicate with, one another and with their respective headquarters back home. Mike found Sergei more talkative than most of his other instructors. In fact, he openly bragged about his knowledge and experience, but Ted didn't seem to mind as he listened in on many of the sessions with interest.

Mike wondered to himself how his government's agents could operate with seeming immunity in a country as strong and vigilant as the United States. He knew from his training and indoctrination that the U.S. had agents posted in the USSR, but they were contained within the embassy staff and were under constant surveillance by the KGB when they left their confines.

Mike was briefed that he would be provided specific details on his contacts and procedures during his pre-departure orientation prior to his posting. Sergei reviewed the different code word identification and verification systems used by agents. They were really quite simple. The codes mostly consisted of the use of a simple system of color, word, or number combination challenges and responses. Color pairs would be issued to an agent with one being the challenge and the other the response. The same would be true with words or numbers. The various combination "pairs" would be given to an agent with an expiration date and then another set of combinations would be issued. The whole idea, Sergei explained, was not to complicate identification and verification procedures.

If an agent challenged another for positive identification and received a questionable response, he could switch from color, to number or word challenge and response, to be absolutely certain that he was communicating with the right person. "Dead letter boxes and drops" were also covered in his indoctrination. A dead letter box or drop might be a hole in the stump of a tree, a niche under a grave stone in a cemetery, a girder "shelf" under a bridge or any number of innocuous places where notes or documents could be left at a pre-designated time for retrieval by a pick-up agent. "Signals" that a drop has been made might include a parked car with its windshield wipers stopped in a mid-position, or the front wheels of the parked car turned a certain direction, a stuffed animal in the back window of the car, clever marks made by shoe polish on the rear window of a parked car that might resemble innocent graffiti, or a chalk mark on a sidewalk or the side of a building.

Any number of agreed-to creative signals might be used to send notice that "something" was waiting in the dead letter box. Other forms of information or materials exchange by agents could include "brush contacts" where agents meet at a pre-designated place, such as a busy street or tourist sightseeing event where the passing of an envelope or package could go unnoticed. The yavka, or secret rendezvous, could be used when two agents meet at a pre-arranged place, exchange passwords, and verbally discuss information, instructions or a particular situation. Sergei also alluded to the fact that once information is collected and passed for review of relative importance, it may be turned over to a KGB contact in the embassy for transfer by diplomatic pouch back to Moscow.

Mike learned from the lecture that, for the most part, identification, communication and information exchanges were creative, but simply devised, procedures that could be committed to memory and were not easily detected by an observer. The last subject of indoctrination which Sergei described was agent "cover stories." The first of these cover stories is the agent's concocted identity and background. This is carefully and meticulously created and developed by experts to provide the most credible life story possible to place an agent in a foreign country. Mike's new identity was a good example of the precision work given to creating an agent and his undeniable cover. In addition to the creation of a new identity, as Sergei explained, was the creation and development of an emergency cover story should an agent be arrested, or otherwise detained by law enforcement officials.

The emergency cover story follows the procedure of being created and developed by the resident agent-manager in the United States. In a worst case situation, it would likely be one that would eventually have him deported yet evade prosecution for espionage. The critical thing for him, or any agent was to avoid being fully exposed as to who they really were. To be successful, other governments in the Soviet Bloc usually participated in emergency covers; i.e., should an agent be arrested for whatever reason, and the police initiate a comprehensive background investigation, the agent might act to confess that he was an immigrant from a Soviet Bloc country who had escaped and entered the United States illegally.

The agent could employ an Eastern European accent as a disguise to dupe the authorities. The police or law enforcement agency would then likely call the embassy of the country claimed by the arrested agent to confirm his story. When the "claimed country" embassy receives such a call, it has the agent's file pre-positioned—that is complete with wanted posters for the "renegade" for just such a contingency. The embassy will confirm the agent's claim of "escape and illegal entry" into the United States and request that he be turned over to the embassy for return to his native country. In most such cases, the police would routinely turn the individual over directly to the requesting embassy or to the immigration authorities for similar disposition. The "knack" is to keep the situation out of the hands of U.S. intelligence agencies.

After three days of lecture and indoctrination on agency operational practices, Sergei was finished. Ted continued with the subject of communication and verification, applying practical application to the procedures. Next came a block of detailed instruction by an agent named Antoli, regarding GRU *residencies* in the United States.

Antoli described the network of agent residencies and *safe houses* located throughout the United States. He revealed, with some reservation in the interest of security and confidentiality, the GRU residency structure. "The GRU undercover residencies," he said, "amount to a network structure of colonies of Soviet intelligence agents ranging from very large groups in principal cities, throughout the United States, and all Western countries, to smaller and sometimes as few as two agents in lesser important areas. The senior GRU 'resident' agent in the U.S. would likely hold the rank of at least major general, with smaller residencies headed by a colonel. The structure is tight," he said. "The chain of command is absolute. The major residences are staffed with communications/crypto experts, technicians and engineers covering the spectrum of interests to Soviet intelligence. All agents assigned to duties in a given country report to an assigned resident officer and look to him entirely for their instructions and support.

The GRU residency chiefs coordinate their activities with the KGB agents within the Soviet Embassy who provide identification documentation: forged passports, visas, drivers license, social security cards, selective service registration, etc." He told Mike that he would be assigned to a residency officer, or agent-manager, for reporting purposes when he arrived in the United States. He advised him that as he progressed through his mission, he may be handed off from one agent-manager to another, each to provide coordinated, precise instructions to be followed. They would provide him with whatever he needed to do his job, including money, transportation, a place to live and so on.

NINE

Mission Execution

Colonel Sokolov, along with another officer whom he identified only as Lt. Colonel Morozov, arrived at the dacha during Mike's seventh week of training. "I continue to receive excellent reports on your progress, Mike," Sokolov said, greeting his *star* student. "I received the training report on your flying instruction last week. According to Major Rozhko, you far excelled his expectations and fully demonstrated not only expert flying schools, but also excellent decision judgments. Well done!"

"Thank you, Sir. Flying and training with Major Rohzko was great," Mike replied.

"Well, Mike, we are ready to discuss the final details of your mission. You have not disappointed us in any way since your selection. You have taken every challenge handed you and met them with loyal and proficient accomplishment." Sokolov continued, "General Tushenskiy has received permission to move forward with your project. We believe the timing is right to proceed. Today I want to go over with you the entire project plan, get your initial reactions, allow you to think about it for a couple of days, and then we will conclude the final details."

Colonel Sokolov proceeded to outline perhaps the most ambitious and provocative plan ever devised by Soviet intelligence agency planners. "You will be positioned in the United States, in the Cleveland, Ohio, urban area. You will be placed under the management of an experienced GRU residence agent while you get your bearings. The agent will be your 'Uncle Oscar,' and your next of kin. Arrangements are concurrently underway with KGB agency contacts to "create" an appointment for 'Mike Scott' to join the United States Air Force as an aviation cadet. You will attend primary and basic pilot training, be commissioned as an officer in the U.S. Air Force, and if the process can be managed properly, you will eventually be assigned to Strategic Air Command (SAC) as a bomber pilot."

Mike was shocked!

"The GKNIIR will coordinate your intelligence work," the colonel continued, "and the potential exploitation of our particular interests in the operations of their 'SAC.' But I can tell you that we are very interested in strategic aircraft systems, especially the forthcoming new B-52 heavy bomber they are planning: bombing and navigation tactics, maintenance concepts, electronic counter-measures systems and applications, for starters. The U.S.'s Strategic Air Command is too secure for us to attempt to "implant" an older agent. Such a ploy would likely be exposed quickly. The notion to *grow* an agent from the bottom up over an extended period was the conceptual idea of General Tushenskiy. This concept is consistent with the theory of the new Soviet leader, Nikita Khrushchev, and the Politburo. They believe that the likelihood of a near-term all out war between the Soviet Union and the West is not likely. Therefore, there should be a strategy of long-term scientific, technical and subversive collection of Western military capabilities."

Colonel Sokolov continued, "Certainly there are considerable risks involved in Tushenskiy's plan, as in any intelligence collection effort. But if executed carefully and methodically by all of us involved, including you, Mike, the results can be dramatic and extremely beneficial to Soviet Military intelligence as it will be detrimental to the United States."

The slow and deliberate development of the scheme possessed all of the possibilities for both success and failure. "How really vulnerable is the United States?" Mike thought to himself.

It was apparent that the Soviet military intelligence leadership thought that the choice selection of a candidate of Mike's caliber provided even more optimism for success to the planners. General Tushenskiy did not want the project managers to become too eager or provocative. Rather, he wanted absolute patience exercised at all levels and in all progressive phases. The first step would be to get Mike successfully transplanted into his new environment. That initial phase posed little risk. The GRU and the KGB were skilled at inserting agents into the U.S. The task of obtaining an appointment for him to join the U.S. Air Force and attend pilot training appeared to the planners to present little challenge. The Cold War and the added pressures of the Korean Conflict had escalated the requirement in the United States for pilots and aircrew members. With the proper credentials already established for Mike, there should be no problem in his being accepted. This could be done without the need of agent "insiders."

Colonel Sokolov further explained, " This is perhaps the most ambitious and long-ranging mission that we have ever undertaken. But with the prospects that the impasse between the Soviet Union and West could extend indefinitely, and even evolve into a conflict involving nuclear weapons, time is on our side. The aggressive U.S. politicians continue to promote the development of sophisticated strategic bombers and weapons systems at a rate much faster than the Soviet Union. All intelligence indicators pointed to a protracted ideological, if not military, conflict. The arms build-up between the two super powers is escalating at a troublesome rate, and the USSR requires every possible advantage to match its adversary."

Mike was completely absorbed and continued to listen intently. His future was being laid out before him. But with everything that he had been exposed to, and the preparations for this moment, surprisingly, he felt none of the earlier pangs of insecurity or uncertainty about his ability to enter into the project. The past seven weeks in the dacha with Ted and Ann had enhanced his confidence considerably. He was ready, even anxious, to get started!

Colonel Sokolov then turned to Lt. Col. Morosov. "Colonel Morosov is assigned to the GKNIIR, our joint intelligence collection coordinating group," he explained, "and is an expert in the Placement Division. He will address some of the details, and the schedule, which you can anticipate during the execution phase of your mission. He and his staff are responsible for arranging and executing the relocation and placement of agents through the matrix of transfer points to the final destination."

"Mike, I am pleased to finally meet you," Morosov began. "I have heard many good things about you. You have generated considerable interest at the Training Center through your excellent performance and dedication. We are delighted with your excellent successes! I must confess when I was first informed of the notion of introducing a candidate trainee so young as yourself, I was skeptical of the outcome. You have proven to me and others that we were wrong. So, permit me to also congratulate you on your successful progress. It is my responsibility now to make the final arrangements to get you 'through the hoops,' as they say, to your destination. But, let me hasten to give you some confidence that we have a high success rate in doing our job. We have placed thousands of our people into key operating locations in every country in the world."

Morosov continued, "You are going to the United States to become an ordinary citizen. As Colonel Sokolov has told you, you are going to serve in their military air force. We have never tried anything like this before. However, I have high confidence we will be successful, and you will safely and successfully carry out your mission!"

"Now, I will briefly go over your schedule. We have completed your documents, passports, visas and all of your personal identification items, such as driver's license, social security card, photostat of your birth certificate, a library card for the Cleveland, Ohio, library and a few other assorted bits of paper to make you look like who you are. You know, receipts for some purchases and so on. I don't want to belittle any of these, but when you begin to handle and study them, you will get the picture. These documents will be given to you before you depart West Germany. Thereafter, you will become them and they you."

"What next? You may well ask." Morosov was a blasé character, full of self-confidence. "You are currently scheduled to depart Moscow on September 10th by train for Warsaw and on to East Berlin. On this initial leg of your journey you will be fully escorted by two of our people. One will be at your side, at all of times, and the other will be a back-up cover man. You may not even see him. Today, I will leave your personal identification documents, cards and papers with you to review and study. We will collect them before you depart, and they will be returned to you when you are safely in the West—West Berlin, that is. Once you are in East Berlin, our office there will take charge of you, and slip you through the *'eye of the needle'* into the Western Sector of the city. Once on the *other side*, one of our agents will intercept and assist you in getting to London. In London, you will become a solo traveler with tickets to fly aboard an American airliner, TWA, I believe, to New York City."

Morosov continued nonstop, "All of this traveling, from Moscow through Germany and England to the United States will take approximately a week to ten days. We don't want to rush ourselves and make a mistake at any point. In any event, you are getting the short version of our transfer and relocation operation. More often than not, we relocate agents in stepping stone fashion through the back door to Warsaw, Budapest, Kiev and Zurich or Geneva, or back the other way over the Tran-Siberian to Vladivostok and Japan, often with a week or so layover in each stop in order to pick up new ID documents. So, Mike, count yourself lucky! We feel that your youth and simplified background development plays in our favor. So you get the *fast sweep* treatment and do not have to be *washed* through several cycles."

Morosov smiled, enjoying his own joke. "Okay, back to the business at hand. Once you arrive in New York, you will be met by one of our people at the airport. He will take charge of your arrangements there. And, the last briefing item on my list—no single agent is fully briefed-in on your project. Therefore, you are not at liberty to discuss details with anyone, except those who will identify their access to you." He was finished. "That's Project *Mackarova*, Mike. Your thoughts?"

Mike had absorbed it all. Not in the minutest of detail, but he had the picture. "It's a bit breathtaking," he responded. "I haven't taken any notes," he said, "but I presume that I will be provided incremental details as I need them. I am deeply honored to have this confidence placed in me. Thank you."

"You are absolutely correct, Mike, no written notes," Morosov agreed. "We will provide you details, almost always verbally, until we get you successfully to your destination. You are a quick study, my friend," he concluded.

"Well, Mike, that's it," Colonel Sokolov concluded. "The 10th of September is your target date. Today is August 12th. You have less than a month before you depart. You will remain here in the dacha with your hosts and continue to hone your preparations between now and then. By the way, I have arranged a weekend visit with your parents before you depart, the weekend of the 29th of August, I believe. Ted will arrange for a car to take you and bring you back. You won't be chaperoned this time, and you may remain over Saturday and Sunday. Enjoy, and please, convey my best to your father. He is one of our honored generals."

Mike was flattered. "Thank you, Sir. I sincerely appreciate your thoughtful kindness," Mike confidently responded.

"Good, we shall depart then," Sokolov acknowledged. "Continue your work, and I will see you before you move on." The three shook hands. Sokolov and Morosov departed the dacha compound, feeling very confident in Mike and the success of the initial stages of their plan, although neither knew where, or how far, the mostly "unwritten" script would take their young candidate agent.

Sasha visited his parents for the last time before departing on his mission. They didn't ask and he didn't share any information regarding his departure. The atmosphere over the weekend was thick with emotion and anxiety, especially for Tatyana. She didn't have to know the details to know that her son was about to leave her, once again. They would likely not see each other again for a very long time. Neither did Viktor have any information on Sasha's work, but he knew that his son was departing for an important and likely long journey.

Bonita came by during his visit. Although she was not very pleased with the news of Sasha's appointment as an officer in the Soviet Air Force, she joined in the celebration of his success. She, like her daughter, continued to hold out the faintest hope that Russia would find itself someday, and young men like Sasha would not be subjected to such dark and questionable futures.

Back at the dacha, Sasha once again became Mike Scott, a matured, highly trained and skilled Soviet officer and GRU agent prepared to depart on his assigned mission of espionage against the avowed enemy of the Soviet People—the United States. The mackarova, "masquerade", was about to begin.

Mackarova

"Passport, please; state your citizenship," the Immigration Officer requested.

"U.S. citizen," responded the newly arrived passenger from London.

"Your place of birth?" The officer asked.

"Cleveland, Ohio," the returning American responded.

"How long have you been out of the United States?" the Immigration Officer continued.

"Two weeks, Sir, visiting friends in Germany and the UK," came the response.

"Where do you go from here?" the immigration official asked.

"I will be visiting here in New York for a few days before I go back home to Cleveland," he replied.

The Immigration Officer "bammed" his stamp on the passport.

"Thank you. Welcome home," he said, as he returned the passport.

John Michael Scott eased his way beyond the Immigration Counter, took in a deep breath and followed the queue to the baggage carousels. He watched the assortment of luggage and boxes come around until he spotted his. He collected his bag and moved on to the area marked, UNITED STATES CUSTOMS. "This is just as they told me it would be. Everything is exactly like the photos I reviewed," he marveled to himself as he rolled over in his mind the last few days of instruction and orientation in East Berlin and London. Meticulous details had been provided prior to his departure. As he made his way to the head of the queue and handed the Customs Officer his declaration form, he looked around and observed the *sea of people* moving slowly through the immigration and customs processing lines. He may well have gone over his tutoring and orientation a thousand times during the flight from London, but to actually find himself here in the United States, and New York City, was almost overwhelming. He was very tired and filled with anxiety, but he was fully alert to his surroundings and the next steps to be accomplished. The Customs Officer took the declaration form, looked at his unpretentious single piece of luggage, his small hand-carried bag, and waved him on.

"Okay," he thought to himself, "what next?" He had memorized every single detail of the departure area of Idlewild International Airport International Terminal—the street side exits, restrooms and public telephone stations. As he casually walked about the area, he thought that by now he would be approached by his 'contact.' "God, I hope he shows up, and soon. I don't think I want to have to move this quickly to a contingency plan," he thought to himself. "I don't want to loiter here too long either, and have a policeman question me." He had already seen his first New York policeman. Although he dreaded a run-in with the police, he was confident that he could handle most any situation. He had rehearsed every possible option to the principle plan should a screw up occur. Trying to look casual as if waiting for someone, which he was, he strolled over to a row of seats near a bank of telephones and sat down. He took a book out of the side pocket of his bag.

As he sat, pretending to read, he looked about. He was struck by the stark contrast between this airport and Sheremetyvo II, the central international airport, in Moscow. The Idlewild terminal was well-lighted, bright and relatively clean. He had only been in the Moscow airport twice, and it was several years ago, but he clearly remembered how dull, dirty and dark it was. Most all of the light bulbs had been stolen from the lounge areas and there were none in the restrooms. Light bulbs and toilet tissue, as he remembered growing up in Moscow, were prized pilfered items in any public facility. His first impressions of the United States were cleanliness and good order.

"Mike, there you are! Good to see you! How was your flight?" The voice came from a casually dressed fellow moving toward him, smiling as he held out his hand. He judged the fellow to be about forty years old. Mike stood and returned the hand shake in response. "How was your visit with old Dan in London, and what's his wife's name?"

Mike smiled and responded, "Wanda is her name. I had a great visit, thanks. Frank, good to see you. How is Ester and the boy? John is fourteen now, isn't he?"

"Ester is fine, and John is fifteen now," came the reply.

The exchange of greetings and simple code word exchanges were as he expected. Mike took in a quiet breath of air. "Thank God, we're on track. Wow!" he muttered to himself.

The "Transfer Indoctrination" in East and West Berlin, and briefly reviewed in London, had been straight-forward enough. His contact agents at each transfer point had given him a minimum list of challenge and response words he could expect to hear, and use, when he arrived in New York City. He had been briefed numerous times that agents committed to memory the minimum amount of information necessary to move from one phase to the next in an operation. This procedure eliminated the requirement to write down anything which might be compromised, in the event a plan should go sour due to an accident or an arrest for some infraction.

The transfer from East into West Berlin had gone smoothly. He had been provided with new identification documents and a "one-day visitor's pass" to visit a "sick relative" in West Berlin. Once safely through "Checkpoint Charley" he was met by an "uncle" who took him to a safe house. The whole process of trashing his old documents and issuing new ones, complete with photo identifications, took just one day. From West Berlin, in possession of his American passport, drivers license, social security card, selective service card and assorted bits and pieces of personal receipts and so forth, he rode the train across East Germany to Frankfort where he was intercepted by another "uncle."

"Home free" in the West, Mike was escorted via automobile across West Germany and Belgium to Ostende and the ferry to England. The few days of transit and transition from Moscow and a Russian citizen and military officer to West Germany, London and into the United States, as an American, reinforced Mike's confidence in Project Mackarova. The elaborate, painstaking preparations developed by "The System," had trained him, brought him this far and would not fail him now.

"Is this your only bag, Mike?" Frank asked.

"Yep, that's it. I traveled very light," he responded, as Frank took his bag by the handle and proceeded toward a street-side exit.

Once they were inside the Chevrolet sedan parked in the lot across the street from the terminal, Frank observed, "Well, my friend, I am delighted to meet you. You are much younger than I expected, even though I was advised that you were a fledgling."

"Good to see you, too, Frank. Is this *Chevy* a '50 or '51 model?" Mike asked.

"It's a '50 model, just a plain vanilla car, but it runs great," Frank answered. Then he asked, "How is your mother?"

"My mother is no longer living, Frank," Mike answered.

Satisfied with the last *"code word"* exchange, Frank said, "Good, I believe that we are finished with the formalities, Mike. We can't be too careful, you know. The Americans are pretty docile about what's going on, but every once in awhile the FBI or CIA gets tricky and tries to put some sand in our gears. We stay pretty well ahead of them," he chuckled.

"Of course, we have to be alert to an occasional one of our own who decides that money is more important than loyalty and patriotism," he said, "and begins to do some *extracurricular* work for the Yankee agencies. When we discover a bad apple, we make quick work of him. Or, if it suits our purposes, we put a close member of his family back home in a vice and get even better mileage out of him here. Double agent, you know," he smiled drolly.

Frank was considerably more open and "talky" than the agents Mike was used to back home. "He must be lonesome for company," Mike thought as he listened carefully to everything Frank said. He was alert to any key words or phrases that might be suspicious. However, he was aroused by none as they drove through the city.

It was turning dusk on this September afternoon as the lights of the vast city of tall buildings began to come on. They drove on through the busy traffic with Frank pointing out landmarks and buildings that Mike had seen only in photographs and movies. He noted the sign indicating the *Lincoln Tunnel, of* which he had seen photos, and the *George Washington Bridge*. He remembered the name of the first President of the United States. He was most overawed by the streets which ran like long, straight ribbons through the canyons formed by the tall structures. The photographs which he had been shown could not do justice to seeing this incredible city for real. He thought Moscow was a great city, but it was nothing in comparison to this metropolis.

"Well, what do you think, Mike? Does your first visit to the great United States impress you?" Frank asked as he drove on to the suburbs and into an area of lower profile buildings and apartment complexes.

"I don't know," Mike responded. "I don't know what to think right now. I do know that I am very tired and need to go to bed soon before I pass out. I am really bushed."

"Well, we are right on time to take care of that," Frank answered as he pulled the car to the curbside on a tree-lined street of small houses somewhere in the suburbs of the city.

As they got out of the Chevy, another vehicle pulled in behind them and turned off its lights. "Hi, Ed," Frank called out. "Everything okay?"

"All clear, Frank. Good ride," the newest member of the *"reception"* committee answered as he strode over and held out his hand to Mike. "Hi, Mike. I'm Ed. Welcome home."

Mike shook hands and nodded in response, "Hi."

As the three walked to the door of the bungalow, Frank said, "Ed is on our team, Mike. He tailed us from the airport to insure that we were secure. We are. You are safely on the ground in the USA, your new home to be. Come in."

The cottage was comfortably furnished and warm inside. Mike welcomed the feeling of security within the house. "Have a seat, Mike. Can I get you something to eat or drink?" Frank offered. "This will be your temporary home for the next two weeks while you get your feet on the ground. It will give you an opportunity to rest up, get oriented and review your next moves."

"Just a glass of water," Mike acknowledged. "I had plenty to eat on the flight. Where are we? Do you both live here?"

"No, neither of us do," Frank answered. "Come on, I'll show you the kitchen and the rest of the place. This house is owned by Ed, who's a real estate agent. We're in a low profile neighborhood in the suburbs. Should you run into any of the neighbors on the street, just tell them you're new in the city and renting this house temporarily until you find something permanent. So as not to arouse any suspicions, you can also say that Ed's wife is your cousin. She will come by in the mornings and tidy up the place. In the meantime, there is food in the refrigerator and in the larder to tide you over. Ed will come by and pick you up around ten tomorrow and bring you to my place for discussions. So, get some rest. If you can't sleep, there is a television and several newspapers and magazines to bring you up to date. Oh, there is a telephone here also, but we will not call you before we meet again. So do not answer it." Frank paused as he observed his new ward. "Are you okay?"

Mike, still a bit in awe of his new friends and surroundings, acknowledged Frank's instructions, "Yeah, I'm fine. A little tired, but I'm okay. Do I just lock the door when you leave and go to bed?"

"It's all yours, Mike. You need to get used to being on your own. You are the newest American, and you can begin living like one. Enjoy," Frank responded. "Goodnight, see you tomorrow." Then, he whispered, "Das Vadanya, Comrade."

The three shook hands, and Frank and Ed departed.

TEN

America

Mike inspected the kitchen and looked into the refrigerator. It contained more food and drink than he had ever seen in a Russian home. He moved on into the larger of the two bedrooms. He undressed, took a quick shower and lay down on the comfortable bed. As he had been prone to many, many times over the past sixteen months, he lay in the quiet room and reflected on how he got to be where he was. "Here I am," he thought. "This is a safe house, a Soviet dacha, and right here in the United States." And, as he would often ponder, "How could this be? Why me? Where would I be and what would I be, doing if all of this had not happened?"

His thoughts returned to these two new people in his life. "Who are they, really? Are they Russian? Frank is definitely," he assured himself. "But, Ed likely is not. He and his wife are Americans, recruited agents on the take. They are on the take and selling out their country and their souls for money." He had been fully indoctrinated about these "stooges". He was aware of how watchful and careful he must be with them. He finally drifted off to sleep and did not wake up until almost nine a.m., according to his new American-made Bulova wristwatch which had been given to him in East Berlin. He could hear an occasional automobile pass by on the street, but otherwise it was very quiet. If this were Moscow, he thought, there would be a clamor of people moving up and down the street, going wherever. He got out of bed, went into the kitchen and filled a kettle with water for tea and put it on the stove. He still had not fully acquired a taste for coffee, although he was working on it, as he had been encouraged to do. "It is the Americans' preferred drink." He would drink it in public, if need be. But in private, he preferred tea.

Taking out a pair of wrinkled trousers and a shirt from his bag, he got dressed. He slipped a sweater over the shirt and drank his tea, but he wasn't really hungry, so he nibbled on some sugar cookies he found in the pantry. Promptly at ten o'clock, he heard a key turn in the front door lock and in walked Ed with a woman, whom he presumed to be his wife.

"Good morning, Mike. I would like for you to meet my wife, Helen." He had not really noticed Ed's distinctive accent the night before, but this morning he was clearly a New Yorker. During his training, he had been exposed to most all of the various accents which he might encounter in the United States. When Helen spoke, she confirmed their origin.

"Good Morning, Ed. I am pleased to meet you, Helen. Well, I didn't mess up the place too much, so I hope you won't have much cleaning to do," Mike acknowledged as he shook hands with the two.

"Not a bother," said Helen. "You men go on, and I will take care of the house."

There was very little conversation or small talk as Mike collected his small hand-carried bag which contained his passport and other documents. He departed with Ed. As they drove along, Ed said very little except to comment on the beautiful *Indian Summer* weather and pointed out an occasional building or landmark. They drove for almost an hour, making an extraordinary number of turns and changes in direction. Mike concluded that this was Ed's modus to ensure that he wasn't being followed. Mike wondered, "Is there really this much to worry about in America? I had been led to believe that they are fairly complacent and not very suspicious of anyone."

Ed finally pulled up in front of a house in a neighborhood not much different than where he had spent the night. They got out of the car. Ed led the way up the sidewalk to the front door and rang the door bell. Frank opened the door, greeted them both with a smile and handshake, and beckoned them in. Once inside, Frank ushered them into a comfortable sitting room. It was not pretentious but roomy with a sofa and several chairs. "Coffee, anyone? Or, something else?" he asked. Mike and Ed both declined. "Well, did you rest well after the long day, long *several* days, I presume?" Frank asked of Mike.

"Yes, I did, thank you. It was a very comfortable bed and a very quiet night," Mike answered.

"Well, Mike, let's get started," Frank began. "As we have already introduced ourselves, and, you met Helen this morning, we will only go by our first names. You don't need to be concerned with any further information about who we are. The less you know, the less you are accountable for. We want to keep everything as simple as possible—uncomplicated, if you will."

Mike noticed immediately that Frank did not share the same accent as Ed and presumably, his wife, Helen. "Mike, we plan to have you stay here in New York for about two weeks to unwind, look around the city, mix with people on the streets and generally observe conduct and habits. Although," Frank chuckled, "New York is not typical America. In fact, it is probably the most different city in America, but it is a place to begin. I have been stationed here for five years, and my job is to provide initial orientation for newcomers like yourself. Ed, here, is my colleague. He will assist in showing you around the city. Most of our time together will be spent in answering any questions you have as you settle in, arrange for any additional documents you may require, schedule your departure when the time arrives and to generally make you comfortable with your new environment." Frank paused and looked at Ed. "Ed, please recheck our schedule for the day. Mike will be ready shortly." That was Ed's cue to leave the room, and to close the door behind him.

Frank continued, "Mike, I do not know what your mission assignment is after you leave New York. We compartmentalize everything we possibly can. Again, if you don't have knowledge of something, you are not responsible for it. Before you depart in a couple of weeks, I will provide you all the information you will need for your contact agent in Cleveland. He will take charge of you there. Likely we will not meet again. That is, until our day of victory over these flaccid capitalists. That will be *our* Resurrection Day," Frank snickered, then promptly returned to his serious tone. "Now, we will take each day one at a time. As I said a moment ago, look, observe and learn."

"By the way, Mike," Frank interrupted himself, "Here is five hundred dollars in American currency, all in small bills. This should get you through your visit here. Ed will take you to a clothier to add to your wardrobe. You will need an overcoat, additional shoes and the usual, nothing flashy, though. We maintain an average to low key profile over here. Also, I suggest that you do not carry too much cash on your person. If something should happen and you are found to have a lot of money on you, the authorities can ask a lot of questions."

Over the next two weeks, Mike read every periodical he could put his hands on. He rode all around the city, suburbs and the countryside with Ed. He couldn't believe the incredible number of automobiles on the streets of New York City, especially the Yellow Cabs! The brightness and colors displayed on everything from automobiles to advertisements to store window displays was awesome in comparison to drab Moscow. He and Ed walked the streets. They ate meals in a variety of restaurants, rode the subway, visited museums and libraries while Mike watched and listened intently to the people in his strange new world.

The most remarkable discovery of all of Mike's ventures were the supermarkets and department stores. He had difficulty believing the choices, variety, quality and abundance of goods in every store he visited. He recalled his mother's stories about her visit to London, but her descriptions did not even come close to what he now witnessed. Ed had him make a few purchases and pay the bills at restaurants to familiarize him with money exchanges and dialogue. He also had Mike drive his automobile to improve his proficiency and to become familiar with high density traffic, signal lights and the laws.

Frank escorted him on a trip by train to Washington, DC, where they spent two days seeing the city, famous landmarks and a "drive by" the Soviet Embassy. "We don't want to show too much interest in *our* embassy," Frank commented. "I can tell you that *it is* under constant surveillance by the local police and the FBI, and likely others," he chuckled. "I have never even been inside there myself!"

He also took him to the Pentagon. They went inside and joined a tourist group and were escorted around the open environs and historical displays by a sharply dressed and courteous U.S. Marine. "Can you believe this?" asked Frank. He whispered, "Could you imagine an American going to Moscow and *just driving up* to the Kremlin and walking in for a tour? This is really a scream! But, this is America. They are naive. They aren't a bit shy or bashful, or worried too much about spies either." Mike was in awe of the whole scene. He watched as men and women in various military service uniforms walked briskly through the vast hallways of the world's largest office building and the centerpiece of the U.S. Department of Defense and military service headquarters. It was difficult for Mike to believe that he was really here and witnessing all of this. It was far beyond anything his indoctrination had conveyed to him and beyond his wildest imaginings.

From the Pentagon, they went to the White House. Frank had made arrangements with his local contacts to obtain tickets to join a tour group there. "Did you ever go inside Stalin's house, Mike?" Frank chided.

"No, I haven't done anything like this in Moscow," Mike murmured quietly. He was truly impressed. He was struck, not only by the openness of the capital city of the United States, but with the sprite cleanliness, compared to Moscow. There was an air of warmth and friendliness that he saw in the people on the streets, in the restaurants and everywhere. Although he had spent the last year being prepped for this, he was still astonished by what he had witnessed thus far. He recognized immediately that he was going to have to be extremely careful not to be taken in by what the Americans presented as democracy and capitalism. On the return trip by train back to New York, Frank hit upon that very issue.

"I don't know what your mission project is while you are here, Mike, but I want to caution you. No, I want to warn you. You will be vulnerable to what you see and are allowed to do, while in the United States. But do not waver, Comrade. The United States and its Western Allies are a house of cards. Everything that they attempt to put out to the public and to foreign visitors is a false *store* front. It is a mackarova, a masquerade. There is no substance behind the front.

Everything is shiny and glossy for the outside world to absorb, but it is an empty shell when you look behind the curtain. I have been here five years, traveled over most of the country, and I have been provided good intelligence reports from our colleagues. So I can tell you that this so-called democracy is a sham and a fraud. Their whole political process is a joke. You'll see." It was obvious that Frank was giving him a tough pep talk and an admonition against being duped.

Mike had heard all of this before, but also before he had been exposed to the U.S. first hand. He listened intently and acknowledged every point in Frank's intense lecture. He had a very important job ahead of him. It would take his full concentration to move into that challenge without becoming distracted with propaganda or anything else.

Back in New York City, Frank took him to his house. "Mike, I have a bus ticket to Cleveland, Ohio, for you. You will depart on the day after tomorrow. Traveling by commercial bus will provide you an exposure to more of the United States and its people. You don't have to worry about the complexities of that form of travel; I will provide you all of the details about the various city station stops, bus changes and so forth. If you encounter any confusion, the drivers and station attendants are very friendly and helpful. Americans are always delighted to help. It makes them feel superior. It will be a good experience for you and an opportunity to observe and absorb. You will be met when you arrive in Cleveland by your "Uncle Oscar." He will take charge of you from that point," Frank concluded. "Any questions?" he asked.

"No, I have enjoyed my stay here in New York. You and Ed have been exceptionally informative and helpful in helping me get started. I am grateful to you both," Mike replied. "Frank, don't worry about my loyalty. I am fully dedicated to my mission and completely loyal to my government. I look forward with eagerness to the accomplishment of my duties." He paused, and then asked, "Is there anything in particular that I need to know about "Uncle Oscar?"

"I don't know Oscar," Frank replied. "He is posted in the Cleveland area and was given to me as your contact. He will know about you, and your next moves, when you arrive."

Mike continued to observe that good agents share no more information than is necessary to accomplish the immediate task. Frank had been friendly enough and more than helpful in assisting him to adjust to his new environment. But Mike still *knew* nothing of him. "Where was he from? Did he have a family?" Mike wondered. After two weeks of visiting and talking, Frank revealed nothing of a particular nature. "But," he thought to himself, "it was the same with Vlad, even after three years!" Although the discipline of Soviet intelligence agents was absolute, occasionally one would slip away. And almost always it was for money, protection and long-term security. Defections happened on both sides of the Cold War counter. Of major concern to the Soviet agent, KGB and GRU alike, was discovery and expulsion. More often than not, the consequences upon returning home were not pleasant. For the would-be Soviet defector, it was almost always fatal.

The Greyhound bus pulled into the station, and the driver announced, "Here we are folks, chilly Cleveland, Ohio."

Uncle Oscar

Mike put on his coat, collected his bag and followed the passengers off the bus. He didn't realize how stiff he was until he stepped down onto the pavement inside the bus shelter. It had been a long, twenty-six hour ride since he left New York City and headed toward the Midwest. He stretched his legs and twisted his body in an attempt to restore some of the circulation in his body as he moved into the baggage collection area.

The ride hadn't been bad, just long, with what seemed like at least a hundred stops along the way. Many passengers boarded and departed along the way. He only had difficulty with one fellow who had obviously imbibed too much before getting on board and sat himself beside Mike.

"Where you from, boy?" the drunk asked through a noxious breath. And, "Where you goin', anyway?"

Mike tried to respond to his droning questions, but he soon learned that it was impossible. He would respond with short, cryptic answers and try to turn away from him. The irritation lasted for about three hours before the drunk decided to depart at one of the stops.

Mike would not have put up with such nonsense back in his home territory. But he did not want to make a scene and draw attention to himself from the other passengers or the driver. He had endured the jerk's nonsensical gibberish until he finally departed. He thought to himself, "Could that character have been an agent? Well, in any event, I kept my cool, but I should have decked him right then and there." He wondered how long he would be paranoid about people in this new environment. "Likely from now on," he thought to himself.

Mike looked around the terminal at the faces of the dozen or so well-wishers who were there to meet the arriving passengers. If "Uncle Oscar" were among them, he didn't stand out. He spotted his suitcase and pulled it from the growing stack of assorted bags and boxes the bus driver was creating. The bus station and the people there reminded him more of "back home" than anything since he arrived. He wandered over to a row of seats in the center of the terminal and took a seat much as he had when he arrived in New York. He was barely seated when a man of fifty or so sat down next to him. Mike observed him from the corner of his eye. He had on a dark suit coat, white shirt and no necktie. He looked typical of the others on the bus and those in the waiting area. The man opened a newspaper and began to thumb through the pages, humming to himself. Mike was becoming a little irritated and started to get up and move to another location when the stranger quietly asked, "How's the weather in New York?"

Mike didn't respond for a moment, then said, "It's warm for September."

The stranger continued to look through his newspaper, then said, "I heard that it was seventy-five degrees yesterday."

"No," replied Mike. "It was sixty-five degrees yesterday."

"Oh," said the stranger. "Then, have the leaves turned brown?"

"No, the leaves are still green," responded Mike.

"Good," replied the man still casually turning the pages of his newspaper. Then in a low voice, "I believe the coast is clear, Mike. I will depart through the double doors to your left. You may follow me in a minute or two. I am parked along the curb about a half a block straight down the street. It is a green Ford, two-door sedan.

The parking lights will be on." Then he folded his paper and departed the terminal.

Mike waited a couple of minutes, looked casually at his watch, collected his suitcase and small bag and followed through the same doors. He approached the green sedan with the parking lights on, opened the curbside door, pulled the front seat forward and put his bags in the back. "Oscar?" he asked, moving into the right front seat.

"No, I am Joseph, but call me Joe," The man behind the steering wheel said, extending his hand.

Mike suddenly felt his heart race to about twice the normal rate. "Damn," he murmured to himself. "Have I screwed up?" As he sat down in the seat he responded with a weak handshake. "Where is Oscar?" he asked.

"You can relax, Mike. Oscar is okay. He couldn't be here to meet you because he had to attend a union meeting. He is a steward in the local Teamsters Union, so he sent me to meet you. Don't worry, everything is on track. Welcome to Cleveland."

Mike felt some relief and settled back into his seat as Joe drove off. Joe continued, "I am going to take you to the house we have set aside for you and let you get settled in. Oscar will come by in the morning and bring you up to speed on where we are with your program."

Mike acknowledged with a nod and then challenged Joe with a question, "What is Oscar's wife's name? I forgot."

Joe smiled and responded, "Martha. She is a real nice lady. Have you met her before?"

"No, I haven't," replied Mike. "I haven't met Oscar, either," he added.

"You will, and you will like him," Joe acknowledged and continued. "I thought we might stop off for a bite to eat if that's okay. I am sure you didn't eat very well on that damned bus."

Mike allowed that he hadn't, and food sounded good. Joe put him at ease, pointing out various parts of the city until they pulled into the parking lot of a restaurant with a lighted marquee advertising steaks and chops. Joe led him inside. A hostess showed them a booth near the back. Joe ordered two draft beers and Mike began to feel more comfortable with his new "friend."

Joe chatted quietly about the city, the Cleveland Browns, their good season, and the fact that winter was coming on. "Cleveland has some tough winters," he said. "You will want to wish that you don't have to be here too long." Mike surprised Joe with his knowledge of the Browns football team. He named a few of the players and their statistics. It gave him an opportunity to practice what he had studied and committed to memory. Joe was impressed. After a couple of beers and a steak dinner, the two were getting along well. Mike had completely relaxed by the time they had finished their dinner.

Back in the car, Joe told Mike that they were going to one of their safe houses, where he would stay pending the next stage of his mission. They drove to a neighborhood, not unlike the one where he stayed in New York. The house, however, was a duplex apartment style. Joe explained that he and his wife lived in one side, and that the other side was used for transient guests such as Mike. Once inside, Joe showed him around and told him that his wife would prepare his lunch and dinner meals when he wasn't otherwise away from the apartment. Mike would be responsible for taking care of his breakfast meal. Again, the pantry and refrigerator were well-stocked with food of all sorts.

After Joe departed, Mike went straight to bed. He was becoming used to managing for himself in strange new places. He awoke the next morning to a tap on his bedroom door. He rolled out of bed, saw that it was almost eight o'clock, slipped on the robe that was hanging in his closet and opened the door.

"Good morning, Mike, I'm Oscar. Sorry I missed your arrival last evening, but I have to make an honest living, you know," he chuckled. "I trust that Joe took good care of you?"

Oscar was a well-built fellow, about fifty, Mike guessed. He was almost bald and gray around his temples and the fringe around his head. Mike had no doubt that he was Russian although he had perfected a very good American accent. "If you want to get dressed, Mike, we can go to a favorite place of mine, have breakfast and begin our discussion."

Mike acknowledged that he would be ready in a few minutes. He proceeded to select a pair of slacks and a shirt, locate his shoes and get dressed, while Oscar wandered around the kitchen and living room, apparently inspecting the place. In a matter of minutes, Mike said he was ready to go. Oscar led the way to his car, and they departed.

On the way, Oscar began to talk in an almost scripted form. "Mike, we are happy to have you here in the United States, and I am especially delighted that my activity was chosen to initiate your work. I have an excellent staff. We are well positioned to work a variety of programs, not only in the Cleveland area, but throughout this part of the U.S. What I can't get done here, my counterpart in Chicago can."

He didn't elaborate on "what" programs he worked on. Mike did not pursue. Oscar continued, "I initiated the preliminaries on your program about six months ago. I am pleased to tell you that we are about ready to go. Your arrival timing is perfect. In a few days, or within a week, you should receive notification of your acceptance into the U.S. Air Force aviation cadet program." Mike felt goose bumps run over his body. Oscar kept talking. "I am sure that you were well-briefed on that and all of the phases of the project, right?"

Mike quickly responded, "Yessir, I was." His nervousness showed.

"Don't yes sir, me, Mike. I am just like you. I have been at this just a little longer is all," Oscar said, smiling. "I am sure that this is all running a little fast for you, but believe me, it is the best way to get started. Sitting around waiting for something to happen, or to get tasked to go do something is not easy, at least not for me." He continued, "It's my job for the present to look after your safety, and needs, until you move on. I am also your Uncle Oscar, and next of kin, when you begin to complete all of the paper work for the Air Force. You will use my home address, phone number and so on. I will give you a brief background paper regarding our kinship, should some oddball question come up. You never know. Did they provide you with all of the necessary identity documents and the profile on your background?"

"Yes, they did. I have a complete file on my historical background as well as all of my necessary personal ID papers, cards and documents. I have committed to memory my background," Mike replied.

"Good," Oscar said. "While we are driving, and in the security of my car, I am going to give you several other bits and pieces of material which you will need to facilitate communications. First, your personal identifier name will be *Mike*. Just file that away in your mind, bring it up once in awhile to remind yourself and be alert should one of us call you by that name to alert you to a possible problem, or if you need to use it to identify yourself. Now, if you encounter a problem or emergency and need assistance, you are to call a special number which I will provide you. Memorize it so that it will always be in the background of your mind for use when necessary. Also commit to memory the name, "Jasper". That is who you will ask for, if and when, you need to make an emergency call. The individual answering the phone will ask who is calling, and you will respond with "Mike." They will likely tell you that Jasper isn't there, but to leave a number and they will have him call you. If at all possible, in fact, unless it is impossible, use a pay phone and give them the pay phone number to call back. We will review this procedure again before you depart, but you need to begin absorbing the procedures now.

"Okay, let's go over one more 'ID' procedure," Oscar explained, reaching into the folder in the seat beside him, "This is your *'Polka Dot Calendar.'* Colorful, isn't it?" The calendar was a typical glossy month-by-month folding type, roughly twelve by fourteen inches in size and hinged with a spiral ring. "Open it up to a month."

Mike opened the calendar to February. The picture above the calendar, hinged to the bottom, depicted a clown bouncing colorful balls or balloons into the air. The calendar showed the month of February laid out in uniform squares of sufficient size to make appointment notes. He observed an array of colored dots similar to the balls or balloons in the picture above, scattered across calendar date squares.

"Mike, you will note that in each day square there are two different colored dots, one on the left side of the square and one on the right. It doesn't matter if the dots are more to the top or to the bottom of each square, but you will note that each dot is definitely skewed to the right or left within the date box. Now you have already used the color code challenge and response system, so this calendar will provide you a daily set of color codes to use to validate calls, contacts or messages. The dot on the left side is *your* color and the dot on the right is the contacts' color. In other words, if I say to you on the 4th of February, "Hi Mike! This is Uncle Oscar. What a blue sky day. How are you doing?" and you might respond with what?" Oscar asked.

Mike looked at February 4th and noted that the right hand dot was blue and the left side dot was green, and he quickly responded, "Hi, Uncle Oscar. These beautiful days really make the *green* grass grow."

"Good," Oscar said. "Now, note that in addition to the day's date, there is a small number in the lower corner which reflects the day of the year. For additional confirmation of identification, you or your contact could challenge with one of the numbers and respond with the other. So, if I said to you, 'I have those eight tubes you ordered for your radio,' you might respond with, 'Did you say that they are 39 cents apiece?' Got it?"

"Yep, I've got it—pretty simple and slick system." Mike was impressed with how precisely and smoothly Oscar moved through the procedures. His polite manner and pleasant attitude contrasted with his rugged appearance.

Oscar pulled into the parking lot of a restaurant advertising Bohemian breakfast and dinner specials. Inside, Oscar was greeted by several of the waitresses indicating that he was a frequent customer. "This is a hangout for union jocks," Oscar said pointing to a corner booth. "We can talk fairly freely here."

Oscar quietly discussed a few more administrative details over breakfast, mostly reiterating some of the previous information and identification procedures. He then began a verbal descriptive overview of the city of Cleveland. He filled in numerous trivia details that Mike had not been provided, or read, in the material he had been given back at the dacha.

Over the next several days, Oscar and Joe alternated showing him around the Cleveland area. They familiarized him with landmarks, the lake shore and the suburbs. Both of them were literal travelogues, pointing out and explaining the features of everything they saw. In between sites, they talked about the local inhabitants: the various ethnic cultures that had settled in the area, the prominent restaurants, the smaller popular ones, labor unions and their influence, the sports teams, the parks, museums, how the postal system worked and about every other conceivable detail about a city. At the end of a week, Mike *knew* Cleveland!

Oscar's prediction was correct. On Wednesday of his second week in Cleveland, Oscar delivered a white envelope addressed to "John Michael Scott." Mike looked at it. This was his first piece of U.S. Mail. He noted the stark bold return address: Department of the Air Force, 1092nd Recruiting Squadron, Lackland Air Force Base, Texas.

"Open it," Oscar said. "Let's see if we have been successful." Oscar was as excited as Mike.

Mike opened the envelope. Inside was an official looking letter with the same letterhead as the return address on the envelope. The letter was, as Oscar had anticipated, the acknowledgment of "Mike's application" to join the U.S. Air Force and to attend pilot training. In part it read: "I am pleased to acknowledge your acceptance as an enlisted airman trainee into the United States Air Force with subsequent assignment as an aviation cadet to Primary Pilot Training, Class 54-H, Moultrie Air Base, Georgia." The letter continued: "You are requested to report to the Air Force Recruiting Office, 320 North Carlson Street, Cleveland, Ohio, between the hours of 0800 and 1100 on Wednesday, 28 October 1953, for further instructions and to arrange your travel to Lackland AFB. If you are unable to comply with the above date and time, please contact this office immediately." The letter requested that he hand-carry with him a picture ID, his driver license or passport would be fine and a copy of his college transcript. It was signed: "Robert M. Conley, Lt. Colonel, USAF."

As Mike read the letter with Oscar, he could only marvel at the cunning, incredibly skilled deception and efficiency of these Soviet trained agents. He had seen the work that went on at Khodinka. It was no more accurate and efficient than what he had witnessed both in New York and in Cleveland. "This is unbelievable!" he whispered out loud.

Oscar chuckled. "I have to agree, Mike. This is one of our best jobs yet! We are getting damn good at spooking these Americans, and this time, right inside their Defense Department *knickers*! My guys will be pleased when I tell them how well they did. Now, Mike, Comrade, it is up to you to carry the ball. Oh," he said. "Take your drivers license, not your passport. No need to subject that document to unnecessary scrutiny, but hang on to it in case you can use it later."

"Okay, I will. I must admit, I am a bit nervous. But you have certainly gone the last mile to assist me and to make me comfortable. I will be okay. I won't let you down."

Oscar smiled. "It isn't for me, Comrade Mike. It is for our great government and the Soviet people. I am impressed with you. I have processed dozens of agents into the U.S. You are by far the best that I have seen come through here. You will succeed at whatever is asked of you."

"Thanks, Oscar, I will do my best."

ELEVEN

Off We Go....

Oscar dropped Mike off a block from the Air Force Recruiting Office entrance at half past eight a.m. He looked much like any other college-age young man reporting for induction. He handed his letter to the Tech Sergeant sitting at the nearest desk. The Sergeant looked over the letter, asked if he had some identification and his college transcript. Mike responded with both. The Sergeant then directed him to a table and handed him a sheaf of forms to complete.

The paperwork took the better part of an hour. Mike gained confidence with each form. He was amazed at how much he had internalized his new identity and background. After he turned in his papers, the Sergeant reviewed them carefully, indicated that he had no further questions, shook hands with him, and welcomed him into the United States Air Force. He instructed him to report back the day after tomorrow, October 30th, at 0800 with one suitcase, a minimum of civilian clothes and a personal toiletry kit for the train trip to San Antonio, Texas.

"Texas," Mike, thought to himself. "This is something! I have heard about Texas most of my life, and now I am going there!" He recalled seeing a few western cowboy movies which were set in Texas. He couldn't imagine anything being like that place. He was now on his way there!

Mike said goodbye to Oscar and Joe as they dropped him off a block away from the recruiting office. They each wished him well.

He entered the recruiting office foyer to find a dozen guys all about his age with similar bags who were obviously headed for Texas. He was a little frightened at first, neglecting to think that he was not the only one that would be traveling to basic training. He stood aloof, listening to the chatter, not wanting to venture into the scattered conversations. A sergeant stepped into the room with a clipboard in his hand. "Okay, you guys, listen up! Answer 'Here,' when I call your name."

With the roll call complete, he proceeded to read the instructions regarding their train trip to San Antonio. "Jones!" he barked. "You are the biggest guy here, so I am putting you in charge of this group until you get them to Texas. YOU understand?"

The guy named Jones was visibly surprised but finally uttered, "Yessir."

"Don't 'Sir' me, Jones! I am an NCO, and you don't *SIR*, NCO's. Got it?" the Sergeant barked.

"Yessir," Jones answered. The sergeant grinned, shook his head and proceeded to give him the travel instructions in a voice loud enough that everyone could hear and understand, in the event that the nervous Jones didn't. The sergeant then led the group out of the office to two waiting vans at curbside. Then they were off to the train station and the ride to Texas.

Once on the train, Mike felt comfortable enough to engage in conversation with several of those around him. It was good practice for him and helped to relieve his anxiety. He learned that not all of the new recruits were headed for pilot training. All of the others, except he and one other, were going to boot camp for regular enlistments as airmen. The two of them promptly became the envy of the remainder of the new enlistees. He observed quickly that becoming a pilot and officer candidate had the same special distinction as it had back in the Soviet Union. He mused for awhile about how his life had so dramatically changed since he boarded the train in Moscow and headed to Volgograd. It all seemed a distant bad dream which hadn't really happened, but, now he was on another train headed to cadet training. He dreaded that it might be as unbearable as Volgograd. Finally, they arrived at the International Great Northern Station in San Antonio, Texas. Mike tried to act nonchalant as he stepped off the train and joined the others on the blue Air Force bus which took them across the city to Lackland Air Force Base. He was all eyes as he marveled at how clean and open the streets seemed to be. Arriving at the base, they were guided into a building where another fifty or seventy- five more new recruits were waiting. They were instructed to find a seat in the theater-like room. A sergeant in stiffly ironed khakis, with more strips on his sleeves than Mike had ever seen before in Russia, walked to the podium as the room fell quiet.

"Welcome to the Gateway to the Air Force," he began in a very pleasant voice and manner. "I will not take much of your time, but each of you should know that you are about to become a member of a team whose past achievements are without precedent in history, and whose future is as bright as the noon day sun. If you haven't read the history of the United States Air Force, and military aviation, you should. Without a knowledge of our history, you cannot appreciate your heritage. Nor can you understand or appreciate the spirit of restlessness that characterizes our Air Force: the daring quest for the unknown, the courage of your predecessors, the constant seeking of faster, swifter and greater heights of new destinies. Learn our history. Grow to appreciate it. Prize it. Above all, add to it."

Mike was completely absorbed in what the sergeant was saying. He had never heard such eloquent words, especially at Volgograd!

"Okay, now," he shifted his voice to a directive tone. "Each of you were handed a number when you entered the room. When you are dismissed from here, you are to take your personal belongings and assemble outside at the respective sign posts that reflect your number. There, you will meet your DI—your Drill Instructor. He will become your mother, father, minister, priest or rabbi for the next four or six weeks depending on which program you are in. Now, get moving!" The entire room of recruits erupted as if shot by a cannon. Everyone headed toward a door.

Mike was assigned to a flight of other recruits who were also en route to aviation cadet and pilot training. The first week of the scheduled four weeks of his "boot" training breezed by. It was like Heaven compared to his memories of Volgograd. He learned more about his *new* service, the U.S. Air Force, in that first week than he ever learned about the Soviet Air Force. The most dramatic difference was the NCO's. They were tough disciplinarians, but they were also teachers. They had established goals and objectives for their students and helped them achieve them. He promptly fell into the disciplined routine and required courtesies. After the first week, he was appointed Flight Leader of his cadet flight.

He liked wearing the uniform and the starched khakis felt good. He just wished *old* Vlad could see him now. During this period, he was too busy to think about where he was. Nor was he very alert to being contacted by an agent. He was sure, however, that there was a Big Brother somewhere in the vicinity looking over him. The network was too complete, and too tight, to permit him to wander very far from the system, even within the United States. This still amazed him. The time during this initial period in his *new* life was filled with a full schedule of activities: marching drill, medical examination, physical fitness, and psychological and aptitude tests. But oddly enough, he thought, "No political indoctrination, no zampolits! I thought the U.S. was an ideological hot bed of political and military anti-Soviet zeal."

The four weeks of basic military indoctrination training was over quickly. He passed his physical examination and the battery of academic tests with flying colors. Mike, in the uniform of an aviation cadet, was again on his way. This time he was traveling by bus to officer training and pilot school.

He arrived in the small Georgia town of Moultrie, along with sixty fellow cadets to begin Pilot Training Class 54-H at Spence Air Base. Spence was one of a half-dozen civilian contractor-operated primary pilot training bases scattered throughout the Southeast United States. Hawthorne School of Aeronautics was the flying training contractor at Spence. All of the academic and flying training instructors at the contract schools were civilians. The tactical officers who were responsible for military training of the cadets were Air Force officers. This unusual arrangement was precipitated by the accelerated requirement for pilots resulting from the Cold War buildup. The various U.S. Cold War responses caused a relaxation in admissions-screening requirements. Therefore, it was not overly difficult for the internal U.S. KGB and GRU agency system to employ their uncanny skills and successfully obtain an appointment for Mike to enter the Air Force.

The cadets were joined in their class with approximately thirty student officers, mostly second lieutenants, who came into the Air Force already commissioned from either one of the Military Academies, a university R.O.T.C.(Reserve Officers Training Corps) program or officers' candidate school. Mike's class was told that the primary phase of their training at Spence would last approximately six months, after which, those who were still in the program would move on to *Basic* pilot training to specialize for either single-engine jets or multi-engine bombers. Mike already *knew* where he would be going, barring some fluke in the process.

Never Alone

Mike was assigned to a two-man room in a barracks building along with the other cadets. His roommate was his age, from Texas, and had two years of college, the *same* as he. He took to the military training and concurrent academic courses easily. With each passing day he gained increasing confidence in his role. As much as he had despised the two years at Volgograd, the experience had conditioned, and prepared, him for this mission. The military training came easily for him. The discipline structure was an absolute cake *walk* compared to the brutality in the cadet program back home. There were no overbearing NCO's or officers harassing the cadets. To the contrary, they were treated with exceptional respect and dignity. Again, he was struck by the near total lack of political indoctrination. The Soviet Union was seldom mentioned except in a joking manner. There was seldom, if ever, a reference by any of his instructors or fellow cadets to the Soviets as "the enemy."

The Korean War was over. The country seemed reasonably tranquil. "It is no wonder," he thought, "that *our* intelligence agencies can operate with immunity in this country. No one really seemed too concerned about an enemy, or threat to the U.S. homeland." Yet, there was an urgency to train pilots for the Air Force to address the "Cold War" requirements.

The pre-flight academics were challenging for Mike as well as the other cadets. He took each course in stride, studied hard, kept mostly to himself and indulged in trying to excel in each endeavor. He sensed that he was the subject of behind-the- scenes gossip about his stand-offish behavior, but he also knew that if he performed well he would gain the respect of the instructors, and that was all that counted. He could not risk becoming too friendly, or personally acquainted, with any of his classmates for fear of discovery. As a result, he did perform well and enjoyed the respect of the school staff.

As the Aircraft Electronics class ended one afternoon, the instructor, Mr. Harris, dismissed the cadets with, "Mr. Scott, will you please remain for a moment?"

Mike's head snapped sharply toward the instructor. These events usually only happened if there was an academic or disciplinary problem. The other cadets gave him only slight notice as he stood at attention beside his desk waiting for the room to clear.

"Have a seat here, Mr. Scott," Mr. Harris said, motioning him to a chair near his desk. Mike put down his briefcase and sat down.

"Mike, you are doing exceptionally well in the pre-flight program. I want to commend you. You will begin your flying instruction soon, and I am sure that you will do equally well. We are proud of you."

Mike was puzzled. "Thank you, Sir," he responded.

"Mike, do you know what today's date is?"

"Yessir, it is December 15th," he answered, even more puzzled by the strange conversation.

"It's also the 349th day of the year," Harris said. "If I were to hand you this *green* pencil, what would you think about its color?"

Mike was put off at first. "What's this?" his thoughts raced quickly. "Harris was an agent; this is a tes!" he assessed. He had grown lax in scanning his calendar since he had been in training and absorbed in his work. He finally remembered that he had glanced at it hanging in the back of his locker that morning and thought he remembered his *color* for the day. "Yellow, Sir," he blurted.

"Good," Harris replied. "We can talk here for a few minutes. I wanted to wait until you were settled in before I made contact with you. How is it going?"

"Fine," he relaxed, exhaling. "You caught me by surprise. I received a letter from Uncle Oscar last Friday, but he did not indicate that anyone would contact me here."

"Well," Harris chuckled. "You are our prize pupil, so we cannot fail to watch over you and to insure that all is going well. It is, I might add. You excelled beautifully at Lackland indoctrination and are off to a good start here. Mike, I want you to plan to come to my home for the Christmas Holiday week. As you know, training will be suspended on the 21st after duty hours and pick up again on Monday, the 4th of January. Oscar and I have coordinated the plan, and it has been cleared with Roger in Washington. This way, you will not have to travel, we can get some work done here and you can relax for a few days. Okay?"

"Sure, fine with me. To be honest, I knew I would have to make plans to do something, but I did not know what. I am still a novice at this and perhaps rely too much on being taken care of, which you are. Thank you. I hope to become more self-sufficient as I gain more experience."

"You will," Harris replied. "Good, I will plan on picking you up at your barracks next Monday afternoon, and we will depart from there. Bring along some casual civilian clothes and shoes so that you can relax. And, don't worry about the other cadets. It is routine for instructors and faculty to invite cadets in for holiday breaks if they don't have any place to go. If you are quizzed about your plans, just tell them I invited you to spend the week with me and my wife, and you accepted."

Mike departed George Harris' classroom with feelings of confidence and reassurance that he wasn't alone; even here, in an American military training program.

George Harris pulled up in front of Mike's barracks building at 5:00 p.m. Mike was waiting on the steps. Other cadets were rushing off to catch buses and cabs to the nearest bus and train stations. Mike enjoyed the ride off base and down the highway among the Georgia pines. He learned along the way that George Harris had been in the United States for a little over three years and had until recently worked as an aircraft electronics technician at the huge U.S. Air Force maintenance complex in San Antonio. He was a GRU agent. He had been previously assigned to collect information and data on U.S. military aircraft overhaul and maintenance procedures. Then he was directed to take a leave of absence, go to Spence Air Base and apply for a job—any job—and be in position when Mike arrived. Harris said he was fortunate that he was qualified to instruct aircraft electronics in the pilot training course and was hired. He also allowed himself to brag that while at the depot, he had successfully collected virtually every heavy bomber and transport aircraft maintenance procedures document in use by the Air Force and delivered them to the Soviet Embassy in Washington. They, in turn, sent the documents to the Military Aviation Technology Exploitation Division at Khodinka. George was very pleased with his work in the United States.

Mike was greeted warmly by George's wife, Emily. She whispered a quiet "dobre di'en," smiling; "Good afternoon." The Russian greeting sounded strange after so many months of English. She seemed excited and beckoned him in. She showed him to his room in the comfortable home in the country outside the city of Moultrie. Some of the instructors and faculty sought homes in the countryside where it was quiet, and they could plant small gardens and enjoy beautiful trees. For George and Emily Harris, it meant partial seclusion without nosy neighbors. As soon as he deposited his belongings in his room, Emily called George to come and sit down. "Guess what?" she asked. "I have a great surprise!"

Before he could respond, she said, "Galina will be here tomorrow! She just called from New York! She will arrive in Atlanta very early in the morning, catch a bus and be here by late afternoon. She will be here for the holidays!" She added that Galina was met on arrival in New York by a U.S. Aid agent. They would put her safely on the flight to Atlanta, and that someone would also take care of her when she arrived there.

Mike listened as George responded, "That's great, Emily!" "Mike," he quickly turned to him. "Galina is our daughter," he said excitedly. "We haven't seen her in almost three years. She has been working in Moscow since she finished public school. We have been working hard to get her a legitimate student visa so that she can come here and be with us while she attends an American university. And, believe it or not, the Soviet Embassy was successful in negotiating just that! Of course, the U.S. authorities have no idea that the Harrises, who lives in Georgia and volunteered to act as her sponsor, are really her parents!"

Mike smiled and congratulated both of them on the good news. He already felt comfortable and at ease with the Harris family; settled into comfortable clothes the next day and watched as the two excited parents prepared for theisr daughter's arrival. He asked if he might stay at their house the next afternoon when they departed for the Greyhound Bus Depot in Moultrie. He wanted to relax. They agreed.

Galina

At dusk, Mike heard their automobile pull into the driveway and the three-way chatter—some Russian mixed with English—as they closed the doors of the car and trod toward the door.

The three entered the living room where Mike was comfortably seated and reading a magazine. "Mike, please meet our daughter, Galina." Mike rose to his feet and then froze as he looked at the tall blonde girl standing before him.

She likewise, was stunned when she saw Mike. Neither showed any expression, just stared at one another.

It had been almost a year and a half since Mike planned to meet Galina, the dining room hostess, inside a Khodinka entrance gate. He had planned to take her to a gypsy operetta, but she never showed up. He couldn't believe his eyes. He quickly put out his hand and proceeded to greet her, as if for the first time. She, not having any idea of what was going on, did the same. The parents, absorbed in the joy of her presence, did not notice the momentary *"start"* on the part of Mike and Galina.

"Mike will be with us over the holidays, Galina," Emily told her. "This is a treat for him to be able to suspend his training for a few days and to relax with us."

It was now apparent to Mike that the Harris' had not revealed his true identity, and why he was really in their home. Emily had prepared a "welcome home" dinner before they departed to meet Galina. They all sat down to a busy exchange of news and information over the meal. Mike listened quietly and exchanged guarded eye contact with Galina across the table. Not long after dinner, Mike excused himself to let the family reunion continue and went to his room.

With mixed feelings of confusion and excitement at this turn of events, he tried to read for awhile before finally going to sleep. He was awake early the next morning and slipped out of the house to walk in the pine woods surrounding the Harris' home. He had decided that he would not make any overtures toward acknowledging he knew Galina. He would allow the situation to play itself out.

Galina slept most of the day trying to overcome the time difference between Moscow and back here in the United States. Mike spent the day with George, discussing his flight training, what might come next and refreshing himself on normal and emergency procedures for his activities. Late in the afternoon, Emily suggested that perhaps Mike and Galina might like to drive into town and go to a movie. She said that it might help Galina relax, get to know Mike who was near her own age and begin boning-up on her English. After an early dinner, Mike and Galina took George's car and drove off toward town with the traditional parental admonitions to drive carefully and have a good time. Neither said anything until they were well out onto the highway. Finally, Mike blurted out,

"I can't believe that you are here! How on earth could all of this come to pass? What happened to you? Where did you go?"

Galina paused, and took in a deep breath. "I can't believe it, either. This is so strange. What are you doing here in the United States, in my parents' home? I have been a wreck since I arrived last evening. I am still a wreck!"

"Has your father not told you about me?

"No, nothing, other than you are a U.S. Air Force cadet undergoing aircraft flight training or something like that."

The two exchanged bits of information back and forth as they drove down the highway. Galina then began to unfold her story. She said, "On the Sunday that I was supposed to meet you at Khodinka, I received a message which was delivered by a man who came to my apartment. He said you could not meet me that afternoon." She took in a deep breath. "This all so unreal! And, it has been so long. But I want to get the facts straight. Later that same afternoon, an older woman knocked on my door. She said she was from the personnel office at Khodinka. And she told me I was being placed on temporary leave with pay while reorganization was being performed with dining facility workers. The woman collected my identification pass and said it would be reissued when I was called back to work."

She continued as Mike drove around various streets in the small town. "I thought that it all seemed strange, but in Moscow we all had learned to accept abrupt and strange events. After that day, Sasha, I never went back to Khodinka, but, everyone was unusually pleasant to me. After about two weeks, I was reassigned to work for Intourist, in the dining room of the National Hotel near Red Square. I tried desperately to contact you at the Center, but no one would talk to me about where you were or anything about you. Meanwhile," she said, "I began the process to apply for a student visa to go to the United States to study. This was mainly because my parents were here and I had not seen them in over three years. And, now I am here! Sasha, isn't this a miracle?"

Mike briefly spoke about his own experiences, leaving out considerable detail (especially that he had trained at Khodinka to become a Soviet agent). He told her that he was a military "exchange" student similar to her status, and through a joint U.S. - Soviet agreement, enrolled in the flight training program with the U.S. Air Force. He told her he had been in training at Khodinka to learn English in preparation for his assignment in the United States. He also said he had been given an *assumed* name so as not to arouse any problems with fellow cadets. He didn't ask Galina directly if she knew that her father was a Soviet agent, although he suspected that she did not know what his *real* job was.

The two of them talked on, almost forgetting about the movie they were supposed to be going to see. Finally, they parked and rushed in to catch the last half of *FROM HERE TO ETERNITY*, but that was enough for Galina to tell her mother about when they arrived back home.

The following day was Christmas Eve. It dawned on Mike that he had no gifts to give for the next day. This gave him an opportunity to ask George if he could borrow his car to go into the city to purchase a few items. He also asked Galina if she would like to go. She jumped at the chance to be with Mike again. They spent the afternoon enjoying each other's company and their renewed friendship.

The next day found Mike reflecting on the Christmas he had spent with his parents the year before. He wondered what they were doing this day, and how they were. The months since he left Khodinka and entered the U.S. had been so busy he had hardly had time to think about his parents. This brief respite from the grind, and pressure, over the holidays had given him time to think about his mother and father as well as the reality of where he was and what may be ahead of him.

The remainder of the holiday break was pleasantly spent with George, Emily, and especially, Galina. All too soon, the end of the week arrived, and Mike was back in his cadet barracks preparing to resume training. Galina, meanwhile, was planning to enroll in a small college in Alabama the following summer, where she had been referred by the Health Welfare and Education offices in Washington. The spring gave her and Mike the opportunity to see each other when he could get away on weekends. George Harris liked the arrangement. It gave him time with Mike to review his progress, provide guidance, and to insure that he *remained* a faithful Soviet.

Flight Training

Pre-flight academics and officer training progressed until time for flight training to begin. When Mike marched with his cadet unit to the flight line for the first time, his adrenalin spiked at the sight of the sprite yellow AT-6 trainers parked uniformly on the ramp. He was surprised by the extraordinary number of aircraft. "There are at least seventy-five or a hundred!" he thought. He was assigned to a flight instructor along with two other cadets and a student officer. Throughout his preflight training, Mike was continuously amazed at the difference between the harsh, and often brutal, discipline that he had endured during the two years at Volgograd compared to the straight-forward business-like training by the NCO's and training officers in the U.S. program. The same proved true with his flight instructor. He was pleasant and engendered confidence in the four student pilots he was assigned to teach.

Mike's turn came to be introduced to the AT-6. He carefully listened to his instructor, as he had with Major Ruzhko, but he gave no indication that he had ever been near this type trainer, nor that he had ever flown one. Finally, he climbed into the front cockpit of the "T-6", as it was more often referred to, strapped into his parachute and followed the instructions to start the engine. He was excited. His recall of the brief exposure to the aircraft at Khodinka easily came back to him.

During his first flight, Mike conducted himself as if he had never flown before and displayed some clumsiness when he was instructed to initiate a few basic maneuvers. But clearly after his second flight, he moved rapidly to head of the class in his flying skill. His instructor praised him after each flight lesson. He raved to the other instructors that Mike was a natural born aviator.

Mike was impressed with the training techniques used by the Air Force. The Basic Flying Handbook contained clever cliché's and thoughtful admonishments: "BE EAGER! BE FIT! BE READY! VISUALIZE THE MANEUVER! ANALYZE! MASTER THE SMALL THINGS and DON'T BECOME DISCOURAGED!" The "Before Take-Off" acronym, "CIG-F-TPRS," meant Controls (move freely), Instruments (set properly), Gas selector set, Flaps up, Trim tabs set properly, Propeller set full pitch, Radio on and checked, and Safety belt and harness locked. Before landing, "GUMP" meant, Gas set on fullest tank, Undercarriage (landing gear) down, Mixture control set Full Rich, and Propeller Control set to 2000 rpm.

Mike memorized every procedure and literally every word in the Flight Manual. He prided himself in demonstrating his professionalism. He soloed the T-6 in minimum time and was the first in his class to be thrown into the base swimming pool by his classmates, carrying out the ritual which commemorated his feat. Likewise, he passed all of his phased flight checks with ease.

The completion of primary flight training came all too soon, especially since he would be leaving Georgia, and Galina as well. There was little doubt on the part of either that they were in love. However, the strict discipline within them prevented them from betraying their feelings. During their final visit, they kissed warmly for the last time. They pledged to remain in touch through letters and to see each other again as soon as possible.

Mike's performance and grades permitted him to choose his next type of training. His instructor insisted that he apply for single-engine basic training which meant that he would go on to fly jet fighters. But Mike told him, falsely, that he had always wanted to fly big airplanes and requested to go to multi-engine training. The choice sent him to Vance Air Force Base near Enid, Oklahoma, where he was trained briefly to fly the T-28, a new single-engine trainer with tricycle landing gear and a more powerful engine. This would be Mike's last opportunity to *feel* like a "fighter pilot."

His class soon moved into the TB-25 twin engine trainer, the same type of light bomber that Jimmy Doolittle and his crews flew off the carrier deck of the USS Hornet to make the daring bombing attack on Japan in 1942. He wasn't disappointed in flying the TB-25. It had more engine power than he had anticipated and had the solid "feel" of real air power.

Mike stayed in touch with Galina by mail. She had enrolled in Troy State College in Alabama and was mastering her studies reasonably well. She also told him that her father, George, and her mother had moved back to Texas, and was again working at the Air Force maintenance complex at San Antonio. This didn't surprise Mike, who by now was getting used to the way *the system* worked. Although he had not been contacted directly by anyone since he arrived in Oklahoma, he felt sure that he was being closely monitored. He continued to receive letters from Oscar, most of which were intended to keep the channel open should he encounter any difficulties.

One evening while he was studying, an Orderly Room clerk knocked on his door and told him that he need to call "Joe," there was a "family emergency." Mike's mouth went dry and his heart pumped as he got dressed while trying to rationally interpret the message. Had it been a call from Oscar, he would have understood it more clearly. but "Why was Joe calling?" He instinctively knew that the phone number given him by the orderly was for a pay phone and that he needed to move quickly to return the call. He got dressed without trying to make the phone message appear routine to his roommate and made his way to the row of pay phone booths outside the orderly room building and placed the call to Joe.

"Mike, what took you so long?" the irritated voice answering the pay phone in Cleveland responded. "I've been guarding this pay phone for half an hour!"

"Sorry," said Mike. He was now more calm than when he first received the message. "It's not easy here to dash out and make a phone call. What's up?"

"Oscar is what's up," Joe answered in a shaky voice. "He's been taken out!"

"What do you mean, taken out?"

"He was arrested this afternoon. He got into a fight with one of those stupid union goons. It looked routine at first when he called me. But when the police got to checking his background, they got suspicious after they kept hitting blind alleys, so they called in the FBI. This ain't good, Mike. He is in real trouble!"

"What do I need to do? Mike asked.

"Nothing. Sit tight and hold your breath. Maybe you will be clear. I went to his house as soon as he called me and went through our *routine*. He had all of our *business* files organized in one place and I took them out. So there should not be a trail to you or me. We will just have to sweat it out."

Mike's mind was running a mile a minute. "Are you sure there are no letters or documents relating to me? Have you notified Roger?"

"I have made the necessary calls and as far as I could tell, Oscar's house is clean. He was very organized and kept perfect records, all in one place just for such an emergency. Do you have any letters or anything with his name on it?"

"No, no letters. I always destroyed them after reading. The only thing I can think of is his name is on file as my only relative. That scares me."

"Yeah, me too. Not now, but later you need to change that. Get his name removed from any of your records. Got it? Don't panic, but get it done routinely. You may not hear from me again, since they may have traced the call he made to me and may come looking. For right now, I have been told to sit tight and if the snoops do come, I will just tell them he was a casual friend, and I didn't know anything about him. In your case, if they come, just play it dumb and say he was your adopted uncle and you don't know anymore than that. Okay? I gotta run. Good luck!"

Mike endured a restless night after the call, but finally he took control of his emotions and prepared for the worst. It never came. He heard no more from Joe. He continued with the final phase of his training, but always with a nagging concern for Oscar's fate in the back of his mind, as well as his own!

Finally the day arrived when flight training was completed along with officer candidate training.

TWELVE

...Into the Wild Blue Yonder

"I John Michael Scott, having been appointed a second lieutenant in the United States Air Force, do accept such appointment and do solemnly swear that I will support and defend the Constitution of the United States against all enemies, foreign and domestic, that I will bear true faith and allegiance to the same; that I take this obligation freely, without any mental reservation or purpose of evasion; and that I will faithfully discharge the duties of the office on which I am about to enter, so help me God."

He heard the words of the oath clearly, but he could not audibly repeat them, only lip-sync silently. Once again, Mike felt the return of the turmoil of stomach discomfort and a familiar twinge in his nervous system as he stood along side his fellow aviation cadets taking the officer's commission oath of office in unison. He recalled taking the oath of a Soviet soldier when he first entered the aviation college at Volgograd, and the threat of severe punishment if he did not fully obey the "laws of the Soviet people." There were no threats in this oath, only a responsibility to "support and defend the Constitution of the United States against all enemies . . ." Suddenly he felt frightened and threatened by where he was and what he was doing. He thought about Oscar. "Where was he? What happened to him?" he pondered. He was also deeply concerned for his own welfare. What if the FBI or someone traced Oscar to him? What then? Would I handle it okay?" But he had continuously assured himself that Oscar was smart, and would "go along" with the authorities, even to the point of being expelled from the United States, if that was what it came down to.

As he contemplated his fate, the commandant of cadets stepped up to him, pinned on his silver pilot's wings and congratulated him for graduating first in his class. He shook the commandant's hand, and mechanically, saluted smartly.

Parents and relatives of the cadets converged on the formation to offer congratulations and to pin on their shiny second lieutenant's bars. Mike stood alone, watching the joyful activities and chatter, when suddenly Galina stood directly before him, looking as beautiful as he could ever remember.

"Hello, Mike," she said. "Congratulations, Lieutenant! You look great in your uniform with your new pilot's wings, but who's going to pin on your gold bars?"

"Galina! I can't believe it. How did you get here? Why didn't you tell me you were coming? How did you find me?"

"Give me the bars," she said. "You can't go very far out of proper uniform!"

She took the gold bars from the grip of Mike's sweaty palm and neatly pinned one on each shoulder epaulet of his uniform. "Well, where do you go from here?" she asked.

Mike, was shocked by Galina's sudden appearance. "Well, where do you go from here?" he smiled.

"I started my Christmas break two days early. My father gave me permission to come. He sent me the bus fare, and he also asked me to invite you to come to San Antonio and be with us for the holidays. Would you like to come?"

Mike looked deeply into her eyes. "Yes, yes I would," he quickly blurted, "more than you know! I can't believe all of this!" A smile spread across his face. "You and your parents are wonderful!"

Two weeks before graduation, Mike bought a late-model used car and had already loaded his few belongings. He told Galina he had to report to James Connally Air Force Base near Waco, Texas, on January 3rd to attend a nine-week airborne observer's course tailored for pilots who were bound for B-47 and B-52 training. His assignment, after Waco, was to be at Castle Air Force Base, California, where the first B-52's would be stationed. He said he

184 | *Chris Adams*

presumed that, after initial training as a B-52 co-pilot, he would likely remain at Castle and be assigned to a combat crew there.

Galina was not happy with the news. His assignments meant that he would be even farther away than he had been here in Oklahoma. Then her spirits brightened. "This is the 22nd of December, so we have almost two weeks before you have to go!"

"Where is your bag?" Mike asked.

"It's over there in your orderly room. They let me put it there while I attended the ceremony."

"Let's go," he said.

Mike and Galina spent an idyllic afternoon and night together before they drove off to San Antonio. It was their first. In their innocence, they professed their love for each other and promised that, no matter what, they would be together always. Their naiveté was touching.

The following morning, in high spirits and very much in love, they drove off in Mike's 1950 model Chevrolet and headed South to San Antonio. He still wondered how much she knew of her father's work, and, for that matter, his. Finally, he dismissed the thought from his mind, concentrated on his driving and being with Galina.

This was the second Christmas holiday that Mike would spend with Galina and her parents. George and Emily were great people, he thought. This was almost like being back home, but in a strange way. He asked George if he knew anything about Oscar. George replied, "I have heard nothing. It is best to forget Oscar. When one of our people is taken out, we let them go from our thoughts. They will not be of any further use to us. So, let us hope that he left no trail that can be followed to anyone." Mike recognized the wisdom of George's practical and unfeeling attitude. The eleven days whisked by with Mike and Galina buzzing all around San Antonio in the bright and pleasant December weather of Southwest Texas. Finally, he once again had to say goodbye to Galina. Mike proceeded to Waco, one hundred and seventy miles up the road from San Antonio. Galina returned to Alabama and school.

The "AOB" course, as it was called, presented little challenge for Mike. The routine amounted to classroom academics on the theory of radar navigation, the use of the equipment and flying training in the Convair T-29 Navigation Trainer. It was the twin-engine military version of the commercial Convair 240/340 series passenger model. The interior of the T-29 was configured with navigation stations complete with operating radar systems for both navigation and simulated bombing. Actually, he found it to be a "fun" course with very little pressure, but he did miss flying in the cockpit of an airplane. By the end of the course, he and his fellow students would be a unique breed of aviator. They would be 'triple rated': pilot, navigator and radar bombardier.

After completing the course at James Connally, Mike had two weeks before reporting to Castle Air Force Base for B-52 training. Since he had no other instructions from *anyone* in the system, he immediately headed for Troy, Alabama, and Galina.

He had never driven so far in his life, but he arrived safely in Troy in the early hours of the morning and found a motel on the edge of town. He felt that he was becoming more *American* with each passing day he spent in the United States, and the thought often haunted him. Since graduation and commissioning, he also felt a new sense of freedom. During his free time he could go 'any where' he wished. At times over the past two months, Mike felt abandoned. He had not heard from anyone since Joe called him about Oscar. He presumed that he was to proceed with his Air Force assignments and await further contact and instructions should there be any. He still did not know the nature of his real mission.

Here he was, an officer and a pilot in the U.S. Air Force. It had been easy enough to get to this point. "But what was next? Who was in charge? Where was this *Roger* agent who was in charge of everything?" He was tempted to call Galina's father, George Harris, but he decided against it. He had visited with him over Christmas, and George had no further instructions for him. The *"system"* knew where he was and would make contact when the time was right. The fact no one had contacted him gave him a sense of self confidence and independence, although in the back of his mind, he still knew that he was being closely monitored. That was the way it worked.

Mike surprised Galina when he called at her dormitory. They enjoyed three wonderful days together before he departed to "find" his way to Merced, California, and his assignment to fly the Air Force's newest strategic bomber, the B-52.

Strategic Air Command

Mike checked into the 93rd Bomb Wing headquarters orderly room two days before he was due to report. He was greeted warmly by the headquarters squadron commander, a major, who gave him a brief orientation of the base and where he would be living. He had been assigned a private BOQ (Bachelor Officers' Quarters) room, which amounted to a small apartment in a two-story complex on the base.

Mike enjoyed the feeling of being an officer. The major told him that he would be assigned to the first operational B-52 squadron for ground training and indoctrination. The first new bomber would be delivered to Strategic Air Command (SAC), a couple months hence, in June. In the meantime, he would join both young pilot training graduates like himself, and many older pilots, in ground school. The older pilots were all former B-47 pilots and radar navigators, coming together in the wing to be the first to fly the new B-52.

"You are very fortunate," the major told him. "There are only half a dozen new pilot training graduates coming into the program. The rest are all old SAC 'heads' with thousands of hours of flying time behind them." He continued, "If you're lucky, you'll be assigned to one of the 'old heads' as a co-pilot trainee and move right along with him. If not, you may go into a cadre of younger pilots and wait your turn to be assigned to a crew. All of that will be determined by the squadron operations officer."

Mike had been fully indoctrinated on the Strategic Air Command during his training at Khodinka. He knew the history of the U.S. Air Forces *elite* strategic fighting force and the threat that it posed to the Soviet Union. "SAC" had evolved out of World War II. It had inherited a legacy of long-range strategic bombing operational capabilities. Under the leadership of Major General Curtis LeMay, U.S. Air Force B-29's had dropped the atomic bombs on Hiroshima and Nagasaki, Japan. This effectively ended the war for the United States. After the war, LeMay directed the airlift that kept the people of Berlin fed and safe when Stalin embargoed the city.

Now, General LeMay was Commander-in-Chief of SAC. This elite U.S. strategic fighting force had grown rapidly from the remnants of leftover B-29 and B-50 bombers, at the outset of the Cold War in 1947, to almost 200,000 officers, airmen and 2,800 aircraft: included were the mighty B-36, the all-jet B-47, prop-driven KC-97 and jet powered KC-135 airborne tankers by 1955. The command had 1,200 B-47's alone, supported by a world-wide airborne tanker force. In all, there were twenty-three wings of B-47's, six wings of B-36's, and one B-52 wing being created. There were also two air refueling wings and a whopping thirty-six air refueling squadrons. Castle Air Force Base had been selected to receive the first B-52 heavy bomber wing. The eight-jet bomber would eventually replace the B-36.

Mike had been oriented on the awesome SAC structure and capability. He attended 'newcomers' sessions intended to welcome newly assigned personnel to the future Castle B-52 operations. He reflected that he had never been told, nor even dreamed, the United States possessed such overwhelming strategic capability. As he listened to the awesome numbers of aircraft, the descriptions of intense training feats and demonstrations of enduring air power, he reflected upon the Soviet's boasts of their own great air force. The most impressive feature of SAC, which he was sure that his superiors back home must be aware, was the virtual "free-roaming" ability of its bomber and tanker forces. Routinely, B-36's flew nonstop from their U.S. home bases to Guam and to North Africa. The B-36's stood by on alert with atomic weapons, should the Soviet Union decide to do something untoward. The B-47's were even more impressive. They flew 10,000 mile nonstop training sorties, supported by tankers, to and from Europe and Japan.

SAC leadership claimed that the bomber and tanker crews were flying 50,000 hours per month training and refining procedures. They also boasted of thirty-two active air force bases, including twelve in overseas locations from Guam to England and North Africa. Looking at a map projected on the huge screen in the theater during one orientation session, Mike reasoned, correctly, that the Soviet Union was virtually "surrounded" by U.S. long-range strategic bombers with atomic bomb carrying capability. Surely, he thought, his father and the Soviet general staff must be aware of all of this. How could they not be?

Yet, here he was, in the middle of all this, exposed to information and factual data with, apparently, no one to talk to nor tell. He shuttered at the thought that his government could make a false move and suddenly be destroyed by the might of the U.S. The first few weeks of orientation progressed, and he prepared to begin training. He waited patiently to be contacted by someone; "anyone," he thought, to discuss what he was learning and what actions he might take. The *system* surely had an agent, or agents, somewhere in the area monitoring all of this!

Following the newcomers' orientation and the routines of checking in to his assigned squadron, Mike was confronted with an unexpected test. He should have anticipated that the personnel system would eventually begin processing him for a security clearance. Sure enough, he was handed a lengthy, multi-page form to complete for a *Secret* clearance. He was told that he would be automatically granted an interim-Secret clearance, but a routine background check would be required to provide him a permanent clearance. He was also advised that, eventually, he would be subjected to an "extended background" check by the Air Force Office of Special Investigation (OSI), or the FBI, in order to grant him a *Top Secret (TS)* clearance. The TS would be required for access to information on atomic and nuclear weapons as well as SAC mission planning. He carefully completed the clearance questionnaire, nervously inserting Oscar's name as his only living relative.

"God," he thought, "I need someone to talk to. At this rate, I could be in more trouble than I could ever get out of!" He finally resolved to let it rest. "What will be, will be," he thought with a shrug. Fortunately, the personnel security system was so overburdened during SAC's rapid build up that Secret clearances were handled and granted routinely, with little more than cursory reviews of the questionnaires to verify the presumed accuracy of the individual completing them. In the case of a commissioned officer, the clearances were virtually automatic. Mike would have to address the Top Secret clearance issue later on. Unfortunately, this gave Mike one more issue to clutter his mind and to bear on his conscience.

Along with both old and new pilots and crew members, he reported to the training squadron to begin B-52 ground school. The class was told that the pilots would spend four weeks studying the new bomber's aircraft systems: electrical, hydraulic, flight controls, radios, radar, fire control and weapons capabilities. After that, they would be paired up for simulator training, "flying on the ground" as a pilot and co-pilot in the B-52 mock up simulator. The simulator could essentially replicate most all aircraft systems operations, as well as assist in developing crew procedures and coordination. Ground school was not at all difficult for Mike. He had long since developed study and learning techniques. Consequently, he virtually "aced" every written exam.

He also quickly earned the reputation as the class *smart ass* by some of the other pilots who did not apply themselves as well. But his performance was not lost on the squadron operations officer who had begun early on pairing up potential training crews to move into the simulator and B-52 flight training. Mike was assigned to fly with a Major Hank Johnson, a former B-47 aircraft commander with several thousand flying hours and a sterling reputation as a SAC pilot. He was the only one of his classmates from AOB school to be assigned directly to a crew although he was advised that he was assigned pending proof of his performance. The others, along with a number of the older pilots, were lumped together and paired to train with each other until their true skills could be determined. Mike was learning fast that SAC discipline and expectations were absolute. "You either cut it or you get cut," was the word that quickly aroused the attention of those who thought that they could just give it "the old college try."

The wing commander of the first B-52 wing was a bright, steely-disciplined brigadier general, handpicked by General LeMay to get this new bomber and its combat crews, up and running in short order and with the same exacting professionalism expected throughout the command. The general's influence became readily apparent as the crews began simulator training. The classes ran in six-hour shifts up to eighteen hours a day. It was not unusual for the general to pop his head in the cockpit of the simulator and observe the pilot's and copilot's performance, coordination, attitude and decorum. He would also "pop" questions to them on how "this" operated or how "that" worked. If the crew's performance was going well and they responded correctly to his questions, they would get a pat on the shoulder and likely not see him again for a while. If they were not, "hell, fire and brimstone" would come pouring down on the unfortunate crew members.

SAC was tough. Mike was impressed. He learned a great deal from Major Johnson about SAC operations and expectations of its assigned people. He wondered if his Soviet strategic bomber crew counterparts in *SOVAC* were as motivated and disciplined as those with whom he now associated within SAC. Johnson told him that, at first, he was disappointed when Mike was assigned to try out as his copilot. But after the second simulator session, he was impressed with Mike's exceptional knowledge of B-52 systems and his self-confidence in performing his duties. Hank also told him that after they completed simulator training, the remainder of the crew members would join them. They would pick up his "old" radar-navigator from his B-47 crew, and they would get a new navigator, ECM officer and an enlisted gunner, all of whom were concurrently undergoing their own individual crew specialty training. Eventually, the six would become an "integrated" SAC combat crew; that is, they would, almost without exception, fly together as a crew. There would be minimal swapping around among crew members. They would literally eat, work, fly and play together as a unit and as a family. He knew that Major Johnson would be a tough disciplinarian, no-nonsense pilot and boss. Mike could see in him an officer who was destined to rise to the top in SAC and the Air Force. He knew Johnson would work his crew and himself very hard to get there.

Mike often felt pangs of guilt and frustration; however, he never let slip from his inner-most thoughts and doctrinal training his true identity and what he must do when called upon by his government. He was first and always a Soviet officer, agent and loyal communist. He would obey any order given him. He had learned to live with his double life and, essentially, a split personality. He found a respite in his private room in the BOQ. After studying everything he could about the B-52 and being a SAC crew member, he would complete the self-study session with a "deep conscious thought" period. He would recall every aspect of his training at Khodinka: at the dacha, in New York and with Oscar in Cleveland. He did not want to lose the edge of who he was and what he might be called upon to do.

He would often go into deep thought about his parents. "Were they okay? Were they well? How was his mother coping with her mixed life of loyalty and disloyalty?" He also developed an ability not to drift too deeply into sentimental reflection or feelings of insecurity. The thoughts of meeting the challenges of performance in his new life in the U.S. Air Force, and now on a B-52 bomber crew, kept him focused and clearheaded. Matching knowledge and performance, wits with Major Johnson were his daily challenges. He met them well. He listened carefully, not only to Johnson, but to anyone he considered credible. He learned quickly. The process became a high-stakes game just as it had from the day Vlad challenged him at Volgograd and he went off to Khodinka. He was now mentally tough, and emotionally strong enough to take on any problem, surprise, or threat.

The sudden *demise* of Oscar had temporarily thrown him a curve, but he had quickly absorbed its impact and potential complications and moved on. Discussions with Galina's father, George Harris, had helped greatly. Although he knew there would be other stressful times ahead, he also knew that if he "played it cool," there would always be a way to solve the problem. This game of psychological reinforcement that he played each night gave him a renewed sense of self-confidence. Each morning he woke early, suited up in his jogging clothes and sprinted any lingering doubts out of his system.

Dan

Several months into B-52 ground school and simulator training, Mike was jogging around the interior perimeter of the base as was his routine, when he was joined by another jogger who came out of nowhere.

"Hi, Mike," greeted the stranger, who was puffing considerably harder than his new running mate. "I'm Dan, a friend of Roger's. It is inconvenient to flash colors at you, but when you return to your room, check out *black* and *red* for today, Monday the sixteenth of May." The stranger then handed him a small folded piece of paper. "Call me tonight after ten o'clock from a pay phone." Then the stranger promptly turned back and jogged in the direction from which he came.

The new contact happened that quickly. The encounter surprised Mike, but it did not alarm him. He was getting used to the routine and knew that sooner or later he would be "back in the loop." As he continued his run, he had mixed feelings about this new agent. This would add another dimension and, undoubtedly, more stress to his routine. On the other hand, he felt a sense of comfort that he "was not alone."

Once again, he had a fellow Soviet agent with him—someone who could reinforce his confidence in his mission. He wondered, "What was next? What were *Dan's* orders and instructions for him? What would he have him do?"

Back in his BOQ room, he quickly looked at his May 1955 calendar hanging in the bedroom. It had been given to him by George Harris over the Christmas break. He had no doubt that the 16th of the month block would have a *black* and a *red* dot in the specified corners. It did.

This Monday was a scheduled day of academics in the B-52 ground school and provided no additional pressure to Mike's thoughts. He continued his study routine after dinner. Shortly before 10:00 p.m., he drove off base a mile or so to a service station with a couple of pay phones located outside. He placed a call to Dan. They exchanged some color codes and personal identifier information. Then he listened to Dan's story. He seemed pleasant enough, not overly directive. He revealed no detectable accent. Neither did he say where he lived, or worked, nor how he came to be jogging on the base that morning. He told Mike that he would be his principal contact at Castle.

"Use this phone number for now," he said. "I will contact you later, and we can meet and get to know one another. In the meantime, I know you're very busy, and you need to continue to work and perform in your training."

"Thanks," Mike replied, "but I do need to talk to you about an important issue which has come up. I need your advice and likely your help."

Dan agreed to get back to him. The issue Mike had in mind was the inevitable requirement to complete the security forms required to initiate an extended background investigation for a Top Secret clearance. The TS clearance processing would have to be at least "in progress" when he began to upgrade as a copilot on a combat ready B-52 crew. All in all, the conversation with Dan did not provide Mike with very much comfort, only that he was in the area if he needed him. He didn't ask him to do anything except to continue what he was doing.

The next evening, however, when Mike arrived back to his BOQ room after a mentally and physically draining six-hour simulator session, he found a note that had been slipped under the door. It read: "Call me for an appointment Dan." The note didn't say when to call. Mike showered, dressed, went by the officers' club for a quick dinner and drove off base around 10:00 p.m.

This time he drove in the opposite direction of the service station where he made his last call. Dan inquired about his schedule for the week, and they made arrangements to meet the following Thursday around six p.m. at a small cafe several miles North of Merced on Highway 99, near the small town of Turlock. "Look for a New York Jets ball cap in the rear window of my car," Dan concluded.

On the designated Thursday at six a.m., Mike and Hank Johnson were scheduled for their last simulator ride which was an evaluation check ride. Mike wanted to get that event out of the way before he met with Dan. The fewer things on his mind the better, he thought. He hoped the meeting with Dan would be a respite from the stress of the day. The simulator check ride went very well. The evaluator was extremely complimentary about the demonstrated proficiency of both Mike and Hank. He stated that their crew coordination was superb, and they made a "great pilot team." Hank told Mike afterward he was doubly pleased to have him on his crew as copilot, and he hoped the other members of the crew would be as dedicated to the job as he was. Hank also invited him to join him and the other members of their crew-to-be for a few beers that afternoon to celebrate. Mike agreed, saying also that he had a dinner appointment later on, so he couldn't stay long.

Hank didn't inquire about his dinner appointment. This greatly relieved Mike. "Hank," he thought, "was going to be okay to work with. He is not inquisitive about my personal life. He keeps everything on a professional basis, and he seems to have only one thing in mind—to command a first-rate SAC bomber crew." Mike looked forward to meeting the other crew members and fervently hoped that he would find the same attitude and demeanor amongst them.

At four p.m., Mike drove over to the officer's club, the appointed time set by Hank to meet the other crew members. He strolled into the dimly lit bar and spotted Hank with several others seated at a corner table. "Hey, Mike!" beckoned Hank when he spotted him. "Come on over and meet our crew."

Hank stood and shook hands with Mike and thanked him for his performance during simulator training. "Guys, I want you to meet the sharpest copilot in SAC! Mike is fresh out of pilot training and AOB school, and I predict he will be a top gun B-52 pilot in the very near future." Hank was euphoric and embarrassed Mike with his laudatory introduction.

Mike shook hands and introduced himself again to each of the fellows seated around the table. Major Bill Clements was the radar navigator from Hank's old B-47 crew. Captain Mac Abrams was the navigator, also from B-47s at another base. The electronic warfare officer was First Lieutenant Toby Clark. He was a former enlisted NCO who had gone to OCS and previously flown B-36's as a flight engineer, and he had volunteered for ECM school so he could fly B-52's. In civilian clothes was Sam Allen, the gunner. He was a tech sergeant and not authorized to be in the officers' club, but Hank broke the rules in this case so that they could all meet together on this first occasion. "Well," said Bill Clements, "it isn't often we see a second lieutenant on a crew, especially on a brand new B-52 crew."

Hank piped in immediately, "Fellows, Mike may be wearing a pair of gold bars, but I want to tell you, and I will in front of him, he is the quickest study and fastest learner in an airplane cockpit I have ever seen." He continued, "I was dubious at first, but after the ops officer told me about his records in flight school and down at AOB, I took a chance. I want to tell you HE IS SHARP!"

Mike was embarrassed. "Thanks, Major," he said looking around sheepishly.

"Okay, the beers are on me!" Hank said, breaking up the timid silence. They all responded with a shout and clap of the hands. "Mike has to leave in an hour for another appointment—a super date, I hope! I wanted to get all of you together for a few minutes to tell you that it's my goal for each of you to make us the best damn B-52 crew in this wing, and help us make the wing the best in SAC!" Again they all responded with tempered "hear, hear's" and hand claps. "Every time one of you screws up," he continued, "the beers will be on you! The first "Buff", (the B-52 was affectionately referred to as the "Big Ugly Fellow" and similar references), is going to be delivered on the 29th of next month, and I hope they come fast after that so we can start flying. In the meantime, I expect each of you to keep your heads in the books. Walk around and ask questions, go over to the ground school, and whenever possible, go sit in your simulator trainers and get to know your systems operations."

Mike observed the developing camaraderie. He also noted the most serious and determined tone in Hank's remarks. He was a professional, and he was going to make sure that everyone on his crew became one also—if they weren't already. Mike liked the situation. The more the seriousness, then the less fun and games, and less socializing with the crew, he hoped.

Mike listened to the talk of the others and only responded when asked a specific question: "Where are you from?" "Married?" "Family?" "What do you think about the Air Force?" "Why did you sign up?" He responded to each query carefully. He had to keep his stories straight and uncomplicated because the questions would likely come up again. At five o'clock, Mike stood and asked Hank to be excused. His new aircraft commander reiterated how pleased he was with the way everything had "really hit the mark" during their training. Mike finally shook hands with the others and left the officers' club.

He went to his room, changed into casual civilian clothes and headed out the main gate of the base and over to Highway 99. He easily found the roadside cafe, just as Dan had described it, and spotted a black Ford sedan with a bright green New York Jets ball cap prominently placed on the rear window shelf. Mike parked his car out of sight of the highway and went inside. It was five minutes to six o'clock. He spotted a lone individual sitting in a rear booth and headed in that direction. Mike hoped to identify the person he had barely caught a glimpse of on the morning of the jogging encounter. Sure enough, it was Dan. He motioned for Mike to have a seat opposite him and held out his hand. Mike shook hands with him as he took his seat in the booth. In a low voice, Dan greeted Mike. "Hello, Comrade. It is good to finally really meet with you."

"Same here," Mike responded as he looked around to see if he could identify any Air Force people from the base in the cafe. He saw none.

They looked over the menu without speaking. Each gave the waitress their order when she arrived. "Mike, I don't want to spend much time here with you since I don't know how risky this place is, so I will give you a few requests from on high and listen to any problems you have. We can meet somewhere else again, later on." Dan got right to the point of the meeting. "We would like to have the latest copy of the new B-52 Dash-1 operating procedures tech order and the Dash-2 performance manual. Are you settled into the organization sufficiently to get spare copies of these documents?"

"Yes," Mike said. He had already anticipated this request and had "picked up" a copy of each that he had seen lying on a table in the squadron study lounge. Some unfortunate pilot likely had to confess that he had lost his tech orders. Although they were not classified, tech orders were not to be casually lost. Mike had not brought along the documents to this meeting, but now wished he had.

"Good," said Dan. "I thought you could. Now here is a more difficult challenge. We also would like to have copies of the B-52 maintenance manuals, engine, electrical, weapon system, avionics, the whole bash. What about that?"

Mike felt a little queasy and replied, "That is a difficult order. I am brand new in the unit and only a second lieutenant at that. I may have some difficulty getting close to those documents since I don't normally *belong* around the maintenance training facility. But," he continued, "I will give it a try. I am finished with my ground training for now until the new bombers begin to arrive next month. I should be able to nose around different areas in the interest of learning more about the airplane and provide you with the operating and performance manuals anytime you want them."

"That's okay. We'll meet again in a few days and I can get them then. In the meantime, work on the heavy duty maintenance books."

The waitress delivered their food, and they diverted their conversation to the weather and pleasant California spring. As they ate, Dan asked, "What about you? Are you doing okay? Have you had any problems? Is there anything I need to do for you?"

Mike thought to himself, "Well, it is about time someone inquired about my welfare." But he didn't speak to that. He said, "I have a potential problem coming up. I have to turn in my forms for processing a Top Secret clearance. When I turn them in, I am told that they will conduct what they call an EBI (extended background investigation) by either the OSI or the FBI. They will go as far back as they can with family, friends, law enforcement, and so on, to determine whether I am a security risk. My concern is that when they look into my past, they are going to hit a brick wall and come back to me. What do you suggest?"

"Okay," Dan acknowledged. "We have had this come up before. I have already begun to run the traps within your personnel office and the local OSI. I may have found a trap door. There is a lady, a secretary, in the OSI office who is responsible for processing clearance requests. I won't go into all the details, but I believe she may be vulnerable to help us. She is divorced, has four kids, and could use some financial help. I want you to drag your feet in turning in your clearance paperwork for as long as you can. First, that will give me time to cultivate the situation. Second, the delay will hopefully allow a big build up of requests. They may not be as meticulous as they ordinarily would be in performing the background checks and processing the clearances."

"What if I am pressured for the clearance forms?" Mike asked. "My aircraft commander is a real tyrant for efficiency."

"Just tell him, or the personnel folks, that you, as an orphan, are trying diligently to fill in as many details as possible and will get it done as soon as possible. My plan is to work as fast as I can to get something working with the lady, but I have to be careful and not risk overplaying the situation by trying to move too fast. I think I have a plan that will work."

Mike preceded, "What about Oscar? Do I put his name on these forms, as I did the others, as my only living relative? Where is he any way?"

Dan was uncomfortable with the questions. "First of all, I hope that dumb ass is under an American jail somewhere. He has made all of this very difficult for us, and your project, in particular. I don't know where he is. His high and mighty temper got him into serious trouble. It could eventually jeopardize this and other projects. We hope not. In any case, you will have to put down his name, as you have done so on other documents in the past. Just hope that I can finesse the situation before it gets out of hand! I will keep you informed and let you know when to submit your papers to the personnel office."

They finished their meal and talked about when and where to meet again. Dan suggested the following week, also on Thursday evening, since it was a relatively slow evening of the week with not too many people wandering about. He said that they should meet at a different restaurant and on the south side of town. He gave Mike the name and address of one and added that Mike should bring anything that he had collected in a paper grocery sack, with a loaf of bread or something similar sticking out the top of the bag. During the entire conversation, there was no mention of who Dan was, where he lived or what his cover or job was in that particular area. Neither could Mike figure out whether he were a Russian or an American. If Dan were Russian, he had been in this country for quite sometime and had successfully integrated himself into the culture. He had not the slightest hint of an accent or any word pronunciation difficulty. He was a natural and a pro!

The intensity and pressure of training settled down considerably over the next several weeks. Hank wanted to meet with his crew a couple of times each week to get to know them better and to insure that they were working diligently on their preparations to begin B-52 flight training once the aircraft began arriving. The additional time gave Mike the opportunity to begin moving around areas of the base and the wing where he hadn't before. This gave him fresh opportunities to "collect" the maintenance documents and manuals that Dan had requested. He found that accomplishing his objective would be relatively easy.

Mike began by showing an interest in the ground crew maintenance classes. He periodically sat in on different ones where various aircraft systems were being taught. He got to know the instructors, and they him. It wasn't unusual for Mike to show up during class instruction or systems demonstrations. He watched for the opportunity to pick up a manual, or related materials, and drop them undetected in his briefcase. He tried not to take any of the student's materials to avoid getting one of them in trouble. As it turned out, there was considerable personal benefit to sitting in on the classes. He began to learn and understand more about the B-52 systems and operating functions than he ever did in the flight crew classes. It was fairly simple to "collect" the reasonably-sized manuals, but considerably more difficult when it came to the five-inch or so, thick and very heavy loose-leaf tech order documents. Deciding to risk staying behind after certain classes, Mike would pretend to show interest in a particular system and to casually remove a section of pages from the notebooks. He carefully noted the section and page numbers once he was back in his BOQ room, so as to avoid duplicating the collection.

To further avoid personal suspicion, Mike would occasionally slip back by the classrooms after hours. More often than not, he found them unlocked and unattended. These excursions provided a gold mine of opportunity for his work; however, he also risked being discovered. If he were ever challenged, he felt confident that he could get by with the explanation of being an inquisitive student. Mike's persistence continued for several weeks. In the end, he had collected copies of virtually every systems manual pertaining to the new B-52 bomber, hiding them under his bed, behind clothes in his closet and in empty suitcases.

In the meantime, he met Dan again on the subsequent Thursday following the first meeting. This time they met at a restaurant in Berenda, a few miles South of Merced where he delivered the crew flight manuals. Over the next several weeks, Mike and Dan rendezvoused at various places in surrounding towns where Mike delivered the maintenance manuals. Dan was impressed. "Mike, you are performing like a pro!" he told him after the first few deliveries. Mike felt good and was satisfied with his work, finally doing something more substantive than going to school and being trained to do something for his own enjoyment and pleasure. Although he had been trained as an agent, he had not really performed as one until now.

Dan advised that he was making progress in clearing a path for the security clearance issue and should have something firmed up by the end of May. The whole security clearance problem made him nervous. Hank had already prompted him twice to get the paperwork in. The squadron operations officer had also told him to Get moving on it. Otherwise, it could delay his and his crew's upgrade training. The last thing he wanted was to get cross-wise with either Hank or his squadron; he wanted to remain "squeaky clean" in every way.

THIRTEEN

The B-52

May 29, 1955, arrived on a bright sunshiny day. The base was hosting an Open House for everyone in the city and surrounding area, to witness the arrival of the first operational B-52B bomber flown in from the Boeing plant in Seattle, Washington. Mike joined his crew on the flight line to witness the landing of the giant bomber.

The wing commander was at the controls of the aircraft as it made its approach and a low pass down the centerline of the runway, then pulled up into a gentle turn and entered the downwind leg in the pattern to land. The assembled crowd was as jubilant as was the future B-52 crew members and military dignitaries, which included General Curtis LeMay himself!

Mike had never seen as many assembled "stars" in his life, not even in Moscow. He edged as close as he could to get a look at General LeMay, the legendary Air Force leader whose name was well-known in the Soviet Union. Mike remembered the stories told by his father about the U.S. General who directed the atomic bombing of Japan and later commanded the Allied relief effort that thwarted the Soviet blockade of Berlin. He was now the Commander-in-Chief of the U.S. Strategic Air Command. Mike was surprised at LeMay's short, stocky stature. He had presumed that General LeMay would be much taller with a commanding presence, but he was duly impressed with the firmness of his look. LeMay was almost bulldog in appearance with heavy set jaws and an unlit long black cigar firmly clenched in his teeth. Mike reasoned that he looked like a general, and he was tough enough as well.

The B-52 made a smooth landing with the dual tires on the aft wheels of the "quadra-cycle" landing gear giving off a wisp of smoke when they made contact with the runway. The bomber loomed even larger as it taxied up to, and in front of, the reviewing stand. The noise of the eight engines was deafening. Several members of the ground crew hurried to their positions, placed ground chocks in front of the tires, plugged in an intercom cord so that the crew chief could communicate with the pilots and give the signal to shutdown the engines. The engines finally whined down and the entrance hatch door dropped open with a short ladder extending almost to the ground.

Two legs appeared on the ladder, and the wing commander stepped to the ground. He smartly saluted and shook hands with General LeMay and the others in the greeting party. Mike stood in awe of this moving event. Then he surveyed the huge bomber; how could anything this large actually fly, and with such apparent ease and smoothness as he observed when it made the low pass and effortless turn to enter the traffic pattern and land. The 185-feet wings seemed to labor under the weight of the eight J-57 jet engines. The eight engines were housed in four pods hung on pylons under the wings. There were two on each side. The stabilizer tail stood 48 feet in the air like an aluminum sail on a schooner. The B-52 fuselage was 140 feet longer in length than the Wright Brothers first flight at Kitty Hawk. Mike had spent many hours "flying" the B-52 simulator with Hank, but to actually "see" the real thing he was going to fly was awe inspiring!

After the dignitaries dispersed, the ground crew and security police placed a rope cordon around the perimeter of the bomber and allowed the crowd to walk around it. Mike and some of his crew members joined in and slowly moved around the giant bird, comparing various aspects of it with their ground school training. Mike commented that he still couldn't imagine thrusting nearly 400,000 pounds of airplane into the air and then cruising along at almost 600 miles per hour.

Sam Allen, the gunner, had a particular interest in his "perch" located at the farthest point of the fuselage in the tail section of the aircraft. Sitting tightly fitted in a pressurized compartment he would face his gun control panel and look to the rear of the bomber. The gunner would have control over four .50 caliber machine guns providing an armed defensive capability. The gunners had already been cautioned that airsickness would become almost a given circumstance, due to the "seesawing" and twisting motion of the lumbering airframe of the B-52. He also had another special concern—bailing out in the event of an emergency. He would be required to pull an ejection handle to remove the tail section of the aircraft, physically pull himself out the hole created, and jump. Even with these potential problems, young airmen still volunteered to fly as gunners aboard the new bomber.

Bill Clements, the radar bombardier, observed that the twenty-eight foot long bomb bay could carry ten thousand pounds and several types of every atomic bomb in the inventory. After observing the fanfare of the arrival ceremony and walking around the new bomber, Mike was pumped and ready to start flying.

Almost two more months elapsed before Mike and the crew could think about flying. In the meantime, Hank Johnson took advantage of every opportunity to get Mike and himself into the simulator to practice their procedures and sharpen their skills. The other crew members also worked on their own proficiency in their respective simulators and trainers.

Finally, two additional B-52's arrived from the Boeing plant, and the instructor crews began to methodically work with the new upgrade crews, including Hank's. Their work paid off. After a couple of training flights, Hank's crew was selected for training to become an instructor crew. This delighted Mike. He liked to be at the top of every challenge.

The additional time before their flying training also gave Dan time to work his plan with the secretary in the office of the OSI. He was successful. Hannah Franks was a divorcee with four children. Although she was completely loyal to her job and her country, she could use the extra money that her new boyfriend, Dan, told her he could get for her if she worked a little paperwork problem for the nephew of a friend. She had been dating Dan for a couple of months.

He had told her that Mike Scott was the nephew of his best friend and, coincidentally, he was now stationed at Castle Air Force Base to fly B-52s. He also told her that Mike was worried that when his paperwork was submitted for his Top Secret clearance the discovery of an incident when he was back in high school could preclude him from getting a clearance and ruin his Air Force career.

Dan said he was a great kid and had been mistakenly arrested. He was caught running with the wrong kids who had been stealing automobiles and stripping them for parts. Mike was tried in court, given a probated sentence, and had never been in trouble again. Because of his concern and desire to become an Air Force pilot, Mike did not report the incident in any of his Air Force application disclosures or his security clearance background questionnaire. Now that he is on the threshold of fulfilling his dream to be a pilot, he and his uncle are worried. When a background investigation is performed, he could be disqualified and perhaps even be put out of the Air Force. There was a secondary motive, of course. Oscar had been arrested and his disposition was not clear. They could not risk having the OSI or FBI connect him with Mike.

Dan was smooth and very convincing, telling Hannah that all she had to do was to hold back Mike's TS clearance questionnaire for a reasonable period of time. Then he said, "Just put the right official stamps on it, sign it with a name you know to make it look official and put it back into the system. That'll work won't it?" he asked.

Hannah was reluctant to the proposal, saying. "Look, Dan, if I got caught doing something like that, I would get fired and never get another job working for the government, or anyone else."

"Listen," he said. "You have been around the system long enough to know that a minor deal like this can be worked with little difficulty. There's so much security clearance processing going on these days. The system is saturated, and no one is ever likely to know the difference. It's just a paper exercise anyway to cover somebody's butt. Besides, this will save a good kid's career, and the Air Force needs people like him."

Then he dropped the clincher. "Hannah, Mike's uncle is very well off. It's worth at least ten thousand dollars to keep Mike on his track and not to lose his goal to be an Air Force pilot. He's an orphan and really deserves not to be sidetracked by a dumb mistake he made as a kid. He really deserves an opportunity to prove himself. Will you help us?"

Hannah was dumbfounded. She did not know what to say or how to respond. The thought of that much money loomed heavily in her thoughts over the next several days. She liked Dan very much, as well. He had been good to her and her children, dropping off surprise gifts and treating her to a delightful social life that she had really never enjoyed.

Dan was skilled at bargaining, smooth with persuasion and persistent in pursuit of his objective. Finally, after two such sessions with Hannah and the promise of five thousand dollars the day Mike submitted his paperwork, and another five thousand when his Top Secret clearance came through, she agreed to try to work the scheme. It was the middle of June, and Dan left a note under Mike's door. "Turn in your paperwork immediately," it read.

One more time, the uncanny work of the Soviet intelligence apparatus succeeded in undermining a small, but very significant, American process.

The next morning Mike went to the personnel office, apologized profusely to the sergeant in charge of processing security requests, explaining that he was an orphan and had some difficulty in tracing his relatives and completing all of the details required in the DD Form 398. After leaving the paperwork, he went on his way, and didn't bother to tell Hank that he had turned in the clearance forms. He didn't want to make a big to do, just let the system work—he hoped!

SAC Crew Duty

Flying training in the new B-52 bomber went exceptionally well. Hank's crew was clear to solo after their fourth flight. Each member of the crew performed just as he expected. After their third solo flight, they passed their instructor crew proficiency check and began teaching the intricacies of the giant bomber to other upgrade crews in the wing. Once Hank became an instructor pilot, he began to work with Mike, allowing him to sit in the left seat of the aircraft commander and to make takeoffs, landings and air refuelings. He pushed Mike to become as good a pilot and aircraft commander as himself.

The training missions were very complex and demanding. The six-man crew of the B-52 were fully integrated into the weapon system. During the tightly planned and coordinated 14 and 20 hour training sorties, there was hardly a spare minute to relax, eat or relieve one's self. Each had not only had his own responsibilities but also interacted with the others in the rapidly moving, on-going events of the mission. There were high altitude and low-level navigation and simulated bombing runs, air refueling, electromagnetic countermeasures testing against simulated enemy radar sites, gunnery practice and simulated enemy fighter attacks. Each activity required absolute attention to detail and fixed concentration. Mike learned early that being a SAC combat crew member was tough. He had heard the story, repeated more than once, that General LeMay had often remarked to SAC crew members: "Fighters are fun, but bombers are important." Mike believed it!

Serving on a SAC bomber crew was not limited to merely flying training missions. The ground study, preparations, mission planning, testing and a multitude of incidental requirements filled every busy day. Mike and the crew attended classes on the theory and operation of the special weapons (atomic bombs) carried in the B-52. The co-pilot and radar bombardier were responsible for understanding the complex intricacies of the various weapons carried by the bomber. They attended special highly classified courses in atomic and nuclear weapons technology and operations. The purpose was to understand the inner-workings and the electronics of the complex powerful bombs.

These "special weapons" were far different than the conventional gravity bombs of World War II which were simply released on a designated target and detonated when they hit the ground. Special weapons required considerable "TLC" and attention to detail by the bomber crew. Additionally, the crew spent inordinate hours studying their assigned "war plans." These were the missions they might be required to fly in the event the "balloon went up." This was the expression which meant "going to war." Their studies included specific sortie navigation routes they would fly, tactics to avoid radar detection, surface-to-air missiles and enemy fighters, planned and emergency air refueling areas, emergency airfields into and out of enemy territory and, lastly, escape and evasion plans in the event they were shot down.

Mike was both absorbed and fascinated by the complexities and depth of knowledge required by SAC combat crew members. He often wondered if the same attention to detail and emphasis on professionalism was required of Soviet air crews. He never got that far, nor was he ever indoctrinated on these types of activities in his training back home.

Perplexed

Mike excelled in his crew position as copilot. With the attention given him by Hank, he learned to fly the B-52 and manage the crew as if he had been flying for several years. He was the envy of both the older pilots and his contemporaries who came to Castle with him. Mike, however, would be confined to flying on the crew as a co-pilot for some time to come. He lacked the minimum total flying hours to become an aircraft commander and was still a second lieutenant for several more months, but without fanfare, his Top Secret security clearance "came through." The personnel office clerk called one day and asked him to drop by and sign the acknowledging paperwork. Dan had done his work well.

Mike stayed in periodic contact with Dan. They met every week or so to keep Dan informed of his progress and to pass on information which appeared to be important and of potential use by his "other" government. Mike worked hard and professionally as a U.S. Air Officer, but he never forgot Who He Was or what his mission in life was. He was a Soviet military officer and secret agent assigned to conduct espionage against the United States in any form or manner requested.

Dan was his present handler. Mike responded to his every request for information, data and documents, delivering them as promptly as he could. He had been at this dual persona for so long now, it had become the very fabric of his being, and he had no qualms about carrying out Dan's requests. Mike remained motivated and prepared to do whatever was asked. In the meantime, he loved being a bomber pilot and SAC combat crew member; however, virtually all of his training and daily requirements were directed at planning and preparing to destroy the Soviet Union. He frequently thought of the whole gestalt as being bizarre, but throughout his life of school, training, discipline and ingrained doctrine, he had little difficulty staying the course set out for him. Bizarre, indeed!

He called Galina at least once a month and more frequently when he felt lonely. She was doing well in her studies and would continue to go to school summer and winter in order to complete her degree program. Her parents remained in San Antonio where he presumed George was carrying out his "work". Galina invited Mike to meet her at her parents the following Christmas if he could get away. "It will have been a whole year!" she pleaded.

Mike agreed to try if his crew could get leave at that time. He explained that he could only take leave if the entire crew did so. "We live together, fly together, eat together, sleep together (almost) and take time off together," he said.

She couldn't understand. She "wanted desperately to see him." Mike felt that he loved Galina, but he also knew that she could not be in any of his immediate plans. His thoughts often drifted back to Mackye as well. He wondered where she was and what she might be doing. "She's likely married by now," he thought. She was the most intellectual and sensitive girl he had ever known or imagined. But, like Galina, she had suddenly come into his life, then vanished just as swiftly. Mike knew, in both instances, Vlad was at the center of their separation from him. As much as he was disgusted with Vlad and the tactics he used to disrupt any personal involvements at Khodinka, first with Mackye and then Galina, he now realized his mission precluded serious liaisons. There were husband and wife teams, of course, but they appeared more like business arrangements than strong personal commitments. The only exceptions he had seen were Ted and Ann at the safe house in Moscow, and Galina's parents. At least they appeared to be normal relationships. He would though, if the opportunity presented itself, try to meet Galina in San Antonio at Christmas or somewhere else soon. He would like to see her.

Hank negotiated a "long week"—Saturday through the following Sunday week—during the Christmas holidays. Mike hitched a ride on a flight from Castle to Scott Air Force Base, and he and Galina spent three days together but only one night away from her home and her parents. Galina was cautious with her questions about Mike's future, but she did try to get him to say when he would complete his "training" in the United States and go back home. Mike remained evasive, telling her he was sure that he would be finished by the time she graduated. He asked, "Will you be going back to Moscow even though your parents are still here?" She said that she presumed so, since her education Green Card permitted her to remain in the U.S. until her schooling was completed. Their dilemma remained at an impasse. They pledged to keep in touch and see each other whenever it was possible, and both returned to their individual pursuits.

Fast Track

The busy days moved into busy weeks and months, as Hank's crew worked diligently to become the top crew in the wing. In the summer of 1956, Mike had served his minimum time in grade and was promoted to first lieutenant. The promotion helped to remove the stigma of "hot shot gold bar pilot," as many of his peers and some of the envious older crew members in the wing referred to him. His earned reputation as a "fast burner" or "comer," flattered Mike. He was busy working hard along with the other crew members and was responding to Hank's leadership and tutoring.

The crew was assigned number "05" in the wing and steadily upgraded to Combat Ready, R-05. By the fall of 1956, they had attained Lead Crew status. In October came eruption growing out of the unrest in Hungary and, finally, riots in the streets of Budapest. The people of that Soviet-dominated state had had enough and wanted out of their shackles. They burned Party buildings and likenesses of Khrushchev and even Stalin who had been dead for over three years.

In the United States, President Eisenhower became sufficiently concerned that he directed SAC to place its forces on ready alert in the event the Soviets decided to move beyond controlling one of their "naughty prodigies." SAC tanker task forces were moved to forward bases to support B-47 bombers should they be required to fly missions from the United States. In North Africa and in the

United Kingdom B-47's were also placed on alert. Along with the few combat ready B-52's in Mike's wing, B-36's were also placed on alert. All of the bombers were fully loaded with atomic weapons and full fuel tanks. This was Mike's first experience with the seriousness of the situation between his own government and the United States. Before this event, more often than not, the antagonism between the two countries was mostly talk. Mike often thought this was for propaganda purposes, to increase military budgets and to "motivate" the troops. Sitting with his crew in a makeshift, hastily-put-together alert facility which had been near the flight line where the bombers were parked, it seemed all too real.

The sparse reports from Budapest of mass killings by Soviet troops alarmed everyone, including Mike. He had considerable difficulty differentiating between what was right on the part of the United States and what was allegedly going wrong in the Soviet Union. Mike and his fellow crew members remained on alert and at the ready to take off on a bombing mission in Eastern Europe, should they be so directed. They conducted comprehensive mission planning and pre-flighted their B-52 every day to insure it was ready. They exchanged stories about rumors and other fragments of news that was passed on to them.

Finally, on October 29th, Khrushchev announced that the Soviets would withdraw from Hungary, and the government would be returned to the people and their deposed premier, Imre Nagy. The U.S. and its Western Allies relaxed and breathed a sigh of relief. The strategic forces stood down from their alert posture. Within a week, the Soviets moved rapidly back into Hungary, killed an estimated 30,000 civilians in Budapest alone, took Premier Nagy to Moscow and executed him. The U.S. and the West stood by this time without responding.

In the aftermath, Mike wondered, "Was the alert posturing a charade or smoke screen, which failed to impress or frighten the Soviets? Or did the United States calculate that the odds were too great to face?" He was desperate for information but found little at his level within his organization. He later consulted Dan, who found the whole U.S. response a joke. He told Mike that the days of the Western Empire and its oppression of communism were numbered.

Returning to training, Hank's crew, L-05, was the new B-52 wing's flagship crew. They excelled in flying performance, bombing and navigation. Three crews were selected in the winter of 1957 to participate in an endurance test to demonstrate the long-range strategic capability of the B-52. Crew L-05 joined two of the other wing's top crews in flying a carefully planned, non-stop flight around the world.

Operation Power Flight demonstrated the far-reaching capability of SAC bombers to strike anywhere in the world and return home. Joining crews in the lead bomber on the mission was the venerable "three star" general and legendary commander of SAC's Fifteenth Air Force. The flight crews were honored to have the "Old Man" on board one of their aircraft. But, Mike was pleased that the general wasn't on his aircraft; otherwise, he would have had to ride the jump seat while the "Old Man" got to make the take-off and landing. The mission demonstration was an overwhelming success.

When the three bombers landed, they were met by the SAC Commander-in-Chief himself, General LeMay. He promptly pinned the Distinguished Flying Cross (DFC) on each crew member, an unusual recognition normally reserved for heroic acts during wartime. LeMay wanted to draw attention to both the greatness of the B-52 and the performance capabilities of the SAC combat crews. Mike thought to himself, "Here I am, barely a pilot in the U.S. Air Force, and I already have a 'Distinguished Flying Cross!' Incredible!"

Meanwhile, Dan had made virtually no requests of Mike over a lengthy period of time, leaving him to work at his assigned duties. Mike, on the other hand, had little to offer except an occasional verbal relay of his unit's operational activities, the alert response to the Hungarian fiasco and what he could learn about the overall growth of SAC. He reported the inventory of bombers, tankers, people, etc. Dan told him he would pass on to his seniors that their young agent, Mike, was already a hero with a medal to prove it.

Mike wasn't amused. He wondered when the next "shoe" would drop, and he would be directed to provide something of importance to his handler. Occasionally, Dan would share some information about what was going on within the system, but there was seldom anything of significance. Soviet agents simply didn't share very much between themselves, either due to their inherent suspicion of one another, paranoia, or both. Mike longed to hear from, or about, his parents; however, he didn't discuss the subject much less ask Dan to inquire. Finally, during a meeting over dinner in early 1957 at a restaurant in Fresno, California, where Dan had asked Mike to meet him, he was hit with a shocker. "Mike, how would you like to go home?"

Mike stared back at him almost speechless. "Go home? You mean to Moscow? For good? Am I finished here? What gives?"

Dan grinned. "I thought you would be shocked out of your shorts. No, not for good; you are far from finished here, Comrade. Roger told me to have you begin working on an extended leave. Nothing urgent, but you will need twenty days, or so, in order for us to get you there and back. The "powers" in Moscow would like for you to come back for a few days' refresher at the Center and to discuss your future. There would also likely be an opportunity for you to visit your family while you're there. What do you think?"

Mike studied his words for a minute or so. Dan continued to eat his dinner. Racing through Mike's mind was the question, "How could he pull this off with Hank and his squadron?" The crew might be coming up for a leave later in the spring or summer, but it would likely be for no more than ten days or two weeks at the most. Hank didn't like to take more leave than that, and the squadron seldom let a crew go for any longer. Finally, he said, "I would give anything to go home, even were it for a day, but I don't know about getting away for twenty days. That is almost impossible, given how we work in this unit. Let me think about it and see what I can work out. I don't think I should arouse any suspicions or draw attention to me. Do you?"

"No, absolutely not! You have performed superbly and are invaluable to us! Just nose around; see if there may be a window of opportunity sometime in the future. Don't get antsy about it. Just look for an opportunity. We are very patient."

Mike drove back up Highway 99 with his mind spinning at full speed. "God, I wish they wouldn't do these things to me. Damn right I would like to go home, but how can I possibly work that much time away without concocting something that might do me in? I've got to think this through. God!"

Out of the blue, the opportunity presented itself. Hank told Mike that he had been nominated to attend Squadron Officers' School (SOS) the following summer. That meant he would be away from the crew and Castle for at least twelve weeks while going to the school located near Montgomery, Alabama. This bothered him, but if he could work an extended leave out it, he would accept the school appointment. His next thoughts were of Galina. She was in Alabama. Troy shouldn't be too far from Montgomery and Maxwell Air Force Base where the SOS was located.

He promptly asked Hank if he could take an additional three weeks of leave, either en route to the school or afterward, to take care of some much neglected personal affairs. Hank reluctantly agreed and jokingly told him, "You had better not be away too long, or I might just find a better co-pilot to take your place." Mike knew he was joking. He and Hank had developed a very healthy and professional respect for one another. Only an occasional twinge of his conscience bothered him. He overcame these mild feelings of guilt by justifying to himself that they were both professionals and each had "a job to do."

SOS was designed to train young Air Force officers, lieutenants and junior captains in basic military studies, policy, administration, leadership and command. The course included a healthy physical fitness program: team play and games. Staff studies and writing were also an integral part of the training. Mike coordinated his plans with Dan. It was decided that it was best for him to attend the school first, then to take leave afterward. This meant that he would be available to depart the country at the end of August and be back by mid-to-late September, "if all went as planned." Mike was nervous about the prospects and potential downside of such a venture. He definitely wanted to go home and see about his parents; he was extremely concerned about what could happen during such a journey. He was also somewhat concerned with why they wanted him back at Khodinka.

"What have I done? Or, not done?" he thought. "Surely Dan would know and give me a clue if something bad is wrong? Maybe something has happened to my mother or father? Surely they would tell me before I suffered through three more months?" Finally, he tucked it all away. He rationalized that the requirement to go home was routine, or they would call for him immediately. If there were a serious problem with him or his conduct, the KGB wouldn't hesitate to act. Mike continued to fly and train with his crew, and he looked forward to the respite of school in June.

SOS was a welcome departure from B-52 crew duty. The school program was structured around twelve officer seminar groups. They attended lectures together, studied together, teamed together in athletic competitions and drank beer together in the rathskeller after duty hours. The course was very competitive individually and collectively: in academics, leadership, officership training and athletics. The situation was ready-made for Mike.

He had alerted Galina that he was coming to Alabama several months before he was due to arrive. She, in turn, had built-up an abundance of excitement and anticipation before he actually arrived. Their reunion was wonderful for both. Galina was doing exceptionally well in her college degree work, and she was looking forward to graduation. Her great concern was Mike and his future. She pressed him for his plans. "When will you complete your training in the United States and go back home?"

Mike continued to counter, truthfully, "I don't know when I will complete my work in the U.S.—as soon as our respective Air Forces think that I have accomplished what they want," he vaguely responded. Galina was due to graduate in a year and a half. She told him after that she was sure she would be required to return to Russia. Mike probed her about her parents' situation. He was convinced she was not aware her father and, likely her mother, as well, were Soviet agents.

She told him her father had informed her they might go back home, at any time, after his work was completed. Mike and Galina were at an impasse, but they did not permit the dilemma to overcome the joy of being able to see one another almost every weekend for three months. Consequently, their affection for one another grew stronger and, perhaps, more dominant than Mike preferred. Throughout his time in the school, he carefully kept Galina away from the officers' club, the base or any place where they might encounter some of his classmates.

His greatest fear was that Galina would reveal he was a "Soviet exchange student." Such a casual reference would promptly bring his world to an end. As an additional safeguard, he would caution her to never say anything about his status. He would say, "The relations between the United States and our country are very strained. People probably wouldn't understand my presence in the U.S." He also told her, "What I am doing here, and your father, as well, is for the good of our two countries. We are, in effect, quiet bridges of peace." Galina was by no means stupid, but she had no reason not to believe him.

The end of August soon arrived. Mike was recognized as a distinguished graduate of the SOS course, adding yet another honor to his growing list of achievements. He bid Galina goodbye, telling her he would be departing on a "lengthy TDY trip" with his crew, and he would be out of touch for awhile. He pledged to see her again as soon as he could. He then proceeded to drive to Atlanta, put his car in a temporary storage facility, and purchased an airline ticket to New York. He was met at the domestic terminal by his first U.S. contact, Frank. They greeted one another warmly. "It's good to see a friendly face," thought Mike. "You look great, Mike!" Frank said. "The Air Force apparently agrees with you."

"Yes, I guess it does," Mike responded. "How have you been?"

"Great, just great," Frank said. "We've been busy, up to our 'you know what's,'" he laughed. "There's a lot going on as you might expect. How is old Dan doing in California? I envy him in that cushy assignment!"

"Dan is fine. I visit with him every week or so. He stays busy, too, I suppose. He doesn't tell me much about his business."

"Good! Okay, here is our plan," Frank continued as he ushered Mike to the baggage area to collect his suitcase. "You brought only one bag, I presume, and no military uniforms, I hope; only civilian clothes and your U.S. passport?"

"Yep, I have my passport, and I left everything else in the trunk of my car in Atlanta. I brought very little: trousers, shirts, sweaters and spare shoes. My shoes are American, so I hope that they will be okay," Mike responded.

"You'll be fine. I made reservations for you to fly to London late this afternoon; from there you are ticketed to Frankfurt. Siegfried

Hauptmann will meet you in Frankfurt tomorrow afternoon. Siegfried will have your new travel documents and escort you on the train to West Berlin. Be sure that you turn over to him, for safekeeping, your U.S. passport, military I.D., American currency and any other personal documents you shouldn't have in your possession. He will return them to you when you arrive back in West Berlin. Siegfried will then hand you off to one of his people for passage over to the Eastern Sector. Then I'm told you will be flown to Moscow. You are getting 'first class' treatment, Mike, my boy!"

"Thank you, Frank. You guys are not only thorough but thoughtful! What time is my flight this evening?"

Frank looked at his watch. "6:40 p.m. Do you want to have a beer or something to eat? We have about three hours."

"Maybe just a beer," Mike responded indifferently.

They passed the time with mostly small talk about politics and speculation about conditions back home. Mike promised to make a few phone calls for Frank while he was in Moscow. He could tell that Frank was homesick, as was he.

"But," he smiled to himself, "I'm going home!"

FOURTEEN

Home

The PANAM flight *ar*rived in London at 7:30 a.m., and wearily, Mike joined the queue of other travelers as they processed through the immigration check points. He was much more confident than he was four years earlier when he first experienced travel outside his native land. Now he was returning, at least for a brief visit. He departed the Immigration Hall and proceeded to the designated departure gate for his flight to Frankfort. He had two hours to wait for his scheduled flight and located a chair near the gate where he thought he might grab a quick snooze. But the anticipation was too great and ended up sitting wide-eyed until the flight departed.

As he walked through the gateway into the Frankfort air terminal, he looked about only momentarily before he heard his name called out in English by someone with a heavy German accent.

"Mike, I am Siegfried. Welcome to Germany! How was your flight?"

"Fine thank you, Siegfried," Mike replied; "nice to meet you."

"Mike, or shall we now call you by your native name, Sasha? I know you must be very tired, but our schedule has us moving onto West Berlin in a few hours. Do you have luggage?"

"Startled at hearing 'Sasha' for the first time in years," he smiled. "I guess I am almost home aren't I. Yes, I have just one bag." he responded. "I am a little tired but ready to move on."

Sasha claimed his single suitcase and followed Siegfried to a waiting car and driver outside the airport. The driver didn't speak, took the bag, put it in the trunk and drove the pair toward the Frankfort train station. Siegfried sat quietly during the drive which was a signal that he also should not talk. Siegfried handled the tickets and the two boarded the train into a private compartment. Once the train departed the station, Siegfried opened his briefcase and handed him an envelope containing a German passport and ID card.

"These are only temporary," Siegfried said, "to get you through the East German checkpoints en route to Berlin. The train will be stopped twice by the East German police to review the passenger list and inspect passports. The train crew will handle the details. The police are not likely to come on board the train; as a matter of fact they are forbidden to, but occasionally they will. If that happens, make sure you are in a deep stupor and unconscious. I will handle them. Now I must collect your American passport and any other personal identification and keep them safely for you until you return. You are Sasha Katsanov now."

Sasha felt uncomfortable surrendering his U.S. passport, drivers' license and military ID card, but he had been told by Frank that this was to be the procedure. The conductor came by shortly and collected their tickets and passports to be cleared by the East German police at the rail corridor checkpoint along the route into the West Berlin sector.

Filled with anxiety and apprehension, Sasha tried to relax and doze as best he could as the train rambled along the 500-kilometer rail line to West Berlin. As Siegfried had predicted, they were stopped twice, once entering the Eastern Sector of Germany and then departing into West Berlin. They arrived the morning of the second day of Sasha's journey. He was bushed, and Siegfried hailed a taxi and drove them to an apartment he kept in a high rise building in the center of the city. After a shower, shave and a hearty breakfast prepared by Siegfried's wife, Gretchen, Sasha felt much better, but he was tired from the forty-eight hour marathon trip.

"Comrade, you have about eight hours to rest before we move onto the airport," Siegfried advised.

Sasha felt ready right then to go on, but there was a schedule that had to be met. He easily fell asleep in the duck down feather decker bed, and Sasha was deep in slumber when Siegfried woke him.

"It is almost time to depart, Comrade. There is cold water in the basin on the dressing table; get dressed and we will leave in fifteen minutes."

Sitting in the back seat of a chauffeur-driven sedan, Siegfried quietly briefed Sasha that they would go directly to "Checkpoint Charlie," the principal gateway into East Berlin.

"When we arrive at the checkpoint," Siegfried instructed, "just hold up your passport for inspection, do not turn loose of it, either on the West Side or the East Side. The security police on this side are reasonably 'friendly' and usually won't hassle you, but over on the other side they often try to take your passport for a close look just to intimidate you. So, we'll keep the windows up and flash our documents, and the driver will keep moving. I hate these petty bureaucratic thugs!"

Sasha noticed the stark contrast between the "two" Berlins. As the car moved around Karl Marx Platz, the center of East Berlin, there were very few people walking the streets and few shops were even open. Many of the buildings were boarded up, and there were many others that bore the obvious damage of World War II bombings, eight years prior. On the other hand, his brief trip through West Berlin reflected a 'New York City' flair. It was busy and prosperous, people moving about in every direction, neon lights and flashy advertising of all sorts of products and goods. He wondered, "Has Moscow changed during his long absence?" They drove onto an airport which appeared to be on the outskirts of the quiet city.

"There is an AN-12 transport waiting for you," Sigfried said. "It is part of the regular courier service between Moscow and Berlin. Some civilians or military may be on board, so keep to yourself. Feign fatigue or drunkenness, and sleep your way to Moscow." He also advised, "If you are questioned by anyone who is a senior military officer or civilian, just tell them in your best Russian that you have been on duty in the West and cannot discuss your presence with them. That is usually enough to stop the questions. If not, tell them you are reporting to General Tushenskiy at Khodinka, which is no lie, and I guarantee that will shut them up," he chuckled.

The flight to Moscow was uneventful, and the transport landed at the Vnukovo military airfield Southwest of the city. Sasha stepped off the plane with his bag and drowsily walked directly into his old 'friend' and former nemesis, Vlad.

"Zdrah'stvooite! Tovarish Sasha," Vlad said, giving him a warm hug and kisses on both cheeks. "It is so very good to see you. Are you okay?"

Still in mild shock at the sight of an older and a sterner appearing Vlad, and hearing his Russian *given name* for the first time in years, Sasha returned the greeting. "Vlad, I am so happy to see a familiar face. It has been some time now. How are you?"

"Fine, Comrade, fine. I remain busy with assignments here and there, but I must tell you, I have never had another venture such as the one you and I endured at the Volgograd academy. That was the worst experience of my life and yours as well, I think. Come, let's go. Is that your only bag?"

"Yes, this is it," Sasha, replied.

Vlad guided them through the terminal building to a waiting sedan at the curbside. Along the way, he was full of talk but no questions about where and what Sasha was specifically doing.

"We are going to your old hang out at Khodinka. Are you surprised, or did someone tell you?"

"Neither," Sasha replied. "I presumed that I would go there and meet with Colonel Sokolov and perhaps the general."

"It is 'General' Sokolov now," Vlad responded. "He was promoted two years ago and is now in charge of international training at the Khodinka Center. He is a fine officer, and I enjoy working for him. General Tushenskiy is now the First Deputy of the GRU. By the way, I am now a "podpolkovnik" (lieutenant colonel)! Who knows? You may hold a rank even higher as a result of all your work," Vlad exuberantly chattered on.

Vlad looked much older to Sasha. The lines in his face were indelible, and he had begun to gray at the temples. He seemed almost hyper, and not the steady and precise Vlad who had been so succinct and in control over every detail in their earlier relationship.

"Congratulations, Vlad, 'er Colonel. I am pleased for you. Have you been at Khodinka ever since I departed?" Sasha interjected.

"Thank you, Sasha. I am still 'Vlad" to you, Comrade. We will always be friends. I'm very proud of you and the way you have matured into just the type of officer I knew that you would. You look great! You are a credit to our great Soviet regime. To answer your question, I was dispatched to the United Kingdom for a year and a half to assist in some work there. I had some difficulty mastering a British accent, but I managed to muddle through. I will tell you about that sometime. Suffice to say, the Brits are very astute and sly when it comes to monitoring our activities there. We have had a few of our people picked up as a result of Brit counter-intelligence and sloppy work by some of our agents. No more on that subject now."

"Vlad, what do you know about my schedule? Who am I to meet with, the likely discussion topics and so forth?" Sasha asked.

"Well, first of all, I know you are exhausted after your trip, so I suggest we drop off your bag in your room and go to the dining room for a bite to eat, then you get some rest. First thing in the morning you will meet with General Sokolov. After that you will likely meet with several of the Center staff directors for debriefing on subjects of their particular interest. All of this may take a day or two. Then I am sure you wish to see your parents. I understand that your father continues to do well. He continues to be a highly respected officer on the General Staff. I don't know about your mother. Have you had any contact with them?"

"No," Sasha responded, "not in four years."

They drove on with mostly small talk about the city of Moscow and how it looked, arriving at the familiar entrance gate to Khodinka. Vlad escorted him through the security guards and the short walk to the dormitory building. He dropped his bag in his room, quickly washed up, and then they departed for the dining hall. After their meal, Vlad told him he wouldn't be disturbed for the rest of the day and to get some rest. Sasha promptly tried to use the telephone in his room to call his parents, but beyond the dial tone, he couldn't dial out. Nothing had changed. Telephone calls could be received but not made outside.

He was dressed and ready when Vlad rapped on his door at seven a.m. the next morning.

"I am afraid these wrinkled trousers, shirt and sweater are the best I can present myself in," Sasha remarked when Vlad entered the room.

"That's fine, Comrade; the general will understand. I am sure you were instructed to travel light, were you not?" Vlad responded. "I will arrange to have your clothes 'rehabilitated' while you are in your meetings today, if you wish."

"That would be great, Vlad, if you can. I feel and look pretty grungy. Here's my room key...but you don't need it, do you?"

"I will drop you off with the general and take care of everything," Vlad smiled.

Sasha was greeted warmly by General Sokolov, who then nodded to Vlad that his services were completed and offered Sasha a seat on the sofa in his office.

"Well, Sasha, it is good to see you again." Sokolov began, "You look very well and healthy. The United States must be agreeing with you."

"Thank you, General. It's good to be home, and, Sir, congratulations on your promotion."

"Thank you, Sasha. We just wanted to bring you back for a few days to meet with you face to face and validate some of the material you have provided us. By the way, all of the information and data have been outstanding, and our exploitation people in operations and engineering are very pleased to learn the details of the new American B-52 bomber. Likewise, you have greatly increased our knowledge on their Strategic Air Command: the force structure, operational planning, inventories and dispersement. Also, the tech data on the aircraft has been very beneficial. Now, tell me, are you happy in your assignment? Is there anything I can do to enhance your situation, short of bringing you back home, of course?" Sokolov chuckled.

"Thank you, Sir. I am pleased to know that what I have been able to provide has been useful, and no, I really don't have any particular requirements. I have been well cared for by all of our agents in the U.S.," Sasha timidly responded, "but I would like to know how I can be of more value and provide more substantive information. I don't really believe that I have accomplished very much."

Sasha surprised himself that he had at his finger tips most of the answers to Sokolov's questions and in considerable detail. He didn't really know if the general *also* knew the answers to the questions, as well, or if this was a genuine debriefing, or merely a verification of his knowledge and diligence toward his assignment. In the end, he decided that it was a little of both.

"Sasha, you are doing fine and carrying out your mission well," Sokolov responded. "We just want you to be comfortable in your assignment. We have never enjoyed the luxury of having an agent posted *inside* such a critically important organization as you are now serving. Be careful and keep up the good work. It is invaluable to our government. You should be completed with the debriefings of the staff by tomorrow afternoon, and then you will be free to visit your parents for the next two days. Is that satisfactory with you?"

"Sir, that will be great," Sasha smiled. "It has been a long time."

Reunion

As he stood and was preparing to leave the general's office to meet with various staff members, Sasha had an impulsive thought. Confident in his standing with the general, he asked, "Sir, may I bother to inquire, do you recall the understudy instructor, Mackye Bolschekovsky, who was here briefly during my training and then departed? I believe she was working with the Humanities Department or perhaps in the American Culture instructional area."

"Yes, indeed I do, Sasha—we can relax with your legitimate name, can't we? Ms. Bolschekovsky has become one of our star staff professors. She completed her doctoral training at Moscow University and has continued to work both here at the Center and at Lubiyanka. She is currently assigned to the staff of GKNIIR, which as you know is the joint organization between GRU and KGB for technical and scientific research. Ms. Bolschekovsky has been invaluable in assisting with the interpretation and filtering of collected data and information for potential exploitation. I see her frequently. Do you wish to see her during your visit? If so, I will arrange it."

Sasha's heart leaped. He couldn't believe that finding her would be so easy. "Yessir, I would, General, if it isn't too much trouble. I just wish to say hello."

"Good, I'll take care of it and let you know. Meanwhile, your work is invaluable to us and our Government. Keep up the good work, and I will see you again before you return. I have notified your father that you will be arriving home as early as tomorrow afternoon, so have a good visit with your parents and also tell your father again that I wish him well."

Sasha departed the general's office and was met by a Soviet Air Force major who introduced himself and said he would be his escort for the day. As they walked out of the building, his thoughts were completely preoccupied with the prospects of seeing Mackye again. He was excited—so much so that he barely acknowledged his escort's comments.

The escort first took him to the strategic exploitation department where he was again quizzed generally about the same information that General Sokolov had expressed interest in, but then more specifically about the B-52. Sasha knew from their questions that they *knew* as much as he did about the bomber, its performance characteristics, capabilities and so forth. This was a validation session. They seemed equally interested in the fact that he had actually flown the bomber, and several of the pilots in the group expressed great envy. He proceeded to meet with most of the departments, including the American Culture Department, where he had been given instruction while he was in training. They were very interested in updating their data base on the conduct of Americans, their political leanings, attitudes, dress trends, popular books and magazines, slang language and even food. Once again, he felt they virtually knew as much as he did but wanted to compare and validate.

Several times during the day he wondered to himself, "Why am I really back here in Moscow? Either they already know most of what I am telling them, or they are very smug and merely infer that what I have to say is old information. Russians are very proud, so probably a little of both," he finally concluded.

The day was long and exhausting, and he was ready to rest his body and his brain when he finally got back to his room. He noticed immediately that his trousers and shirts had been pressed and were hanging neatly in the closet. Vlad had done his work, but within minutes of sitting down to relax, the tap on the door could only mean one thing—Vlad!

"God," he whispered to himself, "Can't he leave me alone for just one minute?"

"Vaidee'te!" he responded in his best practiced Russian. To his surprise, the voice was not Vlad's, and the door didn't open which was Vlad's usual manner.

"Tavarish, Sir. I have a message for you."

Sasha opened the door and a young uniformed soldier handed him an envelope. "Spa'see'ba," Sasha responded.

He opened the envelope and there was a brief scrawl on General Sokolov's letterhead note pad. "Ms. Bolschevsky's telephone number is 226 45 07. Your room telephone is operative. I hope you have a pleasant visit." Signed: "Sokolov."

Sasha couldn't believe the note. He was really getting VIP treatment, and from a general! He could use the phone! He felt as though he had been liberated. It was 6:10 p.m., and he knew he should call his parents, that is if he still had the right number. General Sokolov had already alerted them, and he knew if he got on the phone with his mother it may take an hour to bring her back down to earth. He would just wait until he saw them the next afternoon and promptly called the number Sokolov had written in the note.

"Dah, zdrah'stvooite?" Came the soft response on the other end of the line. At first, Sasha was not prepared to respond. He should have built up his courage more and rehearsed the phone call, but he failed to do either.

Just as she was about to hang up, he regained his nerve. "Mackye, this is Sasha Katsanov. Do you remember me?"

There was a pause, and he could hear her catch her breath.

"Sasha, I can't believe it is you. It has been so long. No, of course I haven't forgotten you, but you dropped out of sight so suddenly while you were still in training. Then I heard you had departed the country and I did not think you would ever call me again. Are you well?"

Her voice was golden to Sasha's ears. She had the same smooth, soft and delicate delivery, very poised, even more so than he remembered.

"I am well," he said. "I have been away, and now I am back for just a few days here at the Center."

He was well aware that his phone call was being monitored and probably taped, so he had to be careful with his words.

"Mackye, I would like very much to visit with you while I am in the city if it is possible."

"Yes, it is possible," she said. "When will you be free to visit?"

Sasha would have liked nothing better than to tell her he was ready right then, but he knew it would be virtually impossible for him to leave the compound. Then he had an impulsive thought.

"Can you come to the Center this evening?" He knew instinctively that he was treading on tenuous ground, that the security snoops were monitoring his call, but he also felt the confidence of his stature with General Sokolov.

Mackye likely knew as well that the phone call was undoubtedly monitored, and she responded in a very formal manner, "Yes, I believe that I can, Mr. Katsanov. I have some business to attend to as well with General Sokolov. I presume you have seen him during your visit?"

"Yes, I have," Sasha answered, reading her message clearly. "I had a very thorough meeting with him this morning and will be seeing him again in a few days. He believes my program is going very well. I am in the officers' dormitory, Room 216, if you wish to contact me here. Or, if you prefer, I can meet you somewhere else."

"Let's make it the Library Hall at 8:00," she replied.

Sasha was thoroughly depleted after the phone conversation. Now, he had to worry about Vlad showing up without notice to louse up his evening. So, he moved with haste, took a shower, shaved and dressed as fast as he could in order to leave the room and "*hide out*" at the library until Mackye arrived. Vlad did not show up and he was mildly surprised.

"He must be slowing down in his old age," he thought.

He was waiting for Mackye in the foyer of the Library Hall when she arrived promptly at eight p.m.

She took his hand warmly and kissed him on both cheeks. "It is good to see you again, Sasha. You look very well and healthy, and I might add, more handsome than ever!"

"So do you, Mackye. More beautiful than ever." They paused and looked at one another. "Where shall we sit and talk?" Sasha said finally.

"It is still light and warm outside. Let's walk through the park," she responded.

As they reached the sidewalk, Vlad hailed: "Sasha, I have been looking for you. I thought we might have dinner together and talk about old times."

Sasha froze. This was "just like old times," he thought. He replied to Vlad as he approached. "Hi, Vlad."

Before Sasha could say anything further, Mackye interjected. "You are Lt. Colonel Yepishev are you not?"

"Yes, I am," Vlad responded.

"Mr. Katsanov and I have important business to discuss this evening, and he is not available to meet with you." Her voice was soft but very firm and official.

It was apparent that she had official clout, and Vlad knew it. "Yes, Madam," he replied with a polite salute. "Sasha, I will look forward to seeing you tomorrow." He promptly turned on his heel and walked away.

"Was that sufficient, Mr. Katsanov?" she asked, grinning.

"Wow, I have never seen him steam off like that unless some colonel or general nailed him. And, Madame, you just nailed him."

They both laughed.

The evening was the most pleasant that Sasha had enjoyed in a great while. He still had strong feelings for Galina, but the ambient quality of Mackye, her distinct manner and intellectual substance were captivating.

Mackye told him about her studies and alluded only vaguely to her present assignment.

"I haven't married," she said, before Sasha even asked, "I have been too busy and absorbed," she smiled, "to get involved with anyone. I hold the civilian government grade equivalent to colonel in the GRU, and the likes of a Vladimir Shepilev don't bother me one bit. Your shadow, Vlad, is a petty 'wanna be.'"

Sasha saw a firm confidence in Mackye that he did not see almost five years before. She was very mature, self-confident, firm in her convictions and even more intellectually accomplished, yet she retained the soft quality of an exquisite lady. Sasha also saw in her a determined communist with complete loyalty to the Party ideology and the Soviet Government.

Mackye did not ask about Sasha's assignment. She only commented that it was apparent he had not used his native Russian language very much, and the American in him showed.

"I have been very busy, Mackye. I am very fortunate to be able to come back home even if it were for a few days. Would you consider going to the United States if the opportunity arose?" "Absolutely not!" she replied. "I have no desire to visit, much less to work there."

They talked until it was very late, and finally she said that she must get back to her apartment and rest for a very busy day tomorrow. They walked to the departure gate, exchanged a soft brief kiss, and she left with a wave. "Call me tomorrow evening after six."

Vlad rapped on Sasha's door promptly at 0630. "Would you like to join me for breakfast?"

This was an unusual gesture for Vlad who usually stated that he was—"ready for this or that and proceeded to lead the way." This morning he seemed subdued and almost apologetic. Neither mentioned the evening before and Vlad's encounter with Mackye. They finished a quiet breakfast with small talk until the major who was assigned to escort Sasha to his appointments showed up to walk him to his first meeting. Vlad bid Sasha goodbye, telling him they may have another opportunity to visit before he departed to return to his assignment. Sasha remained puzzled by the sudden change in Vlad's demeanor, but he let it slip out of his thoughts as the morning of debriefings proceeded.

He finished his last meeting at straight up noon, feeling "brain fatigue" from the morning of questioning and returned to his room with his escort officer to collect his clothes and bag. He was told to return two days later and report to General Sokolov at ten a.m.

The major escorted him through security and to a waiting sedan outside the Center. The driver dropped him on a side street a block from the familiar apartment building where his parents lived. Even after four years, the area remained familiar and unchanged. He made his way up the stairwell to the door of the apartment and, feeling somewhat apprehensive and nervous, he knocked on the door.

Viktor opened the door, and they stood looking at one another as if not believing the moment. Finally Victor put his arms around his son and held him firmly. "Sasha, Son, welcome home! You look great and so well. Come in! Come in!"

Sasha entered the small foyer, putting down his bag and looked around. "Where is mother?" he asked. "In the kitchen, I bet?"

"No, Sasha, she isn't here. The news I have is not very good. I am not entirely sure what happened, but your mother is being detained by the police for questioning on some foolish accusation that she has been unlawfully meeting with a group of dissident intellectuals. The secret police came here very early this morning and asked if she would accompany them to a detention center not far from here to answer some questions."

Sasha froze. "I can't believe this! She is not involved with any such activity." His heart and pulse were pumping so fast he could feel his entire body vibrating. "Who would make such a charge? Did you accompany her to the police center?"

"No. They were very respectful and asked that I not go with them at this time. She left in the company of a male and a female officer, and they assured me that she would be well cared for. They said her detention for questioning was probably routine, and I should not worry. The secret police said that she would likely be returned by the end of the day. I felt helpless, Sasha. My military rank and position mean nothing to the secret police. If this situation does not come to a satisfactory conclusion in a few hours, then I will appeal to the legal officer on the General Staff."

Sasha was livid. He knew in his heart of hearts that Vlad had to be behind this. The coincidence was surreal.

"That bastard," he thought to himself, "is getting even for last night. He has to be the winner in all events. This explains his subdued attitude this morning. He knew what he had done. So much for the promises made to me when I agreed to do all of this five years ago."

His thoughts were reeling. "I'll call General Sokolov. He can straighten this out. No! I need to work it a lower level first, if I can. Mackye is assigned to NKIIR; she will know what to do, but I can't call her until six o'clock."

He was sick to his stomach. "That bastard, that bastard," he murmured over and over. "I will kill him if anything happens to my mother!"

It was 1:30 in the afternoon, four and a half hours before he could call Mackye.

"Father, I have a contact I can call but not until six o'clock. If we have heard nothing by then, I will call, and if this person cannot do anything, I will call General Sokolov himself. This cannot be happening to mother!"

"Fine, Sasha," Viktor cautioned, "but you must be careful. The KGB rules everything now and everyone is considered suspicious if they even appear to step out of line. Now, sit down, I have some other unpleasant news to give you as well. These are not good times."

Viktor put his hand on his son's shoulder and gave him further unpleasant news. "Sasha, Bonita died a few months ago. She took pneumonia in the spring and became very weak. She just gave up. Your mother took her death very badly. We are all sorry."

Sasha remembered his very bright and incisive grandmother. He sat down, letting all of these compounding events settle within him. Viktor brought in a pot of tea from the kitchen. Sasha looked at his father as he sat holding the cup of steaming tea. Even in his smart uniform with the piping and brass buttons, he looked hollow with deep lines in his sallow face; he was no longer the strong and erect man that he once knew.

Sasha felt despair. His mother had been arrested, apparently by the KGB, his grandmother gone and his father appeared to be only a shadow of his former self.

"How could all of this be?" he brooded to himself. "I only have today and tomorrow before I have to leave again for no telling how long." His thoughts raced. "If Mackye can't settle this and if General Sokolov can't or won't involve himself, what can we do? Well, I know what I can do; I will confront that SOB, Vlad, and beat him senseless. Then I will refuse to return to the U.S. They can't make me."

The reality of the situation then set in. He knew that they had him just where they wanted him, and he could do nothing less than to follow their directions. They have his mother and could easily arrest his father and use them to make him do anything they wished. He was trapped. They were all trapped! Who could he trust?

"No one, really," he concluded.

Sasha and Viktor spent the next several hours waiting for a knock on the door or the telephone to ring. Neither occurred. Viktor was interested in his well-being and his job. Sasha didn't reveal anything of importance, not that he was working in the United States, much less serving in the U.S. Air Force! He knew that his father likely knew "something," but neither tipped their hand.

Finally, six p.m. arrived, and he told his father he would make a phone call. Viktor nodded.

Sasha placed a call to Mackye. "Dah," she promptly answered.

"Mackye, I am so glad you are there!" He was nervous but went directly to the issue. "Mackye, I need your help. I hope you will understand."

He told her about the events of the day, what was alleged by the police who came to their apartment, why his father had not officially made any moves and, finally, his strong suspicion that Vlad was at the bottom of it all. He did not tell her what he knew about his mother's suspected involvement with the krushki for fear that she might not be inclined to involve herself.

Mackye listened to his story. "Sasha, stay by the phone. I will do some inquiries and get back to you as soon as I can."

Sasha told his father he had called a friend who might be able to help. They sat quietly drinking tea laced with brandy. Neither wanted anything to eat.

After an anxious hour of waiting, the phone rang and Sasha dashed to answer it.

"Sasha, your mother is fine. She is being detained temporarily at an annex station in your district not far from your parents' apartment building. They have not gotten around to questioning her because of higher priorities; they said. I believe I have convinced the police colonel in charge of that district the information they had received was a hoax, that the individual who passed it onto them was a questionable person and is a suspect himself. I happen to know the colonel and do not think much of him, but he will do this favor for me. He said he will submit a request to release her to go home very shortly. If she is not back there within two hours, call me back. And Sasha, I would also like very much to see you this evening. Call me back soon."

"Mackye, you are an angel! I will call you within an hour or so, either way."

Sasha told his father the news, and once again they sat back waiting for a knock on the door or the phone to ring. Tatyana arrived back at the apartment about forty-five minutes later. She was escorted by a female agent who apologized to both she and Viktor for the misunderstanding and then departed. Tatyana was visibly upset by the events of the day, but after a few minutes with her son, she calmed down.

"Tatyana," Viktor soothed, "Sasha is responsible for your release. He has performed a miracle for us!"

She told them both she was treated very kindly and had spent the day in a comfortable room where she was permitted to read and listen to music. She also confirmed she had not been asked any questions and remained confused about the whole affair. But separately, each of the three knew what the subject of the arrest had been. Only Sasha knew who had likely perpetrated it. After they all had settled back and became more relaxed, he excused himself.

"I must make a phone call to express our appreciation for your release, Mother."

He placed a call. "Mackye, how can I ever thank you for what you have done? She is back home and said she was treated very well. You have performed a miracle!"

"You, Sasha, can thank me by taking me to dinner," she responded curtly.

He was perplexed. "Mackye, I want to see you very badly, but I haven't seen my parents in four years and my mother has been through a terrible experience today." Taking a deep breath, he asked, "Where can I meet you in an hour from now? I will work it out here."

"Sasha, I know you have had a very troubling time of this, and I respect the fact you need to be with your parents. I also believe you also need to relax away from all of that for a while. Don't you agree? I will meet you at the Krista Coffee Bar on Arbat Prospekt in about an hour. Find a table on the sidewalk and wait for me."

Sasha explained to his parents he had to go out to meet with a colleague and offered his apologies to his mother. He asked her to get some rest and they would have all of the next day to catch up. He visited with them for another half an hour and then hugged his mother warmly and departed.

Mackye arrived shortly after he had found the coffee bar and was seated at an outside table. She greeted him with a bright smile and polite kiss, and as always, she was chipper, spirited and in control. She thanked him for meeting her and explained that she had confirmed Vlad was the vex behind his mother's arrest.

Falsely, she alluded that his father's rank and position, as well as his own position, had aided in his mother's release. "Otherwise," she said, "it would not have been so easy."

Mackye the KGB was still suspicious as they always are of anyone whose name is turned into them. "Sasha, you need to advise your mother not to place herself in any undue situations which might bring about the same circumstances again."

"Thank you, Mackye, I will," he replied. "and I will be forever grateful to you."

Mackye did not tell Sasha she knew the secret police district commander, Dimitri Vetrov, all too well. He had pursued her since they met two years before, and while he was an attractive man in his early fifties and several years older than she, he was an arrogant boor. On this evening, he told Mackye that Tatyana Katsanov had been on their suspicion list for years, but there was a "Monitor, but do not arrest," notation in her file. However, last evening his office received a call from a GRU agent at Khodinka Center which directed him to "pick her up for questioning," but neither did Vetrov tell Mackye his intentions were to "retain her for only a few hours just to give her a fright and a warning, and then escort her back home."

Vetrov also told Mackye, "I had no choice but to place a notation in her file that she was suspected of disloyalty against the State." He said also, "Mackye, you are meddling in a very sensitive area, and I would prefer not to make a record of your inquiry into the case. We need to have an informal visit about it." Mackye knew what that meant. She would have to go out with him and likely even more than that to keep him from making serious trouble for her.

Blackmail among GRU and KGB agents was an accepted way of life: "Quid pro quo." Not knowing that Tatyana would be released routinely anyway, Mackye fell victim to Dimitri Vetrov's ploy.

"Something for something, Mackye," he whispered to her over the telephone.

Mackye would take any risk for Sasha. She had agreed to Vetrov's terms, knowing full well he would extract payment for his services or turn her in for meddling and make the allegations far worse than they actually were.

Sasha and Mackye enjoyed a pleasant time together, first at the coffee bar and then at a nearby restaurant for dinner. Mackye told him she instinctively knew that he would be leaving again soon. She hoped he might return to Moscow in the near future and that they could share in their mutual work together for the government. Sasha was extremely fond of Mackye and expressed the same hope, but he knew full well it would likely be several years before he returned again. She told him her code name was "Emerald," and she would attempt to pass any significant information to him regarding his mother or other activities if warranted. She surprised him when she said that she knew his code name was "Mike."

Then as quickly as she appeared, Mackye told Sasha to go home and be with his parents, and she thanked him again for meeting with her. With a casual "goodbye," she was gone. She had given her word to meet Dimitri Vetrov later that evening.

Sasha walked to the Arbat Metro Station and took the train back to his parent's apartment where he found both his mother and father waiting up for him. He apologized for the lateness of the hour and again for leaving them on his first night home. There was no further talk about Tatyana's experience, but he did give her Mackye's caution about guarding against any possible suspicious contacts with questionable people.

The following day was spent visiting and assessing his parents' well-being. Viktor remained at home for the day, responding to phone calls when they came but otherwise being with his son. In the afternoon they visited Bonita's grave located in an Orthodox Church cemetery. Sasha had told them the first thing that morning he would be departing early the next morning. He had no idea when he might return. Although remorseful, Tatyana had long since given up the closeness of her son. He now belonged to the system, and she had no further dreams about what he might have become.

Sasha called Mackye during the last evening with his parents.

"Mackye, I wish to again thank you for all that you have done. I am sure that it was not easy to involve yourself with the police in the affairs of others. I am so grateful. I don't know when I will again return. I will be thinking of you. Da seveedah'neeya."

"Da seveedah'neeya, Sasha; please be careful," her voice trailed off.

Sasha had already decided he would not see her before returning to Khodinka the next morning and departing Moscow later in the day. It was time to return to his other life. Morning came, and he said a tearful goodbye to Viktor and Tatyana as he walked away from the apartment building to meet his prearranged sedan pick up parked a block away. The major who had previously escorted him through his debriefing was waiting for him in the car, and they drove quietly back to Khodinka Center. He dropped his bag by his room with every hope that he would not run into Vlad. If he did, he wondered how he would handle it.

The major escorted him to Sokolov's office where once again the general warmly greeted him. After offering him a seat on the sofa to one side of his desk and working area, he asked, "Sasha, how was your visit with your parents? Are they well?"

If Sokolov was aware of the incident with his mother, he didn't reflect it. After a few minutes of friendly conversation, Sokolov pressed a button near his chair and three well-dressed agents came into the office and were introduced. Sokolov said they were exploitation experts from the Department of Aviation. For the next two hours, they questioned Sasha about every feature concerning the B-52 strategic bomber. They asked what he might know about follow-on improved versions that might be developed later. Sasha told them the "B" model he was flying was the basic aircraft, and several later versions would likely be produced over the next few years.

"There is a rumor about a "G" model B-52 in the design phase that would have more powerful engines, heavier payload and all new avionics," he said.

The agents acknowledged that they were aware of the proposed new American bomber. They told Sasha he needed to collect as much information as he could on the prospective "G" model and report it to his local contact.

They instructed him to also continue working within the American Strategic Air Command to provide any and all information regarding procedures, force structure, plans and special weapons. "All information," they said, "even that which appears to be insignificant or unimportant."

The agents departed and General Sokolov asked Sasha if he had any requests. "Are you being properly supported in the United States? Is there anything personally which I may do for you? I am well aware that your assignment and long absences from home are very strenuous on you, but Sasha, we are greatly indebted to you for all you are doing."

"Yes Sir. I am being supported very well by everyone in the system. I only have one request, Sir. I am concerned with the health and well-being of my mother. I would appreciate being contacted should she become ill or in need." He ventured further, "General, my grandmother died several months ago, and I was never notified. I did not learn of her death until I arrived back home."

"Sasha, I am truly sorry to hear that, but you may be sure I will remain in contact with your father. Should anything of the sort occur, I will personally insure that you are notified; if it is warranted, I will do everything I can to get you back home. I wish you well, Comrade. You are truly a success story within our agency, and we will continue to look for good results from your work," Sokolov responded. Then he said, "I have a surprise for you. Comrade Bolshekovsky is waiting outside to escort you to the airport."

Sasha was caught off guard. "Mackye!" he quickly breathed to himself.

Sokolov gave Sasha a warm bear hug and concluded, "Good luck to you, Sasha."

The Return

Mackye was waiting outside General Sokolov's office. They met with smiles and departed for the waiting sedan. His single piece of luggage was already in the trunk. Mackye held Sasha's hand firmly as they rode in the back seat heading for Vnukovo airfield, each knowing within themselves their next time together may be an eternity away.

As the sedan pulled into the airport grounds and stopped near the waiting AN-12, Mackye looked at him. "Sasha, I have to tell you that Dimitri...Colonel Vetrov, the officer who was responsible for securing your mother's release, I have known for quite sometime and he has petitioned me to marry him. I feel that I must do so. There are complicated circumstances about which I cannot tell you, but I wanted you to know about my situation before you departed. These are difficult and stressful times, and I don't know when I will ever see you again."

Tears were streaming down her face, and Sasha was struck cold with her words. He couldn't respond. The driver got out of the car and opened the rear door on Sasha's side.

As he continued to sit, speechless, absorbing the words, Mackye put her hand on his arm. "Sasha, please know that I love only you, but what I have to do is necessary. I have avoided it for some time, but now I must comply for my own well-being...and yours."

He looked at her in disbelief, hearing the words but not comprehending their meaning.

"Sir, the aircraft is ready to depart," the driver said, standing by the open door and motioning for him to get out of the car.

Mackye leaned over and kissed his cheek. "Da seveedah'neeya, Sasha. Zhelah'yoo oospe'kha!"

"Mackye, are you being forced to do this—blackmail?" he whispered.

"Sasha, go! Now! Goodbye!" she choked the words.

He could barely walk as he stepped out of the rear seat of the sedan. The driver steadied him as he walked to the steps of the aircraft. Sasha looked back at Mackye sitting motionless in the car. He took his bag from the driver and walked up the steps into the transport. There was only one other passenger in the compartment, an East German officer. They nodded to one another and Sasha strapped himself into his seat. He was still shaken by Mackye's abrupt disclosure. He had heard her every word, but they did not come through as genuine. Something in her tone was both desperate and surrendering. This was not at all like her. The self-assurance and confidence were not in her words. For the first time since he had known her, Mackye was frightened, and he couldn't figure out why.

"Was Vlad involved?" he thought. "No, it couldn't be him, at least not directly. She had his *number.*"

He felt completely helpless. There was no way he could contact her again until he returned, and he knew that might be years. This whole event had drained him mentally and physically.

The AN-12 landed in East Berlin. He was met by Siegfried, and they departed promptly to reenter West Berlin, following the same procedures as when they came through Checkpoint Charlie the previous week. Siegfried had little to say, the usual small talk about how well did his visit go, and so forth, but he did not ask any serious questions. That was the procedure. He briefed Sasha that he would escort him once again by train to Frankfort and see him off to London and thence onto his destination. There was no time wasted. They caught the train, secured themselves into their private compartment and completed the journey without incident.

Siegfried returned his passport and personal documents once they were safely through the corridor and back into West Germany, and he gave him airline tickets to fly via Lufthansa to London and PANAM on to New York. The fast pace of his return to the U.S. did not overcome his preoccupation with Mackye's troubling disclosure as he departed. Something was not right, and he felt it deeply.

"Mike Scott" arrived back in New York, and Frank had a reservation for him to fly on to Atlanta where he collected his car from the storage facility. He checked into a nondescript motel and went to bed to try to rest from the marathon return from Moscow. Trying to clear his mind of all that had happened over the all too fast week, he slept fitfully. Finally collecting himself, he headed out on the long drive to California. He drove day and night, stopping at roadside parks only long enough to sleep for an hour or so and then on down the road.

Arriving back at Castle, Don Johnson was delighted to see Mike and welcomed him back. He told Mike that while they had missed him, the crew had done very well during his absence. They had been upgraded to "Select" crew status which meant everyone on the crew had received a "spot" promotion in rank to the next grade. Mike couldn't receive one because he had been temporarily off the crew. Don was now a lieutenant colonel and each of the others were now one grade higher.

Mike was soon back into the world he had left almost four months earlier, and everything began to fall back in place. The staff school he had attended, the fun times with Galina during the period at school, the fast trip to Moscow, his mother's bad experience and lastly, Mackye, now all seemed like a bad dream.

Within days after Mike departed Moscow, Mackye reluctantly married Colonel Dimitri Vetrov. Had she not given in to him, it would have likely not only ended her career, but possibly her arrest by the KGB and no telling what else. Vetrov was a tough and cunning professional, at least twelve or fifteen years older than Mackye, and he had been "around the system for years." He knew all the tricks, as well as how to try and snare an extremely beautiful and bright woman such as Mackye. She understood "the system," and later she would learn how Dimitri had clearly blackmailed her over the incident with Sasha's mother. She had unwittingly fallen into a trap quickly closed by Dimitri. Mackye was not aware that Vlad's little game could have kept Tatyana detained only briefly since she had "protected" status, even though she was high on the dissident criminal list. She could not be charged with any crimes. Dimitri knew her status and that he had to release her after several hours, detaining her only for "cosmetic" purposes.

When Mackye called, Dimitri used the opportunity to draw her into a web of potential conspiracy. He politely, but firmly, told her that she could very well be arrested for "attempting to tamper with a serious criminal case." He also strongly hinted she could easily avoid serious problems if she agreed to spend some time with him. Mackye clearly understood the terms, either give into Dimitri, or be turned over to the worst of other consequences.

San Francisco

"Good Morning, Boss," Jack Collier greeted, as he walked into the office of Bill McClaren, the Special Agent in Charge of the FBI's San Francisco office.

"Hi, Jack. What's up? My secretary said you wanted to see me this morning on a curious subject. What've you found under whose rock this time?" Bill McClaren responded to one of his bright young agents.

"Well, I'm not sure. I had a call from the Air Force OSI office down at Castle Air Force Base. You know, the bomber base near Merced. The call was from a Major Jasper Couch, OSI chief at the base. He said they may be on to something regarding a gal in their office, a civilian admin specialist, who might be peddling security clearances. How does that grab you?"

"Well, it grabs me right here!" McClaren responded, clutching his heart. "What's the story?"

Jack Collier described what he knew. "Major Couch says that one of the other ladies in his office came to him last week and told him that the gal in question had suddenly come into some money several months ago. She couldn't remember exactly when, but all of a sudden the gal—her name is Franks, Hannah Franks— began to show some sudden affluence."

"She is a divorcee with four kids," he continued, "and apparently was barely making ends meet. All of a sudden she had a new car and some pretty flashy clothes. When one of the other administrators asked her about her new wealth, she said she had a new boyfriend who was pretty flush. Well, that all sounded normal until the SAC Inspector General paid a visit to the base recently and conducted an audit of the unit's security clearance procedures. They pulled a few sample TS clearances granted over the past couple of years. The IG became a little suspicious when several sets of clearance paperwork appeared to have irregularities such as," he continued, "not being completely filled-out. Some of the signatures of the OSI officers who conducted the background investigations on some individuals did not appear to be legitimate. The OSI records reflected that some of the investigative officers' names didn't even exist. The major conducted a full audit of all the clearances in the bomber wing and found at least a half dozen individual files that contained irregularities."

McClaren interrupted, "What has the OSI chief done with the suspected employee at this point? How does he know she is a suspect? Has he questioned her?"

"Boss, I presume that he hasn't done anything with her since he called us. He said he thought we ought to get into the issue. The combination of the tattletale story about sudden money in the hands of the Franks gal and the questionable background investigation forms she had processed raised his suspicions. He said he had not questioned her. He wanted to get some guidance from us first, and felt like she might try to give them a snow job, but if we came down and questioned her, and if she has been a party to something, our presence might get quicker action. What do you think?"

"Well, we sure as hell can't ignore it," McClaren replied. "Somebody has got to get into it. If it's true, we could have a Pandora's Box here, full of no telling what! Are there any suspicions of 'mouse play' by any foreigners, Soviets or anybody else? I don't want to get paranoid over something that may be just a paper shuffle to expedite security clearances, but we can't be too careful. Okay, Jack. Go down there and look into it. Keep me informed."

Moving Om

Mike rejoined Don's crew and quickly got back up to speed and proficiency. Dan contacted him shortly after his return just to let him know he was still in the area and available for any information that might be helpful. Mike met him for dinner one evening and assured him he would continue to closely follow events and report any information he felt would be useful.

The following spring Mike was awarded his spot promotion to captain which boosted his morale considerably. He had worked hard and contributed immeasurably to the success of his bomber crew. He continued to call Galina, and they chatted often about their future and when and where he might go. She told him she definitely would return to Moscow when she completed her degree program. Galina was uncertain about what her parents might do.

Mike's feelings cycled between Galina and Mackye. He cared very much for them both, but it appeared if he were going to find happiness it would have to be with Galina. He presumed by now that Mackye had long since married and gone her way. Her situation still puzzled him from time to time, but it was all out of his hands.

Mike had been back from his visit to Moscow almost a year when he met Dan one evening. During their conversation, Dan said casually, "Oh, I have a message for you, Mike. *Emerald* sends greetings and says the *fox* has been dispatched. I suppose you know what that means?"

Mike was taken off guard. "Emerald!" He was surprised and told Dan that Emerald was a friend back home, but he wasn't sure about "the fox." And, he really *wasn't* sure.

"Which *fox?*" he wondered. "Had Vlad been properly taken care of or had she *disposed* of the fellow, Dimitri, who she was supposed to marry?"

Dan's message served only to confuse him. He had mixed feelings about whether he hoped Vlad had been properly dealt with or was Mackye free from her relationship with the Dimitri character. Obviously, though, it was Mackye's well-being that he was far more concerned with. "Vlad can go to Hell. Is that all there is to the message?" he asked.

"That's it," said Dan. "Do you want me to reply? I may have success, and I may not. The system doesn't go along with friendly message exchanges I presume *Emerald* has clout enough to get through to you, so you may have the same success going back. I will try to send a brief response if you wish."

"Yeah, try one for me," Mike offered. "Send a message to Emerald: 'Clarify the fox.'"

Almost two months elapsed before Dan revealed to Mike he had another message from Emerald. "The *fox* has been *de-fanged,* and the maiden remains in the tower."

Mike was reasonably sure then it was Vlad to whom Mackye was alluding. "Well, good riddance!" he concluded.

The remainder of her note served only to distress him further. "Thanks, Dan. I appreciate the note."

Galina completed her college work and traveled by bus to California to see Mike before she departed for home. The meeting was unsettled and strained for both of them. He could make no promises to her, only if she would wait for him, he would one day complete his "exchange work" and return home to Russia.

"Sasha, I will try to write you and, hopefully, the letters will get through. I don't know how the situation is at home now. I wish this whole silly problem between our country and the U.S. would just go away. Americans seem nice enough. I just don't understand," Galina lamented.

"I agree, Galina. Perhaps one day the situation will improve between our governments. Here is an address which you can try to send mail. I will check it frequently." Mike gave her a post office mail box number, and Galina departed.

As the time passed, Mike continued to work and perform diligently as a B-52 co-pilot. Don continued to work with Mike until he was fully capable and qualified to become an aircraft commander any time a "position" opened. Only his lack of seniority and accrued flying time prevented him from upgrading.

A perceptive President Eisenhower directed the Secretary of Defense to place one-third of SAC's bomber and tanker force on ground alert in response to growing concerns with Soviet ICBM developments. On October 1, 1957, SAC implemented the ground alert concept.

Leading up to the ground alert decision, U.S. intelligence sources had indicated the Soviets were showing a marked improvement in their development and potential deployment of intercontinental ballistic missiles. This meant a proven ICBM capability made the United States and its strategic bases vulnerable to a missile attack which could occur before the bombers and tankers, under normal conditions, could be loaded and launched.

In response to the President's directive and in order to be in position to execute an effective and immediate retaliatory attack, SAC developed the ground alert concept to maintain one-third of its bombers and tankers on ground alert and to be prepared to take off with a nominal fifteen minute notification. The bombers placed on alert were fully loaded with their designated nuclear weapons and a full fuel load. The air refueling tankers were also fully loaded to take off and support the en route bombers. The combat crews scheduled for ground alert would be matched to their respective aircraft and be housed in a facility near the flight line and their aircraft.

Just three days after initiating the ground alert posture, the Soviets launched a satellite on October 4, 1957, and placed it in orbit around the world. The capability demonstrated by "Sputnik" brought a chill to Americans who, heretofore, refused to believe that such a backward nation as Russia could pose a serious threat to the Continental United States.

The "out of the blue" event was startling enough, and then came Sputnik II a few days later. The latter satellite weighed an incredible 1,120 pounds, roughly the weight of a Volkswagen "Bug." Mike was in awe of these events. The strides his government was making in weapon systems technologies, and to the surprise of everyone including himself, were incredible. When he finally was able to meet with Dan and discuss the great accomplishments, even he was not aware these things were being accomplished "back home."

To U.S. leaders, the apparent Soviet achievements meant yet another Cold War crisis that had to be dealt with. The increased tensions validated the requirement for the strategic ground alert posturing. Don Johnson's crew was assigned alert duty on the first day. This was a new operating environment for the first few days with the combat crews. The first few alert tours finally became a repetitious and dull routine. The aircraft commanders, such as Don, had to become innovative leaders to ensure that their crews remained sharp and motivated.

They conducted "skull sessions" on planning, procedures and what "if's" should they be called to take off and go to war. SAC improvised its own training and motivating procedures. To keep the crews on their toes, the SAC Command Post would periodically sound the *klaxon* alert signal, sometimes in the middle of the day and sometimes in the dead of night.

The penetrating, ear spitting and agitating sound of the klaxon horn sent the crews scrambling to their aircraft. The ground crews turned on the portable power carts, the pilots jumped into their seats and started the aircraft engines, and the remainder of the crew strapped in and turned on their equipment. The co-pilot listened to the command post radio frequency for further instructions.

Was it the real thing or just a practice alert? In any event, the adrenaline flowed through the bodies of each crew member. Mike pondered these events each and every time they occurred. He really wanted to go home but by no means this way! The single thing that often puzzled him was that his leaders, Don and those above worked at motivating the crew members with lectures on responsibilities, excellent food, games and television. Surprisingly, there were seldom any words seriously spoken about *the enemy*, the Soviet Union.

This would never have been the case back home. The political officers, the zampolits, would take full advantage of the increased tensions and the *captive* combat crews to infuse their venom and hate of the U.S. aggressors. The SAC crew members did maintain their spirit without political lectures; they accepted their responsibilities, and there was seldom any friction or dissention between individuals, nor grousing about their job or their leaders. Mike often thought it was difficult to dislike Americans.

Screw Up

Jack Collier drove down to Castle Air Force Base to follow up on the OSI's report of potential irregularities in the processing of security clearances. When he arrived, he was surprised to learn Major Couch, the OSI detachment commander, had proceeded to question Hannah Franks about the suspected irregularities in her files.

"I don't have good news for you, Mr. Collier. I may have screwed up. I decided to go ahead and confront Ms. Franks with what the IG had found, as well as my own findings. I called her in last Friday to talk to her, pending your arrival. She denied any wrongdoing. We had a lengthy discussion, and she remained very calm. She said she only processed the documents that came back from the field investigations. I told her I had discussed the situation with the FBI, and they would likely be looking into the situation. I also told her to think about it over the weekend, and we would discuss the issue further on Monday." Couch took a deep breath and continued, "but, Ms. Franks didn't report to work on Monday morning. Later in the day, I had my secretary try to contact her. After spending most of the day trying to locate her, we learned she left town over the weekend. She took her kids, had her furniture put in storage for later pick up and disappeared without leaving word where she could be contacted."

Jack Collier listened to Couch's story in dismay. "Well, so much for calling me about this, Major. It looks like you have pretty well wrapped it up."

He thought for a minute, then asked, "What have you done to try to trace her?"

"Nothing yet," Couch replied. "I tried to catch you before you departed San Francisco but missed you. So, I will defer to you for further direction."

"Okay," Collier acknowledged. "Let me see the files in question. Copies need to be made of each of the file folders with as much supplementary information as you can get for me. I want to know where each of the officers in question are located now. Are they still stationed here? Have they been transferred? What are their current job assignments? Everything about each one. I just want the data for now. We are not going to question any of the officers with irregular paperwork until we get a complete profile of the case. I also need you to verify the existence of the suspected phony investigator names and signatures. Let's put out an APB to see if we can locate Ms. Franks. We need to know everything you have on her: her own security clearance file, last known address and any personal information you have regarding her background."

Couch was noticeably embarrassed. "Yes Sir. The place is yours. I will have the staff get everything together for you. Again, I apologize for jumping the gun."

"It's not a problem," Collier sighed. "You were just trying to do your job. I'll stay here until you get all the information together. Then I will have to go back to San Francisco to clean up other things I have hanging fire there. This may take awhile since we don't have our suspect in hand. We need to find her first before I challenge any of the officers in this mix. We don't want to screw up and embarrass ourselves over something that may not be as serious as it sounds."

Jack Collier collected the requested information and went back to San Francisco. He did not attach a high priority to the case since it appeared to be more of a paper shuffle for a few bucks to expedite security clearances for anxious young officers. It could be serious, he knew, but tracking down Soviet agents and monitoring their activities on the West Coast had a higher priority and was much more interesting. He debriefed his boss on the events and put out a routine search and locate order for Hannah Franks.

FIFTEEN

The New Bomber

A year and a half later in early 1959, SAC began to receive the first B-52G model bombers. These new aircraft were a considerable improvement over the initial designs, with larger and more powerful engines, advanced avionics and fire control systems. It was a "Cadillac" according to the combat crews at Travis Air Force Base where the first bombers were assigned. In January, 1960, Dan left a note for Mike to have a dinner meeting with him. During the meeting, he suggested that Mike apply for a transfer to Ramey Air Force Base, Puerto Rico, where the new "G" model B-52 was also being assigned.

Mike was puzzled that Dan was involved in his future Air Force assignments, but he agreed to try and pursue a transfer. Dan also told Mike that he didn't want to alarm him, but the lady who had helped expedite his security clearance might be in serious trouble. He had helped her move and get out of the area. "You have been too busy to worry about such things, and I didn't want to alarm you. She is no longer here. What they don't know, they can't find out from her. But, I believe if you're transferred out of here, it would also be best for all of us."

This didn't set well with Mike. "How long have you known this?" he asked.

Dan tried to be nonchalant. "Oh, she called me several months ago over a weekend and told me an audit had turned up some funny stuff in her files. I made some quick arrangements and got her and her kids relocated. She is being well taken care of, so not to worry. Has anyone asked you about your clearance or anything like that?"

"No," Mike replied, "but, I am glad you told me in the event I am questioned. I hope I can come up with a story." This new twist bothered him considerably.

Mike talked to Hank about applying for an assignment to Ramey and possibly upgrading to aircraft commander in order to fly the B-52G. Hank went to bat for him; he had been loyal, patient and an outstanding member of his crew. Hank's influence paid off and the reassignment came through. Mike received orders to report to the bomb wing at Ramey with instructions he would be upgraded to aircraft commander upon arrival. He had been promoted to captain in the meantime by the regular promotion board and his "spot" promotion confirmed. In short order, Mike prepared to transfer the following summer to Puerto Rico. Dan was delighted with the news of Mike's acceptance to be transferred and said he forwarded the information through channels. He knew the people at Khodinka would be pleased.

The whole notion of essentially *starting a new career* bothered Mike considerably. He was not one to complain, but what could all of this mean in the long run? He could see no light at the end of the endless tunnel of his life. He didn't feel he was accomplishing very much. Homesickness set in from time to time. For all practical purposes, he had lost contact with his mother and father, and their relationship would never be the same. He had met only two Russian girls that meant anything to him, and they were also likely gone forever. He fought hard to overcome bouts of depression, finding little beyond his U.S. duty assignments to keep him motivated. None of the agents, Dan or any of the others which he had made contact with since he had been in the United States, ever provided any follow-on plan for him.

"Just do what you are doing," Dan would say. "It is important to our government."

As summer approached in 1960, Dan casually told Mike over a dinner meeting that there was a good possibility he might go back to Moscow during the period he was transferring from California to Puerto Rico. "Your bosses at Khodinka feel you might need a break in your work, and also they would like to review your work." Dan saw the reaction in Mike's eyes. "Comrade, don't get too excited. First, it may not happen, and second, it will be a very brief visit. We cannot risk having you disappear for too long."

Mike gauged Dan's words. "Listen," he said. "I will take the opportunity to get back home for just one day, if that is all they can arrange. When will you know?"

"I should receive word within a week. I presume you will get at least a 30-day leave when you transfer, won't you?" Dan asked.

"Yes, that is customary, but I haven't requested anything yet," Mike replied.

"Okay, you had better do that, and make all the arrangements to be on leave at some address that is quasi-legitimate. What about Harris in San Antonio? Make his place your leave address. You don't need to contact him—I will. After you get the dates straight on your departure for leave and your reporting date in Puerto Rico, let me know and I will make your airline reservations to New York; and you will be taken care of from there," Dan continued. "I will get a note to you in a week and let you know if this is a "Go". I think you do need a break."

Mike allowed his emotions to begin to freewheel. It had been three years since he was in Moscow. He had heard very little about his parents, only a few vague remarks that Galina tried to work into her letters. "And what of Galina?" he thought. "Was she married by now? Likely so. She couldn't wait around forever. And Mackye? She probably has a couple of kids by now." He faced the prospects of going back to Moscow this time with much less enthusiasm than his last visit.

Finally, his thoughts got around to Khodinka and wondering they wanted this time. He had provided everything that he could scrape up and passed it on to Dan. "Maybe," he thought, "maybe, they want me to come back to stay, and teach at the center or something. I have a lot of experience I could convey to the intelligence people and the students in training to become agents." And then reality would set in. "No, this will be another very fast and busy trip. They will not allow me to stay. A scant visit with my parents, most of the time, will be at the center and nothing more. I will try to locate Galina, but there is no need to look for Mackye." His thoughts and emotions cycled.

He came in from a flight late one night a week after his last meeting with Dan and found one of the neatly folded "Dan notes" he had become accustomed to, slipped under the door of his BOQ room. "The fishing trip is on. Make your plans," Dan had scrawled inside the folded paper. Mike didn't sleep much that night. In his thoughts, he carefully organized everything he had to do: get his "leave en route" requested and approved, make arrangements to ship his personal effects, clothes, etc. to his new base and sell his automobile.

Return to Khodinka

By daybreak, he was "ready to go". "This will be great," he said to himself. "I really need to go home! If they are willing to risk it, so am I." He immediately went to work to take care of all the miscellaneous items required to be accomplished, but mainly he needed to get his leave dates approved so that he could give Dan a schedule to work with.

During the first week of May, an impromptu event occurred that not only disturbed Mike but the entire country as well. A CIA operated U-2 surveillance plane, often referred to as a *spy plane*, took off from Peshawar, Pakistan, to fly a reconnaissance mission over Russia with a pilot named Gary Powers in the cockpit. As the story later unfolded, it was revealed the U-2 was shot down by a Soviet anti-aircraft missile some 1300 miles inside Soviet airspace.

It was during MAY DAY celebrations in the Soviet Union when the word was received about the shoot down. The Eisenhower Administration tried to evade the true story for several days, claiming the aircraft was on a weather reconnaissance flight and had strayed off course. Premier Khrushchev allowed the U.S. to develop their story and then dramatically revealed to Russian and Western reporters and television stations, photographs of the U-2 wreckage and the captured pilot, a "CIA pilot." Not unlike the revelations of the launch and orbit success of the Sputnik's, this was another great triumph by the Soviets. Mike researched every newspaper and news broadcast for information about the incident. When he listened to others discuss the Soviet feat, he had to hide his elation. He couldn't wait to get home to hear more about it.

By the middle of June, Mike was organized to depart on leave after being relieved from Hank's crew. They threw a big party for him at the officers' club, and he was cleared to sign out on the 25th. Leaving the crew and Castle left him with bitter sweet feelings; this had been his home and his job for five and a half years, and Hank had been a true mentor. He never allowed himself to think of the consequences if Hank or anyone else in his wing ever found out who he really was. His world and the *real world* were kept completely compartmented from each other. Dan had made reservations for him to fly out of San Francisco to New York the evening of June 25th, and he would drive Mike to the airport.

His farewell to Dan reflected no emotion on the part of either. Their relationship had been very business-like and completely impersonal. This was typical of Soviet agents operating in foreign countries. Friendship between agents was strongly discouraged. The more one agent knew about another, the greater potential for compromise if either were arrested. Dan told Mike en route to the airport he would be contacted by "Rudy" once he was in place in Puerto Rico. Rudy would be his principle point of contact and provide instructions and support just as Dan had.

Mike arrived in New York and was met by the reliable Frank. Frank could have been an exception to the "no friendship" rule. While he was strictly business, he also had an engaging manner and affable spirit about him. Mike liked him and felt comfortable in his company. Frank had made reservations for Mike to travel to London and then on to Frankfort as he had the previous trip.

"This should be 'old hat' to you now, Mike," Frank chided. "I haven't been home in almost eight years, so I wouldn't even know where I used to live," he chuckled. "I suppose I am doing my job okay or someone would tell me."

Mike detected a restless tone in Frank's words. He felt sorry for him and offered once again to make phone calls for him to family or friends if he wished. Frank declined, saying most of his close family were either dead or nowhere to be found. "So, not to worry," he said. "Have a safe trip, Mike, and I will likely still be here when you return."

Frank had definitely undergone a change in his demeanor, and Mike wondered if he should pass that along to General Sokolov, or just let it go. There was little compassion in the agent business he had learned, so he decided to let it go. Frank was smart and could take care of himself.

His transit through London and on into Frankfort was uneventful, but when he arrived at the Frankfort Mein Airport, he did not see Siegfried or anyone who appeared to be looking for him. He found a seat near the baggage carousel and began to wait. He sat there for over an hour and was beginning to get nervous thinking something had gone wrong when a thin looking man approached him and called him by name.

"I am Hans," he said in good English. "Siegfried has had a bit of difficulty. He sent me to collect you and to accompany you on a flight directly to West Berlin."

Mike was concerned with the change of plans and the whereabouts of Siegfried. The events after his arrival in Frankfort threw Mike off. Siegfried didn't meet him; a stranger named Hans not previously mentioned to him showed up over an hour late, and now he was being rushed to catch a flight and not the train to West Berlin. Finally, he realized he had not challenged Hans to determine if he was legitimate. As they stood in line at the check-in counter for the flight to Berlin, Mike suddenly asked, "Hans, what color is your day?"

Hans grinned and promptly said blue. Mike was immediately relieved; he looked at Hans and said, "Thanks, Hans. I'm a little tired and you showed up and surprised me. Is Siegfried alright?"

In a hushed voice, Hans responded, "Siegfried's wife has been picked up by the police for questioning after a traffic violation."

Hans stepped up to the ticket counter, got their boarding passes and guided Mike to a couple of seats to wait for the flight to be called. He continued, "We don't know what the problem is, but the West Berlin police are very clever. They will often pick up a spouse or close relative on a bogus charge in an attempt to get one of our people to over-react. Siegfried is playing it cool and waiting to see what unfolds. Gretchen is smart and knows the rules—she won't reveal anything. Our main concern is *why* she was arrested for just a minor traffic offense.

It may be legitimate, but we must always be prepared for the worst."

Then Hans said, "It was too risky for Siegfried to leave Berlin to meet you in the event he was being watched. I live here in Frankfort, so it is easy for me to take over from Siegfried and see you to your destination."

Once they were airborne for the flight to Tempelhoff Airport in West Berlin, Hans told Mike once they arrived they would exchange documents the same as he did during his last visit. Mike agreed. Hans instructed him they would follow the same routine in crossing into East Berlin. He had a chauffeur driven sedan waiting; they would proceed through Checkpoint Charlie and show their German passports and visas as if it were old hat to them. Hans apologized for not being able to stop over so that Mike could clean up and rest. He said, "There is a military transport waiting for you in East Berlin."

"If you miss that one," he said, "it will be three days before the next courier flight to Moscow."

Mike said he didn't mind at all, he was happy to keep moving. Hans smiled and said he would send word ahead once he was airborne. They arrived at Tempelhoff Airport; their car was waiting, and the driver headed toward the crossing into East Berlin. En route, Mike turned over his wallet and passport to Hans. In exchange, Hans gave him a Russian passport and East German visa identifying him as Viktor Alexandrovich Katsanov. He also provided him a Russian-made wallet along with sufficient rubles to get him through the trip.

Once again, he was *Sasha* and going home. They crossed over into East Berlin, arriving at the military airport without incident. Sasha boarded the Soviet AN-12 transport, found a seat away from several other military and civilian passengers, strapped into his seat and promptly fell asleep.

He didn't wake up until the aircraft touched down at the Vnukovo military airport near Moscow. Still drowsy, he tried to straighten his wrinkled clothes, found his bag and walked down the steps of the aircraft and into the dimly lit terminal building. Once inside Sasha looked around to determine if anyone indicated that they might be looking for him and then headed straight for the men's room. After he washed up and tried again to make his shirt and trousers look as tidy as he could, he walked back into the terminal lobby.

Dimitri

"Hello Sasha Aleksandrovich," a soft voice came from a few feet away.

Sasha was in momentary shock. "Mackye!" he gasped, as he turned and looked at the slender figure of the beautiful young woman he had all but erased from his thoughts. "I can't believe that you are here!" He was amazed at seeing her after all this time. "Are you here to meet me?"

"Who else?" she asked, revealing the incredible smile that he instantly remembered as the most beautiful and warmest smile he had ever seen. "This is where I dropped you off, so I thought I should come back and collect you." She moved to him and kissed him gently on each cheek. "Are you ready? Is that your only bag? I see that you are still traveling light."

Sasha, still numb from fatigue and the surprise of Mackye's sudden appearance, picked up his bag and followed her to a waiting black sedan at curbside. The driver promptly opened the right rear door and let Mackye in. After taking Sasha's bag, he trotted around to the left side and opened the door. Sasha got in and settled next to Mackye. "I can't believe this," he began. "I feel so shabby to have you see me like this. I have been in these clothes for two days." He couldn't think of anything else to say.

"You are fine. It is so good to see you, Sasha," Mackye said. "You look great. Are you well? Is everything going well for you? I am so glad you are home again. I have been so worried about you."

"I am fine," Sasha replied. "I still can't believe this. Are you okay? Are you well? What are you doing these days? Did you request to come meet me?" And then he stopped short. "I am sorry. I apologize for petitioning you with so many questions. Mackye, you remain so beautiful!"

Mackye smiled and gently put her hand on his, carefully ensuring that the driver had his attention on the street and the traffic. "Thank you, Sasha. The questions are fine. We have so much to talk about. Do you know how long you will be here? I hope we will have an opportunity to visit."

"No, I don't know. This trip came up very suddenly. I wasn't told how long I might stay, but in any event I must be back by the last week in July," he replied.

"My instructions are to take you first to Khodinka and your quarters so you can refresh yourself, and then you will be permitted to proceed today to visit your parents. You are not required to report back to the center for three more days, so that should provide you an opportunity to relax some and catch up with your mother and father." Indicating that she did not want to answer any questions or discuss any details, she put her fore finger to her lips and rolled her eyes toward the driver. "Well, it is good to have you back in Moscow, Sasha. You look very well."

The driver maneuvered the sedan through the Moscow streets of cars, carts and people while Sasha and Mackye exchanged small talk and an occasional smile, as he eased his hand over to touch hers periodically. He looked for familiar landmarks and began to feel depressed as he observed the dismal and dreary sights of the city. The filth and depravation seemed much worse than he had remembered. The sidewalks appeared to be much more burdened with people aimlessly moving in both directions. Most were poorly dressed with blank expressions on their faces. Briefly reflecting on the people and cities in the United States, Sasha wanted to comment to Mackye. He wanted to ask about the situation in Russia, but he declined. They finally arrived at the street side entrance to Khodinka, and the driver swiftly stepped around and opened the door for Mackye. Sasha let himself out, took his bag and followed Mackye into the entrance hall and through the security checks. It was very apparent to him she was recognized as someone of importance to the security guards. They were exceptionally courteous and responsive; of course, her striking beauty was also a factor. She guided him to the officers' quarters apartment building and inside to his assigned room. She had the key and led him in.

Once inside the room, Mackye turned to Sasha and melted into his arms with a lingering kiss. "Oh Sasha, I thought that I might never see you again."

He was caught by surprise greeting. "Mackye, I have missed you so terribly. What has happened to you? I received your two messages, but I confess I could not fully interpret them. Are you okay?" He continued to hold her firmly.

She eased away and moved to sit on the small sofa. "Sasha, take a quick shower, and I will talk to you while you dress."

He moved quickly to pull a pair of slacks, shirt and pull-over sweater out of his suitcase and went into the tiny bathroom and quickly showered. As he emerged, she smiled at him. He wanted to go immediately to her, but she motioned him to get dressed. He moved to the wash basin and mirror to shave.

"Sasha, I am married to Dimitri Vetrov. We were married almost three years ago shortly after your visit. It is a long story, but we will talk about that later. He is now here at Khodinka. The KGB assigned him here to work with the GRU staff. Don't worry; he isn't here at the center this week. He is visiting one of the offices in Kallingrad. When I heard you were coming home, I requested to meet you." Giggling, she said, "You didn't miss Vlad, did you?"

Sasha sneered, "Miss that SOB? I haven't given him a thought since you dispatched him the night we were here at the library. Where is he?"

"Vladimir Shepilev is rotting away in Angola. He received an *unexpected* posting to the embassy in Luanda," she chuckled, "and he is working under one of the toughest bastards in the KGB, who probably got his assignment the same way as Vladimir. The system can always find a special place for distasteful characters who get carried away with their self-importance."

Sasha continued shaving, briefly reflecting on Vlad and all of the cute little tricks he had played. "Good riddance," he finally responded. "Why did you marry this Dimitri?" he asked. "Do you love him?"

"Love is not a factor or issue," She shrugged. "I married Dimitri because I had to. I made a bargain with him—'something for something'. He has been very good to me, and he lavishes me with expensive gifts and treats me very well. I am his *trophy*. He likes to show me off at silly social events. I go along with it. Our relationship is one of requirement. He has two other former wives and two children by each. That is the personal side of it. On the other side, he is a very professional and tough officer of the KGB. He is well-liked by his superiors because he knows how to get things done, not always the conventional way, but he pleases those who count. He will never be promoted above colonel, because his superiors know he would attempt to wield too much power. The *system* wants him just where he is. And, presently he is assigned here at the center as a special assistant to Lieutenant General Anatoli Borodin who succeeded General Sokolov. Oh, I suppose you didn't know that Sokolov has departed. He was reassigned to Norway as the senior GRU officer to assist with problems there. Dimitri told me this. I understand that we have had several agents uncovered and expelled from there and Sweden," she continued while he finished dressing.

"Sasha, you may find General Borodin not as pleasant as Sokolov. He is very direct and overbearing. He came to the center as an exchange officer from the KGB. Of course, like all KGB officers, he has a grudge against GRU and takes it out on the career agents here," she smiled. "As you might expect, he and Dimitri get along fine," she interjected somewhat cynically, and added, "No doubt you will meet Dimitri when he returns."

"Why do you suppose I have been ordered back here?" Sasha asked.

"I believe General Borodin wants to see who you are. He has heard a lot about you, and I understand he has asked a lot of questions about your mission and how much it is costing to support you. And, of course, he wants to know what benefits are being derived from your work," Mackye replied.

"Sasha, I don't know anything about your assignment and I shouldn't know, so I have to be careful, but when Dimitri mentioned your name, I couldn't help but be very interested. As you may recall, it was Dimitri who had your mother arrested and detained after Vladimir turned her in. It was he that I appealed to for her release. And, dear Sasha, you might as well know the rest, Dimitri did not tell me everything he knew about your mother's case at the time. He admitted he could not detain her for more than a few hours because of her special status. Sasha, he blackmailed me into our relationship and marriage. All of the details of his ploy did not come clear to me for over a year. Even then, I was still at fault for inquiring into a case where I had no business. I hope you find your mother well, Sasha. I do not understand Russian people such as she who are borderline dissidents or worse, but because she is your mother, I can be lenient in my thoughts."

Sasha was shocked at hearing all Mackye had to say. He immediately felt twinges of guilt. He had called her and asked for her help when his mother was arrested. He had no idea that the whole event had implicated her and led to her being literally forced into marriage with this rotten character.

"Mackye, I had no idea," Sasha murmured. "I am so sorry. I feel awful. What have I done to you?" He walked over to her and took her hand, slightly pulling her up to him. Holding her in his arms, he asked, "How can you ever forgive me? I am so sorry for what I have caused." He had tears running down his cheeks.

"Shush!" she said. "It was not your fault at all. You didn't know what the circumstances were. I permitted myself to fall into a situation. I should have been smarter, but that is all history now. Everything is fine. I am well. Sasha, I will always love you. What is done is done. You are very important to our government's work, and we likely would have never had the opportunity to carry out our lives together anyway." She lamented, "Now, we must go. I have been here in your quarters much too long. People here observe everything. I will escort you to the drop-off near your parents' apartment building. Your father has been advised you are coming." She kissed him warmly and whispered that she loved him.

"One last thing," she said. "Dimitri knows who you are and has made some cynical remarks about you and your mother. He is also suspicious of my feelings for you because of my involvement in seeking her release. Please be careful. He may goad General Borodin into being tough with you."

"I can handle it," Sasha responded, "but I appreciate the warning. I regret that General Sokolov is no longer in charge of this directorate. I wonder where General Tushenskiy is now."

Mackye looked surprised. "Do you know Tushenskiy? He is the First Deputy of the GRU now. He is here at Khodinka."

"Mackye, General Tushenskiy recruited me for training here at Khodinka and for my mission assignment. I did not see him during my visit three years ago, but I am sure he is still interested in my assignment and continues to monitor my activities," Sasha replied.

"Good," she said. "Sasha, do not hesitate to use his name or to call on him if the situation becomes too difficult with Borodin and Dimitri. I don't trust either," she continued. "Sasha, may I quietly insure that General Tushenskiy is aware you are back at the center for debriefings? I know how to do it without creating a problem."

"Mackye, I am not afraid of these guys, and I know what my assignment is. I have been very successful in carrying it out, but if you believe General Tushenskiy should know I am here, then I trust your judgment."

"Good," she said. "We must go now."

Neither said very much as they drove across Moscow. Mackye reached over and caressed his hand from time to time when the driver was preoccupied with the traffic. As Sasha looked at her, he was absorbed with her natural beauty. She was older, and her facial features were sharper than when he first met her. Mackye was even more striking than he remembered, and when she flashed her bright smile, he melted.

Arriving at the drop off street, Mackye became business-like and said, "Sasha, a driver and escort will pick you up here on Thursday at nine a.m. Dress casual as you are now—perhaps a little less wrinkled," she smiled. "You have an appointment with General Borodin at ten o'clock."

As he stepped out of the car, Mackye slipped a small folded scrap of paper into his hand. He read it as he walked toward the apartment building. It read: "I will call you tonight after nine o'clock if I may. I love you." Sasha wanted to run back to the sedan, but it had departed, and he knew that would have been a mistake anyway.

Sasha bounded up the stairs and then stood breathless when he reached the second floor of the building. He hadn't been to bed in almost two days and fatigue was setting in. He rapped on the door of his parents' apartment. Tatyana opened the door. She stood for a moment as if she didn't recognize her son, and then she slowly put her arms around him and began to sob. "Sasha, Sasha," she cried.

"Mother, I am home. Please don't cry," he whispered.

Sasha was taken by how frail his mother looked. She was visibly much older in appearance than just three years earlier. "She wasn't old," he thought. "Could she be ill?" They chatted and drank tea until Viktor arrived home later in the day. Sasha was equally surprised that his father was beginning to age as well. Neither of them looked well to him, and both were subdued in their demeanor and conversation. Sasha asked about each and how the situation was in Moscow and Russia. Neither commented substantially about their well-being, but each said that they were well, the country is fine and they were generally doing alright. His first day home went reasonably well, but he felt that it was strained.

Tatyana prepared a wonderful Russian dinner which Sasha took delight in. It brought back many memories, but it was so rich he had difficulty doing justice to all of her work. After dinner, the three sat in the small parlor and sipped tea. They exchanged small talk without touching on any sensitive issues such as where he was working or what he was doing, although Sasha felt sure that his father must have some knowledge of his assignment. As the evening wore on, he told Tatyana and Viktor he was expecting a telephone call around nine o'clock and he would answer the phone when it rang if they didn't mind. "I am supposed to get a call from a colleague and may have to go out for a short while," he explained.

A few minutes after nine, the phone rang and Sasha sprang to another room to answer it. "Dah," he responded.

"Sasha, how is your visit going?" Mackye asked. "Are your parents well? Were they surprised and pleased to see you? You don't need to respond to those silly questions. I am sure all is well."

"Mackye, it is good to hear your voice. Yes, all is well with some concerns, of course. How are you? What are you doing?" Sasha responded.

"I am calling you, of course...to ask if you can meet me for a short while."

Sasha responded immediately, "Yes, where?" He hated to leave his parents so soon after arriving, but he really needed to get out of the apartment. He wanted to see Mackye.

"Meet me at the Borovitskaya Metro station, train platform level, near the coupon booth. I will be there before you," she replied.

Sasha hung up the phone and walked back into the parlor. He told Tatyana and Viktor he did have to go out for awhile to meet with a colleague, but he wouldn't be too late and not to wait up for him. They passively acknowledged and cautioned him to be careful. He slipped on a sweater over his cotton shirt, kissed his mother on the cheek and departed.

Mackye was standing next to the coupon booth and immediately flashed a bright smile when she saw Sasha approach. "Have you been waiting very long?" Sasha asked.

"No, I timed it just right, calculating how long it would take you to get here. I have coupons. Come with me," she said.

Mackye guided him to the train platform, and they boarded the next train that arrived. They sat comfortably next to one another as the metro train rumbled along, neither showing any expression. Mackye carefully observed every passenger in the car and each new one that entered at the stops along the way. Russians are curious, if not suspicious of any and everyone, and they stare a lot. Sasha had all but forgotten this peculiar habit, but Mackye was not staring out of habit. She was trained in observing and characterizing. As they approached a station stop, she nudged him to go with her.

They departed the train and took the escalator to the street level. Sasha at once noticed they were in a quiet and dimly-lighted part of the city. He walked beside Mackye as she led him to the entrance of an apartment building. She nodded to the swarthy- looking man in a dark suit standing inside the portico. Sasha recognized the tell-tale features of a KGB *goon*. After she placed her key in the door and opened the outside entrance, he immediately noticed this was not a typical Moscow apartment building. The interior had a highly polished marble floor and was poshly decorated with expensive looking paintings, murals and crystal chandeliers. He had never seen anything like this before. Mackye led him to the elevator. Sasha had never ridden on an *elevator* in Moscow. It hadn't occurred to him they even existed. Again, she inserted her key and the door opened. She pushed the button next to the fifth floor. Stepping out of the elevator, she walked down the lush carpeted hallway to "510." They entered the foyer.

Mackye had not said a word since they departed the metro stop. "Well, what do you think, Sasha?"

Sasha looked around the high ceiling of the foyer with a large chandelier hanging down from the domed ceiling, the mirror covering one entire wall and the deep carpet leading into the main living room. Mackye led the way to a balcony on the far side of the room and opened the French doors. Sasha hadn't spoken and followed her out onto the balcony and the moonlit night.

"Mackye, you have done well. It is clear to me why you found Dimitri a good catch."

She moved to him and pressed against his body. "Sasha, I am not trying to show off or impress you. All of this means very little to me. It is pleasant, and as I told you, I am treated very well, but I would trade it all and anything else if I could have you." She reached up and kissed him warmly. "I just wanted you to see that all in our government is necessarily fair. Very few generals in our army live like this. Dimitri has skillfully maneuvered himself into a position of reward. Just as easily, it can all vanish if he makes an errant move or crosses the wrong bureaucrat, but he won't. He's too clever. Come."

She led him into a large bedroom. "This isn't the master suite," she said.

Sasha spent the next two days visiting mostly with his mother. He went shopping with her, tried to carry on a pleasant conversation and avoided any discussion of her feelings or the incident three years before. She seemed to relax more after a time and talked of his grandmother, Bonita, and how she died a bitter person. His mother said she didn't want to leave the world that way, but prospects of anything different did not appear to be in the offing. "Our country and our people have little hope for the future, Sasha. We all had hopes when the miserable Stalin died, but nothing has changed. It may be even worse," she said. "There is little food for people to find, fear of the government and terror for those who step out of line, continuous talk of invasion and war with America. There is little hope left in my lifetime," she shrugged with a sigh.

Sasha talked with his father some, but he couldn't engage him in any conversation of a substantive nature. He had to realize that his father, although very bright and respected, was not a particularly strong individual. He was a loyal Soviet and apparently worked hard to direct the development of plans to defeat the United States and the West if they initiated an attack. Sasha wished he could openly discuss what he had been doing in the United States and seek his counsel. Even if he broached the subject, he knew his father would instinctively stop the conversation. Viktor, like most disciplined Soviet military officers, would not discuss anything having to do with KGB or GRU secret police activities. They simply didn't want to know.

Sasha tried several times to try and locate the whereabouts of Galina while he was at his parent's apartment, but he had no success. The Moscow telephone system had no semblance of order to it; the phone books were out of date and the information service was an exercise in frustration. He decided to wait until he got back to Khodinka, and maybe someone there might assist him. His visit days at an end, Sasha said goodbye to Tatyana and Viktor and departed for the rendezvous with his waiting sedan. In the back of his mind, he was hoping Mackye would be waiting with the car, but she wasn't.

A black sedan was waiting along with the driver and an escort officer dressed in civilian clothes. The escort didn't introduce himself, he simply nodded for Sasha to get in the backseat. "Must have had a bad day," Sasha thought to himself about the silent escort as they rode silently along to meet General Borodin. "I hope this isn't an indication of things to come!"

The sedan arrived at the entrance portal, and the escort led him through the security checks and on to Borodin's office. He was right on time and had barely sat down in the outer office when the general's door opened. A short, dark barrel-chested man stepped out, looked at him and said, "I'm Borodin. Come in." There was no offer of a handshake or any reflection of friendliness.

Sasha thought to himself, "Oh, shit. This isn't going to be very pleasant." He stood at attention and dipped in a half bow. "Sir, I am Lieutenant Katsanov."

Borodin didn't respond. He walked back into his office and Sasha followed. An aide closed the door, and Borodin sat down in his chair behind his desk. There was another man in the office who Sasha immediately identified as Colonel Dimitri Vetrov. "I am Vetrov," the tall, dark Russian offered. He didn't offer a handshake either. Vetrov was, as Mackye had casually described, nice looking, tall for a Russian, dark hair with graying temples, and he had a self-assured look about himself. Vetrov kept his gaze on Sasha and nodded for him to take a seat.

"Well, Katsanov," Borodin began. "Tell us what you do, not immaterial stuff. I know all of that. What do you do?"

Before Sasha could quickly develop his thoughts to respond to this vague question, Borodin interrupted, "You have been in the United States for seven years. You have cost our government a great deal of money. Our agents have provided you every convenience of American life and coddled you continuously. I want to know what you have done for your government, or have you become so used to the American life that you are now one of them?"

"Sir, if I may," Sasha tried to respond, but was again interrupted, this time by Dimitri. He applied a soft touch.

"Sasha, the general has been thoroughly briefed on your mission, how it all began and where you are now. He has a responsibility to properly manage all of the 'illegal' programs in other countries and must be assured we are getting our money's worth. What he needs to know is where you are in your plan and what can we expect from you in the future. Can you tell us?"

Sasha tried to assimilate the breadth and depth of Dimitri's statement and question. He began again, "Sirs, I believe I have worked diligently to follow the directions which I was given at the outset of my mission and have likewise responded to all the directions provided me by my in-country contacts. I am a Soviet GRU agent who uniquely holds a commission in the United States Air Force. I am a fully qualified B-52 bomber pilot serving under cover in the Strategic Air Command. I have provided every element of information available to me on SAC operations, capabilities, aircraft, weapons systems, planning processes and future programs. I..."

Borodin interrupted, "Katsanov, I hold your father in high regard. You were chosen for this special program in great part because of your father's loyalty and your demonstrated competence, but I must tell you I am disappointed in the products you have delivered. I personally believe you are playing around in the United States, having lots of fun as a hot rock Air Force officer and chasing all of those American girls around. Colonel Vetrov asked you, What are your plans?"

Sasha was burning up inside. He knew by now that no matter what he said, he couldn't satisfy either of these two. He had learned well how to control his feelings as a cadet at Volgograd and how to express himself as a constantly tested combat crew members in SAC. He looked straight into Borodin's eyes and said, "Sir, I have explained to you what I have accomplished to this point. I have responded to every direction which I have been given. I am confident I can accomplish anything that you or my government directs me to do. I believe I have created a posture from which will be able to achieve many great feats for the Soviet Union. I am at your disposal to exploit the United States strategic forces for every capability and technology which they posses or plan for the future. The longer I serve, the greater credibility I will have to accomplish whatever is asked of me. To this point, I have duped the American military and intelligence systems. I am entrusted with one of their highly sensitive Top Secret clearances which grants me access to most everything within my unit's war plans and special weapons activities. I was instructed at every phase during my training and dispatch to the United States to be patient and to exercise caution in the development of my mission and, Sir, I believe I have done just that and accomplished a great deal in the process." Sasha expected to be interrupted at any moment, but wasn't. Borodin fixed his eyes directly back at him.

He took a breath and started to continue with some specific details when Dimitri interjected, "Comrade Sasha, I believe General Borodin is sufficiently impressed with what you have accomplished, but you have yet to answer my question. I ask you again, what are your plans for the future? Are you just going to enjoy all of the pleasures of living in America for the rest of your life, become a general in their air force and retire there? Or, are you going to provide us with good intelligence to use to defeat the capitalist pigs? Can you answer me?"

Sasha was furious and turned to face Dimitri, attempting to gain control of his response when a sharp knock on the door interrupted him. The door opened and in stepped a smiling General Tushenskiy. General Borodin, Dimitri and Sasha all promptly jumped to their feet and snapped to attention. General Tushenskiy nodded and turned his attention to Sasha.

"Sasha Aleksandrovich, how good it is to see you." General Tushenskiy said as he walked over to him, shook his hand and kissed him on both cheeks. "I just heard yesterday that you were here. It is great to see you. You look so good and healthy," he chuckled, and in a low voice said, "America must agree with you! I have heard incredibly good things about your work. You are to be commended! Have you debriefed General Borodin?" He looked at Borodin, "Anatoli, what do you think? Do we not have a gold mine in this fine officer? I have monitored him since before we selected him out of Volgograd Academy. and I believe we have a great hero in our midst."

Borodin was still standing at attention and looked as though he had swallowed a rotten egg. He finally choked out a response, "Yes, General, we have had an excellent discussion with Lieutenant Katsanov and learned very much about his work. He is indeed a fine officer and excellent agent."

General Tushenskiy looked past Sasha to Dimitri and asked, "How about you, Dimitri? I bet that you folks in the KGB have never had an officer as skilled as this young man. Have you?"

Dimitri was no fool. He smiled at Tushenskiy and replied, "General, Sir, Sasha is one of the finest young officers and agents that I have ever met. I am pleased I am here to finally meet him personally. He is a good friend of my wife as you may recall. They were in training here together, and she has nothing but the greatest of respect for him and his potential."

Sasha couldn't believe what he was hearing out of the mouths of Borodin and Dimitri. "This guy, Dimitri, *is* cool though," he thought. Everything that Mackye had said about him was true. He knows how to 'tiptoe through the tulips,' certainly more so than Borodin who was still in shock at Tushenskiy's sudden appearance and his laudatory remarks.

Tushenskiy then turned to Borodin and asked, "Anatoli, are you about finished with Sasha? I wish to invite him to have lunch with me in my office. I also want to introduce him to the Director General."

Borodin had mostly recovered and replied, "Yes, General, I am finished and very satisfied with the report and accomplishments of Sasha." Sasha noted that he almost choked again when he used his given name.

"He may accompany you now if you desire, General," Borodin smiled.

General Tushenskiy took Sasha by the arm. "Good, Sasha, let's be off to my office so we can chat."

SIXTEEN

Vindication

Sasha enjoyed a pleasant visit with General Tushenskiy. He was also introduced to the Head of GRU, Army General Zotov, to whom Tushenskiy also lauded Sasha's work and achievements. He thought to himself during their meeting that General Tushenskiy could almost pass for an *American military officer*. He was extremely courteous and polite, and he demonstrated a genuine interest in people. The general was very interested in American military leaders, and he said he was very impressed with all of them. His two favorite heroes of World War II were Marshall Georgi Zhukov and General Dwight Eisenhower, who was now the President of the United States.

General Tushenskiy lamented that if Zhukov had become Premier instead of being exiled by Stalin, he would have been a great leader of the Soviet people, just as Eisenhower was for the Americans. He asked if Sasha had ever actually seen General Curtis LeMay, the former commander of SAC and now Chief of Staff of the U.S. Air Force. Sasha told him he had seen him twice, and for that matter, he said, General LeMay himself had pinned a Distinguished Flying Cross medal on him when they completed the first B-52 endurance flight. He had not been able to make that point with Borodin and Dimitri, but when he described the events of the flight and the rewards afterward, he thought Tushenskiy was going to faint. He roared with laughter and danced around the room.

"Sasha, you are a great hero, not only in Russia, but also in America, and you are still young! You will be a great leader in our country one day. I am so proud of you! I wish I could tell your father about all of the details of your successes, but one day he will know." And then he asked, "Tell me, did General Borodin give you a hard time today?"

Sasha was completely relaxed by now and replied, "Sir, he has a job to do, and I am sure he is very curious about me and what I may be able to do for our government. He wasn't too difficult with me."

"Sasha, you are also a diplomat. What about Colonel Vetrov?" he asked.

"Again, Sir, he asked some complex questions for which I did not have all of the answers, but he was fair." Then Sasha smiled and said, "But, Sir, I was delighted when you showed up." They both chuckled.

Tushenskiy, with a sigh then commented, "We try hard to get along with the KGB, and the Politburo and the Army continue to attempt to integrate us by exchanging around senior officers. The competition and jealousy between our two agencies is too historical to correct, so we do the best we can do; every once in awhile, I am 'blessed' with a Borodin or a Vetrov, and now I have *two* of them!"

Then he said, "Sasha, how would you like to go to Gorky Park and see first hand the wreckage of the U.S. U-2 spy plane we shot down several weeks ago? I would like for you to also see the pilot, Powers, but that would probably not be a good idea." He smiled. "Besides, the KGB has him so secured over at Lubiyanka that even I can't get a look at him."

Sasha swallowed and said, "Sir, I would like to see the aircraft. I heard the heroic story about our shooting him down before I left to come home. Is the aircraft fairly intact? Was the pilot injured?"

"Yes and No," Tushenskiy responded. "The aircraft being so light in weight came down in relative good condition, beat up badly, but our people have done a remarkable job of piecing it together for public viewing. The pilot bailed out successfully without any injuries. This has been a great military and political feat for our country. I will arrange for you to be given an escorted visit by one of our aviation experts this afternoon."

As they were saying goodbye, Tushenskiy asked Sasha if there was anything he could do for him before he departed to go back to the

United States. Sasha, feeling very confident after the turn of events of the day, said, "Sir, I have one small request, but only if it doesn't require too much work for someone. When I was here in training, there was a young lady I met before she left to work elsewhere, and then when I arrived in the United States, it turned out she is the daughter of one of the agents assigned to guide me through training. I met her again when she came to America on a student visa to attend college. She is back in Moscow now, but I have been unable to locate her." Sasha tried to rush through all of the details without making it too complicated or taking too much time.

"Good! I was hoping I could do something for you," the general said, smiling. He then called in one of his staff officers and asked him to assist Sasha in locating the lady he would describe to him.

Sasha departed General Tushenskiy's office with a Soviet Air Force major who was to escort him to view the U-2 wreckage. He also gave Galina Pakilov's name to the staff officer who, in turn, told Sasha if he were successful in locating the woman, he would leave the information in his room. Sasha was walking on air.

He wished he could contact Mackye and tell her about his most interesting day, which *she* had in fact made happen. She had saved his fat one more time! At the same time, he had mixed emotions about contacting Galina, even if she were located. It didn't seem fair to him to reunite with her after he had rediscovered Mackye, and perhaps even giving her false hopes again. "That is," he thought, "if she isn't already married to someone. Oh well, what th' hell, I have nothing to lose."

Sasha spent the remainder of the afternoon with his escort visiting the U-2 wreckage display set up at Gorky Park for all of Moscow to see. He wondered what the follow-on repercussions of this event might lead to. An American pilot was in the hands of the KGB at Lubiyanka Prison, and it would be anyone's guess what would eventually happen to him. The U-2 wreckage was just that; not much could be determined about the plane's engineering or technological developments. He thought to himself, "What if his government had captured the U-2 intact, forced it to land or something and how great a coup that would have been. What if we captured a B-52 and could exploit all of its development technologies and weapons capabilities."

Sasha's imagination continued to run. If he could make something like that happen, the likes of Borodin and Dimitri would probably blow out their miserable brains.

Back in his room, Sasha found two envelopes on his desk. "Does everyone have a key to my room?" he thought to himself. He opened the first one from the "Office of the First Deputy." The brief note inside read: "Ms. Galina Pakilov may be contacted at 252 95 52. Signed: Igor Vilkov, Lt. Colonel." His first thought was to check the telephone to see if he could call outside the center, and then he looked at the other envelope with "Office of 2nd Directorate, GRU" on the upper left corner. He opened it. The one-page note inside read: "Comrade Katsanov, I would be pleased to meet with you briefly tomorrow morning at 0900 to discuss further your assignment orders and departure arrangements. Signed: *Borodin.*" Sasha felt sudden chills run down his back. "Would he have to go through another session with those two goons?" he thought. As he was about to try the telephone, it rang. He hesitated and then picked up the receiver.

"Sasha, this is Mackye." She didn't need to identify herself. He could always instantly recognize her voice. There was no other like it. "I know that you cannot discuss any details, but did it go okay?"

"Thanks to you, dear lady, it went exceptionally well!" he responded. "I hope to be able to talk to you about it soon."

"I will be at the center tomorrow afternoon, in the library after two o'clock, if you are available. Goodbye." And she was gone.

Sasha then picked up the phone to dial out, and it worked. The number for Galina rang into an office, with the person on the other end answering, "Dah, Intourist Offices."

Sasha inquired, "May I speak to Galina Pakilov?"

Galina's voice came over the telephone. "Hello, may I help you?"

"Galina, you won't believe this, but I am in Moscow."

There was a gasp and then, "Sasha, Sasha! Where are you? When did you get here? When can I see you? Oh, I can't believe it!"

"Galina, I am at the *Center,* and I can't talk very much now, but where can I call you after your work hours tomorrow or the next day? I don't know what my schedule is yet," Sasha hurriedly said. He knew his call was being monitored.

Galina gave him her apartment telephone number and pleaded with him to call as soon as he could. Sasha had a restless night of trying to sleep. He had endured one of the more stressful days than he had in years, he thought. "What on earth can possibly happen tomorrow with Borodin and Dimitri? Could he get away to meet Mackye? Would he be able to see his parents again before he departed? Would he possibly get to see Galina now that he *reopened* the contact with her?"

Sasha reported to General Borodin's office at ten minutes before nine o'clock. He didn't want to be late. Borodin stepped out of his office, greeted him with a handshake and invited him in. "Boy, what a difference a day makes," he thought as he walked into the office and saw Dimitri standing, smiling and offering his hand. "Good morning, Sasha," Dimitri said pleasantly. "Did you rest well? How was your day yesterday? That is, after you left here?" he smiled.

"Fine, thank you, Sir," replied Sasha. He had decided to be as brief as possible with his answers, to provide as little elaboration as he could get by with and to respond to all questions with a Yes Sir or No Sir, and little else as possible.

"Sit down, Sasha," Borodin offered and joined Sasha and Dimitri in the corner sitting area of the office. "I really have little else to discuss with you, Sasha," he began. "I wish to join General Tushenskiy in congratulating you on the excellent job you are doing for us and to wish you well as you go back and pursue the work for us."

Sasha could tell that Borodin was carefully guarding every word and having difficulty being the least bit civil. He thought, "Thank Heavens for Mackye notifying General Tushenskiy's office before yesterday or I would be dead meat by now. And, what a bizarre situation. Here I sit with this tyrant of a KGB general and Mackye's husband. Either one or both would like to kill me!"

Borodin continued, "Sasha, I remain concerned about the end game of your assignment. At some point, we will have to make a decision regarding how long we can afford to have you slowly progress to a position where our investment in you pays off. Do you have any idea when that may be?"

Before Sasha could respond, Borodin proceeded, "There are many constructive things a young officer like you can accomplish here at the center or elsewhere in our system, so at some time in the near future, I would like for you to tell us what you would like to do. In the meantime, the GRU would like for you to continue in your present position and to provide your contacts with as much information about military activities you are associated with as you can. Perhaps that will be worth something," he cynically concluded and sat staring at Sasha, waiting for a response.

"Sir," Sasha began, "I believe there is much I can do and collect from the new unit I am being assigned to. I cannot provide you with specifics at this time, but eventually I believe I can. I have a plan, but I would prefer to try to develop it first and to work with my contact agent to perfect it before I explore it in detail with you if that is permissible?"

Sasha waited for a battery of questions to follow, and he knew he did not have an answer to characterize his "plan" which, in reality, he really didn't have one. The questions didn't come. They likely thought he was spoofing them just to get the meeting over with, and he was.

Borodin finally said he was finished. He said he was very busy with *more important* things and excused Sasha. "Your courier flight does not leave Vnukova until the day after tomorrow night so you are free to visit further with your father if you wish." Sasha noted he did not mention his mother. "My staff will make arrangements for transportation and so forth." Sasha thanked him and said that would be fine. He appreciated it very much. As he was preparing to leave the office, Dimitri asked, "Sasha, have you seen Mackye since you arrived back home?"

He panicked for a moment, not knowing if she had told him she had met him at the airport or anything else, and he was about to try to give a vague reply when he continued, "You should call her. I am sure she would like to hear from you."

"Yes Sir. I will do that. I would also like to talk to her," Sasha replied, feeling like he had dodged another bullet, perhaps literally. He departed Borodin's office feeling drained from the brief session he had endured with the two. He made arrangements to be met and escorted out of the center at four o'clock. That would give him time to meet Mackye at the library before he departed to visit his parents over the next two days.

Mackye came into the library a few minutes after two o'clock. They found a quiet corner table, and he related the events of the day before and that morning. "Do you know you saved my life?" he asked. As he revealed the meeting with Borodin and Dimitri, and finally the interruption by Tushenskiy, it was all Mackye could do to keep from bursting out laughing. She was in stitches and getting great joy out of the story as Sasha told it. He asked her if Dimitri had mentioned anything to her the evening before, and she said he had not. She had met him at a social engagement, and he had drunk too much. He collapsed into bed when they got home. She also said she had not said anything to him about meeting Sasha at the airport or at all. They agreed to keep it that way.

She went on to say Dimitri was never off-guard, and if he had any suspicions about anything, he would "track it to ground level." Then Sasha asked her about his visiting their apartment a few nights before and the man she spoke to outside the building. "He is on my side," she said. "If he ever uttered a word about anything he knows, he would be floating in the Moscow River before dawn." And that was that. They visited for an hour and a half in the library, not daring to go to Sasha's room or anywhere else where they might be seen. Finally, Mackye patted the back of his hand and said she must go. If she could manage it, she would call him at his parents' apartment, and then she departed.

Once back at his parents' apartment, Sasha wanted to spend the remaining two days trying to bond with his mother. She wasn't well and he knew it, although both she and Viktor claimed otherwise. Sasha tried to get her to agree to see a doctor at the military hospital, but she refused. They enjoyed a pleasant dinner that evening and after a time, he placed a call to Galina. She was euphoric and wanted to see him immediately. Sasha begged off with the excuse he was tied up with official business all evening and all of the next day, and it was impossible to get away. He promised to call her the following evening and to see her if they could arrange to see each other. He knew she was disappointed and upset, but he also knew he should be with Viktor and Tatyana as much as he could. He had no idea when he would ever be back home again or if he would ever see his mother again.

The following day, Sasha went with his mother again to visit Bonita's grave. He could tell it was Bonita's death that accounted for a great deal of his mother's morose feelings, along with his own prolonged absence. She had placed so much faith and confidence in her mother and had tried to transfer that with her hopes for a great future for Sasha, but that had escaped her as well. She had little to live for. Her hopes for a recovering Russia and a united family would never be. Viktor could never understand her feelings and had allowed his sympathies for her to fade away. Her only son and any hopes for the future she had for him had vanished as well. Sasha knew in his heart he would never see his mother again after this visit. He had tried the evening before to talk to his father about his concerns when they went out for a short walk after dinner, but Viktor told him he had done everything to bring her around and couldn't. She would not respond to any suggestions or help he tried to give her, nor would she visit a doctor. He had given up as well.

Sasha called Galina that evening and arranged to meet her at a cafe on Arbat Prospekt. He was not in a good mood after the day with his mother and tried to explain it all to Galina. She listened, but she was so taken by his being there with her in Moscow that she paid little attention to the details. She told him about her job and that she had been extremely lonely since she arrived back in the city. Her parents were still in the United States, but she seldom received any word from them. She said she loved him desperately and would wait for him no matter how long it took him to get back for good. It was a very stressful and upsetting meeting for the both of them. Sasha knew that he should have left well enough alone and not called her. He had only made the situation worse.

He gave Galina a new mailing address and fictitious name to write to him after he departed, cautioning her to be completely vague about details, not to mention any names and so on. He also asked her if she would mind visiting his mother while he was away just to keep and eye on her. They talked on for several hours, and finally Sasha told her he must go back to the apartment. He lied to her, saying he would call her the following evening, knowing full well he was leaving the next afternoon.

He arrived home half expecting that Mackye had called and a message would be waiting near the telephone, but she hadn't. It was late and he crashed into bed with a multitude of confusing and conflicting thoughts running through his mind. The visit home had been bitter sweet at best.

The Plan

Mike Scott arrived at Ramey Air Force Base, Puerto Rico, in August 1960. He had much to think about following the journey back to Moscow; the complex situation with his parents and that expected of him by his handlers.

The telephone was ringing when he walked into his BOQ apartment after a bright and warm Puerto Rican Sunday afternoon at the Officers' Club Beach. "Hello, Scott here," he responded lifting the handset.

"Captain Scott, this is Rudolpho Cardenas," a deep, heavily accented voice responded. "My friends call me *Rudy*. I understand you are new to Puerto Rico. Perhaps you are interested in buying a new Volkswagen to drive while you are stationed on our beautiful island? I am with San Juan Motors. We, of course, are the Island's major Volkswagen dealer, and I can offer you the best price available, even better than back in the States." Mike had thought about buying a better automobile than the *"stateside reject,"* a worn-out and rusted Chevy he had picked up from a departing young enlisted airman for $250. He needed something immediately, and it fit the bill. "Yeah," he replied after a brief pause. "I might be interested if the price is right, and I can afford it. How much are new *VW's* running down here?"

"I can put you in a brand spanking new Volkswagen for under $2000, which includes freight costs, taxes and license. That would be for cash, of course," the voice responded, "but, if you cannot come up with cash, I am sure I can make some good arrangements for you to borrow the money. What particular color would you be interested in?"

Mike suddenly remembered the name of his contact in Puerto Rico was to be *Rudy*. He felt his internal alert system react to the words on the phone. The name, the words "cash" and "color" were two of the key words in his "signal system vocabulary," but he couldn't always be sure he was being sent a recognition message until there was further exchange. All of his alert words were common usage and required response exchanges. "I probably can come up with the cash," Mike said, "and I like *red*."

The voice on the phone responded, "Good, I think we can do business. You have the green backs and I have the red car you are looking for." The color exchanges satisfied Mike and the voice on the phone continued, "When can we meet, and I can show you a vehicle?"

Mike responded, "I go on alert duty tomorrow, Monday, and I don't get off until Friday about noon."

"That is perfect. Why don't I come over to your end of the island about mid-afternoon on Friday if you do not have plans otherwise, and I will bring a new model for you and your wife to drive and check out? We can discuss the arrangements for me to put you in the seat of a new red VW." He continued, "Captain, please call me Rudy. My telephone number in San Juan is 546-7800, should your plans change or if you need to adjust the time. I will give you a call from the East Gate of the base when I arrive. Are these arrangements satisfactory with you?"

"The arrangements are fine," Mike responded, "and I am not married." Then he tried one more possible word signal exchange to further validate his caller. "By the way, are white sidewall tires available on the VW?"

"Yes, I believe I can satisfy your desire for the color of both car and tires for your new red car, white on the tires and no wife," he chuckled. "Have a good afternoon Captain Scott, or may I call you *Mike*? I look forward to meeting you on Friday."

"Good bye," said Mike. "Boy, this is quick," he thought. "I have been here just seven weeks, and I already have company." He was comforted by the phone call and the prospects of activating his work again. He felt as though he had been "out of the loop" and had not found an opportunity to carry out any substantial work for a year or so. He had upgraded to aircraft commander before he departed Castle and more recently completed B-52G ground school. He had "hit the ground running" since he arrived at Ramey. His new combat crew members had been assigned to him. His crew had transitioned and checked out in the "G" model. After flying three "solo" training missions as a crew and completing alert duty mission study and planning, his crew was now "combat ready" and certified to go on alert for the first time the next day.

Mike still had lingering thoughts about the distasteful encounter he had endured with General Borodin and Dimitri Vetrov. After the intervention by General Tushenskiy and the pleasant visit with him, he had tried to dismiss Borodin; however, he couldn't help drifting into thoughts about the confrontational and challenging questions put forth by both Borodin and Dimitri. It always left him mildly depressed, so he worked at maintaining a high degree of allegiance to his government and split motivation to work hard and perform well in his present capacity.

Dimitri Vetrov's persistent question, "What are your plans?" nagged at him persistently. Adding further aggravation and frustration were the thoughts of leaving behind his mother whom he knew was ill and despondent. Mackye was in a questionable situation, and Galina, for whom he also cared for very much, he had not treated fairly. He felt in his heart of hearts he had to do something soon to alleviate each of these situations that were beginning to weigh much too heavily upon him. His lengthy stay in the United States was beginning to seriously weigh on him.

SAC Alert Duty

His crew's first tour of alert duty was routine. He took the opportunity to pattern his leadership and management practices from his old AC, Hank Johnson at Castle. Although he had flown with his new crew through upgrade instruction and the three training missions, he used the time they were sequestered in the ground alert facility and virtually devoid of personal and family intervention to get to know each one better. He wanted to try and anticipate potential problems, both personal and professional, and to have them understand what he expected of each of them. Performing SAC alert duty was often boring and tedious. The boring part of the alert tours were the hours and days "waiting" for something to happen.

The tedium usually set in when a crew member had a family or other personal problem to bother him while he waited out the alert tour to end. These were the challenges that faced the aircraft commanders: to know their crew members personally, recognize potential problems, and attempt to keep them professionally sharp and motivated. Mike enjoyed these challenges. He had observed and learned well under Hank's leadership and tutoring, but SAC aircraft commanders also enjoyed a very tangible characteristic embedded in all of their combat crew members—not one of them was a draftee or conscript. They served because they wanted to. Mike marveled at this remarkable feature of the U.S. Air Force. This certainly was not the case in the Soviet Union where conscription was a two-edged sword. It forced young men to seek officer candidate training if they were qualified or be forced to serve in the lowly ranks of a soldier.

In all of the Soviet military forces, conscription was necessary to maintain their manning requirements. As he vividly remembered, the training was brutal and demeaning, but he was still a loyal Soviet and yearned to go home. Mike more often than not, felt as though he was not fulfilling his mission and often questioned his even being where he was, just as Borodin and Dimitri had doubted his usefulness. He had dutifully responded to every request for information and often provided more than he was asked to collect. He often wracked his brain to think of what he might do to further impress his leaders, recognizing that he was limited to only providing data as he had in the past—"rumors" and scraps of information about what his unit was doing.

The first tour with his new crew had gone well. He liked each one of his crew members and had concluded they were all compatible and could work and perform well together. With the exception of Tom Dalton, his radar navigator, the other officers were all near his own age, and Charlie Grimes, his gunner was in his early twenties. This satisfaction helped to somewhat ease his lingering thoughts about the visit and circumstances back to Moscow.

SEVENTEEN

Rudy

Mike showered, dressed in shorts and sandals and met his new contact, Rudy, on Friday afternoon as planned. Rudy was waiting outside the security gate to the base. He had a large smile on his face when Mike parked his old jalopy and walked over to the handsome Puerto Rican sitting in the bright red Volkswagen. Rudy got out of the driver's seat and shook hands with Mike. "Hop in, Comrade," he said smiling; walking around to the passenger's side.

"This is a beauty," Mike said, climbing in behind the wheel, "and, it smells good, too! I have never had a brand new car before."

"Well, it's all yours, Comrade," Rudy responded, still smiling and seemingly happy with his new acquaintance. "Take it for a spin. We can just head down the highway toward Arecibo, and watch out for the ox carts loaded with sugar cane; they are all over the place today."

Mike started the engine, and after a jerky start getting the clutch and four-speed transmission coordinated, they had a few laughs and headed East down the narrow highway. After about ten miles, Rudy motioned for him to pull into the parking area of a small seedy-looking cantina a little ways off the main road.

"Let's have a beer and chat for awhile," Rudy said.

Once inside, Rudy led Mike to a table in one of the dark corners of the room which served as a bar and restaurant. "Well, my friend, I am very happy to meet you. I have anticipated your coming for a couple of months after I was advised you would be here to work with me. Welcome to Puerto Rico."

"Thanks," replied Mike. "I am also pleased to meet you and look forward to assisting wherever I can."

Rudy had already insured they were out of voice range of the three or four other native customers in the room.

"Oh, you can do a lot, my friend. With the new B-52 bombers moving in here, we need to know very much about what they will be doing, what their mission is, profiles on the senior officers, and so forth."

Rudy continued, "You know, Mike, we have to be extra careful as well. This was a sleepy activity around here until an Air Force captain, who was stationed here and was either disgruntled or needed money, did a stupid thing last year. He tossed a bundle of classified documents over the fence of the Soviet Embassy in Washington and got caught. Did you hear about it?"

Mike acknowledged he had heard a little about the incident, but he didn't know the details. Rudy went on to explain that the officer, a navigator, had done the deed, but that the embassy people were suspicious of a trap and turned him in. "What a joke," Rudy said, "and how utterly stupid. It put these security and OSI guys on alert down here. As we work things out for you to do, we just need to be extra cautious until they relax again."

Rudy told Mike he wasn't Puerto Rican but Cuban. Working his way through Miami, he got fixed up with American identification and moved on to San Juan to monitor activities at the Roosevelt Roads Naval Base and the Army facilities. The real interest he told Mike was in the strategic bomber and tanker operations at Ramey.

"I am a devoted disciple of our leader, Fidel Castro, and I believe the only way for our people is to survive is to follow the order of the Soviet Union. Your great country is the only one to come to the aid of Cuban people. The capitalist and smug 'Americanos' are just a stone's throw away, and they spit on us!"

Rudy's hatred for the United States was very deep-seated, and he had pledged his loyalties to help overthrow the Yankee government by any means he could. Mike shared with him the rough going over he had received back in Moscow, and he really needed to produce some tangible evidence of his work here.

Rudy chuckled, "My friend, you are a pilot of those big bombers. Why don't you just load up one and go bomb Washington DC? You would be the biggest hero in the history of both countries!" Then he roared, "Think about it, you steal a B-52 and bomb their own country, and Khrushchev himself would come out to meet you! They both had a good laugh, finished their beers and left the dingy little tavern.

Back in the VW, Mike headed the car back toward the base. He asked Rudy how he wanted him to pay for the VW—"Check or cash?"

Rudy replied, "The car is yours. If you brought your title and license receipt for your junk heap, I will drive it back to San Juan, and we will call it a deal."

"The papers on my car are in the glove compartment, but I don't understand about this one," Mike replied.

"Look, my friend, my operating budget is sufficient to provide you an automobile. After all, we don't want our agents riding around in junkies like yours. I have completed all of the paper work on this car, and it is all in your name. You just need to get it registered with the security police, and you are all set. Compren'de?"

Mike was surprised by all this treatment. He wondered what General Borodin would do if he knew this was going on. They had a good chat on the way back to drop off Rudy. Mike liked his new "handler." He had never been around Spanish-speaking people before, but Rudy was easy to talk to. He had a great sense of humor along with reflecting intuitive intelligence. Mike bid him goodbye at the East Gate parking lot, and Rudy gave him a private telephone number to use in contacting him when he needed to.

"Otherwise," he said, "I won't bother you unless something important comes up. Get yourself settled and keep your eyes and ears open."

To Steal A Bomber

Mike picked up a temporary permit from the security policeman at the gate and drove the new car back to his BOQ. Later that night, lying in bed, he reflected on the meeting with this jubilant new friend.

The conversation with Rudy and the beers had given him a renewed spirit. He was more steamed up than ever over the ridicule that had been heaped upon him by Borodin and Vetrov. "I will get even with those bastards," he whispered to himself. "I will show them I am far superior to their petty jealousy and devious minds." Drowsily, he finally drifted off to sleep. The *cervezas* had both energized his thoughts and left him physically exhausted.

Suddenly, in the wee hours of morning, he bolted from a deep sleep, sat up and swung around to the side of the bed. "That's it!" He almost shouted out loud. "That's it! I will show those bastards. It wouldn't be too difficult on the right mission, to fly a B-52 all the way to Russia!"

Mike knew the notion was bizarre and likely even out of the question, but he thought further, "We will be flying sorties well out over the Atlantic, taking on refuelings from the tankers based in Spain, so with a reasonably good fuel load, what would prevent a pilot from going up the 'Med' and continuing on?"

He was still groggy from the beer and his mind still a jumble after commiserating with Rudy over his treatment by Borodin and Vetrov. He should let it go, he thought, but they had hammered him badly. They were far too devious and undoubtedly bent upon doing him in, if they could!

"Is Dimitri Vetrov aware of the relationship between Mackye and me?" he worried to himself. "Did he set me up to be smashed by General Borodin? Something is behind all of this! I will find a way to show them."

He thought how grateful he was for the confidence and caring of General Tushenskiy. Without him, he knew he would be dead meat with those two animals.

"How can I do it?" He couldn't get his mind off of the notion to take a bomber back to Russia. It wouldn't be a crumpled-up U-2, but a whole airplane. It would far exceed any exploit ever by the KGB, GRU or the whole Soviet army—far more than delivering manuals and tech orders for the engineers to pour over!

"How could I get my crew to go along with such a plan? No way, but if the crew were somehow neutralized, knocked unconscious or put to sleep, it could be done. I can fly the bomber single-handed. That wouldn't be a problem."

Mike was fully awake now and was convincing himself such a plan were feasible, given the right circumstances. He had to think it through. He did not go back to sleep.

He didn't care so much about impressing Borodin and Vetrov. Getting even would be fun, but even more so, General Tushenskiy would be overwhelmed as would Mackye. He continued to allow his thoughts to drift over all of the possibilities, but he could not come up with a feasible way to pull off such a stunt. He couldn't possibly go out to the flight line and just start up one of the eight engine monsters and take off with it. There was never enough fuel on board during their training missions to simply head for Russia. Besides, his crew would prevent any such attempt even if he had sufficient fuel and all of the conditions were right. There were likely too many fighters sitting aboard aircraft carriers and on bases in Africa and Europe that would be alerted to stop such an attempt.

"Pie in the sky." He drifted back into feelings of depression as he got up and began to prepare for the day. "What a genius of an idea! Certainly it may not be feasible, but what a great notion." He showered and dressed, still fixed on the whimsical thoughts.

Mike immersed himself in his work and his crew training responsibilities. They pulled their ground alert tours when they came around and flew the many variety of training missions that were handed to them. In the early sixties, tensions between the U.S., the West and the Soviet Union increased as intelligence sources began to report increasing developments in Soviet air defense missile capabilities. This prompted SAC to realize the potential vulnerability that its bombers faced in attempting to fly high over Soviet territories to launch or drop weapons. Therefore, the low-level tactics were devised to permit the bombers to fly under radar surveillance avoiding suspected missile air defenses. The newly devised maneuvers took on a whole new attitude among the crew force. The flying and navigation skills of the crew had to be perfect to avoid colliding with tall towers, mountains and even trees. The crews trained and practiced the maneuvers initially over water and then when their skill levels were achieved, they flew over specially developed low-level routes throughout the United States. Mike and his crew took on the new challenges with enthusiasm. These new maneuvers were exciting and added new elements to the routines of ordinary mission flying and helped to maintain motivation.

In 1961, SAC began to experiment with additional war fighting tactics. The Commander-in-Chief of the Command told the U.S. Congress he was directing the development of an airborne alert capability. The concept would, under certain periods of tension, place B-52 bombers in the air loaded with nuclear weapons and sustain them there with air refueling for indefinite hours. They would be ready to head toward targets in the Soviet Union if warranted. The purpose of the airborne alert tactic, in addition to being able to avoid bombers being caught on the ground during a missile attack, he said, was to send a strong message to the Soviet leadership that the U.S. has the capability, and it can strike Soviet targets with impunity.

This new dimension of evolving capabilities and tactics challenged the combat crews to new heights.

They trained by taking off with the bomber at maximum gross weights and flying extremely long pre-determined missions, air refueling once or twice to top-off the bomber's tanks which permitted them to remain in the air for up to twenty-four hours or longer. This new airborne alert concept was called "Chromedome." The bomber crews were scheduled to fly at least one Chromedome training mission each month to sharpen their proficiency in heavy weight take-offs, maximum air refueling on-loads and crew endurance.

Mike marveled at the consistent motivation of the air crews in his squadron to take on more and more work and responsibilities. He met with Rudy at least monthly to relay these new events in strategy. There weren't any documents he could put his hands on to convey the substance of these activities. He would meticulously write lengthy descriptions of the tactics and procedures and then pass them on to Rudy. He always included in his analysis the high motivation and positive attitudes of the Air Force crew members. He would lament to Rudy that he wondered if the same were the case with Soviet soldiers and airmen. Mike would tell him the U.S. airmen always stepped-up to new challenges without hesitation. He said they did not require political lectures or reminders that the Soviet Union was the great enemy of the Free World, and they were generally happy in their jobs.

Rudy would often sense despair in Mike's conversation. He frequently reminded him that no matter how powerful the U.S. forces appeared to be, the Soviet Union was stronger because it was fighting for a greater cause.

"We are strong, Mike," and he reminded him of Stalin's words. "I can shake my little finger and there will be no more capitalists in the world. Our leaders are waiting for just the right time to take Western Europe into the fold. America will not be far behind, no matter how they create silly ways to defend themselves. Eventually, they will spend themselves to death. Then see how high and mighty your fellow aviators are when one day they don't get paid."

Mike would listen and agree. He saw many faults in the system around him, but he couldn't readily visualize it collapsing so easily.

An Opening

One weekend over dinner in a San Juan restaurant, Rudy told him, "be on alert for something about to happen in my country. I'm not sure what. Our intelligence says that the United States is up to something, and if they aren't careful, all hell will break loose!" He continued, "Remember last year, Mike, when the U.S. tried to invade us at the *Bahia de Conchinos* (Bay of Pigs) disaster? Castro smashed 'em! The U.S. is a paper tiger. With all of its bombers and might which you talk about, and these aviators that are so brave, they couldn't even knock over little old Cuba! Do you really believe that they could stand up to your great nation?" Rudy chided Mike further. "I still think you should hijack one of those big bombers you fly and take it to Castro. He would reward you graciously," he chuckled.

"Rudy is right," Mike thought. "Our government has successfully moved ahead of the United States in space with the SPUTNIKS. They had shot down a prized U-2 spy plane and captured the pilot. The Bay of Pigs invasion was also a disaster for the United States and a great embarrassment to their newly elected President Kennedy. The planning was bad, and the tactics they employed were apparently just as bad. He had not heard much more about it. Although the Island of Cuba was just a "stone's throw" from where he sat on the base, little was discussed about the event within his unit. Mike had heard of no other such activity as Rudy alluded to from briefings he had received. So he dropped by the wing intelligence office the next week and chatted with an intelligence officer he had cultivated as a buddy. He had no such information either about *anything* unusual going on in Cuba or the Caribbean for that matter. "Castro is always pulling stunts and shouting threats," he said, "but we don't take him seriously. We have a battalion or more of marines sitting on the end of his island at Guantanamo, so he is pretty well penned down."

Sudden Recall

"Captain Scott, this is Special Agent Manuel Flores with the FBI office in San Juan." The clear, distinct voice came over the phone, without a trace of accent. "How are you, Sir?" he asked.

The professional tone of the caller and his identification rang in Mike's ears. He had all but forgotten the incident Dan had revealed to him back in California well over two years before. "Yes, I'm Mike Scott. What can I do for you?" Mike replied evenly.

"Sir, sometime at your convenience I would like to come over to Ramey and chat with you about something that has come to our attention. I'm sure you are very busy. When do you think we might talk?" the caller asked.

"Well, you are right. I am awfully busy these days, and I am sure you must know the reason. How soon would you like to see me?"

"Captain, it isn't incredibly urgent, but let me say, as soon as it is practical."

Mike's mind was a jumble of mixed thoughts. He replied, "Mr. Flores, I think I will be relatively free on the twenty-second—that's Monday. Will that work for you?"

"Yes, that will be fine. Why don't we meet at your officers' club? There are some small rooms where we can talk. Is that satisfactory with you?"

"Yes, that will be fine. What time? Can you tell me the subject you wish to discuss?" Mike asked.

"I will be there at ten o'clock Monday morning," Flores answered, "and I can't at this time. Don't worry yourself. This is just a routine visit."

"Fine," Mike said and hung up the phone.

He was terrified. He had gradually allowed the issue with his security clearance to slip into the past. Dan had never mentioned it again, nor had Rudy. As a matter of fact, he never brought the subject up with Rudy. In any event, he instinctively felt the call from the FBI agent was not good news.

Washington D.C.

Following the Bay of Pigs incident, the only thing the United States could do to keep the pressure on Fidel Castro for his continued bellicose conduct and violation of human rights was to tighten economic embargos. The Soviets, however, continued to supply the island dictator with sufficient food and supplies to support his regime. In the late summer of 1962, U.S. intelligence officials began to notice a dramatic influx of Soviet ships transiting into Cuban harbors. Initially, it was thought the ships were simply increasing the supplies of produce and durable goods for the winter. Then on October 16th, the President was notified by the CIA that a SAC U-2 reconnaissance plane had brought back photographs revealing substantial earth works and construction in several locations on the island. Analysis of the photos clearly reflected evidence that missile sites were being built at some of these locations.

The United States was all too familiar with the construction pattern used by the Soviets to build their own missile launch facilities. The photographic evidence showed similar construction patterns. They reflected not only six medium range ballistic missile launch sites and three intermediate missile launch sites, but five air defense launch facilities, three new fighter airfields and two airfields that could accommodate medium bombers. Intelligence experts had also concluded that nuclear warheads must have also been smuggled into Cuba to be fitted into the types of suspected missiles. All of this had happened virtually overnight and without notice by U.S. observers. The next few days and weeks placed Washington and the White House in a frenzy.

No one in the President's cabinet, or those in whom he confided in the Congress, could believe the Soviets would dare to be so provocative. The dominant feeling was surprise and anger. Just weeks before, Anatoly Dobrynin, the Soviet ambassador to the United States, had offered up an initiative to mutually sign an atmospheric test ban treaty. At that time, the Ambassador had also given reassurance the Soviet's only interest in the Cuban government was the protection of their rights.

"The only weapons which we shall send our Cuban ally is for defensive purposes only," Dobrynin was quoted as saying. On that fateful morning in October, it was fully apparent the Soviets once again had been caught in a flagrant lie. They were shipping missiles, fighter aircraft, and bombers to the island nation and concurrently building facilities to support them. There was ample evidence several thousand Soviet military and civilian workers had also entered the island to construct the facilities. U.S. intelligence agencies had allowed themselves to be duped. They had been lulled into a false sense of security, believing that the Soviets, lacking the sophisticated technology and war fighting capabilities of the United States, wouldn't dare to risk such precipitate actions.

The President assembled his closest advisors, political and military, to address the serious turn of events and to plot a course of necessary actions. The following day, October 17th, further U-2 reconnaissance photographs revealed more than a dozen, and possibly double that, shipping crates which likely contained offensive missiles of sufficient size to range over a thousand miles. That meant not only Washington DC, but Omaha, Chicago and most of the major military installations and cities to the center of the United States would be at risk. Analysts quickly calculated that the Cubans, with the help of Soviet technicians, could have the missiles operational within a week to ten days.

There were several alternative plans submitted to the President. His senior military advisors were split on attacking Cuba immediately and taking out the facilities. General Curtis LeMay, Chief of Staff of the Air Force, led the argument for an immediate and decisive attack on all suspected Cuban military installations. Other members of the Joint Chiefs joined the political argument that such an attack on a sovereign Cuba might very well bring the whole of the Soviet Union in a retaliatory nuclear attack. The President agreed. The risk was too great.

He hit upon the idea to place a naval quarantine around Cuba. He would order the Navy to stop and inspect all vessels inbound to the island for weapons of mass destruction. Before initiating that action, he asked his advisors to study the alternatives and consequences of the limited options at hand and report back to him. For the next five days, his advisors wrestled with options. The Soviets stood fast with their argument that they were not placing strategic weapons on Cuban soil.

Soviet Foreign Minister Andrei Gromyko called on the President. The appointment had been on the calendar for months, so the President agreed to meet with the Foreign Minister. He had decided not to reveal the intelligence findings in Cuba. The President wanted first to hear what Gromyko had to say, then follow with where the course took him. He was astonished by the boldness of the Foreign Minister who took the high road in the discussion. He admonished the United States for its aggressive stand in attempting to "starve the Cuban people." The sole objective of the Soviet Union, he said, was to look after the welfare of Cuba and its poor people—"to give bread to Cuba in order to prevent hunger in the country."

Gromyko further stated that only "defensive weapons" would ever be given to the Castro government, and the United States should never be concerned about "any offensive weapons" being placed on Cuban soil by the Soviet Union. Departing, he reassured the President that"....the only assistance being furnished to Cuba is for agriculture and land development. The Cuban people must be permitted to feed themselves, and they must also have a small amount of defensive weapons to defend themselves."

The Soviets remained intransigent. On October 22nd, President Kennedy went before the nation on television to explain to the American public what the Soviets were doing in Cuba. He denounced the Soviet activity and threatened retaliation if the missiles were not removed. Concurrent with his televised speech, the Joint Chiefs declared DEFCON 3 (Defense Condition - Three), which brought the level of readiness for U.S. strategic and tactical forces up to a war fighting posture. The naval blockade was implemented Navy POLARIS submarine patrols were increased from their day-to-day SLBM (sea launched ballistic missile) delivery capability of 48 warheads to 112. SAC ICBM's were brought up to full alert posture, and most of its B-47 bombers were dispersed to forward locations for immediate launch to attack. SAC's B-52 heavy bombers were alerted to begin preparations to implement their full-up airborne alert posture. This meant that upwards to sixty-six B-52's, fully loaded with nuclear weapons, would be airborne around the clock and loitering very near Soviet borders.

The Kremlin

Chairman of the Supreme Soviet, Nikita Khrushchev, was shocked by the response of the U.S. President to the Soviet intrusions in Cuba. He appealed to the Secretary General of the United Nations for support and pleaded for a peaceful solution to the "aggression by the United States" and the apparent blockade of Soviet "humanitarian aid to Cuba." He argued that the Soviet ships were only transporting food and humanitarian supplies to Cuba. He pleaded for intervention by the U.N. Secretary General to intervene, but he was also very careful to use the most polished of diplomatic language in his messages.

He wrote President Kennedy two letters on October 26th, saying: "Our purpose has been and is to help Cuba, and no one can challenge the humanity of our motives aimed at allowing Cuba to live peacefully and develop as its people desire. You want to relieve your country from danger and this is understandable. However, Cuba also wants this." He continued further along: "But how can we, the Soviet Union and our government, assess your actions which, in effect, mean that you have surrounded the Soviet Union with military bases, surrounded our allies with military bases, set up military bases literally around our country, and stationed your rocket weaponry at them? This is no secret."

Meanwhile, the Soviets made no effort to slow down the on-going construction of military facilities on the island. On October 26th new photographs clearly revealed Il-29 bombers being uncrated and assembled at one of the new airfields.

The Soviets appeared to be provoking a situation which was bringing the world closer to the brink of a potential nuclear war. And, then on October 27th, a SAC U-2 reconnaissance plane was shot down by a Soviet made surface-to-air missile over Cuba. The pilot was killed. Only the patience and tolerance of the President of the United States prevented the death of the U-2 pilot from triggering an all-out nuclear war. He held fast.

Ramey Air Force Base

It was Saturday, the 20th of October, when Mike began to hear rumblings of the unfolding events. He immediately called Rudy. They met briefly at a wayside tavern between the base and San Juan. Rudy was jubilant. "See? I told you! Big things are happening on my island! Your country is trying to come to the rescue." He also implied he had "known" about all of this for some time, but "couldn't" tell Mike everything. He said that he had wanted Mike to test his intelligence sources to determine what they knew. He said, "this could be the beginning of a great test of wills between the United States and the Soviet Union. We will see who is the mightiest! Mike, my friend, you could be going home sooner than you think! You will join your comrades in the great victory over capitalism!" he said.

After Rudy finished rhapsodizing about his delight in the news of the Soviet incursions into his homeland, Mike told him about the call from the FBI agent, Flores.

Rudy was instantly concerned. "What do you think the problem is, Mike? Why would they want to talk to you?"

Mike described what Dan had revealed to him concerning the lady who had "facilitated" his security clearance through the system.

"Well, that has been a long time ago, Mike," Rudy replied. "This is probably something routine; don't worry about it."

Mike drove back to the base after his meeting with Rudy. His mind was spinning with what he already knew about the Cuban situation and what Rudy had said. "This is incredible," he thought. "Can all of this be happening so quickly. What will be the U.S. response? What will I do?"

The call from the FBI agent was nagging in the back of his thoughts. He didn't know how to begin to prepare for the upcoming meeting.

Courage

Mike stood inside the entrance to the officers' club and watched the black Ford sedan pull into a parking spot. He *knew* that the dapper looking Puerto Rican dressed in a colorful island shirt was his FBI man.

"Ah, Captain Scott, I am Manuel Flores," the man said as he instinctively showed Mike his picture identification and badge.

Mike held out his hand and responded. "Yes Sir. I am Mike Scott. I have found a room where we can talk."

"Good, you lead the way," Flores cheerfully responded.

Mike led him to a small party room on the back side of the club, overlooking the cliff and bright beach below.

"Mike, may I call you Mike?" Flores asked.

"Yes, certainly," Mike responded. He was nervous. This fella was smooth, almost too smooth. He flashed back to the KGB types he knew, including Borodin and Vetrov. "They could both take lessons from this guy," he thought.

"Mike, do you know a man by the name of Daniel, or Dan Duncan?"

When he said, "Dan," Mike inwardly winced, but quickly responded, "No, I don't. I don't believe I have ever met anyone by that name." Dan had never given Mike a full name, only Dan. So, he was telling the truth.

"You never met a Dan Duncan while you were stationed at Castle Air Force Base?" Flores pursued.

"No, Sir, not to my knowledge," Mike, now more relaxed, replied and asked. "What did he do? Was he stationed there?"

"No, he was a civilian, living in an apartment in town. We have him in custody back in the states. He is under suspicion of being a foreign agent, or he may be a surrogate agent. We haven't been able to get him to talk. Beyond that, he was turned in by a female who previously worked at the Air Force base. She alleges he paid her to "doctor" some security clearance forms several years ago. Our guys have been searching her for quite some time and finally found her. She hasn't told us much, except she was contacted by this Duncan fella. As a matter of fact, she said she dated him for quite awhile. But, in any case, he used her to do some dirty work on security clearance requests."

Mike was churning inside. He tried hard to maintain an innocent looking composure. He didn't want to flush and look frightened. He could feel his heart pumping against his chest.

Flores continued, in a smooth matter-of-fact manner. "The Franks woman said in addition to this guy paying her considerable attention and money, she got greedy and he offered her, you might say, 'administrative services' to several officers whose clearance requests had hit snags for one reason or another. I think they found a half dozen or so Top Secret clearances in which she had fabricated the background investigations and falsified some investigators' names. Mike, your clearance file popped up as one that had the appearance of being manipulated." Then he quickly asked, "Do you know Hannah Franks?"

Mike looked straight at him and firmly responded, "No. I have never heard of her. Is she the woman who is being questioned?"

"That's her, Flores answered. "Well, Mike, the reason I am here is to try to help the guys back in the States track down the leads in this case. I will tell you I have already run a local background check on you, and I have found you are one of the shining stars in this outfit, according to your bosses. Now, don't be alarmed. When I contacted your squadron commander, I phrased everything in the context of a routine background follow-up. I did not mention anything about suspicious clearances or anything like that. So, rest easy. We don't put people on the spot unnecessarily."

Mike smiled. "Thanks, I appreciate that. What else can I do for you?"

Flores smiled back and responded, "Mike, you have been very pleasant to talk to and very cooperative. I want to come back and visit you after I receive a full report from the interrogation of this guy, Duncan and Ms. Franks. We're sure one of them will eventually tell us what we need to know. In the meantime, I need to tell you our offices in the States will be conducting a recheck on the background investigation processing of your Top Secret clearance. When that is completed, I am sure you will be in great shape. There is nothing further to worry about." Flores stood and shook hands with Mike.

Mike told Flores goodbye and went back to his BOQ. He needed to contact Rudy and tell him about the meeting, but he knew he had better not make any unnecessary phone calls or leave the base for awhile after this experience. "They're probably watching my moves and monitoring phone calls, after all of this," he worriedly mused to himself. He knew that the KGB would follow that modus.

EIGHTEEN

World Disorder

The next morning, October 23rd, the wing's B-52's were loaded with fuel and nuclear weapons in preparation for being placed on alert. This was no practice exercise. Later in the day, the wing commander assembled all of the staff, combat crews and support personnel in the alert facility and told them as much as he knew about the situation in Cuba. He also announced the wing would likely begin airborne alert operations within the next day or so.

"These will not be Chromedome training missions," he said. "If we are executed to fly them, you bomber crews will fly pre-planned sorties up to and closest to the edge of the Soviet Union. The tankers will keep you topped-off with gas, and you will loiter in your orbit patterns until you are executed to fly a strike mission against Soviet targets, or you are released to come back home. We will keep this operation up until the Soviets remove the war fighting capabilities from Cuban soil."

At the conclusion of the briefing, the wing operations officer called out the names of eight aircraft commanders to have them report to the operations-plans office to begin airborne alert mission study and planning. Mike's name was among those called. He was elated. This meant his crew would be among the first to begin flying the actual Chromedome missions. He and his crew members reported immediately to the mission planning room. The crews were briefed on the alert sorties they would fly if directed to do so. The route of flights they were told would be conducted in two ship increments:

Two B-52G's would take off from Ramey together, fly across the Atlantic Ocean, over Gibraltar and up the Mediterranean to an area over the Tyrannean Sea. They would set up widely separated large orbit patterns and remain "on station" until executed to fly a strike mission or return home when their fuel levels dictated. Mike studied the maps and locations carefully. He noticed immediately that his bomber would be orbiting just a few hours from Soviet territory and Russia.

That evening following the intensive planning session, Mike drove off base to a pay phone and contacted Rudy. His crew had not yet been placed on alert, so he wanted to meet with him as soon as the two could rendezvous half way between San Juan and Ramey.

First, he told Rudy about the visit with Flores and that the FBI was conducting a follow-up background investigation. "Rudy," he said, "that will nail me for sure. I am a sitting duck with a blank history as to whether I ever existed. So, we have to capture this opportunity! When my crew takes off on our airborne alert mission in the next few days, my bomber will be within a few hours of a dozen airfields in Russia. If I can find a way to take my crew out of action or put them to sleep, I can fly the B-52 home. What do you think? Can you get things arranged that quickly?"

Rudy's eyes were ablaze. "I told you, my friend, you have the *cajones*! Now, I will need to first get permission from Roger in Washington. I will talk to him tonight. Second, you need to tell me what you need when you fly into Soviet territory."

Mike pulled a huge navigation map out of a paper bag. "I have roughly drawn our planned route of flight on this chart. As you can see, we will be in an orbit pattern right here. If I can eliminate interference from my crew members, I can fly the airplane over, or off the Southern tip of Italy, across the Adriatic into Albania and *zap*, right on home. I can land wherever they want me to! What do you think?"

"This is pure genius! Mike, you are a man of courage! We must act fast. When do you think you may fly your first mission?" Rudy asked.

"I don't know, but it could come within a day or two. My crew is one of eight initially chosen. I could be on the first, second, third or fourth day. I could fake a cold for a day or so and ask to go on the fourth day, but I don't want to lose out all together. Eventually, every crew in the wing will be in the lottery to fly. What can you get me to put in my crew member's drinks or food to knock them out? Now, listen to me, I said temporarily put them to sleep for several hours—four to six—not to injure them! Got it?"

Rudy grew more excited. "This is great!" he said. "I'll take this map with me to guide me. You try to delay as long as you can, but don't overdo it. If you have to fly before we can get things organized that may be okay, too. It may give us more time, that is, if a war doesn't start." He drew a deep breath. "I have a source to get you some strong sedatives that might work on your crew. You don't want to hurt them. I understand. But, what if this all works? What will happen to them when you land?"

"Rudy, I want you to relay to your senior contact—I **do not** want any harm to come to these men—from the highest level or it is no deal." Rudy could see that Mike was deadly serious. He pressured Rudy to emphasize that point.

"Okay, Mike. You have my word," Rudy responded. " Now I must move fast. Call me late tomorrow and give me your status, and I will give you mine. Make your call from off base somewhere if you can. The security snoops may be on alert with all that is going on."

Back in his BOQ room, Mike sat at his desk going over detail after detail regarding how this incredible feat could be done. He knew if he could somehow sedate the other five crew members with something in their drinks or food, it would keep them out of the way for several hours. Then he could successfully navigate his airplane to a designated location.

He began to make a list. "I'll need some navigation aids like VOR (visual omni range) that are compatible with the bomber's receivers. I'll also need a route of flight to be laid out for me to follow point to point, to avoid air defenses or populated areas. I sure don't want to be shot down by 'my own fighters' after getting into home territory! I'll need communications frequencies to talk to ground controllers, or other aircraft, after I arrive in Soviet-controlled airspace. And it's up to the GRU or KGB, but they need to plan for a suitable airfield with equipment to handle the huge bomber when I land." His adrenaline would pump up so high that at times it shook his whole body. Then he would be overcome with feelings of despair, thinking that the whole thing was doomed because of a thousand impediments and risks that stood in the way.

It s A Go

The following morning, Mike was notified that the airborne alert sorties would likely begin within a day or two, and that he was number four. He had feigned a cold and sore throat with his squadron operations officer. The schedule gave him considerable relief and hopefully time for Rudy and his contacts to make plans if they considered the whole thing feasible. He drove off base and called Rudy that evening. When he answered the telephone, Mike could tell Rudy was riding high.

"Mike!" he said in an outburst. "They said go for it! They need to know how much time they have before you will be flying?"

Mike told him that he thought he would not fly for at least a several days. Rudy replied, "I hope that's enough time. I'll report back tonight. In the meantime, tell me what you think you need to do this?"

Mike reviewed his list of requirements. "Navigation aids, communications frequencies, identification of an airfield with sufficient runway length to land the bomber, aircraft handling equipment," and, he added, "by all means safe passage. I don't want to get shot down by my own people!"

Rudy was then serious. "I have the list. Most of it we have already discussed. Work is going on, as we speak, by the people who know how to do this. You have been given the highest priority in the government right now. Our leaders want to come out of this situation over on the other island in good shape. They have told me that they will prolong any negotiations as long as possible to insure that you have time to carry out your mission. By the way," he continued, "I am now speaking directly to you-know-where. I have a coded capability to communicate directly to the highest authorities, so I don't have to go through Roger and wait for a relay. Mike, I believe that they think we are doing a good job here, and they are deadly serious about you carrying out your plan."

"That's good, Rudy," Mike responded. "Now, how about the medication we discussed? Did you locate what is needed?"

"Yes, my friend," he replied. "I will have your prescription filled tomorrow and deliver it to you. You will need to experiment with different ways to administer it. You know, try mixing it with water, coffee or juice. I have been assured it is the latest on the market, and it will do the trick as we discussed. And, Mike, my friend, can I go with you?" Rudy roared with laughter. He was getting a great charge out of all of this.

"Yes, you can go," Mike chuckled. "Now, I must go. Tell your friends I have all the navigation maps I need to get me to the selected destination. The folks here probably have better charts than people elsewhere would expect. I will call you tomorrow evening for an update. Thanks, Rudy, you are a real professional and I will see to it you receive hero honors out all of this."

"Thanks, my friend. Good luck with your work." Rudy hung up.

Wake Up Call

Mike returned to his room after his phone conversation with Rudy and had no sooner dozed off into exhausted sleep when his telephone rang. In a groggy response, he answered, "Scott here."

"Mike, this is Lt. Colonel Mathews. Sorry to wake you, but we have a problem. Bob Sanders is on alert with his crew and he is ill. We need you to come down and fill in as AC on his crew until he can get to the hospital and find out the problem. I hate to do this. You aren't scheduled to fly for three more days, but you can get as much rest in the alert shack as you can there."

Mike was immediately angered by the sudden turn of events. "God," he thought, "this is going to screw up everything. I have to get the info and prescription from Rudy and clean up any coordination with him before we fly." Then he responded to the Ops Officer, "Sir, as you know I have a pretty bad cold myself and have been running a little fever."

Lt. Colonel Mathews didn't have time to quibble. "Mike, you're okay to stand alert. Sanders is puking his head off and may have something serious, so get your gear together and get down here pronto!"

"Yessir, Colonel. I'll be okay, and I'm on my way," Mike quickly responded and began to get into his flight suit while thinking of what he could do to let Rudy know. He made sure he had all his mission materials in his brief case and drove hurriedly to the flight line and the ground alert facility.

When he arrived, the ailing Sanders quickly handed him his "codes envelope". The aircraft commanders and radar navigators were responsible for personally holding the highly classified authentication codes which were to be used to confirm a valid execution order should the nation go to war. They wore them in a plastic packet affixed to a beaded chain around their necks. Mike took the chain and code packet, exchanged nods with Sanders, and the medics took the sick pilot away.

It was late when Mike went to Sander's room which was shared with his copilot, Dennis Lamb. Lamb was fast asleep, so Mike quietly put down his briefcase and jacket and went to the galley for a cup of coffee. The Alert Facility Manager was there and told him he had changed the linens on Sander's bed and sprayed the room with Lysol. Mike thanked him and sat down at a table to ponder his next move. He decided he would wait until morning when there would be considerable activity on the base, including lots of telephone traffic, and then call Rudy. If there were any monitoring of phone conversations by the OSI or anyone else, they would have a difficult time catching everything. He finished his coffee and went to bed.

The next morning he got Sander's crew together and went over their alert preparations. He and Sander's crew navigator, Captain Jim Swanson, spent an hour going over that crew's mission plan in the event the "balloon went up" and he had to fly into combat with this crew. The alert crews had been briefed there would not be any practice responses due to the heightened tensions. Everybody was to sit tight and be prepared for the worst. The Ops Officer and intelligence team came to the alert facility after breakfast and brought the crew members up to date on the evolving situation with Cuba and the Soviet Union.

The ops officer said, "The President has sent a stern warning to Khrushchev to either get the missiles out of Cuba, or potentially suffer the worst of consequences. So far the Soviets are intransigent. The waters around Cuba are all under U.S. control and quarantine, so no additional Soviet ships can enter the island's ports." He continued, " The SAC alert posture has been elevated to DEFCON 2. I am sure all of you know this is the highest level of alert posturing ever by the United State. If we go to DEFCON 1, it will, in effect, be a declaration of war and the last step before execution of the war plan." The words were sobering. No one uttered a word.

The intelligence officer briefed the crews on the heightened status of Soviet defenses, including anti-aircraft sites and fighter-interceptor locations. After the briefings, Mike and his "adopted" crew went out to flight line and their assigned B-52. They conducted the daily pre-flight checks to insure the bomber was ready to fly if their mission was executed. At mid-morning, Mike used a base telephone within the alert facility to make a long distance call to Rudy. He knew it was risky. Telephones might be monitored during the current state of conditions, but he needed to get the sedatives and as much other data as possible in the event he didn't have time before he was scheduled to fly his airborne alert sortie, now only two days away. He would attempt to get the message across to Rudy.

When Rudy answered the phone, Mike quickly responded. "Dr. Cardenas, this is Captain Scott. I just wanted to call and tell you I had to go to work last evening, that is, go on alert, and to see if there was some way you could get my prescription to me since I will not be able to get away for a day or so."

Rudy immediately picked up on the situation. "Yes, Captain, I have your prescription ready and instructions for taking care of yourself. I can come to the base later today if you can instruct me on how to deliver the medicine to you."

Mike spelled out his plan. "Doctor, if you can deliver the prescription package to the East Gate of the base, I'll alert the security police on duty there to take the package from you and deliver it to me here at the alert facility. Is that okay?"

"Perfect, Captain," Rudy answered. "I will package it up along with the instructions and have it to the base by four o'clock this afternoon. Are you feeling alright this morning?"

Mike responded, "Reasonably well, Doctor. I just didn't expect to have to go on alert since I wasn't feeling well, but the fellow whose place I'm taking is in worse shape than me. I really appreciate your accommodating me."

"That's okay, Captain. If you need anything else, please call me," Rudy answered. "And, Sir, you might give me your telephone extension where you are located in the event I might need to call you."

Mike gave Rudy the alert facility phone number and concluded the call. When he hung up, he sat back and reviewed the conversation exchange to determine if either had said anything that might be interpreted as suspicious. He was satisfied that all was okay. Rudy was a sharp agent and easy to work with—the best he had dealt with during all of his years in the States. As he went over the various elements of his plan, it occurred to him he had not completed one critical detail necessary to his mission. He needed to take with him at least two lengths of parachute cord for each of his crew members. He had planned to cut nylon parachute cord into sufficient lengths and to sear the ends so they wouldn't ravel. These would be used to secure the arms and legs, if necessary, of his crew members after he "administered" the sedative Rudy was delivering to him. The cords were a critical part of his plan. He would have to find a way to acquire a sufficient amount to do the job, and he would have to get it while he was now sequestered on alert. He decided to initiate an approach which might work. He sidled up to one of the B-52 crew chiefs assigned to the alert bombers after lunch time and one whom he had gotten to know fairly well. "Hi, James. How goes it? Boy, we've got something going, haven't we?"

"Hi, Captain. What are you doing on alert?"

"Oh, I came on last night after midnight to fill in for Captain Sanders. He came down with a bug, throwing up and fever, so I got th' call," Mike responded, sounding a little depressed. "I had a dozen small things I needed to get done before my crew flies an airborne alert sortie the day after tomorrow, but there'll be time when I come back from that one, I suppose."

"Anything I can do, Captain? I get off alert this afternoon," the crew chief offered.

"Naw, James," Mike replied. "I just have a bunch of odds and ends to take care of. But you know, I've been looking for some parachute cord to use to tie down the cover I bought for my VW. The sun and rain are going to ruin my red paint if I don't cover it when I'm not driving it. Do you know where I can get twenty yards or so?"

"Hey, Sir, not a problem. I've got an *in* over at the parachute shop. I'll pick up some for you. When do you need it?" James asked.

Mike smiled, "That would be great, James! If I could get some while I'm sitting here on alert, I could cut it into the lengths I need and sear the ends. Then I'll be ready to cover my car when I get off alert."

"You've got it, Captain," James said, eager to do a favor for one of his favorite pilots. "I'll make a phone call and have my buddy drop some by here this afternoon."

"Hey, James, thanks! Well, I've got some work to do. Guess I had better get going." Mike shook hands with the crew chief and went back to his room, smiling. He was very proud of the rapport that he had with the NCO's in the wing. Reflecting back on his two years at Volgograd and the scum that called themselves non-commissioned officers, there was no comparison.

"These are professional military men of the highest order. They knew their jobs. They work hard. They have families and are completely reliable. How has our own military gone wrong with its enlisted members? If this were the Soviet Union, we would have officers, even captains and majors, performing as crew chiefs on bombers such as the B-52. NCO's simply can't be trusted, much less they aren't bright enough to have the responsibility," he ruefully mused.

Later in the day, just before the dinner hour, the alert facility manager came by Mike's room and handed him a package with his name imprinted on a San Juan pharmacy label. Rudy had once again mastered a professional touch. He was alone, and Dennis Lamb was in the crew lounge playing cards. Mike opened the package to find a bottle containing two dozen large white capulets. He inspected the paper in which the bottle was wrapped and saw that Rudy had lightly printed a column of three-letter symbols along side a column of numbers which he identified as VOR (omni range) frequencies. Mike took a large navigation chart out of his brief case and identified the three-letter symbols as relating to cities or towns along a route from the Adriatic Sea to the Black Sea and thence north to the Russian city of Kursk, which he calculated to be roughly 300 miles south of Moscow. Rudy had, in very simple form, laid out a complete flight plan route for him. Mike was impressed. "This guy is a lot sharper than I ever suspected," he thought. "He's a real pro!"

He folded the chart and put it back in his brief case along with the wrapping paper "flight plan data." He then inspected the bottle of capulets. The label read: "Doriden (Glutethimide) 500 mg. Take one with water or juice. CAUTION: Hypnotic Sedative. One Tablet Can Induce Sleep For Up to 6 Hours and drowsiness for several hours thereafter. Do Not Take More Than One Tablet Without Instructions From A Physician."

Mike studied the bottle and wondered if they really worked. While he sat on the side of his bed thinking through his plan, Dennis Lamb, his temporary roommate and copilot walked in. "What's up, Captain? You gonna eat dinner?"

"Hey, Dennis," Mike responded, momentarily surprised. "Yeah, I am. Are you ready?"

"Yessir, I am. They're having charcoal grilled T-bones with baked potatoes. Boy, we're getting VIP treatment during this little crisis, aren't we?" Dennis chortled.

Mike responded, "Yeah, we sure are, Dennis. I want to go wash up. I'll meet you in the chow line, or save me a place at a table."

Mike proceeded to the facility latrine and washed up. While he was cleaning up, he struck upon an idea. He thought: "We're not subject to practice alert responses during this crisis, so what if I try out one of the sedative caps on Dennis tonight and see how they work?" As he moved on to the cafeteria line, he pursued his idea: "If I can put one in his coffee after dinner and closely monitor him through the night, there shouldn't be any harm done." And then, he said to himself: "I have to do it. It's the only way to proof-test these things."

He took his food tray and joined Dennis and two other crew members at their table. The four completed their dinner, exchanging talk about the on-going crisis, what it meant and what might happen. Mike noted this was one of the few times he heard crew members discuss the Soviets and their potential intentions. Most conversations while crews were on alert duty centered around plans after their alert tour: girls, leave, flying, wives and kids, in random order, but seldom the enemy.

"Are you going to watch the movie, Captain?" Dennis asked Mike.

"I don't think so, Dennis. I think I'll read awhile and turn in early," Mike replied. "Have you heard anything about how your boss is doing?"

"Yeah," Dennis said. "I talked to his wife a little while ago, and she said he was doing fine, just a twenty-four hour bug. He'll probably come back on alert tomorrow and relieve you. That won't disappoint you, will it?"

Mike smiled and replied, "Hardly, I have to go airborne the day after tomorrow. I would like to get a few personal things done before that."

As the other two crew members excused themselves to leave the table, Mike quickly interjected, "Dennis, I'm going to have a cup of coffee. Can I get you one and maybe a another piece of pie?"

"No pie, Captain, but I will take the coffee if you are going to have a cup."

Mike promptly got up and walked over to the coffee urn and slowly filled two heavy mugs. He had already removed one of the capulets from the bottle and held it in his hand. It then occurred to him that the caps would probably have to be pulverized in order to more easily dissolve. So he looked around making sure he wasn't being observed and quickly mashed up the caplet in a spoon with the handle of another.

Mike felt a sudden chill. "This is crazy. I could be executed over this stupid stunt," he said to himself. The cap remained in crude bits, but he dropped it in one of the mugs and stirred it quickly. He was relieved when it appeared that the bits and pieces either dissolved or sank to the bottom.

He returned to the table and put the mug in front of Dennis. "Sorry that took so long, Dennis. One of the urns was empty and the other was still perking."

"That's fine, thanks," Dennis acknowledged and promptly added two spoons of sugar and stirred it in.

Mike breathed a further sigh of relief as Dennis first tasted and then proceeded to drink the contents. "Good coffee," he said.

They each sipped on their coffee, exchanging small talk. Mike watched Dennis carefully. He hoped against hope that this stuff would take a gradual effect and not result in some dramatic collapse or seizure. If it did, he thought, and the medics came, no telling what might happen. Mike finished his coffee and said he was going to the room. Dennis acknowledged and stood up slightly unsteady. "I think I'll join you and brush my teeth before the movie starts." They headed toward the alert facility dormitory rooms.

Mike walked along side Dennis to insure he didn't stumble or fall. As they entered their room, Dennis smiled and slowly muttered, "I think I'll rest a minute before the movie." He let himself down on his bed and that was it. He was dead asleep, if not fully unconscious.

Mike closed the door to the room, removed Dennis' flight boots and put a blanket over his lower body. He checked his watch. It was 6:50 p.m. He thought to himself, "Boy, that stuff worked fast, almost too fast. If the description is correct, he ought to be out until after midnight. Maybe I should have waited until later in the evening to feed it to him. If he wakes up and is wired for the rest of the night, he'll be miserable. Well—" he rationalized, "I had to test it."

He looked over to his bed and noticed a paper bag. He opened it and found two ten-yard lengths of nylon parachute chord. He re-opened the door to the room so as not to arouse any undue suspicion, turned off the overhead light and turned on the lamp on his night stand. He then took out his switch blade survival knife and proceeded to cut the cord into roughly thirty-inch lengths. Periodically, he checked Dennis' breathing and tried several times to jostle him awake. He remained "dead asleep."

Mike had calculated he would need about the estimated thirty-inch lengths to securely tie down each crew member's wrists to their arm rests of the ejection seats once they were sedated. He felt sudden shudders of anxiety as he thought about what he was planning to do and all of the potential things that could go wrong. He piled the pieces of nylon cord in a heap on the side of his bed to look more like a single length in the event anyone popped their head in and asked what he was doing. He would just say he was cutting the cord to tie down his car cover. When he completed cutting a sufficient number of pieces plus a few spares, he took out a book of matches and carefully seared both ends of each length of cord to keep them from raveling. Just as he finished his work and put the pieces in his flight suit leg pocket, Jim Swanson, the navigator stuck his head in the room, "Hey, Mike. I thought Dennis was going to watch the movie. Looks like he decided to cut some z's instead. Is he okay? Not sick, is he? There are a lot of bugs floating around."

"Hi, Jim. I think he's okay. We came back here after dinner; he said he thought he would rest a minute before the movie, and there he is. These young guys have to get their beauty rest, you know," Mike chuckled. Swanson shrugged and left.

The Worst Of Fears

Mike closed the door around ten p.m., took off his flight suit and fitted the legs down over his boots next to his bed, fireman style, in the event they did get an alert response. He checked Dennis for clear breathing and turned out the light and went to bed. There he lay thinking for the next hour or so, running over and over his plan. He tried to methodically go over every detail from start to finish—the mixing of the sedative in the other crew member's drinks. He hoped he could induce the drug into each one fairly close together. He would have to give himself sufficient lead time in the event something went wrong. What would he do if one or more of them didn't want to drink anything when it was time? Would the navigation aids all be in place in time for him to successfully find his way across his intended route of flight? What if he were intercepted by U.S. or other friendly fighter-interceptors when he departed from his approved flight plan? What if he were intercepted by Soviet MiG's who hadn't gotten the word about him? What if the intended landing airfield was too small to land his bomber? How would his crew be treated once he landed? He finally drifted into a restless sleep, waking up occasionally and listening to Dennis' breathing. He satisfied himself that he was okay, just in a deep sleep. This was good.

Mike thought at first he was dreaming. The klaxon horn was blurting its obnoxious static sound. He quickly turned on the bedside lamp and looked at his watch. It was 3:58 a.m. He could hear a clamor of voices, some shouts and the scrambling of booted crew members heading out of the building toward the flight line. He had been through this routine dozens of times, but they were told that there would NO practice responses during this heightened period tension.

"What th' hell is going on?" he thought to himself as he automatically stepped into his flight boots and pulled his flight suit up over his body. He quickly zipped up his boots, tied the top strings and moved to jostle Dennis awake.

He was able to partially arouse Dennis who was at least showing some life and response. "What's going on?" he asked. "What time is it? We're not having an alert are we? We're not supposed to!"

"Get up, Dennis! We've gotta move. I don't know what's going on, but we've gotta go. Get your boots on and grab your jacket. Let's move!" Mike was almost shouting. He helped him get his boots on. "Hey, guy, come on. Tie your boots up after we get in the airplane. Move it!"

Mike took Dennis by the arm, guided him out the door and hustled him along in the dark toward their B-52. Mike was thinking all the way, "This is the worst of all fears. This can't be happening! What on earth is going on?"

The other crew members had already boarded the bomber and were getting strapped into their seats when Mike arrived with Dennis. He literally shoved him up the crew entrance ladder and into the lower level of the bomber. He quickly climbed up himself and left Dennis, still somewhat dazed and trying to orient himself, standing by the ladder to the upper level and the cockpit. Mike immediately put on his helmet, ensured that auxiliary power was connected to he bomber and the Electrical Power Distribution Panel reflected normal readings. He then had to raise up out of his ejection seat to reach across the empty co-pilot's seat, to the right side control panel and turn on the eight starter switches.

This particular B-52 had been modified with black powder engine start cartridges which permitted the pilots to start all eight engines simultaneously rather than sequentially which was the standard procedure. The engines began to whine as they started. Mike steadily moved each throttle to the idle position as each one reached 12% RPM, and he was assured he had a good start. The crew chief, standing in front of the bomber in the glare of the taxi lights, gave him a thumbs up, indicating everything looked normal.

Dennis finally made it to his seat and quietly strapped himself in without saying anything. It was obvious he was still suffering from the sedative. Mike's mind was on the business at hand. "Is this for real? Are we really going to go?" he despairingly asked himself.

He was listening intently to the radio for instructions from the command post controller. There was no small talk. Everyone was tense. "AC, this is the navigator. What do you think, Mike?" Jim Swanson queried over the interphone.

"Don't know, Jim. We're still waiting for some word from the command post. They're all quiet right now," Mike responded.

Finally: This is Apache Control. You are cleared to shut down your engines. Repeat. You are cleared to shut down your engines." And then, "False alarm, guys. Clean up your checklists and re-cock your birds. Go back to bed." The command post controller coolly announced over the radio.

Everyone sighed a deep breath of relief and proceeded to mechanically go through the engine shut-down and re-cock checklists to place the aircraft configuration back to where it was when they hustled aboard. There was very little spoken, just a few mumbled expletives, but no one complained about not taking off on this mission!

The crew departed the aircraft; Mike walked over, shook hands with the crew chief and thanked him for the flawless work on the ground while they were starting engines and configuring the bomber for taxi and take-off. There was little small talk as the dozens of crew members from the bombers and the tankers returned to the alert facility. Some headed for their rooms; others poured themselves a cup of coffee and sat around the dining room, commiserating about the preceding event. Mike followed Dennis back to their room and asked how he was feeling.

"Fine," he said. "Sir, I'm really sorry how I acted out there. I couldn't seem to wake up. Boy, I feel like I have a hangover. I sure hope I'm not coming down with the flu or something."

Mike patted him on the shoulder. "Dennis, you did fine. This was one we weren't expecting. We were all sort of confused. Let's just be thankful that we didn't go on this one! I suppose we'll find out what happened later in the morning when everything settles down. Meanwhile, I think I will try to grab a few more winks before daybreak."

"Me, too," responded Dennis. "As if I need more sleep. I still feel sorta funny."

Following breakfast, the squadron commander assembled the crews in the lounge and reviewed the events of the "early wake-up." He explained that the alert message came from the SAC command post as a result of "spurious" detection of a suspected incoming ICBM from the direction of the Soviet Union. The spurious event was later attributed to a missile sensor problem resulting in a "ghost" signal. He said the senior controller at SAC had no choice but to sound the alarm, and in closing, he repeated Mike's words to Dennis, "Just be thankful we didn't go on this one!" No one was any more pleased than Mike. His entire "project" had been threatened by an all-out war!

As Mike and the others began to leave the lounge, Bob asked, "Mike, are you ready to get out of this place?" He turned to see Bob Sanders. Sanders continued, "Sorry to do that to you, old Buddy, but the bug hit me before I knew what happened, and then I just learned that you guys got rousted out during the night on top of everything else. Sorry."

"Hi, Bob, how are you feeling? Better, I hope," Mike said turning to him. "Hey, it was no problem. It can happen to anybody. I enjoyed being with your crew. They are a bunch of good troops and came through like champions this morning. I was proud to work with them. Are you here to stay?"

"Yep, I'll take your neck chain and the goodie packet, and operations says you're free to go. I understand you are going to do an airborne alert sortie tomorrow, so thanks a lot for sitting in for me," Sanders replied.

Mike returned to his BOQ room and reviewed his strategy. He needed to call Rudy and let him know he was still on schedule, hopefully, to determine if everything was a "Go" on the other end. He showered, dressed casually and drove off base to a pay phone and called Rudy. "Hey Mike! Good to hear from you. Are you out of jail yet?" Rudy roared with his gusto laugh.

"Yeah, I'm out. And, thanks for the supplies. You do good work, my friend," Mike responded. "As a matter of fact, I tested one of the prescriptions last night, and it worked perfectly."

"Not on yourself, Mike!" Rudy almost shouted.

"No, on one of my colleagues," Mike answered. "He was out like a light for eight hours or so and then still out of it for several more. They work, Rudy. Now, how are the preparations going? Are they ready for me?"

"Mike, I will confirm everything tonight. But, as of last night, everything was on track. I gave you the radio frequencies and check points. Could you understand them?" Rudy continued.

"Yeah, Rudy; you ought to be in my business. You have it perfectly laid out. I plotted the route on my chart and it checks out right to the destination. Speaking of which, Rudy, what do you know about the preparations at the end of the road?"

Rudy replied, "My friend, I am advised that the place they have selected for you to go to is perfect for what you are delivering. They tell me they have already made the necessary arrangements for you to come in. Tonight I will be given the final radio frequencies and calls for you to make. Does that make sense to you?"

"It sure does, Rudy," Mike acknowledged. "What time shall I call you this evening?"

"After nine p.m. at my other number. See you later," Rudy said and hung up.

Final Preparations

Mike returned to his room. He needed to prepare the capulets for easier mixing with liquids. He ground up three of the caps into powder in a spoon using the handle of a dinner knife. He then tested how the powder would mix in water and then juice and finally coffee. Each experiment went very well. Hot coffee was the best and cold water was the most difficult. The powder in water left granules in the bottom. He would have to hope he could get the ground powder in coffee for each of the crew if he could. He counted out five capulets and carefully ground up each one. Then he ground up three more and added half of those each to the five single mixtures. "Might as well be safe than sorry," he said to himself. He placed the powdered substance on separate pieces of foil and carefully folded them into small packets. He also placed these in one of the pockets of the flight suit he intended wearing on the mission.

Mike then rechecked his nylon cord pieces and, satisfied, placed them in the zippered leg pocket of the flight suit. Next, he laid out the navigation chart that would take him from the alert orbit pattern toward his destination. He got very nervous as he carefully drew very light pencil lines from point to point along the route Rudy had provided him.

"This is almost too hard to believe," he said to himself over and over. I can't believe this is really going to happen."

He took a blank piece of paper and created a flight plan log including checkpoints, VOR frequencies, headings and estimated flight times between points.

"God, if I get caught with this, I would be shot before sunrise," he muttered to himself. Finished with his work, he placed the chart and log inside a folder and back into his briefcase. He wouldn't let the briefcase out of his sight until the mission was complete. Exhausted from the activities of the night before, he placed his briefcase under his bed and laid down to rest before he was scheduled to call Rudy.

After an hour or so, Mike decided that trying to nap was a lost cause. He had gone over every detail and possible screw ups several times. He ran his thoughts over his mother, father, Mackye and Galina. He had no idea what he would find when he finally got back home. His mind was a jumble of scattered thoughts. Nothing would come together in a coherent or coordinated manner. He opened his closet door to inspect the collection of clothes he had accumulated over the years.

"I can't take them with me," he thought to himself." He decided to take a favorite jacket, a couple of sweaters and two pair of trousers. He folded them tightly and put them in a canvas A-3 bag. If any of the crew asks about the bag, he would tell them he brought along an extra jacket and some reading material, "just in case."

With anxiety running high, Mike finally grabbed his swim suit and briefcase and he drove to the officers' club swimming pool. He locked his briefcase in his car , changed into his swim suit in the club dressing room and swam for an hour. The exercise relieved his tensions considerably. Back in his room, he called each one of his crew to insure their well-being and readiness to fly the next day. Each was ready.

A little before nine p.m., Mike drove off base. Security was tight when he went through the East Gate. The security policeman stopped him and asked for his military ID and cautioned him to be careful on the highway. Mike told him he was just going for a short drive to get off base for awhile, thanked him and drove on. He called Rudy from a phone several miles away from the base. "Are we all set, Rudy?"

"Mike, everything is set," Rudy responded. "You have a Go. My contact over there is so excited he could hardly contain himself. Of course all of this is being kept at the highest levels and many of the most senior are not aware of what is coming down. As you would expect, the top level security guys are in charge. They want all the credit for this deal if it works."

"Rudy, did you ask about the disposition of my men? I told you my conditions," Mike asked.

"Yes, Mike," he replied. "I have been assured that as soon as you arrive, they will be taken good care of. No funny stuff. Strictly and diplomatically professional. I don't know what all that means. You know those people better than I do. You must hope for the best. Your people will make excellent bartering chips, so they will want them to be kept in the best of condition. Now, the arrival location is all prepared. The directions I gave you are still the same. There is one addition. You are to contact Red Crown after you drop your bomber down to 10,000 feet. Your personal call sign is *Crown One*. I think that's cool, don't you? They also told me the route you take will be clear of any obstacles. You should have clear sailing, so to speak."

"Great, Rudy, thank you, my friend, for everything you have done. Let's see, Red Crown below 10,000 and okay, I'm Crown One. Good, I've got it. I look forward to seeing you again one day, somewhere, Rudy. Take care of yourself and be safe. Oh, by the way, thanks for the VW! Wish I could take it with me. Do you want to come out and reclaim it after I depart?"

"No, Mike, not at all. That is my contribution. Good luck, Mike, my friend," and Rudy hung up.

Mike drove back to the base. He was stopped for an ID check when he arrived at the base entrance gate. The security policeman also wrote down his name and the time of the evening in a log book. "What's that all about?" Mike asked.

"Sir, it's just routine. The higher-ups want to know who's coming and going these days," The security policeman responded.

The brief encounter bothered Mike for awhile as he drove on to his BOQ room, but he soon let it go. It was too late now to allow trivial things to interfere. Back in his room, he rechecked all of his materials and equipment: flight suit, briefcase with its contents and the A-3 bag. He thought several times about not taking the A-3 bag but finally decided he would need some souvenirs from his long visit. He inspected his room carefully for any evidence of his planning and looked around at the few things he would have to leave: his clock-radio, snorkel gear he had used at the beach, several pairs of "great shoes," he thought, and a closet reasonably full of neat clothes.

"I feel like I am on the way to the undertaker," he thought. Oh well, someone will benefit from these things." When he finished his inspection, he was reasonably sure there was no evidence of any of his planning activities nor any personal effects, letters, papers or otherwise that would connect him with anyone. He was ready...

NINETEEN

Closest TO The Edge

The Sverdlovsk, one of the Soviet's flagship floating listening posts, had been hastily relocated from the waters off the coast of Cuba to a position approximately eight miles north of the Western edge of Puerto Rico. The sophisticated trawler-picket ship was now in position to monitor the communications activities of the B-52 launch and recovery operations at Ramey Air Force Base.

"Red Crown, Red Crown, this is *Crimson Monitor*. Over." The specially encrypted call emanated from the Sverdlovsk.

"Dah, Dah. Come in, Comrade. This is Red Crown. Please state your position and operational status." The response, also encrypted, came from a command center deep within the Soviet Union.

"Dah, Red Crown. We are *'closest to the edge'*; we have arrived in position as ordered, and our communications systems are all operational. We are successfully monitoring the local aircraft voice transmissions. The subject aircraft of interest is approaching his departure position. For your information and further tracking, his call sign is: Apache Two-Zero; Over."

"Dah, spasee'ba, Crimson Monitor; please advise when our special 'friend' is safely airborne."

"Red Crown, our friend is now airborne toward the south and has reported he is operational. He will be turning back to the north to his course. He is en route, Comrades. We will remain in our present location until further ordered."

"Dah, Crimson Monitor. Well done. Remain in your present position as long as the *Yankee Vultures* aren't harassing you. Meanwhile, enjoy your Western voyage, Comrades. Victory will soon be ours!"

Moving To The Edge
"Apache Two-Zero, this is Bravo Three-Three. Over."

Bill Self responded, "Roger, Bravo Three-Three. This is Apache Two-Zero. We read you loud and clear; over."

"Roger, Two-Zero. This is Three-Three. We're on our climb-out and estimating rendezvous at four-five past the hour."

"Roger, copy, Three-Three. The rendezvous time checks with us. We're presently one-hundred-fifty miles out, descending from three-niner-zero to two-niner-zero thousand, heading zero-eight-nine degrees. We'll be ready for gas when we get there. Over."

"Roger, Two-Zero. Turn on your beacon, and we'll be on the lookout. I guess we'll do this thing broadcasting in the clear. That's what we were briefed. Do you concur? Over."

"Roger that, Three-Three. The word back at our place was to go ops normal and not hesitate to let 'em know we're out here and heading in their direction. For that matter, we were briefed to give our position reports over HF, un-encrypted and in the clear. So, if Ivan is listening, he knows there is a helluva lot of fire power headed his way, and more to come if he wants it. Over."

"Roger, Two-Zero. We *gas haulers* sorta envy you guys.... *sorta*, I said, I don't see any volunteers holding up their hands here in our bird, but, we've got all the petrol you need to do your job when we hook-up."

"Roger, Three-Three. We're at two-niner-zero thousand and presently headed zero-eight-seven degrees. Our beacon is transmitting."

Repeating the same rendezvous procedures as their earlier refueling shortly after take off, Apache Two-Zero and Bravo Three-Three positioned themselves to transfer the necessary fuel to top off the B-52's tanks in order to fly the airborne alert flight plan. The full fuel tanks provided an estimated four hours on station in the alert orbit pattern, flight to their pre-designated targets in the Soviet Union and thence to a post-strike base in Norway, or if their strike mission isn't executed, they would have sufficient reserve fuel to get their bomber back to Ramey. The rendezvous with the air refueling tanker was uneventful, and Mike completed the fuel off-load flawlessly. They were ready.

John Williams gave Mike a heading to fly across the Mediterranean toward their preplanned orbit position. The conversation between crew members grew quiet and businesslike when anyone made an intercom call. The reality of this *actual* airborne alert mission had begun to dawn on each member of the crew.

Apache Two-One completed the identical rendezvous and fuel off-load as TWO-ZERO and proceeded to his alert orbit position.

"Pilot, this is the EWO. Over," Jack Mayer called.

"Roger, EWO. Pilot here," Mike responded.

"Sir, I am painting an unidentified signal to our aft starboard. I thought at first it was a spurious echo, but it is coming in loud and clear now. Boss, I hate to tell you, but the signal is definitely that from a MiG 15 or 17 tracking radar. There may be two of them," Jack replied.

The EWO had an array of ECM equipment at his disposal on the B-52G which could detect, locate, discriminate and identify radar signals emanating from either ground or airborne systems. If a fighter aircraft were to "lock-on" his tracking and/or air-to-air missile firing radar to the B-52, the EWO had the capability to determine if he were friendly or an enemy and take evasive electronic countermeasure actions accordingly. If it appeared imminent that a fighter-interceptor was about to fire on the bomber, the EWO would attempt to electronically "jam" (throw off course, or nullify) his tracking radar.

"Roger," Mike acknowledged. "EWO; Gunner, are you scanning any targets with your TV tracker to our right rear?"

Charlie Grimes responded. "No Sir, Captain. It's pretty hazy back there and I can't make out anything."

Likewise, the gunner had the ability to visually spot an interceptor with his remote television camera if it came within range and could fire his 50mm guns at the intruder if it demonstrated hostile intentions. In the early years of the Cold War, SAC had employed fighter escorts with its bombers for en route protection, but did away with them in the late 1950's as the much faster and higher flying B-47's and B-52's came into the inventory. These new supersonic bombers in many cases could out-fly and out-maneuver older enemy fighters. Also at issue was the overriding requirement to provide a multitude of airborne tankers to keep the short duration fighter escorts refueled along the way. So, the strategic bombers were left to provide their own protection via electronic intercept and jamming along with the modest defensive guns located in the tail of the aircraft.

"Okay, Guys," Mike cautioned the crew. "Everybody on your toes; we don't know if we have company or not, so tighten your seat belts and be prepared for anything. Bill, see if Apache Two-One is within our UHF range; if so ask him if they have spotted any strangers."

"Roger. Will do," Bill Self acknowledged.

"Gunner, take the safety off your guns and make sure they are operational. Rotate 'em around and see if you can get a bead on anything back there," Mike ordered. "If he gets too close, I will clear you to fire a warning burst in an off-direction, just to let him see the tracers and be aware that we are alert to his presence, but *Sarge*, you advise me before you do any shooting. I will give the order, and you just ensure that you are firing well away from him."

"Roger, Sir. I copy. Will do." Charlie Grimes confirmed.

"AC, this is Radar. We were briefed a few weeks ago that the Moroccan Air Force had received some MiG 15's, and they had Soviet pilots there training them. It could be some of those guys mess' in around. What do you think?"

"Could be," Mike responded. "It just isn't likely those birds are ours, or otherwise other *friendlies* out here. EWO, Gunner, how are you guys doing? Anything else in your scopes?"

"This is the EWO, AC. I'm still painting somebody back there; maybe two *somebodies*, but they are staying well back out of our visual range. Gunner can't pick 'em up visual."

"Roger, Jack. Thanks," Mike acknowledged, "Well guys, we're cruising here at thirty-one thousand and approximately 200 miles or so from the Moroccan Coast. I think if those babies are from out of there, they're stretching their legs to be out here. And if so, they should be peeling off pretty soon and heading for home. Besides, I don't think 15's can get up to our altitude anyway."

"Roger, Pilot. We are just about 200 nautical miles from Oujda, Morocco, which is south of the coast on the Eastern border. So unless those are souped-up MiG 15's or something else, we are fast moving out of their radius of action," John Williams reported.

"Pilot, this is the Co-pilot. I can't raise Apache Two-One so I suppose he is either out of range or off my UHF frequency. Also, I haven't picked up any traffic on HF from anybody else regarding intruders."

"Pilot, EWO," Jack Mayer keyed-on. "I've lost their signals, so I think you and Nav are right. Whoever they were, they've turned back. Probably just out prospecting. About everybody in the universe knows we're out here and where we're headed."

"Thanks, EWO," responded Mike. "Well guys, I didn't think we were in any serious danger, but you never know. It should be clear sailing ahead up the Med to our orbit box, but EWO, you and Charlie keep alert. These are ticklish times. Also, this is probably a good time for any of you to take a break for a while, stretch or whatever. You probably need to do so now. I want everybody on their toes once we get on station."

Each crew member acknowledged, in turn, and, over the next hour or so, the crew took turns getting out of their cramped seats, stretching and moving about the limited space within the crew compartment of the bomber. There wasn't much chatter over the intercom between those maintaining watch in their positions. This mission was a "first" for all of them. They had flown "Chromedome" training sorties before, but never with the aircraft loaded with nuclear weapons and flying up to the "edge" of the Soviet Union.

The crew's Chromedome training sorties had consisted of routinely taking off from Ramey, flying a precision navigation leg up the Caribbean chain of islands to the U.S. mainland. They would coast in over land mass in the vicinity of Miami and proceed to a pre-designated penetration point over Georgia. There they would be cleared to make a rapid descent to enter a low-level training route. The low-level route, called "Oil Burner," allowed the crew to fly a navigation leg at three to five hundred feet above the ground at an airspeed of 400 knots, then arrive at a point to "pop up" and make a simulated bombing run over a planned target complex somewhere on the ground in Mississippi or Louisiana. These simulated bomb drops would replicate the "release" of one or more gravity bombs from the bomber. The crew would be scored electronically by an Air Force radar bomb scoring (RBS) site on the ground near the pre-planned target complex. The mission scenario would then take the crew back to high altitude to make simulated bomb runs over other preplanned targets within large city or industrial complexes, such as Atlanta, Dallas, or Chicago.

The simulated bombing attacks were not designed to go against cities themselves, but always against very discrete and often very difficult to find critical nodes such as a specific building, power distribution center or military center. All of the training targets, both low level and high altitude, were designed to replicate those which might be found in the Soviet Union.

"City busting" was never a declared U.S. policy; in fact, the opposite was the case with all preplanned Soviet targets designated to be struck by a nuclear weapon, either gravity bomb, air-to-ground missile or ICBM. All were carefully planned against targets with either military, industrial or political significance.

Target planning for SAC forces by the JSTPS, located in the super secured underground complex contiguous to SAC Headquarters near Omaha. KC-135 air refueling would also be planned for most training missions. If the training flights called for the exercise of GAM-77 *Hound Dog* air-to-ground to missiles, simulated targets would be fed into the onboard missile guidance system by the Navigator, and bombing runs would be made with the *Hound Dog* as the weapon rather than a gravity nuclear bomb.

The EWO and the Gunner would also practice their skills against SAM sites or "attacking" fighters. Each crew member would be involved in the various phases of the Chromedome training missions with the whole idea being to come as close as possible to duplicating an actual wartime mission. This is the first time that Mike's crew, or any SAC combat crew, had ever launched on a potential nuclear strike mission.

The crunch for the United States came on October 22, 1962, when the President directed the increase in preparedness for U.S. forces and the initiation of airborne alert sorties.

On October 24th, Strategic Air Command and the other U.S. combat forces had been placed in DEFCON 2, the highest readiness condition in which U.S. nuclear forces had ever been placed. Only one additional increase in readiness remained—DEFCON 1 for U.S. forces and then the execution of nuclear weapons against the Soviet Union would be imminent. This was the brink of potential disaster on which the world stood.

Tyrrhenian Sea

"Pilot, this is the Nav. We will be over the IP for entering our alert orbit pattern in about fifteen minutes, at which time we will be at 40 degrees North and 12 degrees East. I will advise you when we are at our orbit entry point and request that you take up a heading of three-five-five degrees. Also, adjust your true airspeed to 400 knots. This will conserve fuel and require us to hold our heading on this leg of the pattern for approximately twenty minutes. After that, we will initiate a standard rate turn to the right to a heading of approximately one seventy-five degrees and hold that heading for about twenty minutes in the opposite direction. Round and round we'll go until we get orders to go strike *Ivan*....Heaven forbid! Depending on the winds, I may ask you to adjust the headings occasionally in order to remain in our designated operating orbit pattern."

"Roger, Nav," Mike acknowledged. "Based on our predicted fuel reserve, how long are we expected to remain in the alert orbit pattern?"

"Sir, I estimate we should remain on station here for three hours and fifty-five minutes, give or take. I will continue to coordinate the fuel status with the copilot and watch the time as we go along. As you know, we will also be mission vulnerable for another two hours or so after we depart the alert pattern and start home, should something break out and our mission is executed." John Williams explained. "If that should happen, we would have to turn around and head in to hit our targets."

"Roger, Nav," Mike responded. "I copied. Keep us on course. The only small problem with your latter comment is that if our sortie is executed after we depart the pattern and head for home, we would be flying this beast on fumes before we could get to our targets, finish our work and find someplace to land. Not a jolly prospect, huh?"

"Roger that, Pilot, unless some angel sent up a tanker for us!" the Navigator joked.

"Where do you think we could find a tanker in this God forsaken part of the world?" Bill Self piped in. "Those tanker jocks only hang-out where bad guys aren't! And we're flying *closest to the edge* of bad guy country, except for Italy, but we don't have any tanks down there...at least, I don't think we do."

On Station

The giant B-52 with its crew of six, a bomb bay loaded with four nuclear bombs, four *Quail* decoy missiles and two powerful air-to-ground *Hound Dog* missiles slung under its wings eased up the Mediterranean Ocean on a course which brought it almost equal distance between Bizerte, Tunis, to the South and Gagliari, Sardinia, to the North.

Mike guided the bomber around to the North as it entered the Tyrrhenian Sea and onto the preplanned orbit entry point. Apache Two-Zero was ready for a *shoot-out*, if the Soviets wanted it that way. Once within the airborne alert orbit pattern, Mike pulled the eight throttles back slightly and established an optimum cruising true airspeed of 400 knots in order to reduce fuel consumption and maximize the amount of time they could remain in orbit and on effective alert. The crew then settled in to await a potential "Execution Order" which would send them directly toward the Soviet Union territories to release their bombs and *HOUND DOG* missiles to destroy critical targets.

If executed, their flight plan would take them to a point to cross the H-Hour Control Line (HHCL). The HHCL would be used by all bomber combat crews to adjust their flight timing. They would effectively cross over the imaginary "line" which was overlaid on their maps at a predetermined precise time in order to coordinate the release of their missiles and drop their bombs. The timing adjustments ensured, to the degree possible, the de-confliction of nuclear detonations and the potential for one bomber flying into the "wake" of another bomber's nuclear bomb detonation cloud.

The HHCL also served to coordinate the release of ICBM's and IRBM's from the United States and Western Europe, permitting the bombers to safely skirt through a virtual "mine field" of incoming nuclear weapons. Mike and his crew had high confidence in their mission plan. They had spent many hours reviewing every detail of the route of flight, their assigned targets and possible contingencies.

These same events were taking place with dozens of other B-52 crews flying in airborne alert orbit points around the globe which were literally encircling the Soviet Union. The world could be at nuclear war for the first time in history if the opposing sides did not reach some agreement to calm the situation.

Mike's thoughts cycled between anxiety and fright. His range of emotions over the past year had continued to grow with increasing stress. "Well, I'm committed to this either way," he lamented to himself. "The FBI agents are no fools. I believe that there is little doubt that Flores knew more than he was telling me. If Dan, that gal, or Oscar, haven't talked already, they will eventually, and my days would be numbered. I regret what I have to do with my crew. These are really great warriors, but *this is war* and they are a part of it. I just hope and trust that General Tushenskiy will have a strong hand in ensuring their safety once I get down. In any event, I have no choice but to carry out my plan."

His thoughts drifted back to Volgograd and the two years of *hell* he endured there with Vlad, his ever-present KGB shadow, who stalked him on through his training at Khodinka. He thought of Mackye and Galina. Where were they? And, what of his mother and father? Were they well? Were they still alive? So many reasons to go home.

Mike had no doubt wh*at* his mission was. He knew that every detail had been thought out in order to carry out his plan successfully. He also knew each step required near perfect timing and precise moves.

In his wildest imagination, he could never have dreamed he would be on an assignment of destiny such as that before him.

TWENTY

The Eagle Is Snared

"Pilot, this is the Navigator. Over," John Williams responded over the intercom.

"Roger, Nav. This is the Pilot. Go ahead."

"You guys are awfully quiet up there, Mike. Just want to advise you we have approximately an hour and a half to go before we depart our alert orbit pattern and head for home".

"Roger, John. Thanks," Mike responded. "I guess we aren't going after Ivan on this trip, are we? I wonder if things have cooled off some back home."

"Dunno", John yawned, "but, it sure has been quiet, just cruising 'round and round' over this spot all day. Guess we'll find out what's going on when we get home in about nine hours or so, unless something breaks between now and home base. Has the co-pilot picked up any unusual message traffic from the position reporting of the other birds up here, or has he been napping?"

"Not a thing," piped in Bill Self, "but there sure are a lot of us Buffs up here flying around Ivan's backyard. I'm having to sit here and wait my turn to give our position and status report. This is wild! It's more like flying an ORI (operational readiness inspection) back home. The only difference is we are *here* and not flying around waiting to make simulated 'bomb runs' on Dallas or Chicago. I would give a couple of bucks to peek in on the big Kremlin command post and listen to all the chatter about the 40 or 50 B-52's they are tracking along their borders while they discuss the failures in American values and their own great political process!"

"You're dead on, Bill," piped-in Jack Mayer. "I'll bet those commie bastards are running around like chickens with their heads cut off, trying to figure out where we all came from and what we might do next."

Mike allowed another forty minutes to elapse. He was getting edgy as the time to act drew closer and he became more and more irritated with Bill's philosophical recitations and the crew's chatter. Then it was time to make his move.

"Okay, I'm getting out of my seat for a minute to hit the *john*," he announced over the intercom. "The bar is open and the drinks are on me; coffee, juice or water." Almost in unison, everybody on the crew responded, welcoming the opportunity to break the monotony and drink or eat something.

"Radar and I both will have coffee, both black, one with sugar," John Williams responded.

"EWO and I will have tomato juice if there is still some left in the cooler," Charlie Grimes, the Gunner, answered.

"AC, you can put a little vodka and a squeeze of lime in mine!" responded Jack Mayer.

"Sure, EWO, you can count on it," replied Mike.

"I will just have some water," the co-pilot responded. "I have the aircraft."

"Roger, got your drink orders. You're a pushy bunch!" Mike chided. "Co-pilot, you have the aircraft." He unbuckled his parachute and seat harnesses and climbed out of his seat, making his way back to the ladder-way that led down to the lower deck. As he made his way to the urinal located in a corner behind the Radar Navigator and Navigator seats, he continued to dwell on Bill Self's commentary about the Kremlin and his perception of the Soviet's philosophy of "searching for failures in American values in comparison with their own political processes. If he only knew!" he thought to himself.

Mike had learned much about the United States and Americans during his training back at Khodinka. By actually living here for the past nine years, he had also learned so much more. He had found few weaknesses in American patriotisms or resolve. If he could take one major conclusion back home with him, it would be that Americans are generally naive about their enemies and too trusting while also often being gullible. Here he was, a Soviet military officer and secret agent who had not only successfully entered the United States as a "citizen," but he had become an officer in their Air Force and a pilot of one of their prized strategic bombers.

Mike fully doubted such a feat could have ever been achieved by a foreign agent inside the Soviet Union. Security and surveillance were too absolute throughout the USSR. True they had suffered a few defectors and likely a few Western agents had penetrated his country but nothing on the scale of this grand ploy he was in the process of executing. If America ever failed and was defeated, it would not likely be by force but through infiltration of their social and political systems. The American military fighting force and their leaders, he was thoroughly convinced, were skilled and dedicated warriors, and likely as disciplined and determined as the Soviets to protect their homeland.

"America's weaknesses are within their abiding trust of the civilian bureaucracy," he murmured to himself. "They are simply soft and vulnerable."

His own B-52 crew and all the others in his squadron and throughout Strategic Air Command were examples of a strong American military posture. He thought to himself that he had no idea how this whole Cuban Crises would end, but he was committed to carry out his part of turning the tide in favor of his own government if he could. His conscience had bothered him from time to time as he pondered the prospect of deserting the friends he had made in the U.S., especially these men on his bomber crew, but he was a soldier himself. He had a responsibility to protect and defend the Soviet people.

This thought always brought him back to his own world and restored his confidence in his ability to carry out the challenging mission before him. He, and he alone, might inflict a disastrous and devastating blow to the security of the American military and the over-confident U.S. politicians.

He finished his personal business, cleaned up with "wet and wipes," and proceeded to pour coffee from the in-flight pot into two paper cups for Tom and John. He kept his back to the two crew members as he opened a packet of sugar and let it flow into one of the cups. Then he took two small foil packets of the powered *Doriden* and stirred one into each of the cups until there was no evidence of residue. His experimentation with mixing the powdered substance with different liquids back in his BOQ kitchen had paid off. The key had been to grind and mash the tablets into as fine a powder as possible.

"Hopefully," he thought, "the pre-measured one and a half 500mg tablets would be more than sufficient to render these guys unconscientious for at least five or six hours and long enough to get the bomber on the ground. It had sure worked well on Dennis."

The last thing he wanted to avoid was to overdose the dosage and injure any of his crew members. These guys had become friends, and although they represented the enemy, they were soldiers in arms. Rudy had assured him that if the operation were successful and he was able to deliver the B-52 to his destination, his crew would be treated fairly and humanely. No one, however, could be sure of what their eventual fate might be. They, like the U-2 pilot, Powers, would undoubtedly become political pawns. Mike felt strongly, though, that the success of his mission would give him considerable influence over their well-being.

He handed the cups of coffee to Tom and John, and then opened the cooler box and retrieved two cans of tomato juice which he opened with a mini-can opener. He took a few pieces of ice from the cooler and put into paper cups along with a packet each of the *Doriden* and stirred in the substance. Placing one cup of juice on an equipment rack, he climbed up the short ladder and handed the other cup to the Gunner. He then reached down and retrieved the second cup and handed it to the EWO. They both began to drink the tomato juice without any evidence of detecting anything unusual. Mike thought to himself, "Four down and one to go!"

Taking his time, he poured drinking water into a cup and mixed in the last packet of powdered sedative. The chilled water required considerable stirring to make the water look normal and not cloudy. None of the crew members noticed his methodical handiwork as he worked his way back to the cockpit and handed Bill the cup of water.

"Thanks, Captain," said the co-pilot, taking the cup of water and downing it with one gulp. "Boy, I get dry up here after awhile. Dehydration, I guess."

"You're right," Mike said. "The body really dries out on these long missions." He strapped himself back into the left seat and advised the crew, "Pilot back on interphone."

After settling back into his seat, Mike looked at his watch. It had taken him less than ten minutes to do his work. As he watched Bill Self nod and drift off to sleep, the adrenaline in his body began to pump even harder than when he was mixing the sedatives. Every vital organ in his body seemed to be vibrating. He had just executed the plan he had been working on since the notion struck him that it might just be feasible enough to be successful. It was such an incredible idea that, more often than not, he doubted it could even come close to becoming reality—and yet, here he was. This day's events were about to culminate nine years of preparation. Up to this point, he felt he had really accomplished very little substantive work as an agent. Now he was going to deliver to his government the latest state-of-the-art American heavy bomber, fully configured and loaded with the most modern nuclear weapons in the U.S. inventory. He would, without a doubt, he mused, become one of the Soviet Union's greatest heroes. He might even be awarded "The Order of Lenin!"

If he were successful, he couldn't wait to see General Borodin's and Dimitri Vetrov's reaction to his feat. His discipline quickly brought him back to reality and the work ahead of him. His mind raced with the multitude of details that now had to be accomplished. He began to concern himself with the 'unknowns'—"Was there a possibility of being detected and intercepted by U.S. or NATO fighters? Can I successfully get the bomber across the Italian peninsula, the Adriatic Sea and into Soviet-controlled airspace without being detected and pursued? Will the propositioned navigation aids be in place and the airfield be ready to safely maneuver and single-handedly land the bomber?"

The rapidly evolving turn of events had forced Rudy and him to move quickly to put all of the details in place. Rudy was extremely excited. "What a great idea I came up with!" he would chuckle, but he was deadly serious, and Mike took note of how really professional he was in planning and taking care of the multitude of details and coordination.

Every CHROMEDOME training mission that Mike had been scheduled to fly, well before the Cuban Crises, held the potential to carry out the plan he was now executing. The advent of the response by the U.S. to the Soviet's encroachment into Cuba, to initiate the airborne alert plan, immediately provided him with an unimagined opportunity. He could not only deliver a B-52G bomber to his government, but one loaded with a variety of nuclear weapons for even more exploitation of U.S. weapon systems technology.

He was convinced more than ever that the success of his project was "meant to be!" The Americans had unwittingly fallen directly into a fortuitous trap set by the brilliant actions of the Soviet leadership, and he was destined to spring it.

There had been a few Soviet-built fighters delivered to the West by non-Soviet defectors during the Korean War and thereafter. Most of them were older aircraft and contained very little in the way of sophisticated technology; however, he was not a defector, he was an agent of the Soviet Government, and he had successfully duped the U.S. military and captured one of their newest and most prized heavy bombers. He felt the pride of his years of training as a young communist swell within him. He had been living and acting like an American for so long and serving in the U.S. Air Force for so many years, that more often than not, he thought of himself as an American. Now it was time to go home.

He shuddered at the ridicule heaped upon him by the pompous ass, General Borodin during his last visit to Moscow. Mackye's husband, Dimitri, the clever and coy KGB operative, was just as bad as Borodin, or worse, baiting Borodin and goading him to..."lay it on me!" he mused. "Those two are jackals for sure, and I am looking forward to *facing* them again! This must be the right thing to do and the right time to do it!" he muttered to himself. "I've got the FBI behind me and Borodin and Vetrov to look forward to ahead of me. I'm damned if I do and damned if I don't!"

As Mike watched his co-pilot drift into deeper and deeper unconsciousness, he smiled to himself, remembering his last act before boarding the bomber. As he was about to step up the ladder, the young assistant crew chief patted him on the back and said, "Good luck, Sir. See you when you get back."

Mike had reached into the zippered breast pocket of his flight suit and took out the keys to his red VW; "Thanks, Jonesie. Here hang on to these and take good care of my VW if I don't get back." He remembered the look of surprise on the young two-stripers face as he proceeded to climb up into his aircraft.

After about ten minutes, he reached across the cockpit and jostled Bill's shoulder to see if he was indeed fast asleep. He was. Mike then rechecked the autopilot to insure it was locked-in on course and altitude, unstrapped his harnesses, got out of his seat and moved back to check the condition of the other four crew members. He first climbed down to the lower deck and assured himself that both Tom and John were unconscious and securely strapped into their seats. He took four pieces of nylon cord from the leg pocket of his flight suit and securely tied each of their wrists to the arms of their ejection seats. He wanted to insure that if either of them woke up prematurely, they could not get out of their seat positions or touch any controls or communications switches.

Once he completed securing their arm movements, he positioned their ejection seat Inertial Reel Control into the LOCKED position. The locked seat harness would restrain the crew members' movement and prevent them from leaning or falling forward. He then turned off all of the navigator's radar equipment in the event the emissions from the systems might be picked up and tracked once he departed the orbit pattern and headed eastward. He proceeded back up to the flight deck and checked the condition of the EWO and Gunner. He then securely tied each of their wrists to their seat arms and manually locked their seat harnesses in the same fashion.

In the process of securing each crew member, he also collected their .38 caliber sidearms, removed the cartridges and put all of them in a garbage bag out of sight. He also unplugged each of their radio and interphone connections. Back in the cockpit, he tied down Bill Self's wrists in the same manner as the others. Because he couldn't reach the co-pilot's legs to tie them back from reaching the rudder pedals, he had to trust he would remain unconscious throughout the remainder of the flight and not become a problem to his plan.

His preparatory deeds done, Mike pulled his pre-prepared flight plan from his briefcase and reviewed the details which he had essentially memorized from going over it a dozen or more times during the past several days. His destination was not back to Ramey Air Force Base, Puerto Rico, but to a Soviet air field near Kursk, 295 nautical miles South of Moscow.

He initiated the scheduled turn in the elliptical orbit pattern and headed South. He ran his finger down the line-by-line entries in his devised "flight plan" and calculated that about three quarters of the way down this leg of the elliptical pattern, he would begin a gentle turn to the left and East. Then he would take up a heading of 100 degrees. Any attempt to precisely time his actions from this point would be strictly by way of calculating "best guess" ground speed and estimated distances between the planned navigation points. He would rely on basic raw navigation and the hopeful intercept of the pre-positioned VOR beacons.

The KGB and Soviet Air Force had only five or six days, at the most, to hurriedly install the portable navigation aids at intervals across Albania, Bulgaria and Ukraine. If they were successful, the VOR beacons would guide him to over-fly known check points on the ground. He would simply proceed on "gut" feel with his first heading for approximately 195 nautical miles and intercept the coast of Southern Italy at about the narrowest point of the "instep" of the "boot" of the peninsula.

Based on a true airspeed of 450 knots and the last upper altitude wind direction and velocity he received from Tom, he would use a calculated ground speed of 480 knots. Mike estimated the time to reach the point to cross over Italy would be about 24 minutes. It was a clear day so he should be able to easily see the coastline and all the way across the isthmus. He would then turn northeast to a heading of 055 degrees and tune his navigation aid receiver to intercept the first VOR beacon which should be located a few miles South of Tirane, Albania, just across the Adriatic Sea.

After over flying the beacon at Tirane, he would take up a heading of approximately 070 degrees and track his course outbound to intercept the next VOR beacon which should be located in the vicinity of Sofia, Bulgaria. From that point, he would take up a heading of 082 degrees which should take him to the next navigation aid just south of Varna located on the coast of the Black Sea. Tracking outbound from the Varna VOR on heading of 044 degrees, he would cross the western coast of the Black Sea toward Cherson, Ukraine.

From over the Cherson navigation check-point, he would turn to the north-northeast and a heading of 010 degrees toward an expected VOR beacon at Kremencug, Ukraine, 155 nautical miles away. His final navigation leg after Kremencug would be on a heading of 032 degrees to his planned destination airfield just South of the city of Kursk, safely inside Soviet Russia, and approximately 295 nautical miles south of Moscow. The overall time to make the flight from his orbit departure point to the landing airfield in Russia should be approximately 3 hours and 25 minutes.

A more direct navigation routing would have been to fly from Tirane across Albania to a position near Bucharest, Romania, and to a point south of Kiev, Ukraine, thence to Kursk. But as Rudy had instructed, the distrust of the Romanians kept the Soviets on edge, and the potential risk of intervention by rogue forces would not be worth the difference in distance.

According to his instructions, Mike would not attempt to make contact with the designated Soviet ground control radio station until within 100 nautical miles from Kursk and at an altitude of less than 10,000 feet. This would minimize potential intercept of his transmission by any others than the Soviet Air Force controllers. He would use his VHF (very high frequency) radio to make contact with "Red Crown," the call sign he had been given for Kursk airfield control, using his own special call sign, *"Crown One."*

He had been trying to sharpen his native tongue by talking to himself over the last several days so that when he spoke over the aircraft radio, he wouldn't embarrass himself. He mouthed a few practice phrases now to insure that he would enunciate his words properly and sound as natural as he could.

Arriving over the estimated point on the South leg of his orbit pattern, Mike turned the autopilot heading knob to initiate a left turn toward the east and the southwest coast of Italy; his stomach and nervous system began to spasm. "Here we go!" he could only say to himself. "I am committed. If all goes as planned, I will be back in my homeland in a few short hours." He was both excited and frightened. The deathly quiet B-52 with its "solo" crew member headed toward a destination never before flown to by an American strategic bomber.

Bill Self had given a position report on the status of Apache Two-Zero less than half an hour before he was put to sleep, so no one would be looking for them for awhile. Mike's major concern was the potential for radar tracking and surveillance from U.S. or NATO ground stations or ships in the area. He had not been briefed on any such facilities in the area of their airborne alert orbit locations, but he was quite certain his bomber was being tracked either directly or routinely by radar sites or ships. The international situation was too tense to expect otherwise. He turned off the aircraft's IFF (Identification -- Friend or Foe) emitter and left only the VHF, UHF and HF radios on to monitor other transmissions and to possibly alert him to any broadcasts calling attention to his bomber's unscheduled maneuvers.

From his cruising altitude of 35,000 feet, Mike could easily make out the Western coast of Italy and as far South as the coast of Sicily, as he proceeded across the Tyrrhenian Sea. He knew he would be across the narrow breadth of the Italian land mass in a matter of minutes. He was also reasonably confident that there shouldn't be any U.S. or NATO aircraft carriers in the ocean area below from which fighters might be launched to intercept him. He checked his fuel gauges and calculated he had an abundance of fuel to get him to his destination with several hours to spare.

As he approached the Italian Coast the worst of his fears surfaced when he heard a call over the UHF emergency frequency: "Aircraft approaching the west coast of Italy from the east, and approximately 50 kilometers south of Maralea. Please identify yourself, Over!"

Mike's stomach tightened. The caller repeated: "Unidentified aircraft, heading easterly and approaching the Italian coastline, please state your call sign, type aircraft and destination. And, squawk Zero-Three-Zero on your IFF, Over!"

He was almost sure the call was coming from a ground or ship transmitter and not a fighter, but he couldn't be sure. The voice had a definite British accent. He sat tight and continued on his course heading. The voice came again and this time more intense: "Unidentified aircraft heading easterly from the Tyrrhenian. If you read me and cannot transmit, please make a right turn for positive ID. Over!" He could imagine the hornet's nest of activity going on wherever the radio transmission was coming from. Under normal circumstances in such cases, a ground station would likely begin a roll call of all known aircraft within an operating area of concern, but this was not "normal circumstances." Whoever was tracking him and trying to contact him would not likely have a complete list of every aircraft in the area. He reasoned that his bomber would not be listed as missing until he failed to make a position report after leaving his previous alert orbit pattern when he headed home. By that time he should be well over his own "friendly" territory. That, in itself would present another worry—safety from Soviet fighter interceptors who may not have gotten the word of his coming.

He thought to himself: "This is not going to be a cake-walk!"

Mike continued to scan the sky below and the horizon around him for the sight of fighters, but he saw none. He did not detect any transmissions from fighter aircraft either, which might be launched in pursuit of his bomber. He did suspect, however, that whoever was trying to contact him did have his direction and airspeed. They also suspected the type of aircraft, which they had profiled and passed the information along up the chain.

Eventually, APACHE TWO- ZERO would be declared missing. He also felt that with all the nuclear weapons and missiles onboard his bomber and the ongoing world crisis, it was doubtful the higher authorities would declare him missing until the situation had been well thought out. The calls to identify himself finally ceased and the airways became quiet except for the continuous chatter of position reporting on HF radios from other airborne alert B-52s.

As he crossed over the narrow boot of Italy, Mike tuned in the first pre-planned VOR frequency and took up a heading of 055 degrees. He would be over the Soviet satellite country of Albania in another half an hour to forty minutes. The VOR signal from the first navigation beacon in his flight plan did not immediately respond and the indicator needle on the VOR dial spun around aimlessly.

He thought to himself, "I can't get too anxious. These VOR nav aids are portable and were hastily set-up, so they might not be too accurate along the way. I will just forge along my pre-planned headings and hope for the best." Meanwhile he stayed busy monitoring the aircraft systems, especially the fuel and engine instruments. He also continued to watch for any movements on the part of the unconscious co-pilot, Bill Self.

Then about ten minutes along his new course, he observed the VOR directional indicator needle lock steadily on the tuned in VOR beacon dead ahead. Mike drew a deep breath. "They know I'm coming and have paved the way!"

He proceeded along his planned flight path, constantly checking and re-checking his headings, distance and estimated time to the next navigation check point. His plan and flight were going along flawlessly. With the exception of the query by the unknown radar tracking facility over southern Italy, Mike had encountered no difficulties. The VOR beacons were apparently in place at the designated locations and were guiding him to his destination.

FBI Special Agents Manuel Flores and Brent Collins again entered Colonel Bill Blair's office at Ramey Air Force Base the morning after their previous visit.

"Come in, Gentlemen the executive officer greeted. "Colonel Blair is in the Command Post. He asked me to call him when you arrived."

"Thank you," Flores responded pensively.

A haggard and somber Blair entered his outer office. He nodded to Flores and Collins without speaking and motioned them to follow him into his private office.

"Good morning," Blair greeted them dryly, fixing his eyes on Flores. "I have some unpleasant news, Manny. We lost radio contact with Captain Scott's aircraft over night and we now fear the worst. It has now been almost ten hours since anyone has had radio or radar contact with his bomber. His sister ship is back in the area and in radio contact with us. They will be landing shortly."

Both agents sat quietly listening. When Colonel Blair paused, Flores spoke.

"What do you think has happened, Colonel?" he asked.

"Manny," Blair replied, starring blankly. "If I had any idea, I would tell you. We are completely at loss for answers at this point. The only thing we can conjecture is that the bomber is down somewhere, more than likely in the ocean. We just don't know. The only possible clue came from a Brit frigate that reported an aircraft on their radar which was headed eastward over Southern Italy. That was sometime late yesterday. I don't put much credence in that report as it applies to our aircraft; it could have been anybody's plane in the area."

"So you believe that the contact by the frigate didn't have anything to do with Captain Scott's aircraft," Flores said. "What are the odds that it was?"

"Manny, that's not logical," Blair emphatically replied. "It isn't possible for his bomber to be over southern Italy; that would put him over two hundred miles or more east of his planned orbit location and headed the wrong way!"

"Well, Colonel, we're truly sorry for you and the families of those men should worse come to worse," Flores replied. "I know you will keep us informed of your findings. Again, we are sorry for the coincidence of our intervention."

The two agents shook hands with the brooding and frustrated wing commander and departed.

Back in their vehicle, Flores mused to Collins, "Brent, I hate to even venture this thought, but with what we believe we know, coupled with what we suspect, our "Captain Scott" and his bomber may be sitting on a Soviet airfield as we speak, with the rest of his American aircrew in a Soviet jail."

Mike Scott had to work hard to control his anxiety. Never in his wildest imagination could he have dreamed this event would be the culmination of all the years of training and patient waiting to honor his government in such a valiant and triumphant way. He was exhilarated by the thought that in a few short hours he would be landing his bomber on an airfield in his homeland and turn over to the Soviet Union one of the prized war fighting possessions in the United States' arsenal. He couldn't control the frequent smile that spread across his face as the prospects of this day and those ahead reeled through his thoughts.

With his emotions and anxiety running high, Mike was feeling very confident about the success of his mission when he noted the expected VOR beacon at Cherson, Ukraine, was not being picked up by his receiver. He re-tuned the programmed frequency several times, including moving it up and down several digits in the event Rudy had not copied it correctly. The distance from his last checkpoint at Varna on the west coast of the Black Sea to Cherson was approximately 265 nautical miles. He estimated that from Varna to Cherson, located a few miles inland on the north coast of the Black Sea and would take about thirty-three minutes. He hoped the upper level winds were still relatively the same, and his ground speed remained as he had estimated it to be.

The bomber was flying high over the Black Sea at this point and could make out the western shore in between the lower cloud breaks. The weather was still very good at his altitude, but there was an increasing undercast of broken clouds well below him which he estimated to be around ten thousand feet or perhaps a little lower. Mike held his course as he watched the VOR indicator needle spin slowly around. He figured either the VOR beacon had failed or maybe they didn't get it installed in time. He just hoped after he arrived over the "guesstimated" navigation point at Cherson and took up his next planned heading, he would be able to intercept the next VOR beacon at Kremencug.

He also worried about the Ukrainians down below. "Had they been alerted to his route of flight?" The Ukrainians were staunch members of the Soviet Union, but they could be very independent at times.

At that moment, Mike suddenly looked over his left shoulder to see two MiG-19's flying along side him and about a quarter mile away. He took a deep breath and watched them as they appeared only to want to look him over with curiosity more than anything else. He could only hope they had been sent up by an air defense controller just to "check him out." Since they had not come in from behind or made an aggressive pass, he presumed they were aware of who he was and would soon head back home. After about ten minutes, they did.

He thought to himself, "Just when I thought this was going too smoothly, all hell breaks loose, first with the VOR beacon and then with those guys!"

His estimated time to be over Cherson elapsed, and while he couldn't see through the clouds below to determine if he were still over the Black Sea, he made a turn to 010 degrees and hopefully toward Kremencug, Ukraine, 155 nautical miles away. He tuned in the VOR beacon frequency for his next checkpoint near Kremencug, and within a few minutes the indicator needle steadied on the direction ahead. He took a deep breath, checked his engine instruments, looked around the cockpit and over at his unconscious co-pilot. He was just a little over an hour from his destination. He figured he would begin a slow descent down to 10,000 feet about halfway between Kremencug and Kursk and attempt to make his first contact with "Red Crown" control when he reached the lower altitude. He hoped the weather at the airfield was clear; he didn't relish attempting an instrument approach at this strange airfield without the benefit of approach plates or any knowledge of the "lay of the land."

"Oh, well, I've come this far and the support has been great, so I can only expect that they are ready for me there."

Nagornaya Air Base

A small but select group of Soviet military officers were gathering at the TU-95 BEAR bomber base near the city of Kursk, several hundred miles south of Moscow. They were arriving by both small aircraft transports and staff cars. The prominent officials in the waiting delegation included General of the Army Dimitriy Tushenskiy, deputy chief of the General Staff of the Soviet Armed Forces, and the new Head of the GRU. Accompanying him was General Anatoli Kashevarov, chief of the KGB. Among the others were Lieutenant General Anatoli Borodin and Colonel Dimitri Vetrov. Representing Chairman Khrushchev was his top military aide, Major General Yuri Kozlov. The remaining half dozen or so included a senior representative from the GRU Aviation Exploitation Directorate and various military and government bureaucrats who had gained special authorization to attend this momentous event. General Tushenskiy had, at first, decided not to invite Borodin and Vetrov because he wanted to keep the group as small as possible for security reasons. When he recognized various others had worked their way on the select list, he relented, acknowledging they were, after all, the managers of Mikeandrovich Katsanov's program.

Tushenskiy remained quiet and mostly to himself during the waiting hours. Inside, he was churning with emotion. They were on the threshold of the culmination of his great experiment. When he made the decision to select a very young agent-candidate to train and infiltrate the U.S. military forces, he had no idea what the final outcome might be. Over the years, he had fought with superiors and peers alike, to justify his project.

"We must be patient, Comrades," he had told his superiors. And, within the GRU, "General Borodin, you must understand that this is *my* special project. I have nurtured it for several years, and I want you to join me in supporting and seeing it through. I have a good feeling about what our government might gain from Katsanov's work, so do not meddle with it, or try to go over my head. Do you understand?"

"I understand, *Dyadya Petya*. I am only interested in the exceptional costs of such a project about which we know very little and over the years have extracted very much useful intelligence," Borodin had patronizingly responded.

Sasha Katsanov's project had been very costly, not only to directly support him, but the network that was necessary to insure his safety and well-being. General Borodin had petitioned Tushenkiy constantly since he arrived at Khodinka, as a KGB agent in residence, to bring Sasha home and "put him to work doing something constructive, and direct the money being spent on him to less complex and better assured means of espionage in the U.S.," Borodin would argue.

And, Tushenskiy himself, now the Head of the GRU was beginning to sway in favor of returning his favorite young operative back to Khodinka and make use of his extraordinary talents and skills. So, when he was notified of Sasha's plan to deliver a fully configured state-of-the-art American bomber, complete with air-to-ground missiles and nuclear weapons, he made an instant call to the Kremlin to gain approval.

He met first with the Minister of Defense and, because of the urgency to set up the necessary communications and airfield arrangements, he was summoned immediately to meet with Khrushchev, himself. Khrushchev had listened carefully as Tushenskiy gave him the background of Sasha's project and how long it had been in work.

"General, can you assure me that this is not an American trap?" Chairman Khrushchev asked.

Tushenskiy was well aware of what would happen to him if there was any possibility of embarrassment or slip-up, and he replied, "Sir, I have the highest confidence in the success of this mission. Lt. Katsanov has been developing this opportunity for years, and now it is a reality. We must act quickly to capture the high ground with the Americans. We will make all of the arrangements to secretly secure the bomber, keep it out of sight and exploit it to the fullest extent. You must understand also, Sir, that this B-52 comes to us fully configured with the latest state-of-the-art nuclear weapons and missiles. This will be a great coup! You, Sir, will be in a position to use the bomber, the weapons and the captured crew in any way you see fit to hold the United States president hostage to your demands."

Finally, he pleaded, "Sir, we must act very quickly to give him the go-ahead." Tushenskiy was to the point of groveling before the tough and imperious Soviet leader.

Tushenskiy recalled how the Chairman had looked sternly around at the assembled staff challenging any one of his advisors to comment. No one spoke. Not one of them were about to "jump" on either side of this discussion. Tushenskiy stood alone.

Finally, Khrushchev grinned and looked at him. "General, this is your day. I trust your judgment to make this a success. I need this victorious feat to put President Kennedy back in his place. Do not fail me."

"Sir, I will not. I will keep you fully informed of the events as they unfold," Tushenskiy had replied. This was a triumphant day, indeed.

Borodin and Vetrov remained in close company of one another during the wait in operations building, drinking tea and quietly talking. While they appeared reserved during their whispered conversations, there was a distinct measure of arrogance along with an occasional joke exchange and chuckle between the two. Neither were well-liked by their GRU peers.

Borodin whispered, "Comrade Dimitri, you are a genius. This event today will once and for all put Tushenskiy's little 'special project' in its proper perspective. It will also 'fix' that cocky pseudo-American who has been free-loading far too long. Heh, heh," he chuckled, and chided Vetrov, "and Demitri, maybe your little wife won't be so smitten by this wise jackal any more."

Vetrov was unabashed by Borodin's 'needle'. "Perhaps not, General, perhaps not," he replied with a slight smile. "I am only waiting to see the look in the eyes of Tushenskiy and these petty zealots when their great hero lands." Vetrov had to choke back a deep robust laugh.

The others assembled in the room of the operations building at the air base gave Borodin and Vetrov an occasional glance when they snickered out loud or chuckled at one another's private jokes. Career agents at Khodinka were all waiting for Borodin's KGB exchange duty to be over with and his going back to the "goon squad," as the GRU professionals quietly referred to the KGB. "He can also take that snake, Vetrov, with him," they would say.

Both Borodin and Vetrov had been a thorn in Tushenskiy's side, and he shared the feelings of his staff. The sooner they are gone, the better. He had tried on a few occasions to negotiate an early departure from Khodinka for the pair, but the bureaucracy prevailed. So here they were, displaying their usual arrogance and secretive smugness. Few of the others bothered to go near them.

Nagoranaya Air Base was chosen as the destination landing place for Mike for several reasons. First, it was a TU-95 heavy bomber base with sufficient runway size to accommodate a B-52, and it had two large aircraft hangars along with the attendant ground support equipment. Second, it was located in a relatively remote area, well out of the city in an agricultural region. Scattered collective farms made up the sparse population. And third, when the base was built, the housing area was located several miles away for security reasons. At the time, the Soviets considered conducting super secret aircraft experiments at the base and wanted to keep nonessential personnel and families as far away as possible.

For the expected arrival of Mike's bomber, the remainder of the base personnel and workers had been sent home. The base had been placed off-limits except for those with special clearances to be there. Only a very few trustworthy and specially skilled aircraft ground handling soldiers remained. Mike had previously provided considerable information on the B-52 and its ground handling requirements. This was used to prepare for the arrival of the bomber.

One of the large hangars had been hurriedly modified so that after landing, the B-52 could be towed into the hangar and placed out of sight where the extensive exploitation work would be conducted. Several of Tushenskiy's aviation experts had already petitioned him to allow them to fly in the bomber after it arrived, in order to fully understand its characteristics and capabilities. They reasoned that "Captain Katsanov can instruct and teach us much more than we can learn crawling around over it and taking it apart."

General Tushenskiy was holding his decision on that until after the bomber safely arrived and Sasha had been thoroughly debriefed. He said he would likely leave the decision up to Sasha as to whether it would be a good idea to fly the bomber, and he reasoned this event is also of such great sensitive political magnitude that the Kremlin had not yet decided how to manage it. There would have to be a great 'mackarova' (masquerade) to cover the story.

Tushenskiy and Kashevarov had worked with the political advisors in the Kremlin to create a plausible story to give to the outside world while keeping the presence of the B-52 totally secret.

"No one, absolutely no one, outside those closest to the program must know about the bomber being in our possession once we get it!" Khrushchev had told both Tushenskiy and Kashevarov. "Under the severest, no one!" he shouted.

The story that seemed most likely to be believed Tushenskiy described to the Kremlin staff: "People along the Albanian coast witnessed the bomber going down in the Aegean Sea. They saw five parachutes come down in the water. Fisherman set out in their boats and retrieved five American airmen. They were turned over to Soviet military authorities and flown to a hospital near Moscow where they were being held for questioning. Each of the five ejected from their bomber and were without injuries and in excellent health.

The authorities had determined from their interrogation of the five that one of their crew was missing. The missing crew member was the pilot, and it was presumed that he crashed with the aircraft. The Soviet Government will retain the five airmen as suspected prisoners of war for crimes against the people, but the benevolent Soviet leadership would perhaps be willing to negotiate some form of repatriation in the future."

Khrushchev and his staff were delighted with the story. Now, they not only had shot down a U-2 spyplane and captured its pilot, but they had captured the crew of a U.S. bomber. They could accuse the United States of provocative acts against the Soviet people by flying a nuclear bomber so close to its borders.

Khrushchev said, "Comrades, this unfolding story has all of the contrived ingredients to embarrass the United States Government into not only settling the Cuban situation, but untold other disagreements."

The Chairman had concluded their second meeting just the evening before: "General Tushenskiy, you are to be commended for developing such a brilliant plan and executing it flawlessly. You shall be justly rewarded. I thank all of you, Comrades, but let me tell you, one word of our possession of that airplane and every head will roll! Good night."

A young staff officer approached Generals Tushenskiy and Kashevarov, "Comrade Generals, the aircraft of interest should be due within an hour."

The generals smiled at one another. "Thank you, Major. Keep us informed," Tushenskiy acknowledged. Then he summoned over to him the colonel in charge of recovery operations for the B-52. "What will your procedures be when the bomber lands?"

The Soviet Air Force colonel promptly responded, "General, we will have vehicles posted on both sides of the runway to follow him through his landing roll-out. At the end of the runway a Follow-Me vehicle will be waiting to guide him around the taxi-way to the apron in front of Hangar One. We will try to get him to align the aircraft with the front doors of the hangar. We will signal him to shut off his engines and open a hatch so a ground crewman can go aboard to assist him."

He watched General Tushenskiy nod approvingly and continued. "We do not have the precise tow-bar to attach this type of aircraft, so we have tried to manufacture something that will work. We will quickly attach it to the front landing gear truck, and one of our heavy duty aircraft tow tractors will carefully pull him into the hangar. We hope his brakes will continue to work after the engines are turned off. After we have the aircraft safely inside the hangar, we will close the doors and the medical personnel will remove the other crew members to ambulances. Security will take over at that point, and the crew will be escorted under guard to the base hospital and isolated. We have also instructed the security team to completely secure the hangar, inside and out. No one without a specially issued badge may enter. Does that satisfy your question, Sir?"

Tushenskiy smiled and nodded, "Yes, excellent. Thank you." Then he said, "Ask the security chief to come over, please."

"Sir, I am Colonel Savrov, in charge of the special security force for this project," the sharp-looking officer reported.

"Good," responded Tushenskiy. "I believe I understand your security arrangements quite well. I was briefed before I left Moscow, but I want to add some additional instructions for you to enforce. There are far too many people involved here today. It was not my idea, but I believe General Kashevarov, here, agrees with me. Do you not, Igor?"

"Indeed, I do, Dimitriy. What are your thoughts?" Kashevarov acknowledged.

"I want Colonel Savrov to go around this room and collect the special access badges from all of the visitors, regardless of rank. No exceptions. Of course, do not interfere with the maintenance and ground handling supervisors. As you collect them, inform each individual to remain in this building until after the aircraft is safely parked inside the hangar. I will then personally re-issue the badges to those whom General Kashevarov and I agree should have immediate and follow-on access to the hangar." Tushenskiy grinned and responded, "Only General Kashevarov and I will accompany the medical and security people into the hangar first. After the situation is under control, I will permit others to come to the hangar."

The colonel acknowledged, "I understand, General. I will collect the badges now."

Tushenskiy looked over at Borodin and Vetrov sitting quietly in two corner chairs and said to Kashevarov, "I don't think we can be too cautious, Igor."

TWENTY ONE

Omaha And Washington

Concurrently, in the super secret Strategic Air Command underground command center near Omaha, Nebraska, SAC generals and their staffs were frantically trying to figure out what had happened to one of their airborne alert B-52G's. It had literally disappeared without a clue. They had received a notice from a British frigate near Sicily that the ship had detected a large aircraft of some type on its radar, but attempts to communicate with it failed. Otherwise, there had been no position reports from Apache Two-Zero for almost four hours. If it were on its scheduled flight plan, it should already be well out of the Mediterranean and into the Atlantic Ocean headed home.

Reluctantly, the Commander in Chief (CINC) of SAC called the Chairman of the Joint Chiefs of Staff in the Pentagon. "Mr. Chairman, I need to inform you we have lost contact with one of our airborne alert B-52's. It is a 'G-model' out of Ramey and now over four hours since he gave his last position report. There have been no radar sightings of him coming down the Med." He went on to say, "Our last known position of the bomber was while it was still in its alert orbit pattern over the Tyrrhenian Sea, so we're at a loss right now to give you any more information."

The Chairman asked, "What are the qualifications of the aircraft commander and the crew, and what is the bomber's weapon configuration?"

The CINC responded, "The crew commander is Captain Mike Scott. He's one of our top young aircraft commanders. Likewise, he has a young but very talented and competent crew. The navigator is an old head, and there would be no problem with navigating the bomber through the mission. This particular sortie is loaded to the hilt. It has four gravities, two HOUND DOG's and four QUAIL decoy missiles."

After a sigh, the Chairman acknowledged, "Okay, thanks. I will notify the Secretary of Defense and the President." In closing he asked. "Can we be sure it is missing or could it be just a radio failure problem?"

The SAC chief responded, "No, I think it is more than radio failure. There is extensive radar coverage from both ground and ships all along the Med as well as at Gibraltar and in Spain. Every other bomber and tanker coming through that area has been identified and accounted for. I believe we have a real problem here, but we will hope for the best."

The Chairman thanked him and then called the Secretary of Defense who advised him to call the President personally and explain the details. The news was not well received. The President thought he had Khrushchev over a barrel. All of the intruding Soviet ships headed to and from Cuba were being stopped and searched. The U.S. was in the highest state of war readiness since World War II. The major exception from previous conflicts and preparations for war was that this heightened state of emergency involved nuclear weapons.

All of the U.S. strategic nuclear forces were on alert and ready to strike the Soviet Union if they provoked a war. The increased posture included the airborne alert sorties of B-52 bombers loaded with nuclear weapons and positioned well within a few hours flying time of targets in Russia and its satellites.

The President was confident he held the upper hand in this stand-off. The missing B-52 was troubling. The country simply did not need an embarrassing incident to add to the ongoing situation. The President listened to the information given to him by the Chairman.

"Thanks Max. That is not good news, today, or any day for that matter. Stay the course, continue with all of the present operational activities and hope for the best. Keep me informed."

A weary U.S. President took a deep breath and weighed the consequences. He remembered, all too well, the embarrassment the country suffered over the Gary Power's U-2 incident and more recently the Bay of Pigs disaster.

Final Approach

Mike made the final navigation adjustment as his bomber passed over the last VOR beacon near Kremencug, Ukraine. He was headed toward the destination airfield.

"I am headed home," he whispered to himself. Calculating where he should begin his descent to the lower altitude of 10,000 feet, Mike looked at his watch and decided he should initiate the descent in sixteen minutes. He rationalized that if he were a little early, it shouldn't matter. He was so sure he was being tracked by Soviet radars; he could almost "feel" their pulses. As the minutes ticked by, he felt the adrenaline build up in his body. After all these years and feeling a lack of real accomplishment, here he was, about to deliver a crown jewel to his government.

He looked over at Bill Self and uttered a promise, "You and the other guys will be okay. You will be treated well by my people and returned to your country as soon as possible." He couldn't help feeling twinges of guilt in bringing them into this, but it could not have been accomplished any other way.

Mike eased back the throttles of the giant bomber and allowed it to begin drifting downward. He slowly raised the air brakes to Position Two in order to increase the rate of descent while maintaining his airspeed. As he was descending through twenty thousand feet, the sudden flash of a fighter dashed across his nose. He watched it as it moved from left to right and disappeared behind him. He caught a glimpse of the aircraft through the co-pilot's side window. Mike identified it as a MiG-21, now flying slightly above him, to the right and several hundred yards away.

"Well, I guess I am getting an escort," he thought to himself.

Mike continued his descent. He had tuned his radio to the prescribed frequency for Red Crown control, but he would not initiate a call until he had reached 10,000 feet altitude. He was still well above the clouds below which appeared to be fairly solid at 8,000 feet or so.

Suddenly, he couldn't believe what was happening. He felt his aircraft vibrate and shudder. There were distinct sounds of riveting and pops. He was being fired on. The MiG was shooting at his aircraft! Mike didn't understand. He was instantly confused.

"What th' hell is going on? Surely they know who I am and where I'm headed!"

He quickly keyed his transmitter: "Red Crown, Red Crown this is Crown One. Over!"

He continued: "Red Crown, Red Crown! Emergency, Emergency! I am being fired on by a MiG-21! Somebody call him off! Over."

There was no response. Mike turned the bomber sharply to the left. He couldn't see the fighter at that point. He thought if he pulled all of the power off his engines, he could descend into the cloud formation and get away from this idiot in the fighter. He knew his aircraft had been hit, but so far all of his instruments read normal and the bomber was still flying okay. Then he felt another barrage of rivet sounds. He was coming in for another pass and firing his guns.

Mike made a sharp turn back to his right, pulled the throttles to idle and pushed the yoke forward, while raising the air brakes to Position Four, in order to increase the rate of descent. He continued to try to call Red Crown control.

Finally, he heard a response. The Russian controller was loud and clear: "This is Red Crown. Come in, Crown One. Are you having difficulties?"

Mike responded, "Red Crown, I am being fired upon by a MiG interceptor. I am being hit. Call him off! Call him off! Tell him who I am! Over."

"Crown One, we are not aware of any fighters in your area. What is your position? Over."

At this point, Mike could only guess where he was. He noted that the VOR indicator needle was pointing about 40 degrees off to the left.

"I am on a heading of zero seven five degrees and your beacon is zero four zero degrees off to my left. I am descending through 12,000 feet and trying to get away from this fool. Call him off, dammit! Do you hear me? Call that bastard off!"

At that instant, the bomber shuddered as an explosion erupted somewhere within the aircraft. Mike looked out to the right side and saw the outboard engine pod was on fire. "My God," he shouted. "He is going to kill us!"

He reached over and grabbed Bill Self's flight suit and tried to shake him awake, shouting, "Wake up, Bill, wake up! We have to get out of here! Wake up!" Bill did not move.

He saw the MiG make a fast pass once again across his nose and disappear back behind him. He tried desperately to contact the fighter on the international emergency radio frequency, but there was no response. Meanwhile, Red Crown continued to ask him questions about his position and altitude. He was too busy to answer. He had to unbuckle his seat harness in order to reach over to the co-pilot's side and shut off the fuel to the right outboard engine pod, but it was still burning. He got back in his seat and buckled himself back in. He checked his ejection seat handles and prepared to arm them. Then he thought: "I can't leave these guys here to die! I can't, I can't!"

There was another explosion. This time it was the left engine pod and it was shooting flames yards to the rear of the aircraft.

"This bastard is taking target practice and killing us a little at a time!" He called again: "Red Crown, Red Crown, what's going on? Get this bastard off my back. We are going to lose this aircraft. Do you understand? Over!"

Red Crown responded: "Crown One, we do not understand what is happening to you. There are no reported fighters anywhere in your area. Do you read? Over."

Once again, Mike unbuckled his harness and reached over to turn off the fuel to the left outboard engine pod. As he buckled himself back into his ejection seat, it happened.

The left inboard engine pod was hit with a heat-seeking missile and the wing buckled. Mike Scott remembered nothing after that.

Peasants working in the field of a collective farm looked up into the cloudy sky and saw a parachute slowly descending to the ground. They also heard a muffled explosion and saw black smoke several miles off in the distance.

Epilogue

"Sasha, Sasha," the soft voice whispered. "May I come in?"

He lay in the hospital bed and could barely move for the huge cast on his left arm. His head was heavily bandaged and his right eye was covered. He rolled over slightly and uttered a whisper, "Come in."

He continued to lay still; heavily sedated and only slightly breathing. His left eye remained closed.

"Who are you?" he asked in a barely audible voice, "Where am I? What is this place? Where is my crew?"

"Sasha, it is me, Mackye," she replied quietly. "You are going to be all right. You have a few injuries, but the doctors say you will be fine. Lay quietly, Dear, don't try to move."

Sasha opened his left eye and tried to focus on the figure standing next to his bed. "Mackye, I can't believe it. Where are we? What happened?"

Mackye took his hand and held it. "Sasha you were in a very bad accident, but you are going to be all right. I am here with you."

He was focusing more clearly now and able to see her. "Mackye, are you all right? What happened to me?"

"Sasha, do you remember jumping out of your airplane?" she asked.

"Yes! I do!" his voice strained with urgency. "What happened to my crew? Where are they?"

"Sasha, they are all gone. They went down with your airplane," she whispered, squeezing his hand tightly.

He lay silent for a long while. Neither spoke as she continued to hold his hand firmly.

Finally he spoke. "Mackye, I have been betrayed. My country betrayed me. Everything I have done is lost. Why would they do this?"

Mackye squeezed his hand slightly. "Sasha, your country did not betray you. Two very evil people betrayed you," she said, "and they have paid."

Becoming more alert, he quickly asked, "What are you saying? Who did what?"

Mackye took a deep breath. "Let me briefly tell you all I know. I don't want to trouble you at this time; you need very much rest in order to get well. Sasha, everyone was waiting for you at Nagoranaya; General Tushenskiy and the Head of the KGB, several other important people. General Borodin and Dimitri Vetrov were also there. Everyone was in shock when you called in to report that you were being attacked. No one could believe it. No one that is, except Borodin and Dimitri. Borodin betrayed you and our government. He secretly ordered the fighter aircraft through his influential channels to shoot down your airplane, but he did not do it alone. He wasn't that bright. Dimitri conceived the tragic plan and goaded Borodin to carry it out. They both hated you and everything you have done. They were overtaken by jealousy, pride and arrogance, so much so, that I don't believe they thought they would get caught. Dimitri believed he had an iron clad plan. They were successful in destroying all of your work and the great prize you were delivering, but in the end they were caught and they paid."

Sasha stared at her, absorbing every word.

Finally, he sighed deeply. "Mackye, they murdered five innocent men. I am equally guilty! I brought them into this trap; this Godforsaken place! I put them to sleep and tied them to their ejection seats. They did not have a chance. I killed them! Before I do anything else, I will settle with those jackals who have done this. Where are they now? What is being done with them?"

Mackye stared blankly at him. "Sasha, you have nothing to do, but get well. Those two are no longer an issue." She took in a deep breath. "Dimitri's body was found last evening in the Moscow River. He had been shot once in the back of the head, KGB style. I was notified and told that no one would claim the body. They said it had been disposed of. Later in the night two men from Lubiyanka came and collected all of Dimitri's personal effects: clothes, shoes, everything that I could find that was attached to his ownership."

Mackye had difficulty continuing and took deep breath. "Borodin was found guilty of treason and stood before a firing squad at midnight last night. Sasha, the two tyrants are no longer your problem. They are gone. You are not to blame for any of this. Sasha, you did your job and did it well. You are a hero!" She smiled, tears running down her face; "A slightly broken hero, but nevertheless, a great hero."

Sasha couldn't respond; he lay quietly staring at the ceiling.

Finally, she said, "There is good news. The doctors say you are very much on the mend. You had a very bad concussion from a severe blow to the head and you have a badly broken arm. The doctor says that all of your vital signs are positive and you should quickly be up and around. Then we will take you back to Moscow."

Sasha was still confused about his condition and all that he had heard. "How did I get hurt? Did my parachute malfunction? Did it not open properly? I distinctly remember coming down smoothly, but I don't remember ejecting from the aircraft."

Mackye looked at him. "No, you apparently parachuted down just fine, but the workers in the collective farm field thought you were an American pilot who was going to drop bombs on them. They viciously attacked you and did all the damage you are suffering. If the farm manager had not gotten to you and intervened, they likely would have killed you. The KGB has arrested all of them for further disposition, poor pitiful wretches. They didn't know any better."

Sasha tried to raise his head. "Mackye," he pleaded, "where is General Tushenskiy? I must talk to him! Those peasants are not to blame. I want them released immediately. I want them rewarded for being loyal and obedient. How can I talk to Tushenskiy?"

Mackye smiled at his sudden awareness. "Sasha, the general was here yesterday, but you were still in a coma. He told me last night when he called to express his regrets about Dimitri, he would be back to see you as soon as he could. He also granted permission for me to come here today. He knows how much I respect and care for you. You are a hero to him, Sasha. I am sure if you want something done for the collectives, he will do it."

"Mackye, how long have I been here? Didn't I just get here today or yesterday? Are we not in Moscow?" Sasha pursued.

Mackye smiled, still holding his hand and explained, "No, Sasha, you are still in Kursk. This is a military medical facility. You have been here for almost ten days, and you have been in and out of consciousness all that time. We were all very worried about you until you began to respond yesterday. General Tushenskiy directed that every medical attention be given to you."

Finally, Sasha asked, "Mackye, are you sad about Dimitri? Did you love him?" Then, he gently squeezed her hand. "I am so sorry for you. I'm sorry I asked such stupid questions."

Mackye smiled. "Those are not stupid questions. No, I am not sad, because of what has happened; I now know just how treacherous and brutal he was. He was a man of many disguises and many horrible characteristics. He is no more. We shall forget him."

General Tushenskiy arrived at the hospital in Kursk two days later. Sasha was now sitting up and walking with some assistance. The bandage that swathed his head and eye had been replaced with a smaller covering over the head wound. He was extremely sore and moved with considerable pain. When Tushenskiy entered the room, he mustered all of his strength to move off the side of the bed and stand at attention. He was not a pretty sight.

Tushenskiy pulled him to his breast and kissed him on each cheek. "Sasha, Sasha, you certainly came home with a bang," he chuckled quietly. "You are a national hero, Sasha. Unfortunately we cannot discuss your exploits too broadly, but it is known in the right places that your great service to the government has been exemplary."

Tushenskiy nodded to his military aide standing near the door. The aide opened the door wider, and in walked Sasha's mother, Tatyana, and his father. Sasha leaned back against his bed. He wilted with emotion.

His mother held him tightly and whispered, "Sasha, Sasha! My Son, my Son! You are home, you are home!"

Then she moved back and allowed Viktor to greet his son.

Neither spoke.

General Tushenskiy moved closer to the three of them and took two military uniform shoulder boards from his aide. They reflected the triangular pattern of three stars reflecting the rank of colonel.

He then carefully pinned one on each shoulder of Sasha's hospital gown.

"Congratulations, Colonel Katsanov," Tushenskiy smiled. "We are very proud of you," and added, "I haven't checked the records, but you may very well be the youngest colonel in the Soviet Air Force. Comrade, you have earned it!"

Sasha was so emotionally overcome with all that was happening so fast that he couldn't respond. Tushenskiy then reached into a velvet box being held by the aide.

"Colonel Katsanov, on behalf of the Chairman of the Supreme Soviet and the Minister of Defense, I wish to decorate you with the *Order of Glory, First Class*. Our government is proud of you for your service and valor. Congratulations, Sasha."

Once again he pulled Sasha's shoulders to him and kissed him on the cheeks.

"Sasha," Tushenskiy continued. "The Chairman was prepared to present you with the Order of Lenin, if the bomber were successfully delivered. That is how strongly he felt about your mission, but alas, you are home safely. That is far more important!"

"Sir, you are too kind to me." Sasha's words were dry and came slowly. "My mission was a failure. I have done nothing for my government. I have two requests, Sir, if I may?"

"Yes, Sasha. What are your requests? They are my command," Tushenskiy quickly responded.

"Sir, please have the peasants who found me, released. They were only doing what they thought was right and they deserve a reward for trying to protect their country."

Tushenskiy smiled. "Sasha, I have already taken care of that. Do not worry yourself. They will not be harmed in any way. You said 'two' requests?"

Sasha was grim and could barely hold back the tears. "General, the five men who crashed with my bomber were all close friends of mine. They were loyal soldiers just like our own. I knew their families, and I helped bring their deaths. What can our government do to somehow compensate for their loss?"

Tushenskiy looked at him firmly. "Sasha, we are in a war with the West. Those men are casualties. It must never be known that your bomber crashed in Soviet territory. That event never happened! I am sorry for them. There is nothing more that I or anyone can do. You must let this incident be closed. Now, get some rest, Comrade."

Mackye had arrived back at the hospital and quietly entered the room. She stood and observed the unfolding events honoring her hero.7

GLOSSARY

Apparatchik	Soviet bureaucrat or politician.
"AC" or Aircraft Commander	Bomber aircrew commander.
"Boomer"	Boom Operator aboard an airborne refueling tanker.
"BUFF"	Big Ugly Fellow, or *similar* affectionate nickname for the B-52 bomber.
Call Sign	Identifying words assigned to an aircraft, ship or command center for communications purposes.
CHEKA	Chrezvychayna Kommisiya, predecessor to the NKVD; Soviet KGB secret police.
CHROMEDOME	SAC airborne alert training missions.
CINC	Commander-in-Chief. The story herein refers to the Commander-in-Chief, Strategic Air Command.
Dah	"Yes," in Cyrillic (Russian).
Da seveedah'neeya!	"Goodbye," in Cyrillic.
DEFCON	Defense Condition. Designates the alert response condition of strategic strike forces.
Do'briy d'ien!	"Good Afternoon!" in Cyrillic.
Do'broye oo'tra!	"Good Morning," in Cyrillic.
Do'briy ve'cher!	"Good Evening!" in Cyrillic.

DOSAAF	Pre-induction and military indoctrination program for Soviet youth.
Dyadya Petya	Pseudonym used in connection with the Chief of Military Intelligence.
ECM	Electronic Counter-measures
EWO	Electronic Warfare Officer. Often referred to as the "E-WHOA"
FBI	Federal Bureau of Investigation.
GKNIIR	Joint coordinating agency between the KGB and the GRU.
Great Patriotic War	Russian term for World War II.
GRU	Intelligence Directorate of the General Staff, Soviet Red Army. Secret police technical exploitation organization.
HF; UHF; VHF	High Frequency; Ultra-"HF; and Very-"HF". Air to ground radio frequency band widths commonly used in military aircraft.
HHCL	H-Hour Control Line. An imaginary line drawn around the Soviet Union which was used for bomber timing coordination.
HOUND DOG (GAM-77)	B-52 air-launched cruise missile with a nuclear warhead.
ICBM	Intercontinental Ballistic Missile.
IFF	Identification - Friend or Foe. An electronic emitter on board an aircraft which specifically identifies

	that aircraft to a querying ground station.
IP	Initial Point. Term to describe a specific position for an aircraft to be at a certain time.
IRBM	Intermediate Range Ballistic Missile.
JSTPS	Joint Strategic Planning Staff. During the Cold War planned for all of the strategic nuclear targets against the Soviet and other communist countries.
KGB	Komitet Gosudarstvennoy Bezopasnosti. Soviet secret police.
KOMSOMOL	The Young Communist League. Youth indoctrination organization for ages 14 to 28 who intend to pursue higher education.
Krasnaya Armiya	Soviet Red Army.
Krushki	"Circle of Devotees", a loosely knitted underground anti-government intellectual dissident faction within in the Soviet Union.
Mackorova (Mas'ka'rova)	Masquerade, in Cyrillic.
Mah'l'cheek	"Boy," in Cyrillic.
NKVD	Narodnyy Komisariat Vnutrennikh Del. Predecessor to the KGB secret police.
ORI	Operational Readiness Inspection. Conducted by military higher headquarters to insure the

	operational readiness of a combat unit.
OSI	Office of Special Investigation (of the U.S. Air Force).
Prospekt	Russian street.
QUAIL	(GAM-72), B-52 air-launched instrumented cruise missile; emanates electronic signals designed to simulate a B-52.
SAC	Strategic Air Command.
"SETTOAC"	Start, Engine, Taxi, Take-Off, Accelerate and Climb checks in the B-52.
Spa'see'ba	"Thank You," in Cyrillic.
Tavarish(chi)	Comrade(s) in Cyrillic.
Vaidee'te!	"Come in," in Cyrillic.
VOR	Visual Omni Range. Aircraft navigation homing station.
Young Pioneers	Soviet youth organization for ages 10 to 15 patterned after *Hitler's Youth* in Nazi Germany.
Zampolit	Soviet political officer.
Zdrah'stvooite	"Hello," in Cyrillic.
Zhelah'yoo oospe'kha	"I wish you success," in Cyrillic.

About The Author:

Chris Adams is a retired U.S. Air Force Major General and former Chief of Staff, Strategic Air Command; former Associate Director, Los Alamos National Laboratory, industry executive and published author. As a basis for this work, he is a former B-52 pilot himself, traveled extensively in the former Soviet States, making some 23 visits over five years. He draws on his extraordinary knowledge and experience in strategic air operations, nuclear weapons and the culture of the former Soviet Union in developing his works. A veteran of the Cold War, including Vietnam, he served 31 years in the Air Force as a bomber pilot, ICBM combat crew commander, wing and air division commander and senior staff officer. He also served three years with the Joint Chiefs of Staff and six years as a senior staff officer with the Defense Nuclear Agency. He has been awarded the nation's highest peacetime decoration, The United States Distinguished Serve Medal as well as, the Department of Defense Meritorious Service Medal, two Legions of Merit, two Air Medals and numerous other awards and decorations. He is also a Distinguished Alumnus Tarleton State University, Texas A&M University~Commerce and is listed in Who's Who in America. His books include three non-fiction Cold War historical treatments and four spy novels.